NIGHTFALL

A FOUNDATION BOOK
DOUBLEDAY
NEW YORK LONDON TORONTO SYDNEY AUCKLAND

**Isaac Asimov
and Robert Silverberg**

NIGHTFALL

A FOUNDATION BOOK
PUBLISHED BY DOUBLEDAY
a division of Bantam Doubleday Dell Publishing Group, Inc.
666 Fifth Avenue, New York, New York 10103

FOUNDATION, DOUBLEDAY, and the portrayal of the letter F
are trademarks of Doubleday,
a division of Bantam Doubleday Dell
Publishing Group, Inc.

This novel is based on the short story "Nightfall" by Isaac Asimov, which first appeared in *Astounding Science Fiction* in 1941. Certain character and place names have been changed at the authors' discretion.

Library of Congress Cataloging-in-Publication Data

Asimov, Isaac, 1920–
Nightfall / by Isaac Asimov and Robert Silverberg. — 1st ed.
p.   cm.
I. Silverberg, Robert. II. Title.
PS3551.S5N5   1990
813'.54—dc20   90-32469
CIP

ISBN 0-385-26341-4
Copyright © 1990 by Nightfall, Inc., and Agberg, Ltd.
All Rights Reserved
Printed in the United States of America
November 1990
First Edition
BVG

In fond and reverent memory of John W. Campbell, Jr.—and of those two terrified kids from Brooklyn who, in fear and trembling, made the awesome pilgrimage to his office, one of them in 1938 and the other in 1952.

TO THE READER

Kalgash is an alien world and it is not our intention to have you think that it is identical to Earth, even though we depict its people as speaking a language that you can understand, and using terms that are familiar to you. Those words should be understood as mere equivalents of alien terms—that is, a conventional set of equivalents of the same sort that a writer of novels uses when he has foreign characters speaking with each other in their own language but nevertheless transcribes their words in the language of the reader. So when the people of Kalgash speak of "miles," or "hands," or "cars," or "computers," they mean *their own* units of distance, *their own* grasping-organs, *their own* ground-transportation devices, *their own* information-processing machines, etc. The computers used on Kalgash are not necessarily compatible with the ones used in New York or London or Stockholm, and the "mile" that we use in this book is not necessarily the American unit of 5,280 feet. But it seemed simpler and more desirable to use these familiar terms in describing events on this wholly alien world than it would have been to invent a long series of wholly Kalgashian terms.

In other words, we could have told you that one of our characters paused to strap on his quonglishes before setting out on a walk of seven vorks along the main gleebish of his native znoob, and everything might have seemed ever so much more thoroughly alien. But it would also have been ever so much more difficult to make sense out of what we were saying, and that did not seem useful. The essence of this story doesn't lie in the quantity of bizarre terms we might have invented; it lies, rather, in the reaction of a group of people somewhat like ourselves, living on a world that is somewhat like ours in all but one highly significant detail, as they react to a challenging situation that is completely different from anything the people of Earth have ever had to deal with. Under the circumstances, it seemed to us better to tell you that someone put on his hiking boots before setting out on a seven-mile walk than to clutter the book with quonglishes, vorks, and gleebishes.

If you prefer, you can imagine that the text reads "vorks" wherever it says "miles," "gliizbiiz" wherever it says "hours," and "sleshtraps" where it says "eyes." Or you can make up your own terms. Vorks or miles, it will make no difference when the Stars come out.

—I.A.
—R.S.

If the stars should appear one night in a thousand years, how would men believe and adore, and preserve for many generations the remembrance of the city of God!

—EMERSON

Other world! There is no other world! Here or nowhere is the whole fact.

—EMERSON

ONE

TWILIGHT

It was a dazzling four-sun afternoon. Great golden Onos was high in the west, and little red Dovim was rising fast on the horizon below it. When you looked the other way you saw the brilliant white points of Trey and Patru bright against the purplish eastern sky. The rolling plains of Kalgash's northernmost continent were flooded with wondrous light. The office of Kelaritan 99, director of the Jonglor Municipal Psychiatric Institute, had huge windows on every side to display the full magnificence of it all.

Sheerin 501 of Saro University, who had arrived in Jonglor a few hours before at Kelaritan's urgent request, wondered why he wasn't in a better mood. Sheerin was basically a cheerful person to begin with; and four-sun days usually gave his normally ebullient spirits an additional lift. But today, for some reason, he was edgy and apprehensive, although he was trying his best to keep that from becoming apparent. He had been summoned to Jonglor as an expert on mental health, after all.

"Would you like to start by talking with some of the victims?" Kelaritan asked. The director of the psychiatric hospital was a gaunt, angular little man, sallow and hollow-chested. Sheerin, who was ruddy and very far from gaunt, was innately suspicious of anyone of adult years who weighed less than half of what he did. Perhaps it's the way Kelaritan looks that's upsetting me, Sheerin thought. He's like a walking skeleton. —"Or do you think it's a better idea for you to get some personal experience of the Tunnel of Mystery first, Dr. Sheerin?"

Sheerin managed a laugh, hoping it didn't sound too forced.

"Maybe I ought to begin by interviewing a victim or three," he said. "That way I might be able to prepare myself a little better for the horrors of the Tunnel."

Kelaritan's dark beady eyes flickered unhappily. But it was

3

Cubello 54, the sleek and polished lawyer for the Jonglor Centennial Exposition, who spoke out. "Oh, come now, Dr. Sheerin! 'The horrors of the Tunnel!' That's a little extreme, don't you think? After all, you've got nothing but newspaper accounts to go by, at this point. And calling the patients 'victims.' That's hardly what they are."

"The term was Dr. Kelaritan's," said Sheerin stiffly.

"I'm sure Dr. Kelaritan used that word only in the most general sense. But there's a presupposition in its use that I find unacceptable."

Sheerin said, giving the lawyer a look compounded equally of distaste and professional dispassion, "I understand that several people died as a result of their journey through the Tunnel of Mystery. Is that not so?"

"There were several deaths in the Tunnel, yes. But there's no necessary reason at this point to think that those people died *as a result* of having gone through the Tunnel, Doctor."

"I can see why you wouldn't want to think so, Counselor," said Sheerin crisply.

Cubello looked in outrage toward the hospital director. "Dr. Kelaritan! If this is the way this inquiry is going to be conducted, I want to register a protest right now. Your Dr. Sheerin is here as an impartial expert, not as a witness for the prosecution!"

Sheerin chuckled. "I was expressing my view of lawyers in general, Counselor, not offering any opinion about what may or may not have happened in the Tunnel of Mystery."

"Dr. Kelaritan!" Cubello exclaimed again, growing red-faced.

"Gentlemen, please," Kelaritan said, his eyes moving back and forth quickly from Cubello to Sheerin, from Sheerin to Cubello. "Let's not be adversaries, shall we? We all have the same objective in this inquiry, as I see it. Which is to discover the truth about what happened in the Tunnel of Mystery, so that a repetition of the—ah—unfortunate events can be avoided."

"Agreed," said Sheerin amiably. It was a waste of time to be sniping at the lawyer this way. There were more important things to be doing.

He offered Cubello a genial smile. "I'm never really much interested in the placing of blame, only in working out ways of heading off situations where people come to feel that blame has to be placed. Suppose you show me one of your patients now, Dr. Kelaritan. And then we can have lunch and discuss the events in the Tunnel as we understand them at this point, and perhaps after we've eaten I might be able to see another patient or two—"

"Lunch?" Kelaritan said vaguely, as though the concept was unfamiliar to him.

"Lunch, yes. The midday meal. An old habit of mine, Doctor. But I can wait just a little while longer. We can certainly visit one of the patients first."

Kelaritan nodded. To the lawyer he said, "Harrim's the one to start with, I think. He's in pretty good shape today. Good enough to withstand interrogation by a stranger, anyway."

"What about Gistin 190?" Cubello asked.

"She's another possibility, but she's not as strong as Harrim. Let him get the basic story from Harrim, and then he can talk to Gistin, and—oh, maybe Chimmilit. After lunch, that is."

"Thank you," said Sheerin.

"If you'll come this way, Dr. Sheerin—"

Kelaritan gestured toward a glassed-in passageway that led from the rear of his office to the hospital itself. It was an airy, open catwalk with a 360-degree view of the sky and the low gray-green hills that encircled the city of Jonglor. The light of the day's four suns came streaming in from all sides.

Pausing for a moment, the hospital director looked to his right, then to his left, taking in the complete panorama. The little man's dour pinched features seemed to glow with sudden youth and vitality as the warm rays of Onos and the tighter, sharply contrasting beams from Dovim, Patru, and Trey converged in a brilliant display.

"What an absolutely splendid day, eh, gentlemen!" Kelaritan cried, with an enthusiasm that Sheerin found startling, coming from someone as restrained and austere as he seemed to be. "How glorious it is to see four of the suns in the sky at the same time! How good it makes me feel when their light strikes my face! Ah, where would we be without our marvelous suns, I wonder?"

"Indeed," said Sheerin.

He was feeling a little better himself, as a matter of fact.

[2]

Half a world away, one of Sheerin 501's Saro University colleagues was staring at the sky also. But the only emotion she felt was horror.

She was Siferra 89, of the Department of Archaeology, who had been conducting excavations for the past year and a half at the ancient site of Beklimot on the remote Sagikan Peninsula. Now she stood rigid with apprehension, watching a catastrophe come rushing toward her.

The sky offered no comfort. In this part of the world the only real light visible just then was that of Tano and Sitha, and their cold, harsh gleam had always seemed joyless, even depressing, to her. Against the deep somber blue of the two-sun-day sky it was a baleful, oppressive illumination, casting jagged, ominous shadows. Dovim was in view also—barely, just rising now—right on the horizon, a short distance above the tips of the distant Horkkan Mountains. The dim glow of the little red sun, though, was hardly any more cheering.

But Siferra knew that the warm yellow light of Onos would come drifting up out of the east before long to cheer things up. What was troubling her was something far more serious than the temporary absence of the main sun.

A killer sandstorm was heading straight toward Beklimot. In another few minutes it would sweep over the site, and then anything might happen. Anything. The tents could be destroyed; the carefully sorted trays of artifacts might be overturned and their contents scattered; their cameras, their drafting equipment, their laboriously compiled stratigraphic drawings—everything that they had worked on for so long might be lost in a moment.

Worse. They could all be killed.

Worse yet. The ancient ruins of Beklimot itself—the cradle

of civilization, the oldest known city on Kalgash—were in jeopardy.

The trial trenches that Siferra had sliced in the surrounding alluvial plain stood wide open. The onrushing wind, if it was strong enough, would lift even more sand than it was already carrying, and hurl it with terrible force against the fragile remains of Beklimot—scouring, eroding, reburying, perhaps even ripping whole foundations loose and hurling them across the parched plain.

Beklimot was a historical treasure that belonged to the entire world. That Siferra had exposed it to possible harm by excavating in it had been a calculated risk. You could never do any sort of archaeological work without destroying something: it was the nature of the job. But to have laid the whole heart of the plain bare like this, and then to have the lousy luck of being hit by the worst sandstorm in a century—

No. No, it was too much. Her name would be blackened for aeons to come if the Beklimot site was shattered by this storm as a result of what she had done here.

Maybe there was a curse on this place, as certain superstitious people were known to say. Siferra 89 had never had much tolerance for crackpots of any sort. But this dig, which she had hoped would be the crowning achievement of her career, had been nothing but headaches ever since she started. And now it threatened to finish her professionally for the rest of her life— if it didn't kill her altogether.

Eilis 18, one of her assistants, came running up. He was a slight, wiry man who looked insignificant beside the tall, athletic figure of Siferra.

"We've got everything nailed down that we were able to!" he called to her, half breathless. "It's all up to the gods now!"

She replied, scowling, "Gods? What gods? Do you see any gods around here, Eilis?"

"I simply meant—"

"I know what you meant. Forget it."

From the other side came Thuvvik 443, the foreman of the workers. He was wild-eyed with fear. "Lady," he said. "Lady, where can we hide? There is no place to hide!"

"I told you, Thuvvik. Down below the cliff."

"We will be buried! We will be smothered!"

7

"The cliff will shelter you, don't worry," Siferra told him, with a conviction she was far from feeling. "Get over there! And make sure everybody else stays there!"

"And you, lady? Why are you not there?"

She gave him a sudden startled glance. Did he think she had some private hiding place where she'd be safer than the rest?

"I'll be there, Thuvvik. Go on! Stop bothering me!"

Across the way, near the six-sided brick building that the early explorers had called the Temple of the Suns, Siferra caught sight of the stocky figure of Balik 338. Squinting, shading his eyes against the chilly light of Tano and Sitha, he stood looking toward the north, the direction from which the sandstorm was coming. The expression on his face was one of anguish.

Balik was their chief stratigrapher, but he was also the expedition's meteorological expert, more or less. It was part of his job to keep the weather records for them and to watch out for the possibility of unusual events.

There wasn't much in the way of weather on the Sagikan Peninsula, normally: the whole place was unthinkably arid, with measurable rainfall no more often than every ten or twenty years. The only unusual climatic event that ever occurred there was a shift in the prevailing pattern of air currents that set cyclonic forces in motion and brought about a sandstorm, and even that didn't happen more than a few times a century.

Was Balik's despondent expression a hint of the guilt he must feel for having failed to foresee the coming of the storm? Or did he look so horrified because he was able now to calculate the full extent of the fury that was about to descend?

Everything might have been different, Siferra told herself, if they'd had a little more time to prepare for the onslaught. In hindsight, she could see that all the telltale signs had been there for those with the wit to notice them—the burst of fierce dry heat, excruciating even by the standards of the Sagikan Peninsula, and the sudden dead calm that replaced the usual steady breeze from the north, and then the strange moist wind that began to blow from the south. The khalla-birds, those weird scrawny scavengers that haunted the area like ghouls, had all taken wing when that wind started blowing, vanishing into the dune-choked western desert as though demons were on their tails.

That should have been the clue, Siferra thought. When the khalla-birds took off and went screaming into the dune country.

But they had all been too busy working at the dig to pay attention to what was going on. Sheer denial, most likely. Pretend that you don't notice the signs of an approaching sandstorm and maybe the sandstorm will go somewhere else.

And then that little gray cloud appearing out of nowhere in the far north, that dull stain on the fierce shield of the desert sky, which ordinarily was always as clear as glass—

Cloud? Do you see a cloud? I don't see any clouds.

Denial again.

Now the cloud was an immense black monster filling half the sky. The wind still blew from the south, but it was no longer moist—a searing furnace-blast was what it was, now—and there was another wind, an even stronger one, bearing down from the opposite direction. One wind fed the other. And when they met—

"Siferra!" Balik yelled. "Here it comes! Take cover!"

"I will! I will!"

She didn't want to. What she wanted to do was run from one zone of the dig to another, looking after everything at once, holding the flaps of the tents down, wrapping her arms around the bundles of precious photographic plates, throwing herself against the face of the newly excavated Octagon House to protect the stunning mosaics that they had discovered the month before. But Balik was right. Siferra had done all she could, this frantic morning, to batten down the site. Now the thing to do was to huddle in, down there below the cliff that loomed at the upper edge of the site, and hope that it would be a bulwark for them against the fullest force of the storm.

She ran for it. Her sturdy, powerful legs carried her easily over the parched, crackling sand. Siferra was not quite forty years old, a tall, strong woman in the prime of her physical strength, and until this moment she had never felt anything but optimism about any aspect of her existence. But suddenly everything was imperiled now: her academic career, her robust good health, maybe even her life itself.

The others were crowded together at the base of the cliff, behind a hastily improvised screen of bare wooden poles with tarpaulins lashed to them. "Move over," Siferra said, pushing her way in among them.

"Lady," Thuvvik moaned. "Lady, make the storm turn back!" As though she were some sort of goddess with magical powers. Siferra laughed harshly. The foreman made some kind of gesture at her—a holy sign, she imagined.

The other workers, all of them men of the little village just east of the ruins, made the same sign and began to mutter at her. Prayers? To *her*? It was a spooky moment. These men, like their fathers and grandfathers, had been digging at Beklimot all their lives in the employ of one archaeologist or another, patiently uncovering the ancient buildings and sifting through the sand for tiny artifacts. Presumably they had been through bad sandstorms before. Were they always this terrified? Or was this some kind of super storm?

"Here it is," Balik said. "This is it." And he covered his face with his hands.

The full power of the sandstorm broke over them.

Siferra remained standing at first, staring through an opening in the tarpaulins at the monumental cyclopean city wall across the way, as though simply by keeping her gaze fixed on the site she would be able to spare it from harm. But after a moment that became impossible. Gusts of incredible heat came sweeping down, so ferocious that she thought her hair and even her eyebrows would burst into flame. She turned away, raising one arm to shield her face.

Then came the sand, and all vision was blotted out.

It was like a rainstorm, a downpour of all too solid rain. There was a tremendous thundering sound, not thunder at all but only the drumming of a myriad tiny sand particles against the ground. Within that great sound were other ones, a slithery whispering sound, a jagged scraping sound, a delicate drumming sound. And a terrible howling. Siferra imagined tons of sand cascading down, burying the walls, burying the temples, burying the vast sprawling foundations of the residential zone, burying the camp.

And burying all of them.

She turned away, face to the wall of the cliff, and waited for the end to come. A little to her surprise and chagrin, she found herself sobbing hysterically, sudden deep wails rising from the core of her body. She didn't want to die. Of course not: who did? But she had never realized until this moment that there might be something worse than dying.

Beklimot, the most famous archaeological site in the world, the oldest known city of mankind, the foundation of civilization, was going to be destroyed—purely as a result of her negligence. Generations of Kalgash's great archaeologists had worked here in the century and a half since Beklimot's discovery: first Galdo 221, the greatest of them all, and then Marpin, Stinnupad, Shelbik, Numoin, the whole glorious roster—and now Siferra, who had foolishly left the whole place uncovered while a sandstorm was approaching.

So long as Beklimot had been buried beneath the sands, the ruins had slumbered peacefully for thousands of years, preserved as they had been on the day when its last inhabitants finally yielded to the harshness of the changing climate and abandoned the place. Each archaeologist who had worked there since Galdo's day had taken care to expose just a small section of the site, and to put up screens and sand-fences to guard against the unlikely but serious danger of a sandstorm. Until now.

She had put up the usual screens and fences too, of course. But not in front of the new digs, not in the sanctuary area where she had focused her investigations. Some of Beklimot's oldest and finest buildings were there. And she, impatient to begin excavating, carried away by her perpetual buoyant urge to go on and on, had failed to take the most elementary precautions. It hadn't seemed that way to her at the time, naturally. But now, with the demonic roaring of the sandstorm in her ears, and the sky black with destruction—

Just as well, Siferra thought, that I won't survive this. And therefore won't have to read what they're going to say about me in every book on archaeology that gets published in the next fifty years. *"The great site of Beklimot, which yielded unparalleled data about the early development of civilization on Kalgash until its unfortunate destruction as a result of the slipshod excavation practices employed by the young, ambitious Siferra 89 of Saro University—"*

11

"I think it's ending," Balik whispered.

"What is?" she said.

"The storm. Listen! It's getting quiet out there."

"We must be buried in so much sand that we can't hear anything, that's all."

"No. We aren't buried, Siferra!" Balik tugged at the tarpaulin in front of them and managed to lift it a little way. Siferra peered out into the open area between the cliff and the wall of the city.

She couldn't believe her eyes.

What she saw was the clear deep blue of the sky. And the gleam of sunlight. It was only the bleak, chilly white glow of the double suns Tano and Sitha, but just now it was the most beautiful light she ever wanted to see.

The storm had passed through. Everything was calm again.

And where was the sand? Why wasn't everything entombed in sand?

The city was still visible: the great blocks of the stone wall, the shimmering glitter of the mosaics, the peaked stone roof of the Temple of the Suns. Even most of their tents were still standing, including nearly all of the important ones. Only the camp where the workers lived had been badly damaged, and that could be repaired in a few hours.

Astounded, still not daring to believe it, Siferra stepped out of the shelter and looked around. The ground was clear of loose sand. The hard-baked, tight-packed dark stratum that had formed the surface of the land in the excavation zone could still be seen. It looked different now, abraded in a curious scrubbed way, but it was clear of any deposit the storm might have brought.

Balik said wonderingly, "First came the sand, and then came wind behind it. And the wind picked up all the sand that got dropped on us, picked it up as fast as it fell, and scooped it right on along to the south. A miracle, Siferra. That's the only thing we can call it. Look—you can see where the ground's been scraped, where the whole shallow upper layer of ground sand's been cleaned away by the wind, maybe fifty years' worth of erosion in five minutes, but—"

Siferra was scarcely listening. She caught Balik by the arm

12

and turned him to the side, away from the main sector of their excavation site.

"Look there," she said.

"Where? What?"

She pointed. "The Hill of Thombo."

The broad-shouldered stratigrapher stared. "Gods! It's been slit right up the middle!"

The Hill of Thombo was an irregular middling-high mound some fifteen minutes' walk south of the main part of the city. No one had worked it in well over a hundred years, not since the second expedition of the great pioneer Galdo 221, and Galdo hadn't found anything of significance in it. It was generally considered to be nothing but a midden-heap on which the citizens of old Beklimot had tossed their kitchen garbage—interesting enough of itself, yes, but trivial in comparison with the wonders that abounded everywhere else in the site.

Apparently, though, the Hill of Thombo had taken the fullest brunt of the storm: and what generations of archaeologists had not bothered to do, the violence of the sandstorm had achieved in only a moment. An erratic zigzagging strip had been ripped from the face of the hill, like some terrible wound laying bare much of the interior of its upper slope. And experienced field workers like Siferra and Balik needed only a single glance to understand the importance of what was now exposed.

"A town site under the midden," Balik murmured.

"More than one, I think. Possibly a series," Siferra said.

"You think?"

"Look. Look there, on the left."

Balik whistled. "Isn't that a wall in crosshatch style, under the corner of that cyclopean foundation?"

"You've got it."

A shiver ran down Siferra's spine. She turned to Balik and saw that he was as astounded as she was. His eyes were wide, his face was pale.

"In the name of Darkness!" he muttered huskily. "What do we have here, Siferra?"

"I'm not sure. But I'm going to start finding out right this minute." She looked back at the shelter under the cliff, where Thuvvik and his men still crouched in terror, making holy signs and babbling prayers in low stunned voices as if unable to

13

comprehend that they were safe from the power of the storm. "Thuvvik!" Siferra yelled, gesturing vigorously, almost angrily, at him. "Come on out of there, you and your men! We've got work to do!"

[3]

Harrim 682 was a big beefy man of about fifty, with great slabs of muscle bulging on his arms and chest, and a good thick insulating layer of fat over that. Sheerin, studying him through the window of the hospital room, knew right away that he and Harrim were going to get along.

"I've always been partial to people who are, well, oversized," the psychologist explained to Kelaritan and Cubello. "Having been one myself for most of my life, you understand. Not that I've ever been a muscleman like this one." Sheerin laughed pleasantly. "I'm blubber through and through. Except for here, of course," he added, tapping the side of his head. —"What kind of work does this Harrim do?"

"Longshoreman," Kelaritan said. "Thirty-five years on the Jonglor docks. He won a ticket to the opening day of the Tunnel of Mystery in a lottery. Took his whole family. They were all affected to some degree, but he was the worst. That's very embarrassing to him, that a great strong man like him should have such a total breakdown."

"I can imagine," Sheerin said. "I'll take that into account. Let's talk with him, shall we?"

They entered the room.

Harrim was sitting up, staring without interest at a spinner cube that was casting light in half a dozen colors on the wall opposite his bed. He smiled affably enough when he saw Kelaritan, but seemed to stiffen when he noticed the lawyer Cubello walking behind the hospital director, and his face turned completely glacial at the sight of Sheerin.

"Who's he?" he asked Kelaritan. "Another lawyer?"

"Not at all. This is Sheerin 501, from Saro University. He's here to help you get well."

14

"Huh," Harrim snorted. "Another double-brain! What good have any of you done for me?"

"Absolutely right," Sheerin said. "The only one who can really help Harrim get well is Harrim, eh? You know that and I know that, and maybe I can persuade the hospital people here to see that too." He sat down on the edge of the bed. It creaked beneath the psychologist's bulk. "At least they have decent beds in this place, though. They must be pretty good if they can hold the two of us at the same time. —Don't like lawyers, I gather? You and me both, friend."

"Miserable troublemakers is all they are," Harrim said. "Full of tricks, they are. They make you say things you don't mean, telling you that they can help you if you say such-and-such, and then they end up using your own words against you. That's the way it seems to me, anyway."

Sheerin looked up at Kelaritan. "Is it absolutely necessary that Cubello be here for this interview? I think it might go a little more smoothly without him."

"I am authorized to take part in any—" Cubello began stiffly.

"Please," Kelaritan said, and the word had more force than politeness behind it. "Sheerin's right. Three visitors at once may be too many for Harrim—today, anyway. And you've already heard his story."

"Well—" Cubello said, his face dark. But after a moment he turned and went out of the room.

Sheerin surreptitiously signaled to Kelaritan that he should take a seat in the far corner.

Then, turning to the man in the bed, he smiled his most agreeable smile and said, "It's been pretty rough, hasn't it?"

"You said it."

"How long have you been in here?"

Harrim shrugged. "I guess a week, two weeks. Or maybe a little more. I don't know, I guess. Ever since—"

He fell silent.

"The Jonglor Exposition?" Sheerin prompted.

"Since I took that ride, yes."

"It's been a little more than just a week or two," Sheerin said.

"Has it?" Harrim's eyes took on a glazed look. He didn't want to hear about how long he'd been in the hospital.

15

Changing tack, Sheerin said, "I bet you never dreamed a day would come when you'd tell yourself you'd be glad to get back to the docks, eh?"

With a grin, Harrim said, "You can say that again! Boy, what I wouldn't give to be slinging those crates around tomorrow." He looked at his hands. Big, powerful hands, the fingers thick, flattened at the tips, one of them crooked from some injury long ago. "I'm getting soft, laying here all this time. By the time I get back to work I won't be any good any more."

"What's keeping you here, then? Why don't you just get up and put your street clothes on and get out of here?"

Kelaritan, from the corner, made a warning sound. Sheerin gestured at him to keep quiet.

Harrim gave Sheerin a startled look. "Just get up and walk out?"

"Why not? You aren't a prisoner."

"But if I did that—if I did that—"

The dockworker's voice trailed off.

"If you did that, what?" Sheerin asked.

For a long while Harrim was silent, face downcast, brow heavily knitted. Several times he began to speak but cut himself off. The psychologist waited patiently. Finally Harrim said, in a tight, husky, half-strangled tone, "I can't go out there. Because of the—because—because of the—" He struggled with himself. "The Darkness," he said.

"The Darkness," said Sheerin.

The word hung there between them like a tangible thing.

Harrim looked troubled by it, even abashed. Sheerin remembered that among people of Harrim's class it was a word that was rarely used in polite company. To Harrim it was, if not actually obscene, then in some sense sacrilegious. No one on Kalgash liked to think about Darkness; but the less education one had, the more threatening it was to let one's mind dwell on the possibility that the six friendly suns might somehow totally disappear from the sky all at once, that utter blackness might reign. The idea was unthinkable—literally unthinkable.

"The Darkness, yes," Harrim said. "What I'm afraid of is that—that if I go outside I'll find myself in the Darkness again. That's what it is. The Dark, all over again."

"Complete symptom reversal in the last few weeks," Kelaritan said in a low voice. "At first it was just the opposite. You couldn't get him to go indoors unless you sedated him. A powerful case of claustrophobia first, that is, and then after some time the total switch to claustrophilia. We think it's a sign that he's healing."

"Maybe so," Sheerin said. "But if you don't mind—"

To Harrim he said, gently, "You were one of the first to ride through the Tunnel of Mystery, weren't you?"

"On the very first day." A note of pride came into Harrim's voice. "There was a city lottery. A hundred people won free rides. There must have been a million tickets sold, and mine was the fifth one picked. Me, my wife, my son, my two daughters, we all went on it. The very first day."

"Do you want to tell me a little about what it was like?"

"Well," Harrim said. "It was—" He paused. "I never was in Darkness ever, you know. Not even a dark room. Not ever. It wasn't something that interested me. We always had a godlight in the bedroom when I was growing up, and when I got married and had my own house I just naturally had one there too. My wife feels the same way. Darkness, it isn't natural. It isn't anything that was meant to be."

"Yet you entered the lottery."

"Well, this was just once. And it was like *entertainment*, you know? Something special. A holiday treat. The big exposition, the five hundredth year of the city, right? Everybody was buying tickets. And I figured, this must be something different, this must be something really good, or why else would they have built it? So I bought the ticket. And when I won, everybody at the docks was jealous, they all wished they had the ticket, some of them even wanted to buy it from me— 'No, sir,' I told them, 'not for sale, me and my family, this is our ticket—' "

"So you were excited about taking the ride in the Tunnel?"

"Yeah. You bet."

"And when you were actually doing it? When the ride started? What did that feel like?"

"Well—" Harrim began. He moistened his lips, and his eyes seemed to look off into a great distance. "There were these little cars, you see, nothing but slats inside for seats, and the cars were open on top. You got in, six people in each one, except

17

they let just the five of us go together, because we were all one family, and it was almost enough to fill a whole car without putting a stranger in with us. And then you heard music and the car started to move into the Tunnel. Very slow, it went, not like a car on the highway would, just creeping along. And then you were inside the Tunnel. And then—then—"

Sheerin waited again.

"Go on," he said after a minute, when Harrim showed no sign of resuming. "Tell me about it. I really want to know what it was like."

"Then the Darkness," Harrim said hoarsely. His big hands were trembling at the recollection. "It came down on you like they dropped a giant hat over you, you know? And everything turned black all at once." The trembling was becoming a violent tremor. "I heard my son Trinit laugh. He's a wise guy, Trinit is. He thought the Darkness was something dirty, I bet you. So he was laughing, and I told him to shut up, and then one of my daughters began to cry a little, and I told her it was okay, that there was nothing to worry about, that it was just going to be for fifteen minutes, and she ought to look at it like it was a treat, not something to be scared of. And then—then—"

Silence again. This time Sheerin didn't prompt.

"Then I felt it closing in on me. Everything was Darkness—Darkness—you can't imagine what it was like—you can't *imagine*—how black it was—how *black*—the Darkness—the Darkness—"

Suddenly Harrim shuddered, and great racking sobs came from him, almost like convulsions.

"The Darkness—oh, God, the Darkness—!"

"Easy, man. There's nothing to be afraid of here. Look at the sunlight! Four suns today, Harrim. Easy, man."

"Let me take care of this," Kelaritan said. He had come rushing to the bedside when the sobbing began. A needle glinted in his hand. He touched it to Harrim's burly arm, and there was a brief whirr of sound. Harrim grew calm almost at once. He slumped back against his pillow, smiling glassily. —"We need to leave him now," said Kelaritan.

"But I've hardly only begun to—"

"He won't make any sense again for hours, now. We might as well go for lunch."

18

"Lunch, yes," Sheerin said halfheartedly. To his own surprise he felt almost no appetite at all. He could scarcely remember a time when he had felt that way. "And he's one of your strongest ones?"

"One of the most stable, yes."

"What are the others like, then?"

"Some are completely catatonic. Others need sedation at least half the time. In the first stage, as I said, they don't want to come in out of the open. When they emerged from the Tunnel they seemed to be in perfect order, you understand, except that they had developed instant claustrophobia. They would refuse to go into buildings—any buildings, including palaces, mansions, apartment houses, tenements, huts, shacks, lean-tos, and tents."

Sheerin felt a profound sense of shock. He had done his doctoral work in darkness-induced disorders. That was why they had asked him to come here. But he had never heard of anything as extreme as this. "They wouldn't go indoors at all? Where'd they sleep?"

"In the open."

"Did anyone try to *force* them inside?"

"Oh, they did, of course they did. Whereupon these people went into violent hysterics. Some of them even became suicidal —they'd run up to a wall and hit their heads against it, things like that. Once you did get them inside, you couldn't keep them there without a straitjacket and a good stiff injection of some strong sedative."

Sheerin looked at the big longshoreman, who was sleeping now, and shook his head.

"The poor devils."

"That was the first phase. Harrim's in the second phase now, the claustrophilic one. He's adapted to being here, and the whole syndrome has swung completely around. He knows that it's safe in the hospital: bright lights all the time. But even though he can see the suns shining through the window he's afraid to go *outside*. He thinks it's dark out there."

"But that's absurd," Sheerin said. "It's *never* dark out there."

The instant he said it, he felt like a fool.

Kelaritan rubbed it in all the same, though. "We all realize that, Dr. Sheerin. Any sane person does. But the trouble with the people who have undergone trauma in the Tunnel of Mystery is that they are no longer sane."

"Yes. So I gather," said Sheerin shamefacedly.

"You can meet some of our other patients later today," Kelaritan said. "Perhaps they'll provide you with some other perspectives on the problem. And then tomorrow we'll take you over to see the Tunnel itself. We have it closed down, of course, now that we know the difficulties, but the city fathers are very eager to find some way to reopen it. The investment, I understand, was immense. But we should have lunch first, yes, Doctor?"

"Lunch, yes," said Sheerin once again, even less enthusiastically than before.

[4]

The great dome of the Saro University Observatory, rising majestically to dominate the forested slopes of Observatory Mount, glinted brilliantly in the light of late afternoon. The small red orb of Dovim had already slipped beyond the horizon, but Onos was still high in the west, and Trey and Patru, crossing the eastern sky on a sharp diagonal, etched shining trails of brightness along the dome's immense face.

Beenay 25, a slender, agile young man with a quick, alert way of carrying himself, darted briskly about the small apartment below the Observatory in Saro City that he shared with his contract-mate, Raissta 717, gathering his books and papers together.

Raissta, sprawled comfortably on the worn green upholstery of their little couch, looked up and frowned.

"Going somewhere, Beenay?"

"To the Observatory."

"It's so *early*, though. You usually don't go there until after Onos sets. And that won't be for hours yet."

"I've got an appointment today, Raissta."

She gave him a warm, seductive look. They were both graduate students in their late twenties, each an assistant professor, he in astronomy, she in biology, and they had been contract-mates only seven months. Their relationship was still in its first bloom of excitement. But problems had already arisen. He did his work in the late hours, when usually only a few of the lesser suns were in the sky. She was at her freshest and best in the period of high daylight, under the golden glow of bright Onos.

Lately he had spent more and more time at the Observatory, and it was getting so that they were almost never awake at the same time. Beenay knew how trying that was for her. It was trying for *him*. All the same, the work he was doing on Kalgash's orbit was demanding stuff, and it was leading him into ever more difficult regions that he found both challenging and frightening. If only Raissta would be patient just another few weeks—a month or two, maybe—

"Can't you stay here a little while longer this evening?" she asked.

His heart sank. Raissta was giving him her come-here-and-let's-play look. Not easy to resist, nor did he really want to. But Yimot and Faro would be waiting.

"I told you. I have an—"

"—appointment, yes. Well, so do I. With you."

"Me?"

"You said yesterday you might have some free time this afternoon. I was counting on that, you know. I cleared a whole swatch of free time of my own—did my lab work in the morning, as a matter of fact, just so—"

Worse and worse, Beenay thought. He did remember saying something about this afternoon, completely overlooking the fact that he had arranged to meet the two younger students.

She was pouting now, and somehow smiling at the same time, a trick that she managed to perfection. Beenay wanted to forget all about Faro and Yimot and go to her right away. But if he did that, he might be an hour late for his appointment with them, which wasn't fair. *Two* hours, maybe.

And he had to admit to himself that he was desperately eager to know whether their calculations had confirmed his own.

It was practically an even struggle: the powerful appeal of Raissta on the one hand, and the desire to put his mind at rest concerning a major scientific issue on the other. And though he had an obligation to be on time for his appointment, Beenay realized in some confusion that he had made an appointment of

21

sorts with Raissta too—and that was a matter not only of obligation but of delight.

"Look," he said, going to the couch and taking her hand in his. "I can't be in two places at once, okay? And when I told you what I did yesterday, it had slipped my mind that Faro and Yimot would be coming to the Observatory to see me. But I'll make a deal with you. Let me get up there and take care of the thing with them, and then I'll skip out and be back here a couple of hours from now. How does that sound?"

"You're supposed to be photographing those asteroids this evening," she said, pouting again, and not smiling at all this time.

"Damn! Well, I'll ask Thilanda to do the camera work for me, or Hikkinan. Or somebody. I'll be back by Onos-set, that's a promise."

"A promise?"

He squeezed her hand and gave her a quick sly grin. "One that I'll actually keep. You can bet on that. Okay? You aren't angry?"

"Well—"

"I'll get Faro and Yimot out of the way as fast as I can."

"You'd better." As he began to assemble his papers again she said, "What *is* this business with Faro and Yimot that's so terribly important, anyway?"

"Lab work. Gravitational studies."

"Doesn't sound all that important to me, I have to say."

"I hope it turns out not to be important to anybody," Beenay replied. "But that's something I need to find out right now."

"I wish I knew what you were talking about."

He glanced at his watch and took a deep breath. He could stay here another minute or two, he supposed. "You know I've been working lately on the problem of the orbital motion of Kalgash around Onos, don't you?"

"Of course."

"All right. A couple of weeks ago I turned up an anomaly. My orbital numbers didn't fit the Theory of Universal Gravitation. So I checked them, naturally, but they came out the same way the second time. And the third. And the fourth. Always the same anomaly, no matter what method of calculation I used."

"Oh, Beenay, I'm so very sorry to hear that. You've worked so hard on this, I know, and to discover that your conclusions aren't right—"

"What if they are, though?"

"But you said—"

"I don't know if my math is right or wrong, at this point. As far as I can tell it is, but it doesn't seem conceivable that that can be so. I've checked and checked and checked, and I get the same result each time, with all sorts of cross-checks built in to tell me that I haven't made an error in computation. But the result that I'm getting is an impossible one. The only explanation I can come up with is that I'm starting from a cockeyed assumption and doing everything else right from then on, in which case I'm going to come up with the same wrong answer no matter which method of checking my calculations I use. I might just be blind to a fundamental problem at the base of my whole set of postulates. If you start with the wrong figure for planetary mass, for instance, you'll get the wrong orbit for your planet no matter how accurate the rest of your calculations may be. Are you following me?"

"So far, yes."

"Therefore I've given the problem to Faro and Yimot, without really telling them what it's all about, and asked them to calculate the whole thing from scratch. They're bright kids. I can count on them to do decent math. And if they end up with the same conclusion I did, even though they're coming at it from an angle that completely excludes whatever error I might have built into my own line of reasoning, then I'll have to admit that my figures are right after all."

"But they can't be right, Beenay. Didn't you say that your findings are contrary to the Universal Law of Gravitation?"

"What if the Universal Law is wrong, Raissta?"

"What? What?"

She stared at him. There was utter bewilderment in her eyes.

"You see the problem?" Beenay asked. "Why I need to know right away what Yimot and Faro have found?"

"No," she said. "No, I don't understand at all."

"We can talk about it later. I promise."

"Beenay—" Half in despair.

"I've got to go. But I'll be back as fast as I can. It's a promise, Raissta! A promise!"

[5]

Siferra paused only long enough to snatch a pick and a brush from the equipment tent, which had been knocked askew by the sandstorm but was still reasonably intact. Then she went scrambling up the side of the Hill of Thombo, with Balik ponderously hauling himself right behind her. Young Eilis 18 had appeared from the shelter by the cliff now, and he stood below, staring up at them. Thuvvik and his corps of workmen were a little farther back, watching, scratching their heads in puzzlement.

"Watch out," Siferra called to Balik, when she had reached the beginning of the open gouge in the hill that the sandstorm had carved. "I'm going to run a trial cut."

"Shouldn't we photograph it first, and—"

"I told you to watch out," she said sharply, as she dug her pick into the hillside and sent a shower of loose soil tumbling down onto his head and shoulders.

He jumped aside, spitting out sand.

"Sorry," she said, without looking down. She cut into the hillside a second time, widening the storm gouge. It wasn't the best of technique, she knew, to be slashing away like this. Her mentor, grand old Shelbik, was probably whirling in his grave. And the founder of their science, the revered Galdo 221, no doubt was looking down from his exalted place in the pantheon of archaeologists and shaking his head sadly.

On the other hand, Shelbik and Galdo had had chances of their own to uncover whatever lay in the Hill of Thombo, and they hadn't done it. If she was a little too excited now, a little too hasty in her attack, well, they would simply have to forgive her. Now that the seeming calamity of the sandstorm had been transformed into serendipitous good fortune, now that the apparent ruination of her career had turned unexpectedly into the making of it, Siferra could not hold herself back from finding out what was buried here. Could not. Absolutely could not.

"Look—" she muttered, knocking a great mass of overburden away and going to work with her brush. "We've got a charred layer here, right at the foundation level of the cyclopean city. The place must have burned clear down to the stone. But you look a little lower on the hill and you can see that the crosshatch-style town is sitting right under the fire line—the cyclopean people simply plunked this whole monumental foundation down on top of the older city—"

"Siferra—" said Balik uneasily.

"I know, I know. But let me at least begin to see what's here. Just a quick probe now, and then we can go back to doing things the proper way." She felt as though she were perspiring from head to toe. Her eyes were starting to ache, so fiercely was she staring. "Look, will you? We're way up on top of the hill, and we've already got two towns. And it's my guess that if we unzip the mound a little further, someplace around where we'd expect to find the foundations of the crosshatch people, we'll— yes! *Yes!* There! By Darkness, will you look at that, Balik! Just look!"

She pointed triumphantly with the tip of her pick.

Another dark line of charcoal was apparent, near the foundations of the crosshatch-style building. The second highest level had also been destroyed by fire just as the cyclopean one had. And from the way things looked, it was sitting atop the ruins of an even older village.

Balik now had caught her fervor too. Together they worked to lay bare the outer face of the hill, midway between ground level and the shattered summit. Eilis called up to them to ask what on Kalgash they were doing, but they ignored him. Aflame with eagerness and curiosity, they cut swiftly through the ancient packing of windblown sand, moving three inches farther down the hill, six, eight—

"Do you see what I see?" Siferra cried, after a time.

"Another village, yes. But what kind of style of architecture is that, would you say?"

She shrugged. "It's a new one on me."

"And me too. Something very archaic, that's for sure."

"No question of it. But I think it's not the most archaic thing

25

we've got here, not by plenty." Siferra peered down toward the distant ground. "You know what I think, Balik? We've got five towns here, six, seven, maybe eight, each one right on top of the next. You and I may spend the rest of our lives digging in this hill!"

They looked at each other in wonder.

"We'd better get down and take some photos now," he said quietly.

"Yes. Yes, we'd better do that." She felt almost calm, suddenly. Enough of this furious hacking and slashing, she thought. It was time to go back to being a professional now. Time to approach this hill like a scholar, not a treasure-hunter or a journalist.

Let Balik take his photographs, first, from every side. Then take the soil samples at the surface level, and put in the first marker stakes, and go through all the rest of the standard preliminary procedures.

Then a trial trench, a bold shaft right through the hill, to give us some idea of what we've really got here.

And then, she told herself, we'll peel this hill layer by layer. We'll take it apart, carving away each stratum to look at the one below it, until we're down to virgin soil. And by the time we're done with that, she vowed, we'll know more about the prehistory of Kalgash than all my predecessors put together have been able to learn since archaeologists first came here to Beklimot to dig.

[6]

Kelaritan said, "We've arranged everything for your inspection of the Tunnel of Mystery, Dr. Sheerin. If you'll be down in front of your hotel in about an hour, our car will pick you up."

"Right," Sheerin said. "See you in about an hour."

The plump psychologist put down the phone and stared solemnly at himself in the mirror opposite his bed.

The face that looked back at him was a troubled one. He seemed so wasted and haggard that he tugged at his cheeks to assure himself that they were still there. Yes, there they were, his familiar fleshy cheeks. He hadn't lost an ounce. The haggardness was all in his mind.

Sheerin had slept badly—had scarcely slept at all, so it seemed to him now—and yesterday he had only picked at his food. Nor did he feel in the least hungry now. The thought of going downstairs for breakfast had no appeal whatever. That was an alien concept to him, not to feel hungry.

Was the bleakness of his mood, he wondered, the result of his interviews with Kelaritan's hapless patients yesterday?

Or was he simply terrified of going through the Tunnel of Mystery?

Certainly seeing those three patients hadn't been easy. It was a long time since he'd done any actual clinical work, and obviously his sojourn among the academics at Saro University had attenuated the professional detachment that allows members of the healing arts to confront the ill without being overwhelmed by compassion and sorrow. Sheerin was surprised at that, how tenderhearted he seemed to have become, how thin-skinned.

That first one, Harrim, the longshoreman—he looked tough enough to withstand anything. And yet fifteen minutes of Darkness on his trip through the Tunnel of Mystery had reduced him to such a state that merely to relive the trauma in memory sent him into babbling hysteria. How terribly sad that was.

And then the other two, in the afternoon—they had been in even worse shape. Gistin 190, the schoolteacher, that lovely frail woman with the dark, intelligent eyes—she hadn't been able to stop sobbing for a moment, and though she was able to speak clearly and well, at least in the beginning, her story had degenerated into mere incoherent blurtings within a few sentences. And Chimmilit 97, the high school athlete, obviously a perfect physical specimen—Sheerin wasn't going quickly to forget how the boy had reacted to the sight of the afternoon sky when Sheerin opened the blinds in his room. There was Onos blazing away in the west, and all that huge handsome boy could manage to say was, "The Darkness—the Darkness—" before he turned away and tried to scuttle down under his bed!

The Darkness—the Darkness—

And now, Sheerin thought gloomily, it's *my* turn to take a ride in the Tunnel of Mystery.

Of course, he could simply refuse. There was nothing in his consulting contract with the Municipality of Jonglor that required him to risk his sanity. He'd be able to render a valid enough opinion without actually sticking his neck into peril.

But something in him rebelled at such timidity. His professional pride, if nothing else, was pushing him toward the Tunnel. He was here to study the phenomenon of mass hysteria, and to help these people work out ways not only of healing the present victims but of preventing recurrences of these tragedies. How could he deign to explain what had happened to the Tunnel's victims if he didn't make a close study of the cause of their disturbances? He *had* to. It would be sheer malfeasance to back out.

Nor did he want anyone, not even these strangers here in Jonglor, to be able to accuse him of cowardice. He remembered the taunts of his childhood: "Fatty is a coward! Fatty is a coward!" All because he hadn't wanted to climb a tree that was obviously beyond the capabilities of his heavy, ill-coordinated body.

But Fatty wasn't a coward. Sheerin knew that. He was content with himself: a sane, well-balanced man. He simply didn't want other people making incorrect assumptions about him because of his unheroic appearance.

Besides, fewer than one out of ten of those who had gone through the Tunnel of Mystery had come out of it showing any symptoms of emotional disturbance. And those people must have been vulnerable in some special way. Precisely *because* he was so sane, Sheerin told himself, because he was so well balanced, he had nothing to fear.

Nothing—

To—

Fear—

He kept repeating those words to himself until he felt almost calm.

Even so, Sheerin was something other than his customary jolly self as he went downstairs to wait for the hospital car to pick him up.

Kelaritan was there, and Cubello, and a striking-looking woman named Varitta 312, who was introduced to him as one of the engineers who had designed the Tunnel. Sheerin greeted

28

them all with hearty handshakes and a broad smile that he hoped seemed convincing.

"A nice day for a trip to the amusement park," he said, trying to sound jovial.

Kelaritan looked at him oddly. "I'm glad you feel that way. Did you sleep well, Dr. Sheerin?"

"Very well, thanks. —As well as could be expected, I should say. After seeing those unhappy people yesterday."

Cubello said, "You aren't optimistic about their chances of recovery, then?"

"I'd like to be," Sheerin told the lawyer ambiguously.

The car moved smoothly down the street.

"It's about a twenty-minute drive to the Centennial Exposition grounds," Kelaritan said. "The Exposition itself will be crowded—it is every day—but we've had a big section of the amusement area roped off so that we won't be disturbed. The Tunnel of Mystery itself, as you know, has been shut down since the full extent of the troubles became apparent."

"You mean the deaths?"

"Obviously we couldn't allow the ride to remain open after that," Cubello said. "But you must realize that we were considering shutting down much earlier. It was a question of determining whether the people who appeared to have been disturbed by their trips through the Tunnel were actually suffering harm or were merely falling in with popular hysteria."

"Of course," Sheerin said, his tone a dry one. "The City Council wouldn't have wanted to close down such a profitable attraction except for a really good reason. Such as having a bunch of the customers drop dead from fright, I suppose."

The atmosphere in the car became exceedingly chilly.

Kelaritan said, after a time, "The Tunnel was not only a profitable attraction but also one that nearly everyone who attended the Exposition was eager to experience, Dr. Sheerin. I understand that thousands of people had to be turned away every day."

"Even though it was obvious from the very first day that some of those who rode through the Tunnel, like Harrim and his family, were coming out of it in psychotic states?"

"*Especially* because of that, Doctor," Cubello said.

29

"What?"

"Forgive me if I seem to be explaining your own specialty to you," the lawyer said unctuously. "But I'd like to remind you that there's a fascination in being frightened *when it's part of a game*. A baby is born with three instinctive fears: of loud noises, of falling, and of the total absence of light. That's why it's considered so funny to jump at someone and shout 'Boo!' That's why it's such fun to ride a roller coaster. And that's why the Tunnel of Mystery was something everybody wanted to see at first hand. People came out of that Darkness shaking, breathless, half dead with fear, but they kept on paying to get in. The fact that a few of those who took the ride came out of it in a rather intense state of shock only added to the appeal."

"Because most people assumed that *they'd* be tough enough to withstand whatever it was that had shaken up the others so much, is that it?"

"Exactly, Doctor."

"And when some people came out not just highly upset but actually dead of fright? Even if the Exposition managers couldn't see their way clear to shutting the thing down after that, I'd imagine that potential customers would have become few and far between, once the news of the deaths got around."

"Ah, quite the contrary," said Cubello, smiling triumphantly. "The same psychological mechanism operated, though even more strongly. After all, if people with weak hearts wanted to go through the Tunnel, it was at their own risk— why be surprised at what happened to them? The City Council discussed the whole thing at great length and agreed finally to put a doctor in the front office and have every customer undergo a physical examination before getting into the car. That actually *boosted* ticket sales."

"In that case," Sheerin said, "why is the Tunnel shut down now? From what you've told me, I'd expect it to be doing terrific business, lines stretching from Jonglor all the way to Khunabar, mobs of people going in the front way and a steady stream of corpses being hauled out the back."

"Dr. Sheerin!"

"Well, why *isn't* it still open, if even the deaths didn't trouble anybody?"

"The liability insurance problem," Cubello said.

"Ah. Of course."

"Despite your grisly little turn of phrase just now, actual deaths were very few and far between—three, I think, or maybe five. The families of those who passed away were given adequate indemnities and the cases were closed. What ultimately became a problem for us was not the death rate but the survival rate among those who underwent traumatic disturbance. It began to become clear that some might require hospitalization for prolonged periods—an ongoing expense, a constant financial drain on the municipality and its insurers."

"I see," Sheerin said morosely. "If they simply fall down dead, it's a one-shot cost. Buy off the relatives and that's that. But if they linger for months or years in a public institution, the price can get to be too high."

"Perhaps a little harshly put," said Cubello. "But that is essentially the calculation the City Council was forced to make."

"Dr. Sheerin seems a little testy this morning," Kelaritan said to the lawyer. "Possibly the idea of going through the Tunnel himself is troublesome to him."

"Absolutely not," said Sheerin at once.

"Of course you understand that there is no real necessity for you to—"

"There is," Sheerin said.

There was silence in the car. Sheerin peered somberly at the changing landscape, the curious angular scaly-barked trees, the bushes with flowers of odd metallic hues, the peculiarly high and narrow houses with pointed eaves. He had rarely been this far north before. There was something very disagreeable about the look of the entire province—and about this crew of mealy-mouthed cynical people, too. He told himself that he'd be glad to get home to Saro again.

But first—the Tunnel of Mystery—

The Jonglor Centennial Exposition was spread over a vast area of parkland just east of the city. It was a mini-city in itself, and quite spectacular in its own way, Sheerin thought. He saw fountains, arcades, shining pink and turquoise towers of iridescent stone-hard plastic. Great exhibit halls offered art treasures from every province of Kalgash, industrial displays, the latest scientific marvels. Wherever he looked there was something unusual and beautiful to engage his eye. Thousands of people,

31

perhaps hundreds of thousands, strolled its glittering, elegant boulevards and avenues.

Sheerin had always heard that the Jonglor Centennial Exposition was one of the marvels of the world, and he saw now that it was true. To be able to visit it was a rare privilege. It was open only once every hundred years, for a three-year run, to commemorate the anniversary of the city's founding—and this, Jonglor's Fifth Centennial Exposition, was said to be the greatest of all. Indeed he felt sudden buoyant excitement, such as he had not known in a long while, as he traveled through its well-manicured grounds. He hoped that he'd have some time later in the week to explore it on his own.

But his mood changed abruptly as the car swung around the perimeter of the Exposition and brought them to an entrance in back that led to the amusement area. Here, just as Kelaritan had said, great sections were roped off; and sullen crowds peered across the ropes in obvious annoyance as Cubello, Kelaritan, and Varitta 312 led him toward the Tunnel of Mystery. Sheerin could hear them muttering angrily, a low harsh growling that he found unsettling and even a little intimidating.

He realized that the lawyer had told the truth: these people were angry because the Tunnel was closed.

They're jealous, Sheerin thought in wonder. They know we're going to the Tunnel, and *they* want to go too. Despite everything that's happened there.

"We can go in this way," Varitta said.

The facade of the Tunnel was an enormous pyramidal structure, tapering away at the sides in an eerie, dizzying perspective. In the center of it was a huge six-sided entrance gate, dramatically outlined in scarlet and gold. Bars had been drawn across it. Varitta produced a key and unlocked a small door to the left of the facade, and they stepped through.

Inside, everything seemed much more ordinary. Sheerin saw a series of metal railings no doubt designed to contain the lines of people waiting to board the ride. Beyond that was a platform much like that in any railway station, with a string of small open cars waiting there. And beyond that—

Darkness.

Cubello said, "If you don't mind signing this first, please, Doctor—"

Sheerin stared at the paper the lawyer had handed him. It was full of words, blurred, dancing about.

"What is this?"

"A release. The standard form."

"Yes. Of course." Airily Sheerin scrawled his name without even trying to read the paper.

You are not afraid, he told himself. *You fear nothing at all.*

Varitta 312 put a small device in his hand. "An abort switch," she explained. "The full ride lasts fifteen minutes, but you just have to press this green panel here as soon as you've been inside long enough to have learned what you need to know—or in case you begin to feel uncomfortable—and lights will come on. Your car will go quickly to the far end of the Tunnel and circle back to the station."

"Thank you," Sheerin said. "I doubt that I'll need it."

"But you should have it. Just in case."

"It's my plan to experience the ride to the fullest," he told her, enjoying his own pomposity.

But there was such a thing as foolhardiness, he reminded himself. He didn't intend to use the abort switch, but it was probably unwise not to take it.

Just in case.

He stepped out on the platform. Kelaritan and Cubello were looking at him in an all too transparent way. He could practically hear them thinking, *This fat old fool is going to turn to jelly in there.* Well, let them think it.

Varitta had disappeared. No doubt she had gone to turn on the Tunnel mechanism.

Yes: there she was now, in a control booth high up to the right, signaling that everything was ready.

"If you'll board the car, Doctor—" Kelaritan said.

"Of course. Of course."

Fewer than one out of ten experienced harmful effects. Very likely they were unusually vulnerable to Darkness disorders to begin with. I am not. I am a very stable individual.

He entered the car. There was a safety belt; he strapped it around his waist, adjusting it with some difficulty to his girth. The car began to roll forward, slowly, very slowly.

Darkness was waiting for him.

Fewer than one out of ten. Fewer than one out of ten.

33

He understood the Darkness syndrome. That would protect him, he was sure: his understanding. Even though all of mankind had an instinctive fear of the absence of light, that did not mean that the absence of light was of itself harmful.

What was harmful, Sheerin knew, was one's *reaction* to the absence of light. The thing to do is to stay calm. Darkness is nothing but darkness, a change of external circumstances. We are conditioned to abhor it because we live in a world where darkness is unnatural, where there is always light, the light of the many suns. At any time there might be as many as four suns shining at once; usually there were three in the sky, and at no time were there ever less than two—and the light of any of them was sufficient all by itself to hold back the Darkness.

The Darkness—

The Darkness—

The Darkness!

Sheerin was in the Tunnel now. Behind him the last vestige of light disappeared, and he peered into an utter void. There was nothing ahead of him: nothing. A pit. An abyss. A zone of total lightlessness. And he was tumbling headlong into it.

He felt sweat breaking out all over him.

His knees began to shake. His forehead throbbed. He held up his hand and was unable to see it in front of his face.

Abort abort abort abort

No. Absolutely not.

He sat upright, back rigid, eyes wide open, gazing stolidly into the nothingness through which he plunged. On and on, ever deeper. Primordial fears bubbled and hissed in the depths of his soul, and he forced them back down and away.

The suns are still shining outside the Tunnel, he told himself.

This is only temporary. In fourteen minutes and thirty seconds I'll be back out there.

Fourteen minutes and twenty seconds.

Fourteen minutes and ten seconds.

Fourteen minutes—

Was he moving at all, though? He couldn't tell. Maybe he wasn't. The car's mechanism was silent; and he had no reference points. What if I'm stuck? he wondered. Just sitting here in the dark, no way to tell where I am, what's happening, how much time is passing? Fifteen minutes, twenty, half an hour? Until I've passed whatever limit my sanity can stand, and then—

There's always the abort switch, though.

But suppose it doesn't work? What if I press it and the lights don't come on?

I could test it, I suppose. Just to see—

Fatty is a coward! Fatty is a coward!

No. No. Don't touch it. Once you turn the lights on you won't be able to turn them off again. You mustn't use the abort switch, or they'll know—they'll all know—

Fatty is a coward, Fatty is a coward—

Suddenly, astonishingly, he hurled the abort switch into the darkness. There was a tiny sound as it fell—*somewhere.* Then silence again. His hand felt terribly empty.

The Darkness—

The Darkness—

There was no end to it. He was tumbling through an infinite abyss. Falling and falling and falling into the night, the endless night, the all-devouring black—

Breathe deeply. Stay calm.

What if there's permanent mental damage?

Stay calm, he told himself. You'll be all right. You've got maybe eleven minutes more of this at the worst, maybe only six or seven. The suns are shining out there. Six or seven minutes and you'll never be in Darkness again, not if you live to be a thousand.

The Darkness—

Oh, God, the Darkness—

Calm. Calm. You're a very stable man, Sheerin. You're extremely sane. You were sane when you went into this thing and you'll be sane when you come out.

Tick. Tick. Tick. Every second gets you closer to the exit. Or does it? This ride may never end. I could be in here forever. Tick. Tick. Tick. Am I moving? Do I have five minutes left, or five seconds, or is this still the first minute?

Tick. Tick.

Why don't they let me out? Can't they tell how I'm suffering in here?

They don't want to let you out. They'll never let you out. They're going to—

Suddenly, a stabbing pain between his eyes. An explosion of agony in his skull.

What's that?

Light!

Could it be? Yes. Yes.

Thank God. Light, yes! Thank any god that might ever have existed!

He was at the end of the Tunnel! He was coming back to the station! It must be. Yes. Yes. His heartbeat, which had become a panicky thunder, was starting to return to normal. His eyes, adjusting now to the return of normal conditions, began to focus on familiar things, blessed things, the stanchions, the platform, the little window in the control booth—

Cubello, Kelaritan, watching him.

He felt ashamed now of his cowardice. *Pull yourself together, Sheerin. It wasn't so bad, really. You're all right. You aren't lying in the bottom of the car sucking your thumb and whimpering. It was scary, it was terrifying, but it didn't destroy you—it wasn't actually anything you couldn't handle—*

"Here we go. Give us your hand, Doctor. Up—up—"

They hauled him to a standing position and steadied him as he clambered out of the car. Sheerin sucked breath deep down into his lungs. He ran his hand across his forehead, wiping away the streaming perspiration.

"The little abort switch," he murmured. "I seem to have lost it somewhere—"

"How are you, Doctor?" Kelaritan asked. "How was it?"

Sheerin teetered. The hospital director caught him by the arm, steadying him, but Sheerin indignantly brushed him away. He wasn't going to let them think that those few minutes in the Tunnel had gotten to him.

But he couldn't deny that he had been affected. Try as he might, there was no way to hide that. Not even from himself.

No force in the world could ever get him to take a second trip through that Tunnel, he realized.

"Doctor? Doctor?"

"I'm—all—right—" he said thickly.

"He says he's all right," came the lawyer's voice. "Stand back. Let him alone."

"His legs are wobbling," Kelaritan said. "He's going to fall."

"No," Sheerin said. "Not a chance. I'm fine, I tell you!"

He lurched and staggered, regained his balance, lurched again. Sweat poured from every pore he had. He glanced over his shoulder, saw the mouth of the Tunnel, and shuddered. Turning away from that dark cave, he pulled his shoulders up high, as if he would have liked to hide his face between them.

"Doctor?" Kelaritan said doubtfully.

No use pretending. This was foolishness, this vain and stubborn attempt at heroism. Let them think he was a coward. Let them think anything. Those fifteen minutes had been the worst nightmare of his life. The impact of it was still sinking in, and sinking in, and sinking in.

"It was—powerful stuff," he said. "Very powerful. Very disturbing."

"But you're basically all right, isn't that so?" the lawyer said eagerly. "A little shaken, yes. Who wouldn't be, going into Darkness? But basically okay. As we knew you'd be. It's only a few, a very few, who undergo any sort of harmful—"

"No," Sheerin said. The lawyer's face was like that of a grinning gargoyle in front of him. Like the face of a demon. He couldn't bear the sight of it. But a good dose of the truth would exorcise the demon. No need to be diplomatic, Sheerin thought. Not when talking with demons. —"It's impossible for anyone to go through that thing without being at grave risk. I'm certain of it now. Even the strongest psyche will take a terrible battering, and the weak ones will simply crumble. If you open that ride again, you'll have every mental hospital in four provinces full up within six months."

"On the contrary, Doctor—"

"Don't 'on the contrary' me! Have you been in the Tunnel, Cubello? No, I didn't think so. But I have. You're paying for my professional opinion: you might as well have it right now. The Tunnel's deadly. It's a simple matter of human nature. Darkness is more than most of us can handle, and that's never going to change, so long as we've got a sun left burning in the sky. Shut the Tunnel down for good, Cubello! In the name of sanity, man, shut the thing down! Shut it down!"

[7]

Parking his motor scooter in the faculty lot just below the Observatory dome, Beenay went jogging quickly up the footpath that led to the main entrance of the huge building. As he began to ascend the wide stone steps of the entranceway itself he was startled to hear someone calling his name from above.

"Beenay! So you *are* here after all."

The astronomer looked up. The tall, heavyset, powerful figure of his friend Theremon 762 of the Saro City *Chronicle* stood framed in the great door of the Observatory.

"Theremon? Were you looking for me?"

"I was. But they told me you weren't due to show up here for another couple of hours. And then, just as I was leaving, there you were anyway. Talk about serendipity!"

Beenay trotted up the last few steps, and they gave each other a quick hug. He had known the newspaperman some three or four years, ever since the time Theremon had come to the Observatory to interview some scientist, any scientist, about the latest manifesto of the crackpot Apostles of Flame group. Gradually he and Theremon had become close friends, even though Theremon was some five years older and came out of a rougher, worldlier background. Beenay liked the idea of having a friend who had no involvement whatsoever in university politics; and Theremon was delighted to know someone who wasn't at all interested in exploiting him for his considerable journalistic influence.

"Is something wrong?" Beenay asked.

"Not in the least. But I need to get you to do the Voice of Science routine again. Mondior's made another of his famous 'Repent, repent, doom is coming' speeches. Now he says he's ready to reveal the exact hour when the world will be destroyed. In case you're interested, it's going to happen next year on the nineteenth of Theptar, as a matter of fact."

"That madman! It's a waste of space printing anything about him. Why does anyone pay the slightest bit of attention to the Apostles, anyway?"

38

Theremon shrugged. "The fact is that people do. A lot of people, Beenay. And if Mondior says the end is nigh, I need to get someone like you to stand up and say, 'Not so, brothers and sisters! Have no fear! All is well!' Or words to that effect. I can count on you, can't I, Beenay?"

"You know you can."

"This evening?"

"This evening? Oh, lord, Theremon, this evening's a real mess. How much of my time do you think you'd have to have?"

"Half an hour? Forty-five minutes?"

"Look," Beenay said, "I've got an urgent appointment right now—that's why I'm here ahead of schedule. After that, I've sworn to Raissta that I'll hustle back home and devote, well, an hour or two to her. We've been on such different tracks lately that we've hardly seen each other at all. And then later in the evening I'm supposed to be here at the Observatory again to supervise taking of a bunch of photographs of—"

"All right," said Theremon. "I see I've picked the wrong time for this. Well, listen, no problem, Beenay. I've got until tomorrow afternoon to turn in my story. What if we talk in the morning?"

"The morning?" Beenay said doubtfully.

"I know morning's an unthinkable concept for you. But what I mean is, I can get back up here at Onos-rise, just as you're finishing up your evening's work. If you could simply manage a little interview with me before you go home to go to sleep—"

"Well—"

"For a friend, Beenay."

Beenay gave the journalist a weary look. "Of course I will. That's not the issue. It's just that I may be so groggy after a whole evening of work that I may not be of any use to you."

Theremon grinned. "That doesn't worry me. I've noticed that you're capable of degroggifying pretty damned quickly when there's anti-scientific nonsense for you to refute. Tomorrow at Onos-rise, then? In your office upstairs?"

"Right."

"A million thanks, pal. I'll owe you one for this."

"Don't mention it."

Theremon saluted and began to head down the steps. "Give

39

my best to that beautiful lady of yours," he called. "And I'll see you in the morning."

"See you in the morning, yes," Beenay echoed.

How odd that sounded. He never saw *anybody*—or anything —in the morning. But he'd make an exception for Theremon. That was what friendship was all about, wasn't it?

Beenay turned and entered the Observatory.

Inside, all was dimly lit and calm, the familiar hush of the great hall of science where he had spent most of his time since his early university days. But the calm was, he knew, a deceptive one. This mighty building, like the more mundane places of the world, was constantly aswirl with conflicts of all sorts, ranging from the loftiest of philosophical disputes down to the pettiest of trivial feuds, spats, and backbiting intrigues. Astronomers, as a group, were no more virtuous than anyone else.

All the same, the Observatory was a sanctuary for Beenay and for most of the others who worked there—a place where they could leave most of the world's problems behind and devote themselves more or less peacefully to the everlasting struggle to answer the great questions that the universe posed.

He walked swiftly down the long main hall, trying as always without success to muffle the clatter of his boots against the marble floor.

As he invariably did, he glanced quickly into the display cases along the wall to the right and left, where some of the sacred artifacts of the history of astronomy were on perpetual exhibit. Here were the crude, almost comical telescopes that such pioneers as Chekktor and Stanta had used, four or five hundred years before. Here were the gnarled black lumps of meteorites that had fallen from the sky over the centuries, enigmatic reminders of the mysteries that lay behind the clouds. Here were first editions of the great astronomical sky-charts and textbooks, and the time-yellowed manuscripts of some of the epoch-making theoretical works of the great thinkers.

Beenay paused for a moment before the last of those manuscripts, which unlike the others seemed fresh and almost new— for it was only a single generation old, Athor 77's classic codification of the Theory of Universal Gravitation, worked out not very long before Beenay himself had been born. Though he was not a particularly religious man, Beenay stared at that thin sheaf of paper with something very much like reverence, and found himself thinking something very much like a prayer.

The Theory of Universal Gravitation was one of the pillars of the cosmos for him: perhaps the most basic pillar. He couldn't imagine what he would do if that pillar were to fall. And it seemed to him now that the pillar might be tottering.

At the end of the hall, behind a handsome bronze door, was Dr. Athor's own office. Beenay glanced at it quickly and hurried past it, up the stairs. The venerable and still formidable Observatory director was the last person in the world, absolutely the last, that Beenay wanted to see at this moment.

Faro and Yimot were waiting for him upstairs in the Chart Room, where they had arranged to meet.

"Sorry I'm a little late," Beenay said. "It's been a complicated afternoon so far."

They gave him nervous, owlish smiles. What a strange pair they are, he thought, not for the first time. They both came from some backwater farming province—Sithin, maybe, or Gatamber. Faro 24 was short and roly-poly, with a languid, almost indolent way of moving. His general style was easygoing and casual. His friend Yimot 70 was incredibly tall and thin, something like a hinged ladder with arms, legs, and a face, and you practically needed a telescope to see his head, looming up there in the stratosphere above you. Yimot was as tense and twitchy as his friend was relaxed. Yet they were inseparable, always had been. Of all the young graduate students, one notch down the Observatory's table of organization from Beenay's level, they were by far the most brilliant.

"We haven't been waiting long," Yimot said at once.

"Only a minute or two, Dr. Beenay," Faro added.

"Not quite 'doctor' yet, thanks," Beenay said. "I've still got the final inquisition to go through. How did you manage with those computations?"

Yimot said, twitching and jerking his impossibly long legs around, "This is gravitational stuff, isn't it, sir?"

Faro nudged him so vigorously in the ribs with his elbow that Beenay expected to hear the sound of crunching bone.

"That's all right," Beenay said. "Yimot's correct, as a matter of fact." He gave the tall young man a pale smile. "I wanted this to be a purely abstract mathematical exercise for you. But

41

it doesn't surprise me that you were able to figure out the context. You figured it out *after* you had your result, didn't you?"

"Yes, sir," said Yimot and Faro at the same time. "We ran all the calculations first," Faro said. "Then we took a second look, and the context became apparent," said Yimot.

"Ah. Yes," Beenay said. These kids were sometimes a little unnerving. They were so young—only six or seven years younger than he, as a matter of fact, but he was an assistant professor and they were students, and to him and them both that was a vast barrier. Young as they were, though, they had such extraordinary minds! He wasn't altogether pleased that they had guessed at the conceptual matrix within which these calculations were located. In fact, he wasn't pleased at all. In another few years they'd be right up here on the faculty with him, perhaps competing for the same professorship he hoped to get, and that might not be fun. But he tried not to think about that.

He reached for their printout.

"May I see?" he asked.

Hands fluttering wildly, Yimot handed it over. Beenay scanned the rows of figures, calmly at first, then with rising agitation.

He had been pondering, all year long, certain implications of the Theory of Universal Gravitation, which his mentor Athor had brought to such a summit of perfection. It had been Athor's great triumph, the making of his lofty reputation, to work out the orbital motions of Kalgash and all six of its suns according to rational principles of attractive forces.

Beenay, using modern computational equipment, had been calculating some aspects of Kalgash's orbit around Onos, its primary sun, when to his horror he observed that his figures didn't check out properly in terms of the Theory of Universal Gravitation. The theory said that at the beginning of the present year Kalgash should have been *here* in relation to Onos, when in undeniable fact Kalgash was *there*.

The deviation was trivial—a matter of a few decimal places—but that wasn't trivial at all, in the larger sense of things. The Theory of Universal Gravitation was so precise that most people preferred to refer to it as the *Law* of Universal Gravitation. Its mathematical underpinning was considered impeccable.

But a theory that purports to explain the movements of the world through space has no room for even small discrepancies. Either it is complete or it is not complete: no middle way was permissible. And a difference of a few decimal places in a short-range calculation would widen into a vast abyss, Beenay knew, if more ambitious computations were attempted. What good was the whole Theory of Universal Gravitation if the position that it said Kalgash was going to hold in the sky a century from now turned out to be halfway around Onos from the planet's actual location then?

Beenay had gone over his figures until he was sick of reworking them. The result was always the same.

But what was he supposed to believe?

His numbers, or Athor's towering master scheme?

His piddling notions of astronomy, or the great Athor's profound insight into the fundamental structure of the universe?

He imagined himself standing right on top of the dome of the Observatory, calling out, "Listen to me, everybody! Athor's theory is wrong! I've got the figures right here that disprove it!" Which would bring forth such gales of laughter that he'd be blown clear across the continent. Who was he to set himself up against the titanic Athor? Who could possibly believe that a callow assistant professor had toppled the Law of Universal Gravitation?

And yet—and yet—

His eyes raced over the printout sheets that Yimot and Faro had prepared. The calculations on the first two pages were unfamiliar to him; he had set up the data for the two students in such a way that the underlying relationships from which the numbers were derived were not at all obvious, and evidently they had approached the problem in a way that any astronomer trying to compute a planetary orbit would regard as quite unorthodox. Which was exactly what Beenay had wanted. The orthodox ways had led him only into catastrophic conclusions; but he had too much information at his own disposal to be able to work in any other mode but the orthodox ones. Faro and Yimot hadn't been hampered in that fashion.

But as he followed along their line of reasoning, Beenay began to notice a discomforting convergence of the numbers. By

43

the third page they had locked in with his own calculations, which he knew by heart by this time.

And from there on, everything followed in an orderly way, step by step by step, to the same dismaying, shattering, inconceivable, totally unacceptable culminating result.

Beenay looked up at the two students, aghast.

"There's no possibility, is there, that you've slipped up somewhere? This string of integrations here, for example—they look pretty tricky—"

"*Sir!*" Yimot cried, sounding shocked to the core. His face was bright red and his arms waved about as if moving of their own accord.

Faro said, more placidly, "I'm afraid they're correct, sir. They tally frontwards and backwards."

"Yes. I imagine they do," said Beenay dully. He struggled to conceal his anguish. But his hands were shaking so badly that the printout sheets began to flutter in his grasp. He started to put them down on the table before him, but his wrist jerked uncontrollably in a very Yimot-like gesture and sent them scattering all over the floor.

Faro knelt to pick them up. He gave Beenay a troubled look.

"Sir, if we've upset you in any way—"

"No. No, not at all. I didn't sleep well today, that's the problem. But this is fine work, unquestionably very fine. I'm proud of you. To take a problem like this, one which has utterly no real-world resonance at all, which in fact is in total contradiction of real-world scientific truth, and to follow so methodically to the conclusion required by the data while succeeding in ignoring the fact that the initial premise is absurd—why, it's a splendid job, an admirable demonstration of your powers of logic, a first-rate thought-experiment—"

He saw them exchange quick glances. He wondered if he was fooling them even slightly.

"And now," he went on, "if you'll excuse me, fellows—I have another conference—"

Rolling the damning papers into a tight cylinder, Beenay shoved them under his arm and rushed past them, out the door, down the hall, practically running, heading for the safety and privacy of his own tiny office.

My God, he thought. My God, my God, my God, what have I done? And what will I do now?

He buried his head in his hands and waited for the throbbing to stop. But it didn't seem to be planning to stop. After a moment he sat up and jabbed his finger against the communicator button on his desk.

"Get me the Saro City *Chronicle*," he told the machine. "Theremon 762."

From the communicator came a long, maddening burst of cracklings and hissings. Then, suddenly, Theremon's deep voice:

"Features desk, Theremon 762."

"Beenay."

"What's that? I can't hear what you're saying!"

Beenay realized that he hadn't managed to get out anything more than a croak. "It's Beenay, I said! I—I want to change our appointment time."

"To change it? Look, fellow, I understand how you feel about mornings, because so do I. But I've absolutely got to talk to you no later than noon tomorrow or I'll have no story here. I'll make it up to you any way I can, but—"

"You don't understand. I want to see you sooner, not later, Theremon."

"What?"

"This evening. Let's say half past nine. Or ten, if you can't make it."

"I thought you had photographs to take at the Observatory."

"The deuce with the photos, man. I need to see you."

"*Need* to? Beenay, what's happened? Is it something with Raissta?"

"It has nothing to do with Raissta in the slightest. Half past nine? At the Six Suns?"

"Six Suns, half past nine, yes," Theremon said. "It's a date."

Beenay broke the contact and sat for a long moment staring at the rolled paper cylinder before him, somberly shaking his head. He felt fractionally calmer now, but only fractionally. Confiding in Theremon would make it easier to bear the burden of all this. He trusted Theremon completely. Newsmen were generally not noted for their trustworthiness, Beenay

45

knew, but Theremon was a friend first, a journalist after that. He had never betrayed Beenay's confidence, not once.

Even so, Beenay didn't have any idea of his next move. Maybe Theremon would be able to come up with something. Maybe.

He left the Observatory by the back stairs, sneaking out by the fire escape like a thief. He didn't dare risk the possibility of running into Athor by going out the main way. It was appalling to him to consider the possibility of seeing Athor now, having to confront him face to face, man to man.

He found the motor scooter ride home a terrifying one. At every moment he was afraid that the laws of gravity would cease to hold true, that he would go soaring off into the heavens. But at last Beenay reached the little apartment that he shared with Raissta 717.

She gasped when she saw him.

"Beenay! You're white as a—"

"Ghost, yes." He reached for her and pulled her close against him. "Hold me," he said. "Hold me."

"What is it? What happened?"

"I'll tell you later," he said. "Just hold me."

[8]

Theremon was at the Six Suns Club a little after nine. It was probably a good idea to get a head start on Beenay, a quick drink or two first, just to lubricate his brain a little. The astronomer had sounded awful—as though he was keeping hysteria at bay only by some tremendous effort. Theremon couldn't imagine what terrible thing could have happened to him, there in the seclusion and stillness of the Observatory, to make such a wreck out of him in so short a time. But plainly Beenay was in big trouble, and plainly he was going to need the highest-quality help Theremon could provide.

"Let me have a Tano Special," Theremon told the waiter. "No, wait—make it a double. A Tano Sitha, okay?"

"Double white light," the waiter said. "Coming up."

The evening was mild. Theremon, who was well known

here and received special treatment, had been given his regular warm-weather table on the terrace overlooking the city. The lights of downtown sparkled gaily. Onos had set an hour or two ago, and only Trey and Patru were in the sky, burning brightly in the east, casting harsh twin shadows as they made their descent toward morning.

Looking at them, Theremon wondered which suns would be in the sky tomorrow. It was different all the time, a brilliant ever changing display. Onos, certainly—you could always be sure of seeing Onos at least part of the time every day of the year, even he knew that—and then what? Dovim, Tano, and Sitha, to make it a four-sun day? He wasn't sure. Maybe it was supposed to be just Tano and Sitha, with Onos visible only for a few hours at midday. That would be gloomy. But then, after a second sip, he reminded himself that this wasn't the season for short Onos-rises. So it would be a three-sun day, most likely, unless it was going to be just Onos and Dovim tomorrow.

It was so hard to keep it all straight—

Well, he could ask to see an almanac, if he really cared. But he didn't. Some people always seemed to know what tomorrow's suns would be like—Beenay was one, naturally—but Theremon took a more happy-go-lucky approach to it all. So long as *some* sun was going to be up there the next day, Theremon didn't especially care which one it was. And there always was one—two or three, actually, or sometimes four. You could count on that. Even five, once in a while.

His drink arrived. He took a deep gulp and exhaled in pleasure. What a delightful thing a Tano Special was! The good strong white rum of the Velkareen Islands, mixed with a shot of the even stronger product, clear and tangy, that they distilled on the coast of Bagilar, and just a dab of sgarrino juice to take the edge off—ah, magnificent! Theremon wasn't a particularly heavy drinker, certainly not the way newspapermen were legendarily supposed to be, but he counted it a shabby day when he couldn't find time for one or two Tano Specials in those quiet dusky hours after Onos had set.

"You look like you're enjoying that, Theremon," a familiar voice said behind him.

"Beenay! You're early!"

"Ten minutes. What are you drinking?"

"The usual. A Tano Special."

"Good. I think I'll have one too."

"*You?*" Theremon stared at his friend. Fruit juice was about Beenay's speed, so far as he knew. He couldn't recall ever having seen the astronomer drink anything stronger.

But Beenay looked strange this evening—haggard, weary, worn. His eyes had an almost feverish glow to them.

"Waiter!" Theremon called.

It was alarming to see Beenay gulp his drink. He gasped after the first slug, as though the impact was a lot greater than he'd been expecting, but then he went back to it quickly for a second deep pull, and a third.

"Easy," Theremon urged. "Your head'll be swimming in five minutes."

"It's swimming already."

"You had a drink before you came here?"

"No, not a drink," Beenay said. "A shock. An upset." He put his drink down and peered balefully at the city lights. After a moment he picked it up again, almost absent-mindedly, and drained what was left. —"I shouldn't have another one so soon, should I, Theremon?"

"I doubt it very much." Theremon reached out and let his hand rest lightly on the astronomer's wrist. "What's going on, fellow? Tell me about it."

"It's—hard to explain."

"Come on. I've been around the track a little, you know. You and Raissta—"

"*No!* I told you before, this has nothing to do with her. Nothing."

"All right. I believe you."

Beenay said, "Maybe I should have that second drink."

"In a little while. Come on, Beenay. What is it?"

Beenay sighed. "You know what the Theory of Universal Gravitation is, don't you, Theremon?"

"Of course I do. I mean, I couldn't tell you what it *means*, exactly—there are only twelve people on Kalgash who truly understand it, isn't that so?—but I can certainly tell you what it *is*—more or less."

"So you believe that garbage too," Beenay said, with a harsh laugh. "About the Theory of Gravitation being so complicated that only twelve people can understand its math."

"That's what I've always heard."

"What you've always heard is ignorant folk wisdom," said Beenay. "I could give you all the essential math in a sentence, and you'd probably understand what I was saying, too."

"You could? I would?"

"No question of it. Look, Theremon: the Law of Universal Gravitation—the Theory of Universal Gravitation, I mean— states that there exists a cohesive force among all bodies of the universe, such that the amount of this force between any two given bodies is proportional to the product of their masses divided by the square of the distance between them. It's that simple."

"That's all there is to it?"

"That's enough! It took four hundred years to develop it."

"Why that long? It seems simple enough, the way you put it."

"Because great laws aren't divined by flashes of inspiration, no matter what you newspaper people like to believe. It usually takes the combined work of a worldful of scientists over a period of centuries. Ever since Genóvi 41 discovered that Kalgash rotates around Onos, rather than vice versa—and that was about four centuries ago—astronomers have been working on the problem of why all six of the suns appear and disappear in the sky as they do. The complex motions of the six were recorded and analyzed and unwoven. Theory after theory was advanced and checked and counterchecked and modified and abandoned and revived and converted to something else. It was a deuce of a job."

Theremon nodded thoughtfully and finished off his drink. He signaled the waiter for two more. Beenay seemed calm enough so long as he was talking about science, he thought.

"It was some thirty years ago," the astronomer continued, "that Athor 77 put the touch of perfection on the whole thing by demonstrating that the Theory of Universal Gravitation accounts exactly for the orbital motions of the six suns. It was an amazing achievement. It was one of the greatest feats of sheer logic anyone has ever accomplished."

"I know how you revere that man," Theremon said. "But what does all this have to do with—"

"I'm getting to the point." Beenay rose and walked to the edge of the terrace, carrying his second drink with him. He stood there in silence for a time, looking out at distant Trey and Patru. It seemed to Theremon that Beenay was growing agitated again. But the newspaperman said nothing. After a time Beenay took a long gulp of his drink. Standing with his back still turned, he said finally, "The problem is this. A few months ago I began working on a recalculation of the motions of Kalgash around Onos, using the big new university computer. I provided the computer with the last six weeks' actual observations of Kalgash's orbit and told it to predict the orbital movements for the rest of the year. I didn't expect any surprises. Mainly I just wanted an excuse to fool around with the computer, I guess. Naturally, I used the gravitational laws in setting up my calculations." He swung around suddenly. His face had a bleak, haunted look. "Theremon, *it didn't come out right.*"

"I don't understand."

"The orbit the computer produced didn't match up with the hypothetical orbit I was expecting to get. I don't mean that I was simply working on the basis of a pure Kalgash-Onos system, you realize. I took into account all perturbations that the other suns would cause. And what I got—what the computer was claiming to be the true orbit of Kalgash—was something very different from the orbit that is indicated by Athor's Theory of Gravitation."

"But you said you used Athor's gravitational laws in setting things up," said Theremon, puzzled.

"I did."

"Then how—" Suddenly Theremon's eyes brightened. "Good lord, man! What a story! Are you telling me that the brand-new supercomputer at Saro University, installed at a cost of I don't want to think how many millions of credits, is *inaccurate?* That there's been a gigantic scandalous waste of the taxpayers' money? That—"

"There's nothing wrong with the computer, Theremon. Believe me."

"Can you be sure of that?"

"Positive."

"Then—what—"

"I might have given the computer erroneous figures, maybe. It's a terrific computer, but it can't get the right answer from the wrong data."

"So that's why you're so upset, Beenay! Listen, man, it's only human to make an error once in a while. You mustn't be so harsh on yourself. You—"

"I needed to be completely certain that I had fed the right numbers into the computer, first of all, and also that I had given it the right theoretical postulates to use in processing those numbers," said Beenay, clutching his glass so tightly that his hand shook. The glass was empty now, Theremon noticed. "As you say, it's only human to make an error once in a while. So I called in a couple of hotshot young graduate students and let *them* work on the problem. They had their results for me today. That was the meeting I had that was so important, when I said I couldn't see you. Theremon, they confirmed my findings. They got the same deviation in the orbit that I did."

"But if the computer was right, then—then—" Theremon shook his head. "Then what? The Theory of Universal Gravitation is wrong? Is that what you're saying?"

"Yes."

The word appeared to have come from Beenay at a terrible price. He seemed stunned, dazed, devastated.

Theremon studied him. No doubt this was confusing for Beenay, and probably very embarrassing. But the journalist still couldn't understand why the impact of all this on him was so powerful.

Then abruptly he understood everything.

"It's Athor! You're afraid of hurting Athor, aren't you?"

"That's it exactly," said Beenay, giving Theremon a look of almost pathetic gratitude for having seen the true situation. He threw himself down in his chair, shoulders hunched, head lowered. In a muffled voice he said, "It would kill the old man to know that someone's poked a hole in his wonderful theory. That *I*, of all people, had poked a hole in it. He's been like a second father to me, Theremon. Everything I've accomplished in the past ten years has been done under his guidance, with his encouragement, with—with, well, his love, in a manner of

51

speaking. And now I repay it like this. I wouldn't just be destroying his life's work—I'd be stabbing him, Theremon, *him.*"

"Have you considered simply suppressing your findings?"

Beenay looked astonished. "You know I couldn't do that!"

"Yes. Yes, I do know. But I had to find out whether you were thinking of it."

"Whether I was thinking of the unthinkable? No, of course not. It never entered my mind. But what am I going to do, Theremon? —I suppose I could just throw all the papers away and pretend I never looked into the whole subject. But that would be monstrous. So what it comes down to is, I have a choice between violating my own scientific conscience and ruining Athor. Ruining the man I look upon not simply as the head of my profession but as my own philosophical mentor."

"He can't have been much of a mentor, then."

The astronomer's eyes widened in astonishment and fury. "What are you saying, Theremon!"

"Easy. Easy." Theremon spread his hands wide in a conciliatory gesture. "It seems to me you're being awfully condescending to him, Beenay. If Athor's really the great man you think he is, he's not going to put his own reputation above scientific truth. Do you see what I mean? Athor's theory is not cast-iron. No theory is and there is always room for improvement. Isn't that so? Science is constructed out of approximations that gradually approach the truth, you told me a long time back, and I've never forgotten it. Well, that means all theories are subject to constant testing and modification, doesn't it? And if it eventually turns out that they're not quite close enough to the truth, they need to be replaced by something that's closer. Right, Beenay? Right?"

Beenay was trembling now. He looked very pale.

"Could you get me another drink, Theremon?"

"No. Listen to me: there's more. You say that you're so worried about Athor—he's old; I suppose he's pretty frail—that you don't have the heart to tell him you've found a flaw in his theory. All right. That's a decent and loving position to take. But think about this, will you? If calculating the orbit of Kalgash is all that important, somebody else is likely to stumble across the same flaw in Athor's theory sooner or later, and that other person isn't likely to be as tactful in letting Athor know

52

about it as you'd be. He might even be a professional rival of Athor's, an outright enemy of his—every scientist has enemies, you've told me so plenty of times. Wouldn't it be better for you to go to Athor and tell him, gently, carefully, of what you've discovered, than for him to find out about it one morning in the *Chronicle?*"

"Yes," Beenay whispered. "You're completely right."

"You'll go to him, then?"

"Yes. Yes. I have to, I suppose." Beenay bit his lip. "I feel miserable about this, Theremon. I feel like a murderer."

"I know you do. But it isn't Athor you'll be murdering, it's a defective theory. Defective theories must never be allowed to persist. You owe it to Athor as well as yourself to let the truth emerge." Theremon hesitated. A sudden startling new idea had occurred to him. "Of course, there's one other possibility. I'm only a layman, you know, and you'll probably laugh. —Is there any chance that the Theory of Gravitation might be correct despite everything, and that the computer's figures for Kalgash's orbit are right also, and that some other factor entirely, something altogether unknown, might be responsible for the discrepancy in your result?"

"That could be, I suppose," said Beenay in a flat, dispirited tone. "But once you begin dragging in mysterious unknown factors, you begin to move into the realm of fantasy. —I'll give you an example. Let's say there's an invisible seventh sun out there—it's got mass, it exerts gravitational force, but we simply can't see it. Since we don't know it's there, we haven't plugged it into our gravitational calculations, and so the figures come out cockeyed. Is that what you mean?"

"Well, why not?"

"Why not *five* invisible suns, then? Why not fifty? Why not an invisible giant who pushed planets around according to his whims? Why not a huge dragon whose breath deflects Kalgash from its proper path? We can't disprove it, can we? When you start in with *why nots*, Theremon, anything becomes possible, and then nothing makes any sense. At least not to me. I can only deal with what I know is real. You may be right that there's an unknown factor, and that therefore the gravitational laws aren't invalid. I certainly hope so. But I can't do serious work on that basis. All I can do is go to Athor, which I will, I

53

promise you that, and tell him what the computer has told me.
I don't dare suggest to him or anybody that I blame the whole
mess on a hitherto undiscovered 'unknown factor.' Otherwise
I'd sound just as crazy as the Apostles of Flame, who claim to
know all sorts of mystic revelations. —Theremon, I really want
that other drink now."

"Yes. All right. And speaking of the Apostles of Flame—"

"You want a statement from me, I remember." Beenay
passed a hand wearily in front of his face. "Yes. Yes. I won't let
you down. You've been a tremendous help to me this evening.
—What is it exactly that the Apostles have said now? I forget."

"It was Mondior 71," said Theremon. "The Grand High
Mumbo-Jumbo himself. What he said was—let me think—that
the time is very near when the gods intend to purge the world
of sin, that he can calculate the exact day, even the exact hour,
when doom will arrive."

Beenay groaned. "So what's new about that? Isn't that what
they've been saying for years?"

"Yes, but they're starting to hand out more of the gory details now. It's the notion of the Apostles, you know, that this
won't be the first time the world has been destroyed. They
teach that the gods have deliberately made mankind imperfect,
as a test, and that they have given us a single year—one of their
divine years, not one of our little ones—in which to shape up.
That's called a Year of Godliness, and it's exactly two thousand
and forty-nine of our years long. Again and again, when the
Year of Godliness has ended, the gods have discovered that
we're still wicked and sinful, and so they have destroyed the
world by sending down heavenly flames from holy places in
the sky that are known as Stars. So say the Apostles, anyway."

"Stars?" Beenay said. "Does he mean the suns?"

"No, Stars. Mondior says that the Stars are specifically different from the six suns. —Haven't you ever paid any attention to
this stuff, Beenay?"

"No. Why in the world should I?"

"Well, in any event, when the Year of Godliness ends and
nothing on Kalgash has improved, morally speaking, these
Stars drop some sort of holy fire on us and burn us up.
Mondior says this has happened any number of times. But each
time it does, the gods are merciful, or at least a faction among

them is: every time the world is destroyed, the kinder gods prevail over the sterner ones and humanity is given one more chance. And so the godliest of the survivors are rescued from the holocaust and a new deadline is set: mankind gets another two thousand and forty-nine years to cast off its evil ways. The time is almost up again, says Mondior. It's just under two thousand and forty-eight years since the last cataclysm. In something like fourteen months the suns will all disappear and these hideous Stars of his will shoot flame down out of a black sky to wipe out the wicked. Next year on Theptar nineteenth, to be specific."

"Fourteen months," Beenay said in a musing way. "The nineteenth of Theptar. He's very precise about it, isn't he? I suppose he knows the exact time of day it'll happen, too."

"So he says, yes. That's why I'd like a statement from somebody connected with the Observatory, preferably you. Mondior's latest announcement is that the exact time of the catastrophe can be calculated *scientifically*—that it isn't simply something that's set forth as dogma in the Book of Revelations, but that it's subject to the same sort of computation that astronomers employ when—when—"

Theremon faltered and halted.

"When we calculate the orbital motions of the suns and the world?" Beenay asked acidly.

"Well, yes," Theremon said, looking abashed.

"Then maybe there's hope for the world after all, if the Apostles can't do any better job of it than we do."

"I need a statement, Beenay."

"Yes. I realize that." The next round of drinks had arrived. Beenay wrapped his hand around his glass. "Try this," he said after a moment. " 'The main task of science is to separate truth from untruth, in the hope of revealing the way the universe really works. Putting truth to work in the service of untruth is not what we at the university think of as the scientific way. We are capable now of predicting the movements of the suns in the heavens, yes—but even if we use our best computer, we are no closer than we ever were to being able to foretell the will of the gods. Nor will we ever be, I suspect.' —How's that?"

"Perfect," Theremon said. "Let's see if I've got it. 'The main

task of science is to separate truth from untruth, in the hope of
—of—' What came next, Beenay?"

Beenay repeated the whole thing word for word, as though
he had memorized it hours before.

Then he drained his third drink at a single astonishing long
gulp.

And then he stood up, smiled for the first time all evening,
and fell flat on his face.

[9]

Athor 77's eyes narrowed, and he scrutinized the little sheaf of
printouts lying before him on his desk as though they were
maps of continents that no one had ever known existed.

He was very calm. He was amazed at how calm he was.

"Very interesting, Beenay," he said slowly. "Very, *very* interesting."

"Of course, sir, there's always the possibility that not only
have I made some crucial error in fundamental assumptions,
but that Yimot and Faro also—"

"All three of you getting your basic postulates wrong? No,
Beenay. I think not."

"I just wanted to indicate that the possibility exists."

"Please," Athor said. "Let me think."

It was midmorning. Onos in full glory blazed in the sky that
was visible through the tall window of the Observatory director's office. Dovim was barely apparent, a small hard red dot of
light, making a high northerly transit.

Athor fingered the papers, moving them about again and
again on his desk. And moved them yet again. How strange to
be taking this so easily, he thought. Beenay was the one who
seemed all wrought up over it; he himself had scarcely reacted
at all.

Perhaps I'm in shock, Athor speculated.

"Over here, sir, I have the orbit of Kalgash according to the
generally accepted almanac computation. And here, on the
printout, we have the orbital prediction that the new computer—"

"Please, Beenay. I said I wanted to think."

Beenay nodded jerkily. Athor smiled at him, not an easy thing for Athor to do. The formidable head of the Observatory, a tall, thin, commanding-looking man with an impressive shock of thick white hair, had allowed himself so long ago to slip into the role of Austere Giant of Science that it was difficult for him to unbend and permit himself to show ordinary human responses. At least, it was difficult for him while he was here at the Observatory, where everyone looked upon him as a sort of demigod. At home, with his wife, with his children, especially with his noisy flock of grandchildren, it was a different matter.

So Universal Gravitation wasn't quite right, was it?

No! No, that was impossible! Every atom of common sense in him protested at the thought. The concept of Universal Gravitation was fundamental to any comprehension of the structure of the universe, Athor was certain. Athor *knew*. It was too clean, too logical, too beautiful, to be wrong.

Take Universal Gravitation away, and the entire logic of the cosmos dissolved into chaos.

Inconceivable. Unimaginable.

But these figures—this damnable printout of Beenay's—

"I can see you're angry, sir." Beenay, chattering again! "And I want to tell you, I can quite understand it—the way this must hit you—anyone would be angry, having his life's work jeopardized this way—"

"Beenay—"

"Just let me say, sir, that I'd give anything not to have had to bring you this today. I know you're furious with me for coming in here with this, but I can only say that I thought long and hard before I did. What I really wanted to do was burn everything and forget I ever got started on any of this. I'm appalled that I found what I did, and appalled that I was the one who—"

"Beenay," Athor said again, in his most ominous voice.

"Sir?"

"I *am* furious with you, yes. But not for the reason you think."

"Sir?"

"Number one, I'm annoyed at the way you've been babbling at me, when all I want to do is sit here and quietly work through the implications of these papers you've just tossed at me. Number two, and much more important, I'm absolutely outraged that you'd have hesitated for so much as a moment to bring me your findings. Why did you wait so long?"

"It was only yesterday that I finished double-checking."

"Yesterday! Then you should have been in here yesterday! Do you really mean to say, Beenay, that you seriously considered *suppressing* all this? That you would simply have tossed your results away and said nothing?"

"No, sir," said Beenay miserably. "I never actually thought about doing that."

"Well, that's a blessing. Tell me, man, do you think I'm so enamored of my own beautiful theory that I'd want one of my most gifted associates to shield me from the unpleasant news that the theory's got a flaw in it?"

"No, sir. Of course not."

"Then why didn't you come running in here with the news the moment you were sure you were right?"

"Because—because, sir—" Beenay looked as though he wanted to vanish into the carpet. "Because I knew how upset you'd be. Because I thought you might—you might be so upset that your health would be affected. So I held back, I talked to a couple of friends, I thought through my own position on all of this, and I came to see that I really had no choice, I had to tell you that the Theory of Univer—"

"So you really do believe I love my own theory more than I do the truth, eh?"

"Oh, no, no, sir!"

Again Athor smiled, and this time it was no effort at all. "But I do, you know. I'm as human as anybody else, believe it or not. The Theory of Universal Gravitation brought me every scientific honor this planet has to offer. It's my passport to immortality, Beenay. You know that. And to have to deal with the possibility that the theory's *wrong*—oh, it's a powerful shock, Beenay, it goes right through me from front to back. Make no mistake about that. —Of course, I still believe that my theory's correct."

"Sir?" said Beenay, all too obviously aghast. "But I've checked and checked and checked again, and—"

"Oh, your findings are correct too, I'm sure of that. For you and Faro and Yimot *all* to have done it wrong—no, no, I've

58

already said I don't see much chance of that. But what you've got here doesn't necessarily overthrow Universal Gravitation."

Beenay blinked a few times. "It doesn't?"

"Certainly not," Athor said, warming to the situation. He felt almost cheerful now. The deathly unreal calm of the first few moments had given way to the very different tranquillity that one feels when one is in pursuit of truth. "What does the Theory of Universal Gravitation say, after all? That every body in the universe exerts a force on all other bodies, proportional to mass and distance. And what did you attempt to do in using Universal Gravitation to compute the orbit of Kalgash? Why, to factor in the gravitational impact that all the various astronomical bodies exert on our world as it travels around Onos. Is that not so?"

"Yes, sir."

"Well, then, there's no need to throw the Theory of Universal Gravitation out, at least not at this point. What we need to do, my friend, is simply to rethink our comprehension of the universe, and determine whether we're ignoring something that should be figured into our calculations—some mysterious factor, that is, which all unbeknownst to us is exerting gravitational force on Kalgash and isn't being taken into account."

Beenay's eyebrows rose alarmingly. He gaped at Athor in what could only have been a look of total astonishment.

Then he began to laugh. He smothered it at first by clamping his jaws, but the laughter insisted on escaping anyway, causing him to hunch his shoulders and emit strangled lurching coughs; and then he had to clap both his hands over his mouth to hold back the torrent of merriment.

Athor watched, flabbergasted.

"An unknown factor!" Beenay blurted, after a moment. "A dragon in the sky! An invisible giant!"

"Dragons? Giants? What are you talking about, boy?"

"Yesterday evening—Theremon 762—oh, sir, I'm sorry, I'm really sorry—" Beenay struggled to regain his self-control. Muscles writhed in his face; he blinked violently and caught his breath; he turned away for an instant, and when he turned back he was almost himself again. Shamefacedly he said, "I had a couple of drinks with Theremon 762 yesterday evening—the newspaper columnist, you know—and told him something about what I'd found, and how uneasy I was about bringing my findings to you."

"You went to a *newspaperman?*"

"A very trustworthy one. A close friend."

"They're all scoundrels, Beenay. Believe me."

"Not this one, sir. I know him, and I know he'd never do anything to hurt me or offend me. In fact Theremon gave me some excellent advice, by which I mean he said I absolutely had to come here, which is why I did. But also—trying to offer me some hope, you see, some consolation—he said the same thing you did, that maybe there was an 'unknown factor'—his exact phrase, an unknown factor—that was confusing our understanding of Kalgash's orbit. And I laughed and told him that it was useless to drag unknown factors into the situation, that it was too easy a solution. I suggested—sarcastically, of course—that if we allowed any such hypothesis, then we might as well tell ourselves that it was an invisible giant that was pushing Kalgash out of orbit, or the breath of a giant dragon. And now here you are, sir, taking the same line of reasoning—not a layman like Theremon, but the greatest astronomer in the world! —Do you see how foolish I feel, sir?"

"I think I do," said Athor. All this was becoming a little trying. He ran his hand through his imposing white mane and gave Beenay a look of mingled irritation and compassion. "You were right to tell your friend that inventing fantasies to solve a problem isn't very useful. But the random suggestions of laymen aren't always without merit. For all we know, there *is* some unknown factor at work on Kalgash's orbit. We need at least to consider that possibility before we toss the theory overboard. I think what we need to do here is to make use of Thargola's Sword. You know what that is, Beenay?"

"Of course, sir. The principle of parsimony. First put forth by the medieval philosopher Thargola 14, who said, 'We must drive a sword through any hypothesis that is not strictly necessary,' or words to that effect."

"Very good, Beenay. Though the way I was taught it, it's 'If we are offered several hypotheses, we should begin our considerations by striking the most complex of them with our sword.' Here we have the hypothesis that the Theory of Universal Gravitation is in error, versus the hypothesis that you've left out some unknown and perhaps unknowable factor in making your calculations of the orbit of Kalgash. If we accept the first hypothesis, then everything we think we know about the structure of the universe tumbles into chaos. If we accept the second one, all we need to do is locate the unknown factor, and the fundamental order of things is preserved. It's a lot simpler to try to find something we may have overlooked than it would be to come up with a new general law governing the movements of heavenly bodies. So the hypothesis that the Theory of Gravitation is wrong falls before Thargola's Sword and we begin our investigations by working with the simpler explanation of the problem. Eh, Beenay? What do you say?"

Beenay looked radiant.

"Then I haven't overthrown Universal Gravitation after all!"

"Not yet, anyway. You've probably won a place in scientific history for yourself, but we don't know yet whether it's as a debunker or as an originator. Let's pray it's the latter. And now we need to do some very hard thinking, young man." Athor 77 closed his eyes and rubbed his forehead, which was beginning to ache. It had been a long time since he'd done any real science, he realized. He'd occupied himself almost entirely with administrative matters at the Observatory for the past eight or ten years. But the mind that had produced the Theory of Universal Gravitation might yet have a thought or two left in it, he told himself. —"First, I want to take a closer look at these calculations of yours," he said. "And then, I suppose, a closer look at my own theory."

[10]

The headquarters of the Apostles of Flame was a slender but magnificent tower of gleaming golden stone, rising like a shining javelin above the Seppitan River, in the exclusive Birigam quarter of Saro City. That soaring tower, Theremon thought, must be one of the most valuable pieces of real estate in the entire capital.

He had never stopped to consider it before, but the Apostles had to be an exceedingly wealthy group. They owned their own radio and television stations, they published magazines and newspapers, they had this tremendous tower. And probably they controlled all sorts of other assets too that were less visibly theirs. He wondered how that was possible. A bunch of fanatic puritan monks? Where would they have managed to get their hands on so many hundreds of millions of credits?

But, he realized, such well-known industrialists as Bottiker 888 and Vivin 99 were outspoken adherents of the teachings of Mondior and his Apostles. It wouldn't surprise him to know that men like Bottiker and Vivin, and others like them, were heavy contributors to the Apostles' treasury.

And if the organization was even a tenth as old as it claimed to be—ten thousand years, was what they said!—and if it had invested its money wisely over the centuries, there was no telling what the Apostles could have achieved through the miracle of compound interest, Theremon thought. They might be worth billions. They might secretly own half of Saro City.

It was worth looking into, he told himself.

He entered the vast, echoing entrance hall of the great tower and peered about in awe. Though he had never been here before, he had heard it was an extraordinarily lavish building both inside and out. But nothing he had heard had prepared him for the reality of the cultist's building.

A polished marble floor, with inlays in half a dozen brilliant colors, stretched as far as he could see. The walls were covered with glittering golden mosaics in abstract patterns, rising to arched vaults high overhead. Chandeliers of woven gold and silver threw a shimmering shower of brightness over everything.

At the opposite end from the entrance Theremon saw what seemed to be a model of the whole universe, fashioned, apparently, entirely of precious metals and gems: immense suspended globes, which seemed to represent the six suns, hung from the ceiling by invisible wires. Each of them cast an eerie light: a golden beam from the largest of them, which must be Onos, and a dim red glow from the Dovim globe, and cold hard blue-white from the Tano-Sitha pair, and a gentler white light from Patru and Trey. A seventh globe that must be Kalgash moved slowly among them like a drifting balloon, its own colors changing as the shifting pattern of the suns' light played over its surface.

As Theremon stood gaping in astonishment, a voice coming from nowhere in particular said, "May we have your name?"

"I'm Theremon 762. I have an appointment with Mondior."

"Yes. Please enter the chamber on your immediate left, Theremon 762."

He saw no chamber on his immediate left. But then a segment of the mosaic-covered wall slid noiselessly open, revealing a small oval room, more an antechamber than a chamber. Green velvet hangings covered the walls and a single bar of amber light provided illumination.

He shrugged and stepped in. At once the door closed behind him and he felt a distinct sensation of motion. This wasn't a room, it was a lift! Yes, he was rising, he was certain of it. Up and up and up he went, in a very unhurried way. It took half an eternity before the lift chamber came to a halt and the door slid open once again.

A black-robed figure was waiting for him.

"Would you come this way, please?"

A narrow hallway led a short distance into a kind of waiting room, where a large portrait of Mondior 71 occupied most of one entire wall. As Theremon entered, the portrait seemed to light up, coming strangely to life and glowing, so that Mondior's dark, intense eyes looked straight at him and the High Apostle's stern face took on a luminous inner radiance that made him seem almost beautiful, in a fierce sort of way.

Theremon met the portrait's gaze coolly enough. But even the tough-minded newspaperman found himself ever so slightly unnerved to think that very shortly he would be interviewing this very person. Mondior on radio or television was one thing, just some crazed preacher with an absurd message to peddle. But Mondior in the flesh—awesome, hypnotic, mysterious, if this portrait was any indication—might be something else again. Theremon warned himself to be on his guard.

The black-robed monk said, "If you'll step inside, please—"

The wall just to the left of the portrait opened. An office became visible within, as sparsely decorated as a cell, nothing in it but a bare desk made of a single slab of polished stone and a low backless chair, cut from a chunk of some unusual red-streaked gray wood, placed in front of it. Behind the desk sat a man of obvious force and authority, wearing the black Apostles' robe with red trim along the hood.

He was very impressive. But he wasn't Mondior 71.

Mondior, judging by his photographs and the way he seemed on television, had to be a man of sixty-five or seventy, with a kind of intense masculine force about him. His hair was thick and wavy, black with broad streaks of white, and he had a full, fleshy face, a wide mouth, a strong nose, heavy jet-black eyebrows, dark, compelling eyes. But this one was young, surely not yet forty, and though he seemed powerful and highly masculine too, it was in an entirely different way: he was very thin, with a sharp, narrow face and tight, pursed lips. His hair, curling down over his forehead under his hood, was a strange brick-red color, and his eyes were a cold, unrelenting blue.

No doubt this man was some high functionary in the organization. But Theremon's appointment was with Mondior.

He had decided just this morning, after writing his story on the Apostles' latest fulmination, that he needed to know more about this mysterious cult. Everything they had ever said struck him as nonsense, of course, but it was beginning to seem like interesting nonsense, worth writing about in some detail. How better to learn more about them than to go straight to the top man? Assuming that was possible, that is. But to his surprise they had told him, when he called, that he could have an audience with Mondior 71 that very day. It had seemed too easy.

Now he began to realize that it *had* been too easy.

"I am Folimun 66," the sharp-faced man said in a light, flexible voice with none of Mondior's compelling thunder. Yet it was, Theremon suspected, the voice of someone who was accustomed to being obeyed. "I am the public-relations adjutant for the home district of our organization. It will be my pleasure to answer any questions you may have."

"My appointment was with Mondior himself," Theremon said.

Folimun 66's chilly eyes betrayed no sign of surprise. "You may think of me as the voice of Mondior."

"I understood it would be a *personal* audience."

"It is. Anything said to me is shared with Mondior; anything that comes from me is the word of Mondior. This should be understood."

"Nevertheless, I was given assurances that I'd be allowed to talk with Mondior. I have no doubt that what you tell me would be authoritative, but it isn't just information that I'm looking for. I'd like to form some opinion of what sort of man Mondior is, what his views are on other things besides the prophesied destruction of the world, what he thinks about—"

"I can only repeat what I have already said," Folimun declared, cutting in smoothly. "You may think of me as the voice of Mondior. His Serenity will not be able to see you in person today."

"Then I would prefer to return on another day, when His Serenity will be—"

"Permit me to inform you that Mondior does not make himself available for personal interviews, not ever. Not *ever*. His Serenity's work is much too urgent, now that only a matter of months stands between us and the Time of Flame." Folimun smiled suddenly, an unexpectedly warm and human smile, perhaps intended to take some of the sting out of the refusal and out of that melodramatic-sounding phrase, "the Time of Flame." Almost gently he said, "I would guess that there's been a misunderstanding, that you didn't realize that your appointment would be with a spokesman for Mondior rather than with the High Apostle himself. But that's the way it must be. If you don't wish to speak with me, well, I regret that you've wasted your trip today. But I'm the most useful source of information you're going to be able to find here, now or at any other time."

Again the smile. It was the smile of a man who was coolly and unapologetically closing a door in Theremon's face.

"Very well," Theremon said after a moment or two of consideration. "I see I don't have much choice. I get you or I get nobody. All right: let's talk. How much time do I have?"

"As much as you need, though this first meeting will have to be a fairly brief one. And also"—a grin, a surprising one, almost mischievous—"you must bear in mind that we have only fourteen months altogether. And I've got a few other things to do during that time."

"So I imagine. Fourteen months, you say? And then what?"

"You haven't read the Book of Revelations, then, I assume."

"Not recently, actually."

"Permit me, then." Folimun produced a thin red-bound volume from some crevice of his apparently empty desk and slid it toward Theremon. "This is for you. You'll find much nourishment in it, I hope. Meanwhile I can summarize the theme that appears to be of the greatest interest to you. Very shortly—exactly four hundred and eighteen days from now, to be extremely precise, on the nineteenth of Theptar next—a great transformation will come over our comfortable, familiar world. The six suns will enter the Cave of Darkness and disappear, the Stars will make themselves manifest to us, and all Kalgash will be set ablaze."

He made it sound very casual. As though he might be talking about the coming of a rainstorm tomorrow afternoon, or the expected blossoming of some rare plant next week in the Municipal Botanical Garden. All Kalgash set ablaze. The six suns entering the Cave of Darkness. The Stars.

"The Stars," Theremon said aloud. "And what, in fact, may they be?"

"They are the instruments of the gods."

"Can you be more specific, do you think?"

"The nature of the Stars will be made more than amply clear to us," said Folimun 66, "in a matter of four hundred and eighteen days."

"When the current Year of Godliness comes to its end," said Theremon. "On Theptar nineteenth of next year."

Folimun looked pleasantly surprised. "So you *have* been studying our teachings."

"To some extent. I've listened to Mondior's recent speeches, at any rate. I know about the two-thousand-and-forty-nine-year cycle. —And the event you call the Time of Flame? I suppose you can't provide me with any sort of advance description of that, either."

"You'll find something along those lines in the fifth chapter of the Book of Revelations. No, you needn't search for it now: I can quote it for you. 'From the Stars there then reached down the Heavenly Flames, that was the bearer of the will of the gods; and where the flames touched, the cities of Kalgash were consumed even to utter destruction, so that of man and the works of man nothing whatever remained.'"

Theremon nodded. "A sudden terrible cataclysm. Why?"

"The will of the gods. They have warned us against our wickedness and have given us a span of years in which to redeem ourselves. That span is what we call the Year of Godliness, a 'year' two thousand and forty-nine human years long, about which you already appear to know. The current Year of Godliness is nearly at its end."

"And then we'll all be wiped out, you think?"

"Not all of us. But most will; and our civilization will be destroyed. Those few who survive will face the immense task of rebuilding. This is, as you seem already to be aware, a melancholy repetitive cycle in human events. What is soon due to occur will not be the first time that mankind has failed the test of the gods. We have been struck down more than once before; and now we are on the verge of being struck down yet again."

The curious thing, Theremon thought, was that Folimun didn't seem at all crazy.

Except for his odd robe, he could have been any sort of youngish businessman sitting in his handsome office—a loan applications officer, for instance, or an investment banker. He was obviously intelligent. He spoke clearly and well, in a crisp, direct tone. He neither ranted nor raved. But the things he was saying, in his crisp, direct way, were the wildest sort of nonsensical babble. The contrast between what Folimun said and the way he said it was hard to take.

Now he sat quietly, looking relaxed, waiting for the newspaperman to ask the next question.

"I'll be frank," Theremon said after a little while. "Like many people, I have difficulty accepting something this big which is handed to me simply as a revelation. I need solid proofs. But you don't show us any. Take it on faith, you say. There's no tangible evidence to demonstrate, of course, that's what you tell us, but we'd all better just believe what you're offering us, because you've heard all this from the gods, and you know the gods aren't lying to you. Can you show me why I *should* believe you, though? Faith alone isn't enough for people like me."

"Why do you think there is no evidence?" Folimun asked.

"Is there? Other than the Book of Revelations itself? Circular evidence isn't evidence to me."

"We are a very ancient organization, you know."

"Ten thousand years old, so the story goes."

A brief flickering smile crossed Folimun's thin lips. "An arbitrary figure, perhaps exaggerated somewhat for popular effect. All that we claim among ourselves is that we go back to prehistoric times."

"So your group is at least *two* thousand years old, then."

"A little more than that, at the minimum. We can trace ourselves back to a time before the last cataclysm—so we are certainly more than two thousand and forty-nine years old. Probably much more, but we have no proof of that, at least not proof of the sort which you'd be likely to accept. We think the Apostles may go back *several* cycles of destruction, which is to say possibly as much as six thousand years. All that really matters is that we are precataclysmic in origin. We have been quietly active as an organization for more than one Year of Godliness. And so we are in possession of information giving highly specific details of the catastrophe that lies in store for us. We know what will happen because we are aware of what has happened many times before."

"But you won't show anyone the information you claim to have. The evidence, the proofs."

"The Book of Revelations is what we offer the world."

Round and round and round. This was leading nowhere. Theremon began to feel restless. It was all a big bluff, obviously. All a cynical fake, probably designed to pull in fat contributions from the gullible likes of Bottiker and Vivin and other wealthy folk desperate to buy their way into escaping the threat of doom. Despite Folimun's obvious appearance of sincerity and intelligence, he had to be either a willing co-conspirator in this gigantic enterprise of fraudulent fantasy, or else merely one of Mondior's many dupes.

"All right," the newspaperman said. "Let's assume for the time being that there *will* be some sort of worldwide catastrophe next year, of which your group has advance detailed knowledge. What is it, exactly, that you want the rest of us to do? Go flocking into your chapels and beg the gods to have mercy on us?"

"It's much too late for that."

"There's no hope at all, then? In that case, why are you bothering even to warn us?"

Folimun smiled again, without irony this time. "For two reasons. One, yes, we *do* want people to come to our chapels, not so that they can try to influence the gods, but so that they can listen to our teachings in so far as they concern matters of morality and everyday decency. We think we have a message that is of value to the world in those areas. But second, and more urgent: we want to convince people of the reality of what is coming, so that they will take measures to protect themselves against it. The worst of the catastrophe *can* be headed off. Steps *can* be taken to avert the complete destruction of our civilization. The Flames are inevitable, yes, human nature being what it is—the gods have spoken, the time of their vengeance is already on the way—but within the general madness and horror there will be some who survive. I assure you that we Apostles most definitely will. We will be here, as we have been before, to lead humanity into the new cycle of rebirth. And we offer our hand—in love, in charity, to anyone else who will accept it. Who will join with us in guarding themselves against the turmoil that is coming. Does that sound like madness to you, Theremon? Does that sound as though we're dangerous crackpots?"

"If I could only accept your basic assumption—"

"That the Flames will come next year? You will. You will. What remains to be seen is whether you accept it long enough in advance to become one of the survivors, one of the guardians of our heritage, or discover only in the moment of destruction, in the moment of your own agony, that we were speaking the truth all along."

"I wonder which it'll be," said Theremon.

"Permit me to hope that you'll be on our side on the day that this Year of Godliness comes to its close," Folimun said. Abruptly he rose and offered Theremon his hand. "I have to go now. His Serenity the High Apostle expects me in a few minutes. But we'll have further conversations, of that I'm sure. A day's notice, or less, perhaps—I'll try to make myself available to you. I look forward to speaking with you again. Odd as this may sound, I feel that you and I are destined to work very closely together. We have much in common, you know."

"Do we?"

"In the matter of faith, no. In the matter of the desire to survive—and to help others to survive—yes, I think so, very definitely. A time will come when you and I will seek each other out, I suspect, and join forces to fight against the Darkness that is coming. I'm certain of it, in fact."

Sure, Theremon thought. I'd better go get fitted for my black robe right away.

But there was no sense in offending Folimun with any sort of rudeness. This cult of Apostles was growing, apparently, day by day. There was a big story here; and Folimun was probably the one he was going to have to depend on for most of it.

Theremon slipped the copy of the Book of Revelations into his briefcase and stood up.

"I'll call you in a few weeks," he said. "After I've had a chance to peruse this with some care. There'll be other things I'll want to ask you then. —And how far in advance do I need to call for an audience with Mondior 71?"

Folimun couldn't be snared so simply. "As I've already explained, His Serenity's work from here until the Time of Flame is so critical that he'll be unable to make himself available for such things as personal interviews. I'm truly sorry. There's no way I can alter that." Folimun put out his hand. "It's been a pleasure."

"And for me," said Theremon.

Folimun laughed. "Has it, really? To spend half an hour talking with a madman? A crackpot? A fanatic? A cultist?"

"I don't remember using those words."

"It wouldn't amaze me to be told that you'd thought them, though." The Apostle gave Theremon another of his curiously disarming smiles. "You'd be half right, anyway. I *am* a fanatic. And a cultist, I suppose. But not a madman. Not a crackpot. I only wish I were. And you will too."

He waved Theremon out. The monk who had guided him in was waiting outside the door to take him to the lift-chamber.

A strange half hour, the newspaperman thought. And not very fruitful, really. In some ways he knew even less about the Apostles than he had before he had come here.

That they were cranks and superstition-mongers was still obvious to Theremon. Plainly they didn't have a shred of anything like real evidence that some gigantic cataclysm was in store for the world soon. Whether they were mere self-deluding fools, though, or outright frauds looking to line their own pockets, was something that he could not yet clearly decide.

It was all pretty confusing. There was an element of fanaticism, of puritanism, about their movement that was not at all to his liking. And yet, and yet . . . this Folimun, this spokesman of theirs, had seemed an unexpectedly attractive person. He was intelligent, articulate—even, in his way, rational. The fact that he appeared to have a sense of humor of sorts was a surprise, and a point in his favor. Theremon had never heard of a maniac who was capable of even the slightest self-mockery—or a fanatic, either. —Unless it was all part of Folimun's public-relations act: unless Folimun had been deliberately projecting the kind of persona that someone like Theremon would be likely to find appealing.

Be careful, he told himself. Folimun wants to use you.

But that was all right. His position with the newspaper was an influential one. *Everyone* wanted to use him.

Well, Theremon thought, we'll see who uses whom.

His footsteps echoed sharply as he walked at a brisk pace through the immense entrance hall of the Apostles' headquarters and out into the brilliance of a three-sun afternoon.

Back to the *Chronicle* office now. A couple of pious hours devoted to a close study of the Book of Revelations; and then it was time to begin thinking about tomorrow's column.

[11]

The summer rainy season was in full spate the afternoon Sheerin 501 returned to Saro City. The plump psychologist stepped out of the plane into a stupendous downpour that had turned the airfield into something close to a lake. Gray torrents of rain rode almost horizontally on fierce gusts of wind.

Gray—gray—everything gray—

The suns had to be up there somewhere in all that murk. That faint glimmer in the west was probably Onos, and there were hints of the chilly light of Tano and Sitha off the other

71

way. But the cloud cover was so thick that the day was disagreeably dark. Uncomfortably dark for Sheerin, who still—despite what he had told his hosts in Jonglor—was troubled by the aftereffects of his fifteen-minute ride through the Tunnel of Mystery.

He would have gone on a ten-day fast sooner than he'd admit it to Kelaritan and Cubello and the rest of those people. But he had come perilously close to the danger point in there.

For three or four days thereafter Sheerin had experienced a touch, only a touch, of the kind of claustrophobia that had sent so many citizens of Jonglor to the mental hospital. He would be in his hotel room, working on his report, when suddenly he would feel Darkness closing in on him, and he would find it necessary to get up and go out on his terrace, or even to leave the building entirely for a long stroll in the hotel garden. *Necessary?* Well, maybe not. But preferable. Certainly preferable. And he always felt better for doing it.

Or he would be asleep and the Darkness would come to him then. Naturally the godlight would be on in his room when he slept—he always slept with one on, he knew nobody who didn't—and since the Tunnel ride he had taken to using an auxiliary godlight too, in case the battery of the first one should fail, though the indicator clearly said it had six months' power left. Even so, Sheerin's sleeping mind would become convinced that his room had been plunged into the depths of lightlessness, utterly black, the true and complete Darkness. And he would awaken, trembling, sweating, convinced he was in Darkness even though the friendly glow of the two godlights was right there on either side of him to tell him that he was not.

So now, to step from his plane into this somber twilight landscape—well, he was glad to be home, but he would have preferred a sunnier arrival. He had to fight off mild distress, or perhaps not so mild, as he entered the flexiglass foul-weather passageway that led from his plane to the terminal. He wished they hadn't put the passageway up. Better not to be enclosed right now, Sheerin thought, even if it did mean getting wet. Better to be out there under the open sky, under the comforting light (however faint just now, however hidden by clouds) of the friendly suns.

But the queasiness passed. By the time he had claimed his

baggage, the cheering reality of being back home again in Saro City had triumphed over the lingering effects of his brush with Darkness.

Liliath 221 was waiting for him outside the baggage pickup area with her car. That made him feel better too. She was a slender, pleasant-looking woman in her late forties, a fellow member of the Psychology Department, though her work was experimental, animals in mazes, no overlap at all with his. They had known each other ten or fifteen years. Sheerin would probably have asked her to marry him long ago if he had been the marrying type. But he wasn't; nor, for all the indication she had ever given him, was she. Still, the relationship they did have seemed to suit them both.

"Of all the miserable days to pick for coming home—" he said, as he slipped in beside her and reached across to give her a quick friendly kiss.

"It's been like this for three days. And they say we're in for three more of it, until next Onos Day. We'll all be drowned by then, I suppose. —You look as if you've lost some weight up there in Jonglor, Sheerin!"

"Have I? Well, you know, northern food—not really to my taste—"

He hadn't expected that it would be so apparent. A man of his girth ought to be able to drop ten or fifteen pounds without its being noticeable at all. But Liliath had always had sharp eyes. And perhaps he had dropped more than ten or fifteen pounds. Ever since the Tunnel, he had simply pecked at his food. Him! It was hard for him to believe how little he had eaten.

"You look good," she said. "Healthy. Vigorous."

"Do I?"

"Not that I think you need to be skinny, not at this late date. But it can't hurt to take a little off. So you enjoyed yourself in Jonglor?"

"Well—"

"Get to see the Exposition?"

"Yes. Fabulous." He couldn't muster much enthusiasm. "My God, this rain, Liliath!"

"It wasn't raining in Jonglor?"

"Clear and dry all the time. The way it was when I left Saro."

"Well, seasons change, Sheerin. You can't hope to have the same weather for six months at a stretch, you know. With a different set of suns in the ascendant every day, we can't expect the patterns of climate to hold still very long."

"I can't tell whether you sound more like a meteorologist or an astrologer," Sheerin said.

"Neither. I sound like a psychologist. —Aren't you going to tell me anything about your trip, Sheerin?"

He hesitated. "The Exposition was very fine. I'm sorry you missed it. But most of the time I was hard at work. They've got a real mess on their hands up north, this Tunnel of Mystery thing."

"Is it really true that people have been dying in it?"

"A few. But mainly they've been coming out traumatized, disoriented. Claustrophobic. I spoke with some of the victims. They'll be months recovering. For some it'll be permanent disability. And even so the Tunnel stayed open for weeks."

"After the problems began?"

"Nobody seemed to care. Least of all the people who run the Exposition. They were just interested in selling tickets. And the fairgoers were curious about Darkness. Curious about Darkness, can you imagine that, Liliath? They lined up eagerly to put their minds in jeopardy! Of course, they were all convinced that nothing bad was going to happen to *them*. And nothing bad did, to a lot of them. But not all. —I took a ride in the Tunnel myself."

"You did?" she said, sounding astonished. "What was it like?"

"A nasty business. I'd pay a good deal not to have to do it again."

"But obviously you came out all right."

"Obviously," he said carefully. "I might come out all right if I swallowed half a dozen live fish, too. But it's not something I'd be likely to want to repeat. I told them to shut their damned Tunnel down. That was my professional opinion, and I think they're going to abide by it. We simply weren't designed to withstand that much Darkness, Liliath. A minute, two minutes, maybe—then we start to snap. It's an innate thing, I'm convinced of it, millions of years of evolution shaping us to be what we are. Darkness is the most unnatural thing in the world. And the idea of selling it to people as *entertainment*—" He shuddered. "Well, I've had my trip to Jonglor, and now I'm back. What's been going on at the university?"

"Nothing much," Liliath replied. "The usual stupid little squabbles, the usual faculty meetings, lofty declarations of outrage over this and that burning social issue—*you* know." She fell silent for a moment, both hands clinging to the steering stick as she guided the car through deep pools of water that flooded the highway. "There's apparently some sort of fuss over at the Observatory, by the way. Your friend Beenay 25 came around looking for you. He didn't tell me very much, but it seems they're having a big reevaluation of one of their key theories. Everybody's in an uproar. Old Athor himself is leading the research, can you imagine it? I thought his mind had ossified a century ago. —Beenay had some newspaperman with him, somebody who writes a popular column. Theremon, I think that was his name. Theremon 762. I didn't care for him much."

"He's very well known. Something of a firebrand, I think, though I'm not exactly sure what kind of causes he fulminates about. He and Beenay spend a lot of time together."

Sheerin made a mental note to call the young astronomer after he had unpacked. For close to a year now Beenay had been living with Sheerin's sister's girl, Raissta 717, and Sheerin had struck up a close friendship with him, as close as was possible considering the difference of twenty-odd years in their ages. Sheerin had an amateur's interest in astronomy: that was one of the bonds that drew them together.

Athor back doing theoretical work! Imagine that! What could it all be about? Had some upstart published a paper attacking the Law of Universal Gravitation? No, Sheerin thought—nobody would dare.

"And you?" Sheerin asked. "You haven't said a word about what you did all the time I was away."

"What do you think I did, Sheerin? Go power-soaring in the mountains? Attend meetings of the Apostles of Flame? Take a course in political science? I read books. I taught my classes. I ran my experiments. I waited for you to come home. I planned the dinner I'd cook when you *did* come home. —You're sure you aren't on a diet, now?"

"Of course not." He let his hand rest fondly on hers for a moment. "I thought about you all the time, Liliath."

"I'm sure you did."

"And I can hardly wait for dinnertime."

"At least that much sounds plausible."

The rain suddenly grew even more dense. A great swolloping mass of it struck the windshield and it was all Liliath could do to keep the car on the road, though she managed it. They were going past the Pantheon, the magnificent Cathedral of All the Gods. It didn't seem quite so magnificent now, with rivers of rain sluicing down its brick facade.

The sky darkened another degree or two in the worsening storm. Sheerin cringed away from the blackness outside and looked toward the brightly lit controls of the car's dashboard for comfort.

He didn't want to be in the enclosed space of the car any more. He wanted to be outside in the open fields, storm or no storm. But that was crazy. He'd be soaked in an instant out there. He might even drown, the puddles were so deep.

Think happy thoughts, he told himself. Think warm bright thoughts. Think about sunshine, the golden sunshine of Onos, the warm light of Patru and Trey, even the chilly light of Sitha and Tano, the faint red light of Dovim. Think about this evening's dinner. Liliath has made a feast for you to welcome you back. She's such a good cook, Liliath is.

He realized that he still wasn't hungry at all. Not on a miserable gray day like this—so dark—so dark—

But Liliath was very sensitive about her cooking. Especially when she cooked for him. He'd eat everything she put before him, he resolved, even if he had to force himself. A funny notion, he thought: he, Sheerin, the great gourmand, thinking about *forcing* himself to eat!

Liliath glanced toward him at the sound of his laughter.

"What's so funny?"

"I—ah—that Athor should be back doing research again," he said hastily. "After having been content so long with being the

76

Lord High Emperor of Astronomy and doing purely administrative stuff. I'll have to call Beenay right away. What in the
world can be going on over at the Observatory?"

[12]

This was Siferra 89's third day back at Saro University, and it
hadn't stopped raining yet. Quite a refreshing contrast to the
bone-dry desert environment of the Sagikan Peninsula. She
hadn't seen rain in so long that she found herself wonderstruck
at the whole idea that water could fall from the skies.

In Sagikan, every drop of water was enormously precious.
You calculated its use with the greatest precision and recycled
whatever was recyclable. Now here it was, pouring down out
of the heavens as though from a gigantic reservoir that could
never run dry. Siferra felt a powerful urge to strip her clothes
off and sprint across the great green lawns of the campus, letting the rainfall flow down her body in an unending delicious
stream to wash her clean at last of the infernal desert dust.

That was all they'd need to see. That cool, aloof, unromantic
professor of archaeology, Siferra 89, running naked in the rain!
It would be worth doing if only to enjoy the sight of their
astounded faces peering out of every window of the university
as she went flying past.

Not very likely, though, Siferra thought.

Not my style at all.

And there was too much to do, really. She hadn't wasted any
time getting down to work. Most of the artifacts she had excavated at the Beklimot site were following along by cargo ship
and wouldn't be here for many weeks. But there were charts to
arrange, sketches to finish, Balik's stratigraphic photographs to
analyze, the soil samples to prepare for the radiography lab, a
million and one things to do. —And then, too, there were the
Thombo tablets to discuss with Mudrin 505 of the Department
of Paleography.

The Thombo tablets! The find of finds, the premier discovery of the entire year and a half! Or so she felt. Of course, it all
depended on whether anyone could make any sense out of

them. At any rate, she would waste no time getting Mudrin working on them. At the least, the tablets were fascinating things; but they might be much more than that. There was the possibility that they might revolutionize the entire study of the prehistoric world. That was why she hadn't entrusted them to the freight shippers, but had carried them back from Sagikan in her own hands.

A knock at the door.

"Siferra? Siferra, are you there?"

"Come on in, Balik."

The broad-shouldered stratigrapher was soaking wet. "This foul abominable rain," he muttered, shaking himself off. "You wouldn't believe how drenched I got just crossing the quad from Uland Library to here!"

"I love the rain," Siferra said. "I hope it never stops. After all those months baking out in the desert—the sand in your eyes all the time, the dust in your throat, the heat, the dryness—no, let it rain, Balik!"

"But I see you're keeping yourself indoors. It's a whole lot easier to appreciate rain when you're looking at it from a nice dry office. —Playing with your tablets again, are you?"

He indicated the six ragged, battered slabs of hard red clay that Siferra had arranged atop her desk in two groups of three, the square ones in one row and the oblong ones below them.

"Aren't they beautiful?" Siferra said exultantly. "I can't leave them alone. I keep staring at them as if they'll suddenly become intelligible if only I look at them long enough."

Balik leaned forward and shook his head. "Chicken-scratches. That's all it looks like to me."

"Come on! I've already identified distinct word-patterns," Siferra said. "And I'm no paleographer. Here—look—you see this group of six characters here? It repeats over here. And these three, with the wedges setting them off—"

"Has Mudrin seen them yet?"

"Not yet. I've asked him to stop by a little later."

"You know that word has gotten out about what we've found, don't you? The successive Thombo town-sites?"

Siferra looked at him in amazement. "What? Who—?"

"One of the students," Balik said. "I don't know who it was

—Veloran, is my guess, though Eilis thinks it was Sten. I suppose it was unavoidable, don't you?"

"I warned them not to say anything to—"

"Yes, but they're kids, Siferra, only kids, nineteen years old and on their first important dig! And the expedition stumbles on something utterly astounding—seven previously unknown prehistoric cities one on top of the next, going back the gods only know how many thousands of years—"

"Nine cities, Balik."

"Seven, nine, it's colossal either way. And I think it's seven." Balik smiled.

"I know you do. You're wrong. —But who's been talking about it? In the department, I mean."

"Hilliko. And Brangin. I heard them this morning, in the faculty lounge. They're extremely skeptical, I have to tell you. Passionately skeptical. Neither one of them thinks it's even remotely possible for there to be even one settlement older than Beklimot at that site, let alone nine, or seven, or however many there are."

"They haven't seen the photographs. They haven't seen the charts. They haven't seen the tablets. They haven't seen anything. And already they have an opinion." Siferra's eyes blazed with rage. "What do they know? Have they ever so much as set foot on the Sagikan Peninsula? Have they been to Beklimot even as *tourists?* And they dare to have an opinion on a dig that hasn't been published, that hasn't even been informally discussed within the department—!"

"Siferra—"

"I'd like to flay them both! And Veloran and Sten also. They knew they weren't supposed to shoot their mouths off! Where do those two come off breaking priority, even verbally? I'll show them. I'll get them both in here and find out which one of them's responsible for leaking the story to Hilliko and Brangin, and if that one thinks he's ever going to get a doctorate in this university, or she, whichever one it was—"

"Please, Siferra," Balik said soothingly. "You're getting all worked up over nothing."

"Nothing! My priority blown, and—"

"Nobody's blown anything for you. It all remains just a rumor until you make your own preliminary statement. As for

Veloran and Sten, we don't really know that either of them is the one that let the story get out, and if one of them did, well, remember that you were young once too."

"Yes," Siferra said. "Three geological epochs ago."

"Don't be silly. You're younger than I am, and I'm hardly ancient, you know."

Siferra nodded indifferently. She looked toward the window. Suddenly the rain didn't seem so pleasing. Everything was dark outside, disturbingly dark.

"Still, to hear that our findings are already controversial, and not even published yet—"

"They *have* to be controversial, Siferra. Everybody's wagons are going to be upset by what we found in that hill—not just in our department, but History, Philosophy, even Theology, they'll all be affected. And you can bet they'll fight to defend their established notions of the way civilization developed. Wouldn't you, if somebody came along with a radical new idea that threatened everything you believe? —Be realistic, Siferra. We've known from the start that there'd be a storm over this."

"I suppose. I wasn't ready for it to begin so soon. I've hardly begun unpacking."

"That's the real problem. You've plunged back into the thick of things so fast, without taking any time to decompress. — Look, I've got an idea. We're entitled to a little time off before we get back to full-time academic loads. Why don't you and I run away from the rain and take a little holiday together? Up to Jonglor, say, to see the Exposition? I was talking to Sheerin yesterday—he was just there, you know, and he says—"

She stared at Balik in disbelief. "What?"

"A holiday, I said. You and me."

"You're making a *pass* at me, Balik?"

"You could call it that, I suppose. But is that so incredible? We aren't exactly strangers. We've known each other since we were graduate students. We've just come back from a year and a half spent in the desert together."

"Together? We were at the same dig, yes. You had your tent, I had mine. There's never been anything between us. And now, out of the blue—"

Balik's stolid features showed dismay and annoyance. "It's not as though I asked you to *marry* me, Siferra. I just suggested a quick little trip to the Jonglor Exposition, five or six days, some sunshine, a decent resort hotel instead of a tent pegged out in the middle of the desert, a few quiet dinners, some good wine—" He turned his palms outward in a gesture of irritation. "You're making me feel like a silly schoolboy, Siferra."

"You're acting like one," she said. "Our relationship has always been purely professional, Balik. Let's keep it that way, shall we?"

He began to reply, evidently thought better of it, clamped his lips tight shut.

They looked at each other uncomfortably for a long moment.

Siferra's head was pounding. All this was unexpected and disagreeable—the news that the other members of the department were already taking positions on the Thombo finds, and Balik's clumsy attempt at seducing her as well. Seducing? Well, at establishing some sort of romantic rapport with her, anyway. How utterly astonished he looked at being rejected, too.

She wondered if she had ever accidentally seemed to be leading him on in some way, to give him a hint of feelings that had never existed.

No. No. She couldn't believe that she had. She had no interest in going to north-country resorts and sipping wine in romantically lit restaurants with Balik or anyone else. She had her work. That was enough. For twenty-odd years, ever since her teens, men had been offering themselves to her, telling her how beautiful, how wonderful, how fascinating she was. It was flattering, she supposed. Better that they think her beautiful and fascinating than ugly and boring. But she wasn't interested. Never had been. Didn't want to be. How tiresome of Balik to have created this awkwardness between them now, when they still had all the labor of organizing the Beklimot material ahead of them—the two of them, working side by side—

There was another knock at the door. She was immensely grateful for the interruption.

"Who's there?"

"Mudrin 505," a quavering voice replied.

"Come in. Please."

"I'll leave now," Balik said.

"No. He's here to see the tablets. They're your tablets as much as mine, aren't they?"

"Siferra, I'm sorry if—"

"Forget it. *Forget it!*"

Mudrin came doddering in. He was a frail, desiccated-looking man in his late seventies, well past retirement age, but still retained as a member of the faculty in a nonteaching post so that he could continue his paleographic studies. His mild gray-green eyes, watery from a lifetime of poring over old faded manuscripts, peered out from behind thick spectacles. Yet Siferra knew that their watery appearance was deceptive: those were the sharpest eyes she had ever known, at least where ancient inscriptions were concerned.

"So these are the famous tablets," Mudrin said. "You know I've thought about nothing else since you told me." But he made no immediate move to examine them. —"Can you give me a little information about the context, the matrix?"

"Here's Balik's master photo," Siferra said, handing him the huge glossy enlargement. "The Hill of Thombo, the old midden-heap south of Beklimot Major. When the sandstorm slit it open, this was the view we had. And then we ran our trench down here—and down to *here*, next—we laid the whole thing open. Can you make out this dark line here?"

"Charcoal?" Mudrin asked.

"Exactly. A fire line here, the whole town burned. Now we skip down to here and we see a second batch of foundations, and a second fire line. And if you look here—and here—"

Mudrin studied the photograph a long while. "What do you have here? Eight successive settlement sites?"

"Seven," Balik blurted.

"Nine, I think," said Siferra curtly. "But I agree it gets pretty difficult to tell, down toward the base of the hill. We'll need chemical analysis to clear it up, and radiographic testing. But obviously there was a whole series of conflagrations here. And the Thombo people went on building and rebuilding, time after time."

"But this site must be incredibly ancient, if that's the case!" Mudrin said.

"My guess is that the occupation period was a span of at least five thousand years. Perhaps much more. Perhaps ten or fifteen. We won't know until we've fully uncovered the lowest level, and that'll have to wait for the next expedition. Or the one after that."

"Five thousand years, you say? Can it be?"

"To build and rebuild and rebuild again? Five thousand at a *minimum.*"

"But no site we've ever excavated anywhere in the world is remotely as old as that," Mudrin said, looking startled. "Beklimot itself is less than two thousand years old, isn't that so? And we regard it as the oldest known human settlement on Kalgash."

"The oldest *known* settlement," Siferra said. "But what's to say that there aren't older ones? Much older ones? Mudrin, this photo gives you your own answer. Here's a site that has to be older than Beklimot—there are Beklimot-style artifacts in its *highest* level, and it goes down a long way from there. Beklimot must be a very recent settlement as human history goes. The Thombo settlement, which was ancient before Beklimot ever existed, must have burned and burned and burned again, and was rebuilt every time, down through what must have been hundreds of generations."

"A very unlucky place, then," Mudrin observed. "Hardly beloved of the gods, was it?"

"Eventually that must have occurred to them," Balik said.

Siferra nodded. "Yes. Finally they must have decided there was a curse on the place. So instead of rebuilding it after the last fire in the series they moved a short distance away and built Beklimot. But before that they must have occupied Thombo a long, long time. We were able to recognize the architectural styles of the two topmost settlements—see, it's cyclopean middle-Beklimot here, and proto-Beklimot crosshatch beneath. But the third town down, what there is left of it, is like nothing I can identify. The fourth is even stranger, and very crude. The fifth makes the fourth look sophisticated by comparison. Below that, everything's such a primitive jumble that it's not easy to tell which town is which. But each one is separated by a burn line from the one above it, or so we think. And the tablets—"

"Yes, the tablets," Mudrin said, trembling with excitement.

"We found this set, the square ones, in the third level. The oblong ones came from the fifth one. I can't even begin to make any sense out of them, of course, but I'm no paleographer."

"How wonderful it would be," Balik began, "if these tablets contained some kind of account of the destruction and rebuilding of the Thombo towns, and—"

Siferra shot him a poisonous glance. "How wonderful it would be, Balik, if you wouldn't spin cozy little wish-fulfillment fantasies like that!"

"I'm sorry, Siferra," he said icily. "Forgive me for breathing."

Mudrin took no need of their bickering. He was at Siferra's desk, head bent low over the square tablets for a long while, then over the oblong ones.

Finally the paleographer said, "Astonishing! Absolutely astonishing!"

"Can you read them?" Siferra asked.

The old man chuckled. "Read them? Of course not. Do you want miracles? But I see word-groups here."

"Yes. So did I," Siferra said.

"And I can almost recognize letters. Not on the older tablets —they're done in a completely unfamiliar script, very likely a syllabic one, too many different characters for it to be alphabetic. But the square tablets seem to be written in a very primitive form of the Beklimot script. See, this is a quhas here, I'd almost be willing to wager on it, and this appears to be a somewhat distorted form of the letter tifjak—it *is* a tifjak, wouldn't you say? —I need to work on these, Siferra. With my own lighting equipment, my cameras, my scanning screens. May I take them with me?"

"Take them?" she said, as if he had asked to borrow some of her fingers.

"It's the only way I can begin to decipher them."

"Do you think you *can* decipher them?" Balik asked.

"I offer no guarantees. But if this character is a tifjak and this a quhas, then I should be able to find other letters ancestral to the Beklimot ones, and at least produce a transliteration. Whether we can understand the language once we read the script, that's hard to say. And I doubt I can get very far with the oblong tablets unless you've uncovered a bilingual that will give me some way of approaching this even older script. But let me try, Siferra. Let me try."

"Yes. Here."

Lovingly she gathered up the tablets and put them back in the container in which she had carried them all the way from Sagikan. It pained her to let them go out of her possession. But Mudrin was right. He couldn't do anything with them at a quick glance; he had to subject them to laboratory analysis.

She watched ruefully until the paleographer had gone doddering from the room, his precious bundle clasped close against his hollow chest. Now she and Balik were alone again.

"Siferra—about what I said before—"

"I told you to forget it. I already have. Do you mind if I get about my work now, Balik?"

[13]

"Well, how did he take it?" Theremon asked. "Better than you expected he would, is my guess."

"He was completely marvelous," said Beenay. They were on the terrace at the Six Suns Club. The rains had ended for the time being, and the evening was a splendid one, with the strange clarity of the atmosphere that always came after a prolonged period of rain: Tano and Sitha in the west, casting their hard white ghostly light with more than usual intensity, and red Dovim in the opposing sector of the dusky sky, burning like a tiny gem. "He hardly even seemed upset, except when I indicated that I'd almost been tempted to suppress the whole thing for the sake of protecting his feelings. *Then* he flew off the handle. He really chewed me out—as I deserved. But the funniest thing was— Waiter! Waiter! A Tano Special for me, please! And one for my friend. Make them doubles!"

"You're really turning into a drinker, aren't you?" Theremon remarked.

Beenay shrugged. "Only when I'm here. There's something about this terrace, the view of the city, the whole atmosphere—"

"That's how it begins. You get to like it little by little, you develop jolly associations between one particular place and drinking, then after a while you experiment with having a drink or two somewhere else, and then a drink or three—"

"Theremon! You sound like an Apostle of Flame! They think drinking's evil too, don't they?"

"They think everything's evil. But drinking certainly is. That's what's so wonderful about it, eh, my friend?" Theremon laughed. "You were telling me about Athor."

"Yes. The really comical thing. Do you remember that wild notion you had that some unknown factor might be pushing Kalgash away from the orbit we'd expect it to have?"

"The invisible giant, yes. The dragon huffing and puffing in the sky."

"Well, Athor took exactly the same position!"

"He thinks there's a dragon in the sky?"

Beenay guffawed. "Don't be silly. But some sort of unknown factor, yes. A dark sun, maybe, or some other world that's located at a position that's impossible for us to see, but which nevertheless is exerting gravitational force on Kalgash—"

"Isn't that all a little on the fantastic side?" Theremon asked.

"Of course it is. But Athor reminded me of the old philosophical chestnut of Thargola's Sword. Which we use—metaphorically, I mean—to smite the more complex premise when we're trying to decide between two hypotheses. It's simpler to go looking for a dark sun than it is to have to produce an entirely new Theory of Universal Gravitation. And therefore—"

"A dark sun? But isn't that a contradiction in terms? A sun is a source of light. If it's dark, how can it be a sun?"

"That's just one of the possibilities Athor tossed at us. It isn't necessarily one that he takes seriously. What we've been doing, these last few days, is throwing around all kinds of astronomical notions, hoping that one of them will make enough sense so that we can begin to put together an explanation for— Look, there's Sheerin." Beenay waved at the rotund psychologist, who had just entered the club. "Sheerin! Sheerin! Come out here and have a drink with us, will you?"

Sheerin stepped carefully through the narrow doorway.

"So you've taken up some new vices, have you, Beenay?"

"Not very many. But Theremon's exposed me to the Tano

Special, and I'm afraid I've caught a taste for it. You know Theremon, don't you? He writes the column in the *Chronicle.*"

"I don't think we've actually met," Sheerin said. He offered his hand. "I've certainly heard a lot about you, though. I'm Raissta 717's uncle."

"The psych professor," Theremon said. "You've been at the Jonglor Exposition, right?"

Sheerin looked startled. "You keep up with everything, don't you?"

"I try to." The waiter was back. "What can we get you? Tano Special?"

"Too strong for me," Sheerin said. "And a little too sweet. —Do you have neltigir, by any chance?"

"The Jonglorian brandy? I'm not sure. How do you want it, if I can find some?"

"Straight," said Sheerin. "Please." To Theremon and Beenay he said, "I developed a liking for it while I was up north. The food's awful in Jonglor, but at least they can distill a decent brandy."

"I hear they've had a lot of trouble at the Exposition," Theremon said. "Some problem in their amusement park—a ride through Darkness that was driving people crazy, literally driving them out of their heads—"

"The Tunnel of Mystery, yes. That was the reason I was there: as a consultant called in by the city and its lawyers for an opinion."

Theremon sat forward. "Is it true that people were dying of shock in that tunnel, and they kept it open anyway?"

"Everyone's been asking me that," replied Sheerin. "There were a few deaths, yes. But they didn't seem to harm the ride's popularity. People insisted on taking the risk anyway. And a lot of them came out very badly deranged. I took a ride in the Tunnel of Mystery myself," he said, shuddering. "Well, they've shut the thing down, now. I told them it was either that or fork over millions of credits in liability suits, that it was absurd to expect people to be able to tolerate Darkness at that level of intensity. They saw the logic of that."

"We do have some neltigir, sir," the waiter broke in, putting a glass of somber brownish brandy on the table in front of Sheerin. "Just one bottle, so you'd better go easy." The psychologist nodded and scooped up his drink, downing about half of it before the waiter had left the table.

"Sir, I said—"

Sheerin smiled at him. "I heard what you said. I'll take it easier after this one." He turned to Beenay. "I understand there was some excitement at the Observatory while I was up north. Liliath told me. But she wasn't too clear on what was going on. Some new theory, I think she said—"

Grinning, Beenay said, "Theremon and I were just talking about that. Not a new theory, no. A challenge to an established one. I was running some calculations on Kalgash's orbit, and—"

Sheerin listened to the story with increasing astonishment. "The Theory of Universal Gravitation's invalid?" he cried when Beenay was halfway through. "Good lord, man! Does that mean that if I put my glass down, it's likely to go floating up into the sky? I'd better finish off my neltigir first, then!" And he did.

Beenay laughed. "The theory's still on the books. What we're trying to do—what *Athor* is trying to do; he's been spearheading the work, and it's amazing to watch him go at it—is to come up with a mathematical explanation for why our figures don't come out the way we think they ought to."

"Massaging the data, I think it's called," Theremon added.

"Sounds suspicious to me," Sheerin said. "You don't like the result, so you rearrange your findings, is that it, Beenay? Make everything fit, by hook or by crook?"

"Well, not exactly—"

"Admit it! Admit it!" Sheerin roared with laughter. "Waiter! Another neltigir! And one more Tano Special for my unethical young friend here! —Theremon, can I get you a drink too?"

"Please."

Sheerin said in the same broad tone as before, "This is all very disillusioning, Beenay. I thought it was only us psychologists who made the data fit the theories and called the result 'science.' Seems more like something the Apostles of Flame might do!"

"Sheerin! Cut it out!"

"The Apostles claim to be scientists too," Theremon put in. Beenay and Sheerin turned to look at him. "Last week just before the rain started I had an interview with one of their big people," he went on. "I had hoped to see Mondior, but I got a certain Folimun 66 instead, their public-relations man, very slick, very bright, very personable. He spent half an hour explaining to me that the Apostles have reliable scientific proof that next year on the nineteenth of Theptar the suns are going to go out and we'll all be plunged into Darkness and everyone will go insane."

"The whole world turned into one big Tunnel of Mystery, is that it?" Sheerin said jovially. "We won't have enough mental hospitals to hold the entire population, you know. Or enough psychiatrists to treat them. Besides, the psychiatrists will be crazy too."

"Aren't they already?" Beenay asked.

"Good point," said Sheerin.

"The madness isn't the worst of it," Theremon said. "According to Folimun, the sky will be filled with something called Stars that will shoot fire down upon us and set everything ablaze. And there we'll be, a world full of gibbering maniacs, wandering around in cities that are burning down around our ears. Thank heaven it's nothing but Mondior's bad dream."

"But what if it isn't?" Sheerin said, suddenly sobering. His round face grew long and thoughtful. "What if there's something to it?"

"What an appalling notion," Beenay said. "I think it calls for another drink."

"You haven't finished the one you've got," Sheerin reminded the young astronomer.

"Well, what of it? It *still* calls for another one afterward. Waiter! Waiter!"

[14]

Athor 77 felt fatigue sweeping through him in shimmering waves. The Observatory director had lost all track of time. Had he really been at his desk sixteen straight hours? And yesterday the same. And the day before—

That was what Nyilda claimed, anyway. He had spoken to

her just a little while before. His wife's face on the screen had been tense, drawn, unmistakably worried.

"Won't you come home for a rest, Athor? You've been going at it practically around the clock."

"Have I?"

"You aren't a young man, you know."

"I'm not a senile one, either, Nyilda. And this is exhilarating work. After a decade of initialing budget reports and reading other people's research papers I'm finally doing some real work again. I love it."

She looked even more troubled. "But you don't *need* to be doing research at your age. Your reputation is secure, Athor!"

"Ah, is it?"

"Your name will be famous in the history of astronomy forever."

"Or infamous," he said balefully.

"Athor, I don't understand what you—"

"Let me be, Nyilda. I'm not going to keel over at my desk, believe me. I feel rejuvenated by what I'm doing here. And it's work that only I can do. If that sounds pigheaded, so be it, but it's absolutely essential that I—"

She sighed. "Yes, of course. But don't overdo it, Athor. That's all I ask."

Was he overdoing it? he wondered now. Yes, yes, of course he was. There wasn't any other way. You couldn't dabble in these matters. You had to throw yourself wholeheartedly into them. When he was working out Universal Gravitation he had worked sixteen-, eighteen-, twenty-hour days for weeks on end, sleeping only when sleep became unavoidable, snatching brief naps and awakening ready and eager for work, with his mind still bubbling with the equations he had left unfinished a little while before.

But he had been only thirty-five or so, then. He was nearly seventy now. There was no denying the inroads of age. His head ached, his throat was dry, there was a nasty pounding in his chest. Despite the warmth of his office his fingertips were chilly with weariness. His knees were throbbing. Every part of his body protested the strain he had been putting on it.

Just a little while longer today, he promised himself, and then I'll go home.

Just a little while longer.

Postulate Eight—

"Sir?"

"What is it?" he asked.

But his voice must have turned the question into some sort of fierce snarl, for when he glanced around he saw young Yimot standing in the doorway doing a bizarre series of wild twitches and convulsions, as though he were dancing on hot embers. There was terror in the boy's eyes. Of course Yimot *always* seemed intimidated by the Observatory director—everybody around here was, not just graduate students, and Athor was used to it. Athor was awesome and he knew it. But this went beyond the ordinary. Yimot was gazing at him in undisguised fear mingled with what seemed like astonishment.

Yimot struggled visibly to find his voice and said huskily, "The calculations you wanted, sir—"

"Oh. Yes. Yes. Here, give me."

Athor's hand was trembling violently as he reached for the printouts Yimot had brought him. Both of them stared at it, aghast. The long bony fingers were pale as death and they were quivering with a vehemence that not even Yimot, famed for his remarkable nervous reactions, could have equaled. Athor willed his hand to be still, but it would not. He might just as well have been willing Onos to spin backward across the sky.

With an effort he snatched the papers from Yimot and slapped them down on the desk.

Yimot said, "If there's anything I can get you, sir—"

"Medication, you mean? How dare you suggest—"

"I just meant something to eat, or maybe a cold drink," Yimot said in a barely audible whisper. He backed slowly away as if expecting Athor to growl and leap for his throat.

"Ah. Ah. I see. No, I'm fine, Yimot. Fine!"

"Yes, sir."

The student went out. Athor closed his eyes a moment, took three or four deep breaths, struggled to calm himself. He was near the end of his task, of that he was sure. These figures that he had asked Yimot to work out for him were almost certainly the last confirmation he needed. But the question now was whether the work was going to finish him before he finished the work.

91

He looked at Yimot's numbers.

Three screens sat before him on his desk. On the left-hand one was the orbit of Kalgash as calculated according to conventional reckoning under the Theory of Universal Gravitation, outlined in blazing red. On the right-hand screen, in fiery yellow, was the revised orbit that Beenay had produced, using the new university computer and the most recent observations of Kalgash's actual position. The middle screen carried both orbits plotted one over the other. In the past five days Athor had produced seven different postulates to account for the deviation between the theoretical orbit and the observed one, and he could call up any of those seven postulates on the middle screen with a single key-stroke.

The trouble was that all seven of them were nonsense, and he knew it. Each one had a fatal flaw at its heart—an assumption that was there not because the calculations justified it, but only because the situation called for some such sort of special assumption in order to make the numbers turn out the right way. Nothing was provable, nothing was confirmable. It was as though in each case he had simply decreed, at some point in the chain of logic, that a fairy godmother would step in and adjust the gravitational interactions to account for the deviation. In truth that was precisely what Athor knew he needed to find. But it had to be a *real* fairy godmother.

Postulate Eight, now—

He began keying in Yimot's calculations. Several times his trembling fingers betrayed him and he made an error; but his mind was still sharp enough to tell him instantly that he had hit the wrong key, and he backed up and repaired the damage each time. Twice, as he worked, he nearly blacked out from the intensity of his effort. But he forced himself to go on.

You are the only person in the world who can possibly do this, he told himself as he worked. *And so you must.*

It sounded foolish to him, and madly egocentric, and perhaps a little insane. It probably wasn't even true. But at this stage in his exhaustion he couldn't allow himself to consider any other premise but that of his own indispensability. All the basic concepts of this project were held in his mind, and his mind alone. He had to push himself onward until he had closed the last link in the chain. Until—

There.

The last of Yimot's numbers went into the computer.

Athor hit the key that brought the two orbits up into view simultaneously on the middle screen, and hit the key that integrated the new number with the existing patterns.

The brilliant red ellipse that was the original theoretical orbit wavered and shifted, and suddenly it was gone. So was the yellow one of the observed orbit. Now there was only a single line on the screen, a deep, intense orange, the two orbital simulations overlapping to the last decimal place.

Athor gasped. For a long moment he studied the screen, and then he closed his eyes again and bowed his head against the edge of the desk. The orange ellipse blazed like a ring of flame against his closed eyelids.

He felt a curious sense of exultation mixed with dismay.

He had his answer, now; he had a hypothesis that he was certain would stand up to the closest scrutiny. The Theory of Universal Gravitation was valid after all: the epochal chain of reasoning on which his fame was based would not be overthrown.

But at the same time he knew now that the model of the solar system with which he was so familiar was in fact erroneous. The unknown factor for which they had sought, the invisible giant, the dragon in the sky, was real. Athor found that profoundly upsetting, even if it *had* rescued his famous theory. He had thought for years that he fully understood the rhythm of the heavens, and now it was clear to him that his knowledge had been incomplete, that a great strangeness existed in the midst of the known universe, that things were not as he had always believed them to be. It was hard, at his age, to swallow that.

After a time Athor looked up. Nothing had changed on the screen. He punched in a few interrogative equations, and still nothing changed. He saw one orbit, not two.

Very well, he told himself. *So the universe is not quite as you thought it was. You'd better rearrange your beliefs, then. Because you certainly can't rearrange the universe.*

"Yimot!" he called. "Faro! Beenay! All of you!"

Roly-poly little Faro was the first through the door, with beanpole Yimot just behind him, and then the rest of the Astronomy Department, Beenay, Thilanda, Klet, Simbron, and some others. They clustered just inside the entrance to his office. Athor saw by the expression of shock on their faces that he must be a frightful sight indeed, no doubt wild and haggard, his white hair standing out in all directions, his face pale, his whole appearance that of an old man right on the edge of collapse.

It was important to defuse their fears right away. This was no moment for melodrama.

Quietly he said, "Yes, I'm very tired and I know it. And I probably look like some demon out of the nether realms. But I've got something here that looks like it works."

"The gravitational lens idea?" Beenay said.

"The gravitational lens is a completely hopeless concept," Athor said frostily. "The same with the burned-out sun, the fold in space, the zone of negative mass, and the other fantastical notions we've been playing with all week. They're all very pretty ideas but they don't stand up to hard scrutiny. There is one that does, though."

He watched their eyes widen.

Turning to the screen, he began once again to set up the numbers of Postulate Eight. His weariness dropped away as he worked: he struck no wrong keys this time, he felt no aches and pains. He had moved into a realm beyond fatigue.

"In this postulate we assume," he said, "a non-luminous planetary body similar to Kalgash, which is in orbit not around Onos but around Kalgash itself. Its mass is considerable, in fact is nearly the same as that of Kalgash itself: sufficient to exert a gravitational force on our world that causes the perturbations of our orbit which Beenay has called to our attention."

Athor keyed in the visuals and the solar system appeared on the screen in stylized form: the six suns, Kalgash, and the postulated satellite of Kalgash.

He turned back to face the others. They were all looking at each other uneasily. Though they were half his age, or even less, they must be having as much trouble coming to an intellectual and emotional acceptance of the whole idea of another major heavenly body in the universe as he had had. Or else they simply must think he had become senile, and somehow had slipped up in his calculations.

"The numbers supporting Postulate Eight are correct," Athor said. "I pledge you that. And the postulate has withstood every test I could apply."

He glared at them defiantly, looking ferociously at each of them in turn, as if to remind them that he was the Athor 77 who had given the world the Theory of Universal Gravitation, and that he had not yet taken leave of his faculties.

Beenay said softly, "And the reason why we are unable to see this satellite, sir—?"

"Two reasons," replied Athor serenely. "Like Kalgash itself, this planetary body would shine only by reflected light. If we assume that its surface is made up largely of bluish rock—not an implausible geological likelihood—then the light reflected from it would be positioned along the spectrum in such a way that the eternal blaze of the six suns, combined with the light-scattering properties of our own atmosphere, would completely mask its presence. In a sky where several suns are shining at virtually every moment, such a satellite would be invisible to us."

Faro said, "Provided the orbit of the satellite is an extremely large one, isn't that so, sir?"

"Right." Athor keyed in the second visual. "Here's a closer look. As you see, our unknown and invisible satellite travels around us on an enormous ellipse that carries it extremely far from us for many years at a time. Not so distant that we don't display the orbital effects of its presence in the heavens—but far enough so that ordinarily there is no possibility of our getting a naked-eye view of this dim rocky mass in the sky, and very little possibility of our discovering it even with our telescopes. Since we have no way of knowing it's there by ordinary observation, it would be only by the wildest chance that we'd have detected it astronomically."

"But of course we can go looking for it now," said Thilanda 191, whose specialty was astrophotography.

"And of course we will," Athor told her. They were coming around to the idea now, he saw. Every one of them. He knew them well enough to see that there were no secret scoffers. "Though you may find the search harder than you suspect, very definitely a needle-in-a-haystack proposition. But there'll be an immediate appropriation for the work, that I pledge you."

Beenay said, "One question, sir."

"Go on."

"If the orbit's as eccentric as your postulate supposes, and therefore this satellite of ours, this—Kalgash Two, let's call it for the moment—Kalgash Two is extremely distant from us during certain parts of its orbital cycle, then it stands to reason that at other parts of its cycle it's bound to move into a position that's very much closer to us. There has to be some range of variation even in the most perfect orbit, and a satellite traveling in a large elliptical orbit is likely to have an extreme range between the farthest and the closest points of approach to the primary."

"That would be logical, yes," Athor said.

"But then, sir," Beenay went on, "if we assume that Kalgash Two has been so far from us during the entire period of modern astronomical science that we've been unable to discover its very existence except by the indirect means of measuring its effect on our own world's orbit, wouldn't you agree that it's probably coming back from its farthest distance right now? That it must currently be approaching us?"

"That doesn't necessarily follow," Yimot said, with a great flurry of his arms. "We don't have any idea where it is along its orbital path right now, or how long it takes to make one complete circuit around Kalgash. It might be a ten-thousand-year orbit and Kalgash Two could still be heading away from us after an approach in prehistoric times that no one remembers."

"True," Beenay admitted. "We can't really say whether it's coming or going at the present moment. Not yet, anyway."

"But we can try to find out," Faro said. "Thilanda has the right idea. Even though all the numbers check out, we need to see whether Kalgash Two is actually out there. Once we find it we can begin to calculate its orbit."

"We should be able to calculate its orbit simply from the perturbations it causes in ours," said Klet, who was the department's best mathematician.

"Yes," Simbron put in—she was a cosmographer—"and we can also figure out whether it's approaching or heading away from us. Gods! What if it's heading this way? What an amazing event that would be! A dark planetary body cutting across the sky—passing between us and the suns! Possibly even blotting out the light of some of them for a couple of hours!"

"How strange that would be," Beenay mused. "An eclipse, I suppose you could call it. You know: the visual effect that occurs when some object gets between a viewer and the thing he's looking at. But could it happen? The suns are so huge—how could Kalgash Two actually conceal one of them from view?"

"If it came close enough to us it might," Faro said. "Why, I could imagine a situation in which—"

"Yes, work out all possible scenarios, why don't you?" Athor interjected suddenly, cutting Faro off with such brutal abruptness that everyone in the room turned to stare at him. "Play with the idea, all of you. Push it this way and that, and see what you get."

Suddenly he couldn't bear to sit here any longer. He had to get away.

The exhilaration he had felt since putting the last piece into place had abruptly deserted him. He felt a terrible leaden weariness, as though he were a thousand years old. Chills were running along his arms down into his fingers, and something was squirming frantically in the muscles of his back. He knew that he had pushed himself beyond all endurance now. It was time for younger workers to relieve him of this enterprise.

Rising from his chair before the screens, Athor took one uncertain reeling step toward the middle of the room, recovered himself before he could stumble, and walked slowly and with all the dignity he could muster past the Observatory staff. "I'm going home," he said. "I could use some sleep."

[15]

Beenay said, "Am I to understand that the village was destroyed by fire *nine times in a row*, Siferra? And they rebuilt it every time?"

"My colleague Balik thinks there may be only seven villages piled up in the Hill of Thombo," the archaeologist replied.

"And he may be right, actually. Things are pretty jumbled down toward the lowest levels. But seven villages, nine villages —no matter how many it is exactly, it doesn't change the fundamental concept. Here: look at these charts. I've worked them up from my excavation notes. Of course what we did was just a preliminary dig, a quick slice through the whole hill, with the really meticulous work left for a later expedition. We discovered the hill too late in our work to do anything else. But these charts'll give you an idea. —You aren't going to be bored, are you? All this stuff does interest you, doesn't it, Beenay?"

"I find it completely fascinating. Do you think I'm so totally preoccupied with astronomy that I can't pay attention to any of the other disciplines? —Besides, archaeology and astronomy sometimes go hand in hand. We've learned more than a little about the movements of the suns through the heavens by studying the ancient astronomical monuments that you people have been digging up here and there around the world. Here, let me see."

They were in Siferra's office. She had asked Beenay to come there to discuss a problem which she said had unexpectedly arisen in the course of her research. Which puzzled him, because he didn't immediately see how an astronomer could help an archaeologist in her work, despite what he had just said about archaeology and astronomy sometimes going hand in hand. But he was always glad to have a chance to visit with Siferra.

They had met initially five years before, when they were working together on an interdisciplinary faculty committee that was planning the expansion of the university library. Though Siferra had been out of the country most of the time since then doing field work, she and Beenay did enjoy meeting for lunch now and then when she was there. He found her challenging, highly intelligent, and abrasive in a refreshing sort of way. What she saw in him he had no idea: perhaps just an intellectually stimulating young man who wasn't involved in the poisonous rivalries and feuds of her own field and had no apparent designs on her body.

Siferra unfolded the charts, huge sheets of thin parchment-like paper on which complex, elegant diagrams had been ruled with pencil, and she and Beenay bent forward to examine them at close range.

He had been telling the truth when he said he was fascinated by archaeology. Ever since he'd been a boy, he had enjoyed reading the narratives of the great explorers of antiquity, such men as Marpin, Shelbik, and of course Galdo 221. He found the remote past nearly as exciting to think about as the remote reaches of interstellar space.

His contract-mate Raissta wasn't greatly pleased by his friendship with Siferra. She had rather testily implied, a couple of times, that it was Siferra herself who fascinated him, not her field of research. But Beenay thought Raissta's jealousy was absurd. Certainly Siferra was an attractive woman—it would be disingenuous to pretend otherwise—but she was relentlessly non-romantic and every man on campus knew it. Besides, she was something like ten years older than Beenay. Handsome as she was, Beenay had never thought of her with any sort of intimate intentions.

"What we have here, first, is a cross section of the entire hill," Siferra told him. "I've plotted each separate level of occupation in a schematic way. The newest settlement's at the top, naturally—huge stone walls, what we call the cyclopean style of architecture, typical of the Beklimot culture in its mature period of development. This line here in the level of the cyclopean walls represents a layer of charcoal remains—enough charcoal to indicate a widespread conflagration that must have utterly wiped the city out. And here, below the cyclopean level and the burn line, is the next oldest settlement."

"Which is constructed in a different style."

"Exactly. You see how I've drawn the stones of the walls? It's what we call the crosshatch style, characteristic of the early Beklimot culture, or perhaps the culture that developed into Beklimot. Both these styles can be seen in the Beklimot-era ruins that surround the Hill of Thombo. The main ruins are cyclopean, and here and there we've found a little crosshatch stuff, just a mere outcropping or two, which we call proto-Beklimot. Now, look here, at the border between the crosshatch settlement and the cyclopean ruins above it."

"Another fire line?" Beenay said.

"Another fire line, yes. What we have in this hill is like a sandwich—a layer of human occupation, a layer of charcoal, another layer of human occupation, another layer of charcoal. So what I think happened is something like this. During the time of the crosshatch people there was a devastating fire that scorched a pretty good chunk of the Sagikan Peninsula and forced the abandonment of the Thombo village and other crosshatch-style villages nearby. Afterward, when the inhabitants came back and began to rebuild, they used a brand-new and more elaborate architectural style, which we call cyclopean because of the huge building-stones. But then came *another* fire and wiped out the cyclopean settlement. At that point the people of the area gave up trying to build cities on the Hill of Thombo and this time when they rebuilt they chose another site nearby, which we term Beklimot Major. We've believed for a long time that Beklimot Major was the first true human city, emerging from the smaller crosshatch-type proto-Beklimot-period settlements scattered all around it. What Thombo tells us is that there was at least one important cyclopean city in the area before Beklimot Major existed."

"And the Beklimot Major site," Beenay said, "shows no trace of fire damage?"

"No. So it wasn't there when the city on top of Thombo was burned. Eventually the whole Beklimot culture collapsed and Beklimot Major itself was abandoned, but that was for other reasons having to do with climatic shifts. Fire had nothing to do with it. That was perhaps a thousand years ago. But the fire that wrecked the topmost Thombo village seems to have been much earlier than that. I'd guess about a thousand years earlier. The radiocarbon dates from the charcoal samples will give us a more precise figure when we get them from the lab."

"And the crosshatch settlement—how old is that?"

"Orthodox archaeological belief has been that the fragmentary crosshatch structures we've found here and there on the Sagikan Peninsula are only a few generations older than the Beklimot Major site. After the Thombo excavation, I don't think so. My guess is that the crosshatch settlement on that hill is two thousand years older than the cyclopean buildings on top of it."

"Two *thousand*—? And you say there are other settlements below that one?"

"Look at the chart," Siferra said. "Here's number three—a kind of architecture we've never seen before, nothing at all like crosshatch work. Then another burn line. Settlement number four. And a burn line. Number five. A burn line. Then numbers six, seven, eight, and nine—or, if Balik's reading is correct, just numbers six and seven."

"And each one destroyed by a great fire! That seems pretty remarkable to me. A deadly cycle of destruction, striking again and again and again in the same place."

"The remarkable thing," said Siferra in a curiously somber tone, "is that each of these settlements appears to have flourished for approximately the same length of time before being destroyed by fire. The layers of occupation are quite extraordinarily similar in thickness. We're still waiting for the lab reports, you understand. But I don't think my eyeball estimate is very far off. And Balik's figures are the same as mine. Unless we're completely mistaken, we're looking at a minimum of fourteen thousand years of prehistory in the Hill of Thombo. And during those fourteen thousand years the hill was periodically swept by massive fires that forced its abandonment with clockwork regularity—one fire every two thousand years, just about exactly!"

"What?"

A shiver traveled along Beenay's spine. His mind was beginning to leap to all manner of improbable and disturbing conclusions.

"Wait," Siferra said. "There's more."

She opened a drawer and took out a stack of glossy photographs.

"These are pictures of the Thombo tablets. Mudrin 505 has the originals—the paleographer, you know. He's been trying to decipher them. They're made of baked clay. We found these three in Level Three, and these in Level Five. They're both written in extremely primitive scripts, and the writing on the older ones is so ancient that Mudrin can't even make a start on them. But he's been able very tentatively to puzzle out a couple of dozen words from the Level Three tablets, which are written in an early form of the Beklimot script. So far as he can tell at this point, they're an account of the destruction of a city by fire—the work of angry gods who periodically find it necessary to punish mankind for wickedness."

"*Periodically?*"

"That's right. Does it begin to sound familiar?"

"The Apostles of Flame! My God, Siferra, what have you stumbled on here?"

"That's what I've been asking myself since Mudrin brought me the first sketchy translations." The archaeologist swung around to face Beenay, and for the first time Beenay saw how bleary her eyes were, how tense and drawn her face. She looked almost distraught. "Do you see now why I asked you to come here? I can't talk about this with anyone in the department. Beenay, what am I going to do? If any of this becomes public, Mondior 71 and his whole crazy crew will proclaim it from the rooftops that I've discovered firm archaeological proof of their crackpot theories!"

"You think so?"

"What else?" Siferra tapped the charts. "Here's evidence of repeated fiery destruction at two-thousand-year intervals, roughly, over a period of many thousands of years. And these tablets—the way it looks now, they might actually be some sort of prehistoric version of the Book of Revelations. Taken together, they provide, if not actual confirmation of the rantings of the Apostles, then at least a solid rational underpinning for their whole mythology."

"But repeated fires at a single site don't prove that there was worldwide devastation," Beenay objected.

"It's the periodicity that worries me," said Siferra. "It's too neat, and too close to what Mondior's been saying. I've been looking at the Book of Revelations. The Sagikan Peninsula is a holy place to the Apostles, did you know that? The sacred site where the gods formerly made themselves visible to humanity, so they say. And therefore it stands to reason—listen to me, it stands to *reason,*" she said, laughing bitterly—"that the gods would preserve Sagikan as a warning to mankind of the doom that will come again and again if we don't alter our wicked ways."

Beenay stared at her, stunned.

He knew very little about the Apostles and their teachings, really. Such pathological fantasizing had never held any interest for him, and he had been too busy with his scientific work to pay heed to Mondior's windy apocalyptic prophecies.

But now the memory of the conversation he had had some weeks before with Theremon 762 at the Six Suns Club burst with furious impact into his consciousness. *". . . won't be the first time the world has been destroyed . . . the gods have deliberately made mankind imperfect and given us a single year—one of their divine years, not one of our little ones—in which to shape up. That's called a Year of Godliness, and it's exactly two thousand and forty-nine of our years long."*

No. No. No. No. Idiocy! Claptrap! Hysterical folly!

There was more. *"Again and again, when the Year of Godliness has ended, the gods have discovered that we're still wicked and sinful, and so they have destroyed the world by sending down heavenly flames. . . . So say the Apostles, anyway."*

No! No!

"Beenay?" Siferra said. "Are you all right?"

"Just thinking," he told her. "By Darkness, it's true! You'd give the Apostles complete confirmation!"

"Not necessarily. It would still be possible for people who are capable of thinking clearly to reject Mondior's ideas. The destruction of Thombo by fire—even the *repeated* destruction of Thombo at apparently regular intervals of approximately two thousand years—doesn't in any way prove that the whole world was destroyed by fire. Or that some such great fire must inevitably come again. Why should the past necessarily be recapitulated in the future? But people who are capable of thinking clearly are in a minority, of course. The rest of them will be swayed by Mondior's use of my findings and go into an immediate panic. You know, don't you, that the Apostles claim the next great world-destroying fire is due to strike us next year?"

"Yes," Beenay said hoarsely. "Theremon tells me that they've pinpointed the exact day. It's a two-thousand-and-forty-nine-year cycle, actually, and this is the two-thousand-and-forty-eighth year, and in something like eleven or twelve more months, if you believe Mondior, the sky will turn black and fire will descend on us. I think the nineteenth of Theptar is when it's supposed to happen."

"Theremon? The newspaperman?"

"Yes. He's a friend of mine, actually. He's interested in the whole Apostles thing and he's been interviewing one of their high priests, or whatever. Theremon told me—"

Siferra's hand shot out and caught Beenay's arm, her fingers digging in with astonishing force.

"You've got to promise me you won't say a word about any of this to him, Beenay!"

"To Theremon? No, of course not! You haven't published your findings yet. It wouldn't be proper for me to say anything to anybody! —But of course he's a very honorable man."

Her iron grip relaxed, but only a little.

"Sometimes things get said between friends, off the record— but you know, Beenay, there's no such thing as 'off the record' when you're talking to someone like Theremon. If he sees a reason to use it, he'll use it, no matter what he may have promised you. Or however 'honorable' you like to think he is."

"Well—perhaps—"

"Trust me. And if Theremon were to find out what I've come up with here, you can bet your ears it'll be all over the *Chronicle* half a day later. That would ruin me professionally, Beenay. It would be all I need, to become known as the scientist who provided the Apostles with proof of their absurd claims. The Apostles are totally repugnant to me, Beenay. I don't want to offer them any sort of aid and comfort, and I certainly don't want to seem to be publicly espousing their crackpot ideas."

"Don't worry," Beenay said. "I won't breathe a word."

"You mustn't. As I say, it would wreck me. I've come back to the university to have my research grant renewed. My Thombo findings are already stirring up controversy in the department, because they challenge the established view of Beklimot as the oldest urban center. But if Theremon somehow manages to wrap the Apostles of Flame around my neck on top of everything else—"

But Beenay was barely listening. He was sympathetic to Siferra's problem, and certainly he would do nothing to cause difficulties for her. Theremon would hear not one word about her research from him.

His mind had moved on, though, to other things, vastly troublesome things. Phrases out of Theremon's account of the teachings of the Apostles continued to churn in his memory.

"—*In something like fourteen months the suns will all disappear*—"

"—*the Stars will shoot flame down out of a black sky*—"

"—*the exact time of the catastrophe can be calculated scientifically*—"

"—*a black sky*—"

"—*the suns will all disappear*—"

"Darkness!" Beenay muttered harshly. "Can it be possible?"

Siferra had gone on talking. At his outburst she halted in mid-sentence.

"You aren't paying attention to me, Beenay!"

"I—what? Oh. Oh. Yes, of course I'm paying attention! You were saying that I mustn't let Theremon know anything about this, because it would harm your reputation, and—and—listen, Siferra, do you think we could continue discussing this some other time? This evening, or tomorrow afternoon, or whenever? I've got to get over to the Observatory right away."

"Don't let me detain you, then," she said coldly.

"No. I don't mean it that way. What you've been telling me is of the most colossal interest to me—and importance, tremendous importance, more than I can even say at this point. But I've got to check something. Something with a direct bearing on everything we've been discussing."

She gave him a close look. "Your face is flushed. Your eyes are wild, Beenay. You seem so strange, all of a sudden. Your mind's a million miles away. What's going on?"

"I'll tell you later," he said, halfway out the door. "Later! I promise you!"

[16]

At this hour the Observatory was practically deserted. No one was there but Faro and Thilanda. To Beenay's relief, Athor 77 was nowhere to be seen. Good, Beenay thought. The old man was exhausted enough from the effort he had devoted to working out the Kalgash Two concept. He didn't need more stress loaded upon him this evening.

And it would be just fine, having only Faro and Thilanda here. Faro had exactly the kind of quick, untrammeled mind that Beenay needed right now. And Thilanda, who had spent so many years scanning the empty spaces of the heavens with her telescope and camera, might be able to fill in some of the conceptual material Beenay would require.

Thilanda said at once, "I've been developing plates all day, Beenay. But it's no go. I'd stake my life on it: there's nothing up there in the sky except the six suns. You don't think the great man's finally gone around the bend, do you?"

"I think his mind is as sharp as ever."

"But these photos—" Thilanda said. "I've been running a random scan of every quadrant of the universe for days now. The program's all-inclusive. Snap, move down a couple of degrees, snap, move, snap. Methodically sweeping the entire sky. And look at what I'm getting, Beenay. A bunch of pictures of nothing at all!"

"If the unknown satellite is invisible, Thilanda, then it can't be seen. It's as simple as that."

"Invisible to the naked eye, maybe. But the camera ought to be able to—"

"Listen, never mind that now. I need some help from you two, purely theoretical stuff. Related to Athor's new theory."

"But if the unknown satellite's nothing but pie in the sky—" Thilanda protested.

"Invisible pie might still be real pie," Beenay snapped. "And we won't like it when it comes hurtling out of nowhere and hits us in the face. Will you help me or won't you?"

"Well—"

"Good. What I want you to do is prepare computer projections of the movements of all six suns covering a period of forty-two hundred years."

Thilanda gaped incredulously. "*Four thousand two hundred,* is that what you said, Beenay?"

"I know that you don't remotely have records of stellar movements over any such span. But I said computer projections, Thilanda. You've got at least a hundred years of reliable records, right?"

"More than that."

"Even better. Set them up and project them backward and forward in time. Have the computer tell you what every daily combination of the six suns was for the last twenty-one centu-

106

ries, and for the twenty-one centuries to come. If you can't do it, I'm sure Faro will be glad to help you write the program."

"I think I can manage it," said Thilanda in a glacial tone. "And would you mind telling me what this is all about? Are we going into the almanac business now? Even the almanac is content to settle for just the next few years of solar data. So what are you up to?"

"I'll tell you later," Beenay said. "That's a promise."

He left her fuming at her desk and walked across the Observatory to Athor's work area, where he took a seat in front of the three computer screens on which Athor had calculated the Kalgash Two theory. For a long moment Beenay stared thoughtfully at the center screen, showing the orbit of Kalgash as perturbed by the hypothetical Kalgash Two.

Then he touched a key and the proposed orbital line of Kalgash Two became visible in bright green, a huge eccentric ellipse splayed out across Kalgash's own more compact and nearly circular orbit. He studied it for a while; then he hit the keys that would bring the suns onto the screen, and peered broodingly at them for perhaps an hour, summoning them in all their varying configurations, now Onos in the sky with Tano and Sitha, Onos with Trey and Patru, Onos and Dovim with Trey and Patru, Dovim with Trey and Patru, Dovim with Tano and Sitha, Patru and Trey alone—

The normal patterns, yes.

But what about abnormal patterns?

Tano and Sitha alone? No, it couldn't happen. The relationship of that double-sun system's position in the heavens to the location of the closer suns was such that Tano and Sitha could never appear in the sky in this hemisphere unless either Onos or Dovim, or both of them, were visible at the same time. Maybe it had been possible hundreds or thousands of years ago, he thought, though he doubted it. But certainly not now.

Trey and Patru and Tano and Sitha?

"Another no. The two sets of double suns were on opposite sides of Kalgash; whenever one pair was in the sky, the other one generally was hidden by the planet's own bulk. Now and then the four of them did manage to get together in the sky, but Onos always was visible when such two-pair conjunctions occurred. Those were the famous five-sun days—which produced the equally distinctive Dovim-only days in the opposite hemisphere. They happened only every few years."

Trey without Patru? Tano without Sitha?

Well, technically, yes. When one of the double-sun pairs was close to the horizon, one sun would be above the horizon and one of them below it for a brief period. But that wasn't really a significant solar event, just a momentary aberration. The double suns were still together, but transiently separated by the line of the horizon.

All six suns in the sky at once?

Impossible!

Worse than that—unthinkable!

Yet he had just thought it. Beenay shivered at the idea. If all six of them were above the horizon simultaneously, then there would have to be a region in the other hemisphere where no sunlight whatever could be seen. Darkness! Darkness! But Darkness was unknown everywhere on Kalgash, except as an abstract concept. There could never have been a time when the six suns moved together and a major part of the world was plunged into utter lightlessness. Could there have been?

Could there?

Beenay pondered the chilling possibility. Once more he heard Theremon's deep voice explaining the theories of the Apostles to him:

"—the suns will all disappear—"

"—the Stars will shoot flame down out of a black sky—"

He shook his head. Everything he knew about the movements of the suns in the heavens rebelled against the idea of the six of them somehow bunching up on one side of Kalgash at the same time. It just couldn't happen, short of a miracle. Beenay didn't believe in miracles. The way the suns were arranged in the sky, there always had to be at least one or two of them shining over every part of Kalgash at any given moment.

Forget the six-suns-here, Darkness-there hypothesis.

What was left?

Dovim alone, he thought. The little red sun all alone in the sky?

Well, yes, it did happen, though not often. On those occasional five-sun days when Tano, Sitha, Trey, Patru, and Onos all were in conjunction in the same hemisphere: that left only

108

Dovim for the other side of the world. Beenay wondered whether that might be the moment when the Darkness came.

Could it be? Dovim by itself might cast so little light, just its cool and feeble reddish-purple gleam, that people might mistake it for Darkness.

But that didn't really make sense. Even little Dovim should be able to provide enough light to keep people from plunging into terror. Besides, Dovim-only days occurred somewhere in the world every few years. They were uncommon, but not all that extraordinary. Surely, if the effects of seeing nothing but a single small dim sun in the sky could cause vast psychological upheavals, then everybody would be worrying about the next Dovim-only event, which was due, as Beenay recalled, in just another year or so. And in fact nobody was thinking about it at all.

But if Dovim alone were in the sky, and something happened, some special thing, some truly uncommon thing, to blot out what little light it provided—

Thilanda appeared at his shoulder and said sourly, "All right, Beenay, I've got your solar projections all set up. Not just forty-two hundred years, either, but an infinite regression. Faro gave me a suggestion for the math and we've done the program so that it'll run clear to the end of time if you want it to, or backward to the beginning of the universe."

"Fine. Pipe it over to the computer I'm using, will you? —And will you come here, Faro?"

The pudgy little graduate student ambled over. His dark eyes were agleam with curiosity. Obviously he was bubbling with questions about what Beenay was doing; but he observed student-professor protocol and said nothing, merely waited to hear what Beenay would tell him.

"What I've got here on my screen," Beenay began, "is Athor's suggested orbit for the hypothetical Kalgash Two. I'm going to assume that the orbit's a correct one, since Athor has told us that it accurately accounts for all the perturbations in our own orbit, and I have faith that Athor knows what he's doing. I also have here, or at any rate I will when Thilanda has finished the data transfer, the program that you and she have just worked out for solar movements over a long span of time. What I'm going to do now is to attempt to work out a correlation between the presence of just *one* sun in the sky and the close approach of Kalgash Two to this planet, so that—"

"So that you can calculate the frequency of eclipses?" Faro blurted. "Is that it, sir?"

The boy's quickness was amusing and also a little disconcerting. "As a matter of fact, it is. You have eclipses on your mind too, do you?"

"I was thinking about them when Athor told us all about Kalgash Two the first time. Simbron, you remember, mentioned that the strange satellite might hide the light of some of the suns for a little while, and you said that that would be called an eclipse, and then I started to work out some of the possibilities. But Athor cut me off before I could say anything, because he was tired and wanted to go home."

"And you haven't said anything about it since?"

"No one's asked me," Faro said.

"Well, here's your moment. I'm going to transfer everything that's on my computer to yours, and you and I are going to sit down in this room separately and begin pushing the numbers around. What I'm searching for is a very special case in which Kalgash Two is at its closest point of approach to Kalgash and there's only one sun in the sky."

Faro nodded. He headed for his computer at a speed faster than Beenay had ever seen him move before.

Beenay didn't expect to be the first to finish the computation. Faro was notoriously quick at such things. But the point was to have each of them work on the problem independently, to provide separate validation of the result. So when Faro made a snorting sound of triumph after a little while and jumped up to say something, Beenay irritably waved at him to be silent and went on working. It took him ten embarrassing eternal minutes more.

Then the numbers began coming up on his screen.

If every assumption that he had fed into the computer was correct—Athor's calculation of the unknown satellite's probable mass and orbit, Thilanda's calculation of the movements of the six suns in the heavens—then it wasn't very likely that Darkness was going to come. The only possibility that would bring total Darkness was a Dovim-only day. But it didn't look as if Kalgash Two stood much chance of eclipsing Dovim.

Dovim-only days were such rarities that the likelihood of Dovim's being alone in the sky at the time when Kalgash Two was anywhere near Kalgash in its long orbit was infinitesimal, Beenay knew.

Or were they?

No. Not infinitesimal.

Not at all. He took a careful look at the figures on the screen. There seemed to be a slim possibility of a convergence. The calculation wasn't complete, but things were heading in that direction as the computer worked over each Kalgash-Kalgash Two conjunction in the forty-two-hundred-year period of the inquiry. Every time Kalgash Two came round on its orbit, it reached Kalgash's vicinity closer and closer to a Dovim-only day. The numbers continued to appear, as the computer processed all the astronomical possibilities. Beenay watched in mounting awe and disbelief.

There it was, finally. All three bodies lined up in just the right way. Kalgash—Kalgash Two—Dovim!

Yes! It *was* possible for Kalgash Two to cause a total eclipse of Dovim when Dovim was the only sun visible in the sky.

But that configuration was an extreme rarity. Dovim had to be alone in its hemisphere and at maximum distance from Kalgash, while Kalgash Two had to be at its minimum distance. Kalgash Two's apparent diameter would then be seven times that of Dovim. That was sufficient to hide Dovim's light for well over half a day, so that no spot on the planet would escape the effects of Darkness. The computer showed that such a highly special circumstance was capable of occurring only once every—

Beenay gasped. He didn't want to believe it.

He turned to Faro. The young graduate student's round face was pale with shock.

Huskily Beenay said, "All right. I'm done, and I've got a number. But first you tell me yours."

"Eclipse of Dovim by Kalgash Two, periodicity of two thousand and forty-nine years."

"Yes," Beenay said leadenly. "My number exactly. Once every two thousand and forty-nine years."

He felt dizzy. The entire universe seemed to be reeling around him.

111

Once every two thousand and forty-nine years. The exact length of a Year of Godliness, according to the Apostles of Flame. The very same figure that was given in the Book of Revelations.

"*—the suns will all disappear—*"

"*—the Stars will shoot flame down out of a black sky—*"

He didn't know what Stars were. But Siferra had discovered a hill on the Sagikan Peninsula where cities had been destroyed by flame with astonishing regularity, approximately every two thousand years. When she had had a chance to run exact carbon-14 tests, would the precise figure of the time between each conflagration on the Hill of Thombo turn out to be—two thousand and forty-nine years?

"*—a black sky—*"

Beenay stared helplessly across the room at Faro.

"When's the next Dovim-only day due to occur?" he asked.

"In eleven months and four days," Faro said grimly. "On the nineteenth of Theptar."

"Yes," Beenay said. "The same day when, Mondior 71 tells us, the sky is going to turn black and the fire of the gods is going to descend and destroy our civilization."

[17]

"For the first time in my life," Athor said, "I find myself praying with all my heart that my calculations are wrong. But I fear the gods have granted me no such mercy. We find ourselves inexorably swept along toward a conclusion that is terrible to contemplate."

He looked around the room, letting his gaze rest for a moment on each of the people he had called together. Young Beenay 25, of course. Sheerin 501, from the Psychology Department. Siferra 89, the archaeologist.

By sheer force of will alone Athor fought to conceal from them the vast fatigue he felt, the sense of growing despair, the crushing impact of all that he had learned in the weeks just past. He fought to conceal all those things even from himself. Now and then lately he had found himself thinking that he had lived too long, found himself wishing that he had been allowed to go to his rest a year or two ago. But he swept such thoughts mercilessly from his mind. An iron will and unflagging strength of spirit had always been Athor's prime characteristics. He refused now, with age making inroads on his vigor, to let those traits slip away.

To Sheerin he said, "Your field, as I understand it, is the study of Darkness?"

The plump psychologist seemed amused. "I suppose that's one way of putting it. My doctoral thesis was on Darkness-related mental disorders. But Darkness research has been only one facet of my work. I'm interested in mass hysteria of all sorts—in the irrational responses of the human mind to overwhelming stimuli. The whole roster of human nuttiness, that's what keeps the bread on my table."

"Very well," Athor said coolly. "Be that as it may. Beenay 25 says you're the ranking authority on Darkness at the university. You've just seen our little astronomical demonstration on the computer screen. I assume you comprehend the essential implications of what we've discovered."

The old astronomer could not find some way of preventing that from sounding patronizing. But Sheerin didn't seem particularly offended.

Calmly he said, "I think I grasped it well enough. You're saying that there's a mysterious invisible planetary-sized astronomical body of such-and-such mass in orbit around Kalgash at such-and-such a distance, and what with one such-and-such and the other, its force of attraction exactly accounts for certain deviations from theory in Kalgash's orbit that my friend Beenay here has discovered. Am I right so far?"

"Yes," Athor said. "Quite correct."

"Well," Sheerin continued, "it turns out that sometimes this body would get between us and one of our suns. This is termed an eclipse. But only one sun lies in its plane of revolutions in such a way that it can ever be eclipsed, and that sun is Dovim. It has been shown that the eclipse will occur only when"—Sheerin paused, frowning,—"when Dovim is the only sun in the sky, and both it and this so-called Kalgash Two are lined up in such a way that Kalgash Two completely covers the disk of

Dovim and no light at all gets through to us. Am I still doing okay?"

Athor nodded. "You've grasped it perfectly."

"I was afraid of that. I was hoping I had misunderstood."

"Now, as to the effects of the eclipse—" Athor said.

Sheerin took a deep breath. "All right. The eclipse—which happens only once every two thousand and forty-nine years, the gods be thanked!—will cause an extended period of universal Darkness on Kalgash. As the world turns, each continent will be totally dark for periods ranging from—what did you say?—nine to fourteen hours, depending on latitude."

"Now: if you please," Athor said, "what is your opinion, as a professional psychologist, of the effect that this will create in the minds of human beings?"

"The effect," Sheerin said unhesitatingly, "will be madness."

It was suddenly very quiet in the room.

At length Athor said, "Universal madness, is that what you're predicting?"

"Very likely. Universal Darkness, universal madness. My guess is that people will be affected to varying degrees, ranging from short-range disorientation and depression to complete and permanent destruction of the reasoning powers. The greater the psychological stability one has to begin with, naturally, the less likely one is to be entirely shattered by the impact of the absence of all light. But no one, I think, will be entirely unscathed."

"I don't understand," Beenay said. "What is there in Darkness to drive people mad?"

Sheerin smiled. "We simply aren't adapted for it. Imagine, if you can, a world that has only *one* sun. As that world rotates on its axis, each hemisphere will receive light for half the day and will be entirely dark for the other half."

Beenay made an involuntary gesture of horror.

"Do you see?" Sheerin cried. "You don't even like the sound of it! But the inhabitants of that planet will be quite accustomed to a daily dose of Darkness. Very likely they'll find the daylight hours cheerier and more to their liking, but they'll shrug off the Darkness as an ordinary everyday event, nothing to get excited about, just something to sleep through while waiting for morning to come. Not us, though. We've evolved under conditions of perpetual sunlight, every hour of the day, all year round. If Onos isn't in the sky, Tano and Sitha and Dovim are, or Patru and Trey, and so forth. Our minds, even the physiologies of our bodies, are accustomed to constant brightness. We don't like even a brief moment without it. You sleep with a godlight on in your room, I take it?"

"Of course," Beenay said.

"Of course? Why 'of course'?"

"Why—? But *everybody* sleeps with a godlight!"

"My point exactly. Tell me this: have you ever experienced Darkness, friend Beenay?"

Beenay leaned against the wall next to the big picture window and considered. "No. Can't say I have. But I know what it is. Just—uh—" He made vague motions with his fingers, and then brightened. "Just an absence of light. Like in caves."

"Have you ever been in a cave?"

"In a *cave!* Of course I haven't been in a cave."

"I thought not. *I* tried, once, long ago when I was beginning my studies of Darkness-induced disorders. But I got out in a hurry. I went in until the mouth of the cave was just visible as a blur of light, with black everywhere else." Sheerin chuckled pleasantly. "I never thought a person of my weight could run that fast."

Almost defiantly Beenay said, "Well, if it comes to that, I guess I wouldn't have run, if I had been there."

The psychologist smiled gently at the young astronomer.

"Bravely said! I admire your courage, my friend." Turning to Athor, Sheerin said, "May I have your permission, sir, to perform a little psychological experiment?"

"Whatever you wish."

"Thank you." Sheerin looked toward Beenay again. "Do you mind drawing the curtain next to you, friend Beenay?"

Beenay looked surprised. "What for?"

"Just draw the curtain. Then come over here and sit down next to me."

"Well, if you insist—"

Heavy red draperies hung by the windows. Athor couldn't remember a time when they had ever been drawn, and this room had been his office for some forty years. Beenay, with a shrug, reached for the tasseled string and jerked. The red curtain slid across the wide window, the brass rings hissing their way along the crossbar. For a moment the dusk-red light of Dovim could still be seen. Then all was in shadows, and even the shadows became indistinct.

Beenay's footsteps sounded hollowly in the silence as he made his way to the table, and then they stopped halfway.

"I can't see you, Sheerin," he whispered forlornly.

"Feel your way," Sheerin ordered in a strained voice.

"But I can't see you!" The young astronomer was breathing harshly. "I can't see anything!"

"What did you expect? This is Darkness." Sheerin waited a moment. "Come on. You must know your way around this room even with your eyes closed. Just walk over here and sit down."

The footsteps sounded again, waveringly. There was the sound of someone fumbling with a chair. Beenay's voice came thinly: "Here I am."

"How do you feel?"

"I'm—*ulp*—all right."

"You like it, do you?"

A long pause.

"No."

"No, Beenay?"

"Not at all. It's awful. It's as if the walls are—" He paused again. "They seem to be closing in on me. I keep wanting to push them away. —But I'm not going mad at all. In fact, I think I'm getting used to it."

"All right. Siferra? What about you?"

"I can take a little Darkness. I've gone crawling around in some underground passages now and then. But I can't say I care for it much."

"Athor?"

"I'm also still surviving. But I think you've proved your point, Dr. Sheerin," said the Observatory head, sharply.

"All right. Beenay, draw the curtains back again."

There were cautious footsteps through the dark, the rustle of Beenay's body against the curtain as he felt for the tassel, and then the relief of hearing the curtain's *ro-o-osh* as it slithered open. The red light of Dovim flooded the room, and with a cry of joy Beenay looked out the window at the smallest of the six suns.

Sheerin wiped the moistness off his forehead with the back of a hand and said shakily, "And that was just a few minutes in a dark room."

"It can be tolerated," said Beenay lightly.

"Yes, a dark room can. At least for a short while. But you all know about the Jonglor Centennial Exposition, don't you? The Tunnel of Mystery scandal? Beenay, I told you the story that evening last summer at the Six Suns Club, when you were with that newspaperman Theremon."

"Yes. I remember. The people who took that ride through Darkness in the amusement park and came out insane."

"Just a mile-long tunnel—with no lights. You got into a little open car and jolted along through Darkness for fifteen minutes. Some who took the ride died of fright. Others came out permanently deranged."

"And why was that? What drove them crazy?"

"Essentially the same thing that was operating on you just now when we had the curtain closed and you thought the walls of the room were crushing in on you in the dark. There's a psychological term for mankind's instinctive fear of the absence of light. We call it 'claustrophobia,' because the lack of light is always tied up with enclosed places, so that the fear of one is fear of the other. You see?"

"And those people of the Tunnel who went crazy?"

"Those people of the Tunnel who went—ah—crazy, to use your word, were those unfortunate ones who didn't have sufficient psychological resilience to overcome the claustrophobia that engulfed them in the Darkness. It was a powerful feeling. Believe me. I took the Tunnel ride myself. You had only a couple of minutes without light just now, and I believe you were fairly upset. Now imagine *fifteen* minutes."

"But didn't they recover afterward?"

"Some did. But some will suffer for years, or perhaps for the rest of their lives, from claustrophobic fixations. Their latent fear of Darkness and enclosed places has crystallized and become, so far as we can tell, permanent. And some, as I said, died of shock. No recovery for them, eh? *That's* what fifteen minutes in the dark can do."

"To some people," Beenay said stubbornly. His forehead wrinkled slowly into a frown. "I still don't believe it's going to be that bad for most of us. Certainly not for me."

Sheerin sighed in exasperation. "Imagine Darkness—everywhere. No light, as far as you can see. The houses, the trees, the fields, the earth, the sky—*black!* And Stars thrown in, if you listen to the preaching of the Apostles—Stars, whatever *they* are. Can you conceive it?"

"Yes, I can," declared Beenay, even more truculently.

"No! No, you can't!" Sheerin slammed his fist down upon the table in sudden passion. "You're fooling yourself! You can't conceive that. Your brain wasn't built for the concept any more than —Look, Beenay, you're a mathematician, aren't you? Can your brain really and truly conceive of the concept of infinity? Of eternity? You can only talk about it. Reduce it to equations and pretend that the abstract numbers are the reality, when in fact they're just marks on paper. But when you try really to encompass the idea of infinity in your mind you start getting dizzy pretty fast, I'm certain of that. A fraction of the reality upsets you. The same with the little bit of Darkness you just tasted. And when the real thing comes, your brain is going to be presented with a phenomenon outside its limits of comprehension. You'll go insane, Beenay. Completely and permanently. I have no doubt of that whatever!"

Once again there was a sudden terrible silence in the room.

Athor said, at last, "That's your final conclusion, Dr. Sheerin? Widespread insanity?"

"At least seventy-five percent of the population made irrational to a disabling degree. Perhaps eighty-five percent. Perhaps even a hundred percent."

Athor shook his head. "Monstrous. Hideous. A calamity beyond belief. Though I must tell you I feel somewhat the way Beenay does—that we will get through this somehow, that the effects will be less cataclysmic than your opinion would indicate. Old as I am, I can't help feeling a certain optimism, a certain sense of hope—"

Siferra said suddenly, "May I speak, Dr. Athor?"

"Of course. Of course! That's why you're here."

The archaeologist rose and came to the center of the room. "In some ways it surprises me that I'm here at all. When I first discussed my Sagikan Peninsula discoveries with Beenay here, I begged him to keep them absolutely confidential. I was fearful for my scientific reputation, because I saw that the data I had uncovered could very easily be construed as giving support to the most irrational, the most frightening, the most dangerous religious movement that exists within our society. I'm speaking, naturally, of the Apostles of Flame.

"But then, when Beenay came back to me a little while later with *his* new findings, the discovery of the periodicity of these eclipses of Dovim, I knew I had to reveal what I know. I have here photographs and charts of my excavation at the Hill of Thombo, near the Beklimot site on the Sagikan Peninsula. Beenay, you've already seen them, but if you'll be good enough to pass them to Dr. Athor and Dr. Sheerin—"

Siferra waited until they had had a chance to glance at the material. Then she resumed speaking.

"The charts will be easier to understand if you think of the Hill of Thombo as a giant layer cake of ancient settlements, each built upon its immediate predecessor—the youngest one at the top of the hill, naturally. That one is a city of what we call the Beklimot culture. Below it is one built by those same people, we think, in an earlier phase of their civilization, and then down and down and down, for a total of at least seven different periods of settlement, perhaps even more.

"Each of those settlements, gentlemen, came to an end because it was destroyed by fire. You can see, I think, the dark boundaries between the layers. Those are the burn lines—charcoal remnants. My original guess, based purely on an intuitive sense of how long it might have taken for these cities to have arisen, flourished, decayed, and crumbled, is that each of these great fires happened something like two thousand years apart, with the most recent of them taking place about two thousand years ago, just prior to the unfolding of the Beklimot culture that we regard as the beginning of the historical period.

"But charcoal is particularly well suited for radiocarbon dating, which gives us a fairly precise indication of the age of a site. Ever since my Thombo material reached Saro City, our departmental lab has been busy doing radiocarbon analysis, and now we have our figures. I can tell you what they are from memory. The youngest of the Thombo settlements was destroyed by fire two thousand and fifty years ago, with a statistical deviation of plus or minus twenty years. The charcoal from the settlement below that is forty-one hundred years old, with a deviation of plus or minus forty years. The third settlement from the top was destroyed by fire sixty-two hundred years ago, with a deviation of plus or minus eighty years. The fourth settlement down shows a radiocarbon age of eighty-three hundred years, plus or minus a hundred. The fifth—"

"Great gods!" Sheerin cried. "Are they all spaced as evenly as that?"

"Every one of them. The fires occurred at intervals of a little more than twenty centuries. Allowing for the slight inaccuracies that are inevitable in radiocarbon dating, it's still altogether permissible to propose that in fact they took place *exactly* two thousand and forty-nine years apart. Which, as Beenay has demonstrated, is precisely the frequency at which eclipses of Dovim occur. —And also," Siferra added in a bleak voice, "the length of what the Apostles of Flame call a Year of Godliness, at the end of which the world is supposed to be destroyed by fire."

"An effect of the mass insanity, yes," Sheerin said hollowly. "When the Darkness comes, people will want light—of any sort. Torches. Bonfires. Burn anything! Burn the furniture. Burn houses."

"No," Beenay muttered.

"Remember," Sheerin said, "these people won't be sane. They'll be like small children—but they'll have the bodies of adults and the remnants of the minds of adults. They'll know how to use matches. They just won't remember the consequences of lighting a lot of fires all over the place."

"No," Beenay said again, hopelessly. "No. No." It wasn't a statement of disbelief any longer.

Siferra said, "It could be argued originally that the fires at Thombo were a purely local event—an odd coincidence, such a rigid pattern of regular occurrence over such an immense span of time, but confined only to that one place, perhaps even a peculiar ritual cleansing practiced there. Since no other ancient sites as old as those of Sagikan have been found anywhere else on Kalgash, we couldn't say otherwise. But Beenay's calculations have changed everything. Now we see that every two thousand and forty-nine years the world is—apparently—plunged into Darkness. As Sheerin says, fires would be lit. And would get out of control. Whatever other settlements existed at the time of the Thombo fires, anywhere in the world, would have been destroyed just as the Thombo cities were, and for the same reason. But Thombo is all we have left from the prehistoric era. As the Apostles of Flame say of it, it is a holy place, the place where the gods have made themselves manifest to humanity."

"And perhaps are making themselves manifest once more," said Athor darkly. "By providing us with evidence of the fires of past epochs."

Beenay looked at him. "So you have come to believe the Apostles' teachings, sir?"

To Athor, Beenay's statement seemed almost like a blunt accusation of madness. It was a moment before he could reply.

But then he said, as calmly as he could, "Believe them? No. No, not quite. But they interest me, Beenay. I'm horrified at the need even to pose this question: but what if the Apostles are right? We have clear indications now that Darkness does come at just the two-thousand-and-forty-nine-year interval that they've mentioned in their Book of Revelations. Sheerin here says that the world would go mad if that happened, and we have Siferra's evidence that one small section of the world, at least, *did* go mad, again and again, its houses swept by fire at that two-thousand-and-forty-nine-year interval that we keep coming upon."

"What are you suggesting, then?" Beenay asked. "That we join the Apostles?"

Again Athor had to fight off anger. "No, Beenay. Simply that we look into their beliefs and see what sort of use we can make of them!"

"Use?" cried Sheerin and Siferra, almost at the same moment.

"Yes! Use!" Athor knotted his great gaunt hands together and swung around to face them all. "Don't you see that the survival of human civilization may depend entirely on the four of us? It comes down to just that, doesn't it? Melodramatic as it sounds, we four are in possession of what is beginning to look like incontrovertible proof that the end of the world is sweep-

121

ing down on us. Universal Darkness—bringing universal madness—a worldwide conflagration—our cities in flames, our society shattered. But there is already in existence another group that has been predicting, on the basis of who knows what evidence, the very same calamity—to the year, to the day."

"Theptar nineteenth," Beenay murmured.

"Theptar nineteenth, yes. The day when only Dovim will shine in the sky—and, if we are right, Kalgash Two will arrive, rising out of its invisibility to fill our sky and blot out all light. That day, the Apostles tell us, fire will engulf our cities. How do they know? A lucky guess? Mere myth-spinning?"

"Some of what they say makes no sense at all," Beenay pointed out. "For example, they say Stars will appear in the heavens. What are Stars? Where are they going to come from?"

Athor shrugged. "I have no idea. That part of the Apostles' teachings may very well be a fable. But they seem to have some sort of record of past eclipses, out of which they've built their current dire predictions. We need to know more about those records."

"Why us?" Beenay asked.

"Because we—as scientists—can serve as leaders, figures of authority, in the struggle to save civilization that lies ahead," said Athor. "Only if the nature of the danger is made known right here and now does society stand any chance of protecting itself against what's going to happen. But as it is, only the gullible and ignorant pay any heed to the Apostles. Most intelligent, rational folk look upon them the same way we do—as cranks, as fools, as madmen, perhaps as swindlers. What we need to do is persuade the Apostles to share their astronomical and archaelogical data, if they have any, with us. And then we go public. We reveal our findings, and we back them up with the material we receive, if we do, from the Apostles. In essence we form an alliance with them against the chaos that both we and they think is coming. That way we can gain the attention of all strata of society, from the most credulous to the most critical."

"So you want us to stop being scientists and enter the world of politics?" Siferra asked. "I don't like that. This isn't our job at all. I vote for turning our material over to the government, and letting them—"

"The government!" Beenay snorted.

"Beenay's right," said Sheerin. "I know what government people are like. They'll form a committee, and issue a report—eventually—and file the report away, and then later on they'll form another committee to dig out whatever it was that the first committee discovered, and then take a vote, and —No, we don't have the time for all that. It's our duty to speak out ourselves. I know at first hand what Darkness does to people's minds. Athor and Beenay, you have mathematical proof that Darkness is coming soon. You, Siferra, you've seen what Darkness has done to past civilizations."

"But do we dare seek out the Apostles?" Beenay asked. "Won't we be endangering our own reputations for scientific responsibility if we have anything to do with them?"

"Good point," Siferra said. "We have to keep away from them!"

Athor frowned. "Perhaps you're right. It may have been naive of me to suggest that we could form any sort of working partnership with those people. I withdraw the suggestion."

"Wait," said Beenay. "I have a friend—you know him, Sheerin, he's the newspaperman Theremon—who's already been in touch with some high official of the Apostles. He might be able to arrange a secret meeting between Athor and that High Apostle. You could sound the Apostles out, sir, and see if they know anything worth our having—just by way of obtaining even more confirming evidence for ourselves—and we can always deny the meeting took place, if it turns out they don't."

"That's a possibility," Athor said. "Distasteful as it would be, I'd be willing to meet with them. —I assume, then, that none of you has any fundamental dispute now with my basic suggestion? You agree with me that it's essential that we four take some action in response to what we've discovered?"

"I do now," Beenay said, glancing at Sheerin. "I still intend to survive the Darkness myself. But everything that's been said here today leads me to realize that a lot of others won't. Nor will civilization itself—unless we do something."

Athor nodded. "Very well. Talk to your friend Theremon. Cautiously, though. You know how I feel about the press. Journalists aren't much more to my liking than the Apostles are.

But very carefully let your Theremon understand that I'd like to meet privately with this Apostle he knows."

"I will, sir."

"You, Sheerin: get together all the literature you can find concerning the effects of exposure to prolonged Darkness, and let me have it."

"No problem there, Doctor."

"And you, Siferra—may I have a report, suitable for the understanding of laymen, on your Thombo excavation? With every scrap of evidence you are able to supply concerning this repetitive-conflagration business."

"Some of it's not ready yet, Dr. Athor. Material I didn't discuss today."

Athor's brows furrowed. "What do you mean?"

"Inscribed clay tablets," she said. "Found in the third and fifth levels from the top. Dr. Mudrin is attempting the very difficult task of translating them. His preliminary opinion is that they're some kind of priestly warning of the coming fire."

"The first edition of the Book of Revelations!" Beenay shouted.

"Well, yes, perhaps that is what they are," Siferra said, laughing without much sign of amusement. "At any rate, I hope to have the tablet texts soon. And then I'll get all the material together for you, Dr. Athor."

"Good," Athor said. "We'll need everything we can get. This is going to be the job of our lives." He glanced once more at each of the others in turn. "One important thing to remember, though: my willingness to engage in an approach to the Apostles does not mean that I intend in any way to provide a blanket of respectability for them. I merely hope to find out what they have that will help us to convince the world of what's about to happen, period. Otherwise I'll do what I can to distance myself from them. I want no mysticism involved here. I don't believe a shred of their mumbo-jumbo—I simply want to know how they've arrived at their conclusions of catastrophe. And I want the rest of you to be similarly on your guard in any dealings with them. Understood?"

"This is all like a dream," Beenay said softly.

"A very bad one," said Athor. "Every atom in my soul cries out that this isn't happening, that it's utter fantasy, that the world will keep right on going past next Theptar nineteenth without any harm coming to it. Unfortunately, the figures tell the story." He looked out the window. Onos now was gone from the sky, and Dovim was only a dot against the horizon. Twilight had descended, and the only real illumination that was visible was the ghostly, uncomforting light of Patru and Trey. "There's no longer any way for us to doubt it. Darkness will come. Perhaps the Stars, whatever they may be, really will shine forth. Fires will blaze. The end of the world as we know it is at hand. The end of the world!"

TWO

NIGHTFALL

[18]

"You'd better be careful," Beenay said. He was beginning to feel tense. Evening was coming on—the evening of the eclipse, so long awaited by him with fear and trembling. "Athor's furious with you, Theremon. I can't believe you came here now. You know you're not supposed to be anywhere on the premises. Especially not *this* evening, of all times to show up. You ought to be able to understand that, when you consider the sort of things you've been writing about him lately—"

The journalist chuckled. "I told you. I can calm him down."

"Don't be too sure of that, Theremon. You basically called him a superannuated crackbrain in your column, remember? The old man's calm and steely most of the time, but when he's pushed too far he's got an amazing temper."

Theremon said, with a shrug, "Look, Beenay, before I was a big-shot columnist I was a kid reporter who specialized in doing all sorts of impossible interviews, and I mean *impossible*. I'd come home every evening with bruises, black eyes, sometimes a broken bone or two, but I always got my story. You develop a certain degree of confidence in yourself after you've spent a few years routinely driving people out of their minds for the sake of getting a story. I'll be able to take care of Athor."

"Driving people out of their minds?" Beenay said. He glanced meaningfully toward the calendar-plate high in the wall of the corridor. In gleaming green letters it announced the date: 19 THEPTAR. The day of days, the one that had been blazing in everyone's mind, here at the Observatory, month after month. The last day of sanity that many, perhaps most, of the people of Kalgash would ever know. "Not the best choice of words this evening, wouldn't you say?"

Theremon smiled. "Maybe you're right. We'll see." He

pointed toward the closed door of Athor's office. "Who's in there right now?"

"Athor, of course. And Thilanda—she's one of the astronomers. Davnit, Simbron, Hikkinan, all Observatory staffers. That's about it."

"What about Siferra? She said she'd be here."

"Well, she isn't, not yet."

A look of surprise appeared on Theremon's face. "Really? When I asked her the other day if she would opt for the Sanctuary she practically laughed in my face. She was dead set on watching the eclipse from here. I can't believe she's changed her mind. That woman isn't afraid of anything, Beenay. Well, maybe she's tidying up a few last-minute things over at her office."

"Very likely."

"And our chubby friend Sheerin? He's not here either?"

"No, not Sheerin. He's in the Sanctuary."

"Not the bravest of men, is he, our Sheerin?"

"At least he's got the good sense to admit it. Raissta's at the Sanctuary too, and Athor's wife Nyilda, and just about everybody else I know, except us few Observatory people. If you were smart you'd be there yourself, Theremon. When the Darkness gets here this evening you'll wish that you were."

"The Apostle Folimun 66 said more or less the same thing to me over a year ago, only it was his Sanctuary he was inviting me into, not yours. But I'm fully prepared to face the worst terrors the gods can throw at me, my friend. There's a story to cover this evening, and I won't be able to cover it if I'm holed up in some snug little underground hideout, will I?"

"There won't be any newspaper tomorrow for you to write that story for, Theremon."

"You think so?" Theremon caught Beenay by the arm and drew close to him, almost nose to nose. In a low, intense tone he said, "Tell me this, Beenay. Just between friends. Do you actually and truly think that any such incredible thing as Nightfall is going to happen this evening?"

"Yes. I do."

"Gods! Are you serious, man?"

"As serious as I've ever been in my life, Theremon."

"I can't believe it. You seem so steady, Beenay. So solid, so

responsible. And yet you've taken a bunch of admittedly specu-
lative astronomical calculations, and some bits of charcoal dug
up in a desert thousands of miles from here, and some wild
frothings out of the mouths of a crew of wild-eyed cultists, and
rolled them up together into the craziest damned mess of apocalyptic nonsense I ever—"

"It isn't crazy," Beenay insisted quietly. "It isn't nonsense."

"So the world is really coming to an end this evening."

"The world *we* know and love, yes."

Theremon released his grip on Beenay's arm and threw his
hands up in exasperation. "Gods! Even you! By Darkness,
Beenay, I've been trying for better than a year to put some
faith in all this stuff, and I can't, I absolutely can't. No matter
what you say, or Athor, or Siferra, or Folimun 66, or Mondior,
or—"

"Just wait," Beenay said. "Only another few hours."

"You really are sincere!" Theremon said wonderingly. "By
all the gods, you're as big a crackpot as Mondior himself. Bah!
That's what I say, Beenay. *Bah!* —Take me in to see Athor, will
you?"

"I warn you, he doesn't want to see you."

"You said that already. Take me in there anyway."

[19]

Theremon had never really expected to find himself taking a
stance hostile to the Observatory scientists. Things had simply
worked out that way, very gradually, in the months leading up
to the nineteenth of Theptar.

It was basically a matter of journalistic integrity, he told
himself. Beenay was his longtime friend, yes; Dr. Athor was
unquestionably a great astronomer, Sheerin was genial and
straightforward and likable; and Siferra was—well, an attractive and interesting woman and an important archaeologist. He
had no desire at all to position himself as an enemy of such
people.

But he had to write what he believed. And what he believed,
to the depths of his soul, was that the Observatory group was

every bit as loopy as the Apostles of Flame, and just as dangerous to the stability of society.

There was no way he could make himself take what they said
seriously. The more time he spent around the Observatory, the
nuttier it all seemed to him.

An invisible and apparently undetectable planet soaring
through the sky on an orbit that brought it close to Kalgash
every few decades? A combination of solar positions that would
leave only Dovim overhead when the invisible planet arrived
this time? Dovim's light thereby blotted out, throwing the
world into Darkness? And everyone going insane as a result?
No, no, he couldn't buy it.

To Theremon, all of it seemed just as wild as the stuff the
Apostles of Flame had been peddling for so many years. The
only extra thing that the Apostles threw in was the mysterious
advent of the phenomenon known as Stars. Even the Observatory people had the good grace to admit that they couldn't
imagine what Stars were. Some other sort of invisible heavenly
bodies, apparently, which suddenly came into view when the
Year of Godliness ended and the wrath of the gods descended
on Kalgash—so the Apostles indicated.

"It can't be," Beenay had told him, one evening at the Six
Suns Club. It was still six months before the date of the eclipse.
"The eclipse and the Darkness, yes. The Stars, no. There's
nothing in the universe except our world and the six suns and
some insignificant asteroids—and Kalgash Two. If there are
Stars also, why can't we measure their presence? Why can't we
detect them by orbital perturbations, the way we've detected
Kalgash Two? No, Theremon, if there are Stars out there, then
something's got to be wrong with the Theory of Universal
Gravitation. And we know the theory's all right."

"We *know* the theory's all right," that was what Beenay had
said. But wasn't that just like Folimun saying, "We know that
the Book of Revelations is a book of truth"?

In the beginning, when Beenay and Sheerin first told him of
their emerging awareness that there was going to be a devastating period of Darkness upon all the world, Theremon, half
skeptical and half awed and impressed by their apocalyptic vi-
sions, had indeed done his best to be helpful. "Athor wants to
meet with Folimun," Beenay said. "He's trying to find out if

the Apostles have any sort of ancient astronomical records that might confirm what we've found. Can you do anything to arrange it?"

"A funny notion," Theremon said. "The irascible old man of science asking to see the spokesman of the forces of anti-science, of non-science. But I'll see what I can do."

That meeting had turned out to be surprisingly easy to arrange. Theremon had been intending to interview Folimun again anyway. The sharp-faced Apostle granted Theremon an audience for the following day.

"Athor?" Folimun said, when the newspaperman had passed Beenay's message along. "Why would he want to see *me?*"

"Perhaps he's planning to become an Apostle," Theremon suggested playfully.

Folimun laughed. "Not very likely. From what I know of him, he'd sooner paint himself purple and go for a stroll in the nude down Saro Boulevard."

"Well, maybe he's undergone a conversion," said Theremon. Cautiously he added, after a tantalizing pause, "I know for a fact that he and his staff have turned up some data that might just tend to support your belief that Darkness is going to sweep over the world on the nineteenth of Theptar next."

Folimun allowed himself the smallest sort of carefully controlled display of interest, an almost imperceptible raising of one eyebrow. "How fascinating, if it's true," he said calmly.

"You'll have to see him yourself to find that out."

"I may just do that," the Apostle said.

And indeed he did. Exactly what the nature of the meeting between Folimun and Athor was, Theremon never succeeded in finding out, despite all his best efforts. Athor and Folimun were the only ones present, and neither of them said a thing to anyone else about it afterward, so far as Theremon could discover. Beenay, Theremon's chief link to the Observatory, was able to offer only vague guesses.

"It had something to do with the ancient astronomical records that the Chief believes are in the Apostles' possession, that's all I can tell you," Beenay reported. "Athor suspects that they've been handing things down over the centuries, maybe even since before the last eclipse. Some of the passages in the

Book of Revelations are in an old forgotten language, you know."

"Old forgotten gibberish, you mean. Nobody's ever been able to make any sense out of that stuff."

"Well, I certainly can't," said Beenay. "But it's the opinion of some quite respectable philologists that those passages may be actual prehistoric texts. What if the Apostles actually have a way of deciphering that language? But they keep it to themselves, thus concealing whatever astronomical data may be recorded in the Book of Revelations. That may be the key Athor's after."

Theremon was astonished. "You mean to say that the preeminent astronomer of our time, perhaps of all time, feels the need to consult a pack of hysterical cultists on a scientific issue?"

With a shrug, Beenay said, "All I know is that Athor doesn't like the Apostles and their teachings any more than you do, but he thought there was something important to gain by meeting with your friend Folimun."

"No friend of mine! He's strictly a professional acquaintance."

Beenay said, "Well, whatever you want to call—"

Theremon cut him off. Real wrath was rising in him now, a little to his own surprise. "And it's not going to sit very well with me, let me tell you, if it turns out that you people and the Apostles have cut some sort of deal. So far as I'm concerned, the Apostles represent Darkness itself—the blackest, most hateful sort of reactionary ideas. Give them their way and they'll have us all living medieval lives of fasting and chastity and flagellation again. It's bad enough we have psychotics like them spewing forth demented delirious prophecies to disturb the tranquillity of everyday life, but if a man of Athor's prestige is going to dignify those ludicrous creeps by incorporating some of their babble into his own findings, I'm going to be very, very suspicious, my friend, of anything at all that emanates from your Observatory from this point onward."

Dismay was evident on Beenay's face.

"If you only knew, Theremon, how scornfully Athor speaks of the Apostles, how little regard he has for anything they've ever advocated—"

"Then why is he deigning to speak with them?"

"You've talked with Folimun yourself!"

"That's different. Like it or not, Folimun's helping to make news these days. It's my job to find out what's going on in his mind."

"Well," Beenay said hotly, "maybe Athor takes the same view."

That was the point where they had let the discussion drop. It was beginning to change from a discussion into a quarrel, and neither one of them wanted that. Since Beenay really had no idea what kind of understanding, if any, Athor and Folimun might have worked out with each other, Theremon saw there wasn't much sense in belaboring him about it.

But, Theremon realized afterward, that conversation with Beenay was exactly when his attitude toward Beenay and Sheerin and the rest of the Observatory people had begun to shift—when he had started to move from sympathetic and curious onlooker to jeering, scornful critic. Even though he himself had been instrumental in bringing it about, the meeting between the Observatory director and the Apostle now seemed to Theremon to be a sellout of the most disastrous kind, a naive capitulation on Athor's part to the forces of reaction and blind ignorance.

Although he had never really been able to make himself believe the theories of the scientists—despite all the so-called "evidence" they had allowed him to inspect—Theremon had taken a generally neutral position in his column when the first news stories about the impending eclipse began to appear in the *Chronicle.*

"A startling announcement," he had called it, "and very frightening—if true. As Athor 77 quite rightly says, any prolonged period of sudden worldwide Darkness would be a calamity such as the world has never known. But from the other side of the world comes a dissenting view this morning. 'With all due respect to the great Athor 77,' declares Heranian 1104, Astronomer Royal of the Imperial Observatory of Kanipilitiniuk, 'there is still no firm evidence that the so-called Kalgash Two satellite exists at all, let alone that it is capable of causing such an eclipse as the Saro group predicts. We must bear in mind that suns—even a small sun such as Dovim—are immensely larger than any wandering space satellite could possi-

135

bly be, and it strikes us as highly unlikely that such a satellite would be able to enter precisely the position in the heavens necessary to intercept all solar illumination that might reach the surface of our world—' "

But then came Mondior 71's speech of Umilithar thirteenth, in which the High Apostle proudly declared that the world's greatest man of science had given his support to the word of the Book of Revelations. "The voice of science is now one with the voice of heaven," Mondior cried. "I urge you now: put no further hope in miracles and dreams. What must come must come. Nothing can save the world from the wrath of the gods, nothing except a willingness to abandon sin, to give up evil, to devote oneself to the path of virtue and righteousness."

Mondior's booming pronouncement had pushed Theremon out of his neutrality. In loyalty to Beenay's friendship he had allowed himself to take the eclipse hypothesis more or less seriously, for a while. But now he began to see it as pure silly-season stuff—a bunch of earnest, self-deluding scientists, swept away by their own enthusiasm for a lot of circumstantial evidence and reasoning from mere coincidence, willing to kid themselves into a belief in the century's most nonsensical bit of insanity.

The next day Theremon's column asked, "Are you wondering how the Apostles of Flame ever managed to gain Athor 77 as a convert? Of all people, the grand old man of astronomy seems about the least likely to line up in support of those robed and hooded purveyors of claptrap and abracadabra. Did some silver-tongued Apostle charm the great scientist out of his wits? Or is it simply the case, as we've heard whispered behind the ivy-covered walls of Saro University, that the mandatory faculty retirement age has been pegged a few years too high?"

And that was only the beginning.

Theremon saw what role he had to play now. If people started taking this eclipse thing seriously, there would be mental breakdowns on all sides, even without the coming of general Darkness to start the trouble off.

Let everyone actually begin believing that doom would arrive on the evening of Theptar nineteenth, and there would be panic in the streets long before that, universal hysteria, a collapse of law and order, a prolonged period of general instability and troublesome apprehension—followed by the gods only knew what sort of emotional upheavals when the dreaded day came and went harmlessly. It would have to be his task to deflate the fear of Nightfall, of Darkness, of Doomsday, by poking it with the sharp spear of laughter.

So when Mondior thundered ferociously that the vengeance of the gods was on the way, Theremon 762 replied with light-hearted sketches of what the world would be like if the Apostles succeeded in "reforming" society as they wanted to—people going to the beach bundled up in ankle-length swimsuits, long sessions of prayer between each bit of action at sports events, all the great books and classic plays and shows rewritten to eliminate the slightest hint of impiety.

And when Athor and his group released diagrams showing the movements of the unseen and apparently unseeable Kalgash Two across the sky on its shadowy rendezvous with the pallid red light of Dovim, Theremon made amiable remarks about dragons, invisible giants, and other mythological monsters cavorting through the heavens.

When Mondior waved the scientific authority of Athor 77 around as an argument demonstrating secular support of the Apostles' teachings, Theremon responded by asking how seriously anyone could take Athor 77's scientific authority, now that he was obviously just as deranged as Mondior himself.

When Athor called for a crash program to store food supplies, scientific and technical information, and everything else that would be needed by mankind after the general insanity broke loose, Theremon suggested that in some quarters the general insanity had *already* broken loose, and provided his own list of essential items to put away in your basement ("can openers, thumbtacks, copies of the multiplication table, playing cards. . . . Don't forget to write your name on a tag and tie it around your right wrist, in case you don't remember it after the Darkness comes. . . . Put a tag on your left wrist that says, *To find out your name, see tag on other wrist.* . . .")

By the time Theremon had finished working the story over, it was hard for his readers to decide which group was more absurd—the ripsnorting doomsayers of the Apostles of Flame, or the pathetic, gullible skywatchers of the Saro University Observatory. But one thing was certain: thanks to Theremon,

137

hardly any member of the general public believed that anything out of the ordinary was going to take place on the evening of Theptar nineteenth.

[20]

Athor thrust out a belligerent lower lip and glared in rage at the man from the *Chronicle.* He was able to restrain himself only by a supreme effort.

"You here? Despite everything I said? Of all the audacity!"

Theremon's hand was outstretched in greeting as though he really had expected Athor to accept it. But after a moment he lowered it, and stood regarding the Observatory director with astonishing insouciance.

In a voice trembling with barely controlled emotion Athor said, "You display an infernal gall, sir, in coming here this evening. It astounds me that you'd dare to show your face among us."

From a corner of the room, Beenay, running the tip of his tongue nervously across his lips, interposed nervously, "Now, sir, after all—"

"Did you invite him to be here? When you knew I had expressly forbidden—"

"Sir, I—"

"It was Dr. Siferra," Theremon said. "She urged me very vigorously to come. I'm here at her invitation."

"Siferra? Siferra? I doubt that very much. She told me only a few weeks ago that she thinks you're an irresponsible fool. She spoke of you in the harshest possible manner." Athor looked around. "Where is she, by the way? She was supposed to be here, wasn't she?" No answer came. Turning to Beenay, Athor said, "You're the one who brought this newspaperman in, Beenay. I'm utterly amazed that you'd do such a thing. This isn't the moment for insubordination. The Observatory is closed to journalists this evening. And it's been closed to this particular journalist for a long time now. Show him out at once."

138

"Director Athor," Theremon said, "if you'll only let me explain what my reason for—"

"I don't believe, young man, that anything you could say now would do much to outweigh your insufferable daily columns of these last two months. You have led a vast newspaper campaign against the efforts of my colleagues and myself to organize the world against the menace that is about to overwhelm us. You have done your best with your highly personal attacks to make the staff of this Observatory objects of ridicule."

He lifted the copy of the Saro City *Chronicle* on the table and shook it at Theremon furiously. "Even a person of your well-known impudence should have hesitated before coming to me with a request that he be allowed to cover today's events for this paper. Of all newsmen—*you!*"

Athor dashed the newspaper to the floor, strode to the window, and clasped his arms behind his back.

"You are to leave immediately," he snapped over his shoulder. "Beenay, get him out of here."

Athor's head was throbbing. It was important, he knew, to get his anger under control. He could not afford to allow anything to distract him from the vast and cataclysmic event that was about to occur.

Moodily he stared out at the Saro City skyline and forced himself back toward calmness, as much calmness as he was likely to be able to attain this evening.

Onos was beginning now to sink toward the horizon. In a little while it would fade and vanish into the distant mists. Athor watched it as it descended.

He knew he would never see it again as a sane man.

The cold white gleam of Sitha also was visible, low in the sky, far across the city at the other end of the horizon. Sitha's twin, Tano, was nowhere to be seen—already set, gliding now through the skies of the opposite hemisphere, which soon would be enjoying the extraordinary phenomenon of a five-sun day—and Sitha itself was also swiftly vanishing from view. In another moment it too would disappear.

Behind him he heard Beenay and Theremon whispering.

"Is that man still here?" Athor asked ominously.

Beenay said, "Sir, I think you ought to listen to what he has to tell you."

"You do? You think I ought to listen to him?" Athor whirled, his eyes gleaming fiercely. "Oh, no, Beenay. No, he'll be the one to listen to me!" He beckoned peremptorily to the newspaperman, who had made no motion at all to leave. "Come here, young man! I'll give you your story."

Theremon walked slowly toward him.

Athor gestured outward. "Sitha is about to set—no, it already has. Onos will be gone also, in another moment or two. Of all the six suns, only Dovim will be left in the sky. Do you see it?"

The question was scarcely necessary to ask. The red dwarf sun looked even smaller than usual this evening, smaller than it had appeared in decades. But it was almost at zenith, and its ruddy light streamed down awesomely, flooding the landscape with an extraordinary blood-red illumination as the brilliant rays of setting Onos died.

Athor's upturned face flushed redly in the Dovim-light. "In just under four hours," he said, "civilization, as we have known it, will come to an end. It will do so because, as you see, Dovim will be the only sun in the sky." He narrowed his eyes, stared toward the horizon. The last yellow blink of Onos now was gone. "There. Dovim is alone! We have four hours, now, until the finish of everything. Print that! But there'll be no one to read it."

"But if it turns out that four hours pass—and another four— and nothing happens?" asked Theremon softly.

"Don't let that worry you. Plenty will happen, I assure you."

"Perhaps. But if it doesn't?"

Athor fought against his rising rage. "If you don't leave, sir, and Beenay refuses to conduct you out, then I'll call the university guards, and— No. On civilization's last evening, I'll allow no discourtesies here. You have five minutes, young man, to say what you have come here to say. At the end of that time, I will either agree to allow you to stay to view the eclipse, or you will leave of your own accord. Is that understood?"

Theremon hesitated only a moment. "Fair enough."

Athor took out his pocket watch. "Five minutes, then."

"Good! All right, first thing: what difference would it make

140

if you allowed me to take down an eyewitness account of what's to come? If your prediction comes true, my presence won't matter at all—the world will end, there'll be no newspaper tomorrow, I won't be able to hurt you in any way. On the other hand, what if there *isn't* any eclipse? You people will be the subject of such ridicule as the world has never known. Don't you think it would be wise to leave that ridicule to friendly hands?"

Athor snorted. "Do you mean *your* hands?"

"Certainly!" Theremon flung himself down casually in the most comfortable chair in the room and crossed his legs. "My columns may have been a little rough at times, agreed, but I let you people have the benefit of the doubt whenever possible. Beenay's a friend of mine, after all. He's the one who first gave me an inkling of what was going on here, and you may recall that at the beginning I was quite sympathetic to your research. But—I ask you, Dr. Athor—how can you, one of the greatest of all scientists in all of history, turn your back on the awareness that the present century is a time of the triumph of reason over superstition, of fact over fantasy, of knowledge over blind fear? The Apostles of Flame are an absurd anachronism. The Book of Revelations is a muddled mass of foolishness. Everyone intelligent, everyone *modern*, knows that. And so people are annoyed, even angered, to have scientists turn about face and tell us that these cultists are preaching the truth. They—"

"No such thing, young man," interrupted Athor. "While some of our data has been supplied us by the Apostles, our results contain none of the Apostles' mysticism. Facts are facts, and there's no denying that the Apostles' so-called 'foolishness' does have certain facts behind it. We discovered that to our own chagrin, let me assure you. But we've scorned their mythologizing and done whatever we could to separate their quite genuine warnings of impending disaster from their quite preposterous and untenable program for transforming and 'reforming' society. I assure you that the Apostles hate us now even more than you do."

"I don't hate you. I'm just trying to tell you that the public is in an ugly humor. They're angry."

Athor twisted his mouth in derision. "Let them be angry!"

"Yes, but what about tomorrow?"

141

"There'll be no tomorrow!"

"But if there is. Say that there is—just for the sake of argument. That anger might take shape as something serious. After all, you know, the whole financial world's been in a nose-dive the last few months. The stock market has crashed three separate times, or haven't you noticed? Sensible investors don't really believe the world is coming to an end, but they think *other* investors might start to think so, and so the smart ones sell out before the panic begins—thus touching off the panic themselves. And then they buy back afterward, and sell again as soon as the market rallies, and begin the whole downward cycle all over again. And what do you think has happened to business? Johnny Public doesn't believe you either, but there's no sense buying new porch furniture just now, is there? Better to hang on to your money, just in case, or put it into canned goods and ammunition, and let the furniture wait.

"You see the point, Dr. Athor. Just as soon as this is all over, the business interests will be after your hide. They'll say that if crackpots—begging your pardon—crackpots in the guise of serious scientists can upset the world's entire economy any time they want simply by making some cockeyed prediction, then it's up to the world to keep such things from happening. The sparks will fly, Doctor."

Athor regarded the columnist indifferently. The five minutes were almost up.

"And just what were you proposing to do to help the situation?"

"Well," Theremon said, grinning, "what I have in mind is this: starting tomorrow, I'll serve as your unofficial public-relations representative. By which I mean that I can try to quell the anger you're going to face, the same way that I've been trying to ease the tension the nation has been feeling—through humor, through ridicule, if necessary. I know—I know—it would be hard to stand, I admit, because I'd have to make you all out to be a bunch of gibbering idiots. But if I can get people laughing at you, they might just forget to be angry. In return for that, all I ask is the exclusive right to cover the scene at the Observatory this evening."

Athor was silent. Beenay burst out, "Sir, it's worth considering. I know that we've examined every possibility, but there's always a million-to-one chance, a *billion*-to-one chance, that there's an error somewhere in our theory or in our calculations. And if there is—"

The others in the room were murmuring now, and it sounded to Athor like murmurs of agreement. By the gods, was the whole department turning against him? Athor's expression became that of one who found his mouth full of something bitter and couldn't get rid of it.

"Let you remain with us so that you'll be better able to ridicule us tomorrow? You must think I'm far gone in senility, young man!"

Theremon said, "But I've explained that my being here won't make any difference. If there *is* an eclipse, if Darkness does come, you can expect nothing but the most reverent treatment from me, and all the help I can give in any crisis that might follow. And if nothing unusual happens after all, I'm willing to offer my services in the hope of protecting you, Dr. Athor, against the wrath of the angry citizens who—"

"Please," a new voice said. "Let him stay, Dr. Athor."

Athor looked around. Siferra had come in, unnoticed by him.

"I'm sorry I'm late. We had a little last-minute problem at the Archaeology office that upset things a little, and—" She and Theremon exchanged glances. To Athor she said, "Please don't be offended. I know how cruelly he's mocked us. But I asked him to come here this evening, so that he could find out at first hand that we really were right. He's—my guest, Doctor."

Athor closed his eyes a moment. Siferra's guest! It was too much. Why not invite Folimun too? Why not invite Mondior!

But he had lost his appetite for further dispute. Time was running short. And obviously none of the others minded having Theremon here during the eclipse.

What did it matter?

What did anything matter now?

Resignedly Athor said, "All right. Stay, if that's what you want. But you will kindly refrain from hampering us in our duties in any fashion. Understood? You'll keep out of the way as much as possible. You will also remember that I am in charge of all activities here, and in spite of your opinions as expressed in your columns, I will expect full cooperation and full respect—"

[21]

Siferra crossed the room to Theremon's side and said quietly, "I didn't seriously expect you to come here this evening."

"Why not? The invitation was serious, wasn't it?"

"Of course. But you were so savage in your mockery, in all those columns you wrote about us—so cruel—"

" 'Irresponsible' is the word you used," Theremon said.

She reddened. "That too. I didn't imagine you'd be able to look Athor in the eye after all those horrid things you said about him."

"I'll do more than look him in the eye, if it turns out that his dire predictions were on the mark. I'll go down on both knees before him and humbly beg his pardon."

"And if his predictions turn out not to have been on the mark?"

"Then he'll need me," Theremon said. "You all will. This is the right place for me to be, this evening."

Siferra gave the newspaperman a startled glance. He was always saying the unexpected thing. She hadn't managed to figure him out yet. She disliked him, of course—that went without saying. Everything about him—his profession, his manner of speaking, the flashy clothes he usually wore—struck her as tawdry and commonplace. His entire persona was a symbol, to her, of the crude, crass, dreary, ordinary, repellent world beyond the university walls that she had always detested.

And yet, and yet, and yet—

There were aspects of this Theremon that had managed to win her grudging admiration, despite everything. He was tough, for one thing, absolutely unswervable in his pursuit of whatever he might be after. She could appreciate that. He was straightforward, even blunt: quite a contrast to the slippery, manipulative, power-chasing academic types who swarmed all around her on the campus. He was intelligent, too, no question about that, even though he had chosen to devote his particular brand of sinewy, probing intelligence to a trivial, meaningless field like newspaper journalism. And she respected his robust physical vigor: he was tall and sturdy-looking and in obvious good health. Siferra had never had much esteem for weaklings. She had taken good care not to be one herself.

In truth she realized—improbable as it was, uncomfortable as it made her feel—that in some way she was attracted to him. An attraction of opposites? she thought. Yes, yes, that was an accurate way of putting it. But not entirely. Beneath the surface dissimilarities, Siferra knew, she had more in common with Theremon than she was willing to admit.

She looked uneasily toward the window. "Getting dark out there," she said. "Darker than I've ever seen it before."

"Frightened?" Theremon asked.

"Of the Darkness? No, not really. But I'm frightened of what's going to come after it. You should be too."

"What's going to come after it," he said, "is Onos-rise, and I suppose some of the other suns will be shining too, and everything's going to be as it was before."

"You sound very confident of that."

Theremon laughed. "Onos has risen every morning of my life. Why shouldn't I be confident it'll rise tomorrow?"

Siferra shook her head. He was beginning to annoy her again with his pigheadedness. Hard to believe that she had been telling herself only moments before that she found him attractive.

She said coolly, "Onos *will* rise tomorrow. And will look down on such a scene of devastation as a person of your limited imagination is evidently incapable of anticipating."

"Everything on fire, you mean? And everyone walking around drooling and gibbering while the city burns?"

"The archaeological evidence indicates—"

"Fires, yes. Repeated holocausts. But only in one small site, thousands of miles from here and thousands of years ago." Theremon's eyes flashed with sudden vitality. "And where's your archaeological evidence for outbreaks of mass insanity? Are you extrapolating from all those fires? How can you be sure that those weren't purely ritual fires, lit by perfectly sane men and women in the hope that they would bring back the suns and banish the Darkness? Fire which got out of hand each time and caused widespread damage, sure, but which were in

145

no way related to any mental impairment on the part of the population?"

She gazed at him levelly. "There's archaeological evidence of that too. The widespread mental impairment, I mean."

"There is?"

"The tablet texts. Which only this morning we just finished keying in against the philological data provided by the Apostles of Flame—"

Theremon guffawed. "The Apostles of Flame! Wonderful! So you're an Apostle too! What a shame, Siferra. A woman with a figure like yours, and from now on you'll have to muffle yourself up in one of those terrible shapeless bulky robes of theirs—"

"Oh!" she cried, stifling a red burst of anger and loathing. "You don't know how to do anything but mock, do you? You're so convinced of your own righteousness that even when you're staring right at the truth all you can do is make some pitiful joke! Oh—you—you impossible man—"

She swung around and headed swiftly across the room.

"Siferra—Siferra, wait—"

She ignored him. Her heart was pounding in rage. She saw now that it had been a terrible mistake to invite someone like Theremon to be here on the evening of the eclipse. A mistake, in fact, ever to have had anything to do with him.

It was Beenay's fault, she thought. *Everything* was Beenay's fault.

It was Beenay, after all, who had introduced her to Theremon, one day at the Faculty Club many months before. Apparently the newspaperman and the young astronomer had known each other a long time and Theremon regularly consulted Beenay on scientific matters that were making news.

What was making news just then was the prediction of Mondior 71 that the world would end on Theptar nineteenth— which at that time was something close to a year in the future. Of course nobody at the university held Mondior and his Apostles in any sort of regard, but it was just about at the same moment that Beenay had come up with his observations of the apparent irregularities in Kalgash's orbit, and Siferra had reported her findings of fires at two-thousand-year intervals at the Hill of Thombo. Both of which discoveries, of course, had

146

the dismaying quality of reinforcing the plausibility of the Apostles' beliefs.

Theremon had seemed to know all about Siferra's work at Thombo. When the newspaperman entered the Faculty Club—Siferra and Beenay were already there, though not by any pre-arranged appointment—Beenay merely had to say, "Theremon, this is my friend Dr. Siferra of the Archaeology Department." And Theremon replied instantly, "Oh, yes. The burned villages piled up on that ancient hill."

Siferra smiled coolly. "You've heard of that, have you?"

Beenay said quickly, "I told him. I know I promised not to say a word about it to him, but after you revealed everything to Athor and Sheerin and the rest, I figured that it wouldn't matter any more if I let him know—so long as I swore him to secrecy—I mean, Siferra, I *trust* this man, I really do, and I was absolutely confident that—"

"It's all right, Beenay," Siferra said, making an effort not to seem as annoyed as in fact she was. "You really shouldn't have said anything. But I forgive you."

Theremon said, "No harm's been done. Beenay swore me to a terrible oath that I wouldn't print anything about it. But it's fascinating. Absolutely fascinating! How old is the one at the bottom, would you say? Fifty thousand years, is it?"

"More like fourteen or sixteen," Siferra said. "Which is quite immensely old enough, when you consider that Beklimot—you know of Beklimot, don't you?—is only about twenty centuries old, and we used to think that was the earliest settlement on Kalgash. —You aren't planning to write a story about my discoveries, are you?"

"I wasn't, actually. I told you, I gave Beenay my word. Besides, it seemed a little abstract for the *Chronicle*'s readers, a little remote from their daily concerns. But I think now there's a real story there. If you'd be willing to meet with me and give me the details—"

"I'd rather not," Siferra said quickly.

"Which? Meet with me? Or give me the details?"

His quick flip reply suddenly cast the entire conversation in a new light for her. She saw, to her mild annoyance and slight surprise, that the newspaperman was in fact attracted to her. She realized now, thinking back over the past few minutes, that

Theremon must have been wondering, all the while, whether there might be something romantic going on between her and Beenay, since he had found them sitting here in the club together. And had decided at last that there wasn't, and so had chosen to offer that first lightly flirtatious line.

Well, that was his problem, Siferra thought.

She said in a deliberately neutral way, "I haven't published my Thombo work in the scientific journals yet. It would be best if nothing about it gets into the public press until I have."

"I quite understand that. But if I promise that I'll abide by your release date, would you be willing to go over your material with me ahead of time?"

"Well—"

She looked at Beenay. What was a newspaperman's promise worth, anyway?

Beenay said, "You can trust Theremon. I've told you already: he's as honorable as they get, in his line of work."

"Which isn't saying much," Theremon put in, laughing. "But I know better than to break my word on an issue of scientific publication priority. If I jumped the gun on your story, Beenay here would see that my name was mud all over the university. And I depend on my university contacts for some of my most interesting stories. —So can I count on an interview with you? Say, the day after next?"

And that was how it began.

Theremon was very persuasive. She agreed finally to have lunch with him, and slowly, cunningly, he pried the details of the Thombo dig out of her. Afterward she regretted it—she expected to see a stupid, sensational piece in the *Chronicle* the very next day—but Theremon kept his word and published nothing about her. He did ask to see her laboratory, though. Again she yielded, and he inspected the charts, the photographs, the ash samples. He asked some intelligent questions.

"You aren't going to write me up, are you?" she asked nervously. "Now that you've seen all this?"

"I promised that I wouldn't. I meant it. Although the moment you tell me that you've arranged to publish your findings in one of the scientific journals, I'll regard myself as free to tell the whole thing. What would you say to dinner at the Six Suns Club tomorrow evening?"

"Well—"

"Or the evening after that?"

Siferra rarely went to places like the Six Suns. She hated to give anyone the false impression that she was interested in getting into social entanglements.

But Theremon wasn't easy to turn down. Gently, cheerfully, skillfully, he maneuvered her into a position where she couldn't avoid a date with him—for ten days hence. Well, what of it? she thought. He was personable enough. She could use a change of pace from the steady grind of her work. She met him at the Six Suns, where everyone seemed to know him. They had drinks, dinner, a fine wine from Thamian Province. He moved the conversation this way and that, very adroitly: a little bit about her life, her fascination with archaeology, her excavations at Beklimot. He found out that she'd never been married and had never been interested in marrying. He spoke of the Apostles with her, their wild prophecies, the surprising relationship of her Thombo finds to Mondior's claims. Everything he said was tactful, perceptive, interesting. He was very charming—and also very manipulative, she thought.

At the end of the evening he asked her—gently, cheerfully, skillfully—if he could accompany her home. But she drew the line at that.

He didn't seem troubled. He simply asked her out again.

They had gone out two or three more times altogether after that, over a period of perhaps two months. The format was the same each time: dinner at some elegant place, well-managed conversation, ultimately a delicately constructed invitation for her to spend the sleep-period with him. Siferra deflected him just as delicately each time. It was becoming a pleasant game, this lighthearted pursuit. She wondered how long it would go on. She still had no particular wish to go to bed with him, but the odd thing was that she had no particular wish any longer *not* to go to bed with him, either. It was a long time since she had felt that way about any man.

Then came the first of the series of columns in which he denounced the Observatory theories, questioned Athor's sanity, compared the scientists' prediction of the eclipse to the mad ravings of the Apostles of Flame.

Siferra didn't believe it, at first. Was this some sort of joke?

Beenay's friend—*her* friend now, for that matter—attacking them so viciously?

A couple of months went by. The attacks continued. She didn't hear from Theremon.

Finally she couldn't remain silent any longer.

She called him at the newspaper office.

"Siferra! What a delight! Believe it or not, I was going to call you later this afternoon, to ask if you'd be interested in going to—"

"I wouldn't," she said. "Theremon, what are you *doing?*"

"Doing?"

"These columns about Athor and the Observatory."

There was silence at the other end of the line for a long while.

Then he said, "Ah. You're upset."

"Upset? I'm livid!"

"You think I've been a little too harsh. Look, Siferra, when you write for a large audience of ordinary folks, some of them *very* ordinary, you've got to put things in black and white terms or run the risk of being misunderstood. I can't simply say that I think Athor and Beenay are wrong. I've got to say that they're *nuts.* Do you follow me?"

"Since when do you think they're wrong? Does Beenay know how you feel?"

"Well—"

"You've been covering the story for months. Now you've turned around a hundred eighty degrees. To listen to you, one would think that everyone at the campus is a disciple of Mondior and that we're all out of our minds besides. If you needed to find somebody to be the butt of your jokes, couldn't you have looked somewhere else than the university?"

"These aren't just jokes, Siferra," Theremon said quietly.

"You believe what you're writing?"

"I do. I honestly do. There isn't going to be any cataclysm, that's what I think. And here's Athor pulling on the fire alarm in a crowded theater. By my jokes, my poking a little good-natured fun here and there, I'm trying to tell people that they don't necessarily have to take him seriously—not to panic, not to get into an uproar—"

"What?" she cried. "But there *is* going to be a fire, There-

N I G H T F A L L

mon! And you're playing a dangerous game with everyone's welfare by your mockery. Listen to me: I've seen the ashes of past fires, fires thousands of years old. I know what's going to happen. The Flames will come. I have no doubt about that whatsoever. You've seen the evidence too. And for you to take the position you're taking now is the most destructive imaginable thing you could do, Theremon. It's cruel and foolish and hateful. And utterly irresponsible."

"Siferra—"

"I thought you were an intelligent man. I see now that you're exactly like all the rest of them out there."

"Sifer—"

She broke the contact.

And kept it broken, refusing to return any of his calls, until just a few weeks before the fateful day itself.

Early in the month of Theptar, Theremon called once more, and Siferra found herself on the line with him before she knew who it was.

"Don't hang up," he said quickly. "Just give me a minute."

"I'd rather not."

"Listen, Siferra. You can hate me all you like, but I want you to know this: I'm not cruel and I'm not foolish."

"Whoever said you were?"

"You did, months ago, the last time we spoke. But it isn't so. Everything I've written in my column about the eclipse has been there because I believe it."

"Then you *are* foolish. Or stupid, at any rate. Which may be slightly different, but not any better."

"I've looked at the evidence. I think you people have all been jumping to conclusions."

She said coldly, "Well, we'll all know whether that's so on the nineteenth, won't we?"

"I wish I *could* believe you, because you and Beenay and the rest of you are all such fine people, so obviously dedicated and brilliant and all. But I can't. I'm a skeptic by nature. I have been all my life. I can't accept any kind of dogma that other people want to sell me. It's a serious flaw in my character, I suppose—it makes me seem frivolous. Maybe I *am* frivolous. But at least I'm honest. I simply don't think there'll be an eclipse, or madness, or fires."

"It's no dogma, Theremon. It's a hypothesis."

"That's playing with words. I'm sorry if what I've written has offended you, but I can't help it, Siferra."

She was quiet a moment. Something in his voice had oddly moved her. She said at last, "Dogma, hypothesis, whatever it is, it's going to be tested in a few weeks. I'll be at the Observatory on the evening of the nineteenth. You come there too, and we'll see which one of us is right."

"But hasn't Beenay told you? Athor's declared me persona non grata at the Observatory!"

"Has that ever stopped you?"

"He refuses even to talk to me. You know, I have a proposal for him, something that could be of great help to him after the nineteenth when all this tremendous buildup misfires into whopping anticlimax and the world comes yelling for his skin, but Beenay says there's no chance he'll talk to me at all, let alone allow me to come in that evening."

"Come as my guest. My *date*," she said acidly. "Athor'll be too busy to care. I want you to be in the room when the sky turns black and the fires start. I want to see the look on your face. I want to see if you're as experienced at apologizing as you are at seduction, Theremon."

[22]

That had been three weeks ago. Fleeing angrily from Theremon now, Siferra rushed to the far side of the room and caught sight of Athor, standing by himself, looking through a set of computer printouts. He was sadly turning the pages over and over and over as though he hoped to find a reprieve for the world buried somewhere in the dense columns. Then he looked up and saw her.

Color came to her face.

"Dr. Athor, I feel I ought to ask your pardon for inviting that man to be here this evening, after all he's said about us, about you, about—" She shook her head. "I genuinely thought it would be instructive for him to be among us when—when—

152

Well, I was wrong. He's even more shallow and foolish than I imagined. I should never have told him to come."

Wanly Athor said, "It scarcely is of any importance now, is it? So long as he keeps out of my way, I hardly care whether he's here or not. A few more hours and then nothing will make any difference." He pointed through the window, toward the sky. "So dark! So very dark! And yet not nearly as dark as it will be. —I wonder where Faro and Yimot are. You haven't seen them, have you? No? —When you came in, Dr. Siferra, you said there'd been a last-minute problem at your office. Not a serious one, I hope."

"The Thombo tablets have disappeared," she said.

"*Disappeared?*"

"They were in the artifact safe, of course. Just before I left to come over here, Dr. Mudrin came to see me. He was on his way to the Sanctuary, but he wanted to check one last thing in his translation, one new notion he'd had. So we opened the safe, and—nothing. Gone, all six of them. We have copies, naturally. But still—the originals, the authentic ancient objects—"

"How can this have happened?" Athor asked.

Bitterly Siferra said, "Isn't it obvious? The Apostles have stolen them. Probably to use as some kind of holy talismans, after the—the Darkness has come and done its work."

"Are there any clues?"

"I'm no detective, Dr. Athor. There's no evidence that would mean anything to me. But it had to be the Apostles. They've wanted them ever since they knew I had them. Oh, I wish I'd never said a word to them about them! I wish I'd never mentioned those tablets to anyone!"

Athor took her by the hands. "You mustn't get so upset, my girl."

My girl! She glared at him, astonished. No one had called her that in twenty-five years! But she choked back her anger. He was old, after all. And only trying to be kind.

He said, "Let them have them, Siferra. It makes no difference now. Thanks to that man over there, *nothing* makes any difference, does it?"

She shrugged. "I still hate the thought that some thief in an Apostle's robe was sniffing around in my office—jimmying my safe—taking things that I had uncovered with my own hands.

It's like a violation of my body, almost. Can you understand that, Dr. Athor? To have been robbed of those tablets—it's almost like a rape."

"I know how upset you are," Athor said, in a tone that indicated he didn't really understand at all. "Look—look there. How bright Dovim is this evening! And in just a little while how dark everything will be."

She managed a vague smile and turned away from him.

All about her, people were buzzing to and fro, checking this, discussing that, running to the window, pointing, murmuring. Now and then someone would come rushing in with some new data from the telescope dome. She felt like a complete outsider among these astronomers. And altogether bleak, altogether hopeless. Some of Athor's fatalism must have rubbed off on me, she thought. He seemed so depressed, so lost. It wasn't at all like him to be that way.

She wanted to remind him that it wasn't the world that would end this evening, it was just the present cycle of civilization. They would rebuild. Those who had gone into hiding would come forth and start everything over, as had happened a dozen times before—or twenty, or a hundred—since the beginning of civilization on Kalgash.

But for her to tell Athor that would probably do no more good than for him to have told her not to worry about the loss of the tablets. He had hoped all the world would prepare itself against the catastrophe. And instead only a small fraction had paid any heed to the warning. Just those few who had gone to the university Sanctuary, and whatever other sanctuaries might have been set up elsewhere—

Beenay came over to her. "What's this I hear from Athor? The tablets are gone?"

"Gone, yes. Stolen. I knew I never should have allowed myself to have any sort of contact with the Apostles."

Beenay said, "You think *they* stole them?"

"I'm sure of it," she said bitterly. "They sent word to me, after the existence of the Thombo tablets first became a matter of public knowledge, that they had information that would be of use to me. Didn't I tell you? I guess not. What they wanted was a deal similar to the one Athor worked out with that high priest, or whatever he is: Folimun 66. 'We have maintained a knowledge of the old language,' Folimun said, 'the language spoken in the previous Year of Godliness.' And so they had, apparently—texts of some sort, dictionaries, alphabets of the old script, perhaps a lot more."

"Which Athor was able to obtain from them?"

"Some of it. Enough, at any rate, to determine that the Apostles did have genuine astronomical records of the previous eclipse—enough, Athor said, to prove that the world had been through such a cataclysm at least once before."

Athor, she went on to tell Beenay, had given her copies of the few astronomical text fragments he had received from Folimun, and she had shown them to Mudrin. Who indeed had found them valuable in his own translation of the tablets. But Siferra had balked at sharing her tablets with the Apostles, at least not on their terms. The Apostles claimed to be in possession of a key to the early clay-tablet script, and perhaps they were. Folimun had insisted, though, that she give him the actual tablets to be copied and translated, rather than his giving her the decoding material that he had. He wouldn't settle for copies of the tablet texts. It had to be the original artifacts, or else no deal.

"But you drew the line at that," Beenay said.

"Absolutely. The tablets mustn't leave the university. 'Give us the textual key,' I said to Folimun, 'and we'll provide you with copies of the tablet texts. Then we can each attempt a translation.' "

But Folimun had refused. Copies of the texts were of no use to him, since they could all too easily be dismissed as forgeries. As for giving her his own documents, no, absolutely not. What he had, he said, was sacred material, which could only be made available to Apostles. Give *him* the tablets and he would provide translations of them for her. But no outsider was going to get a look at the texts already in his possession.

"I was actually tempted to join the Apostles for a moment," Siferra said, "just for the sake of getting access to the key."

"You? An Apostle?"

"Only to get their textual material. But the idea repelled me. I turned Folimun down." And Mudrin had had to toil on at his translations without the help of whatever material the Apostles might have. It became apparent that the tablets did indeed seem to talk about some fiery doom that the gods had sent upon the world—but Mudrin's translations were sketchy, hesitant, sparse.

Well, now the Apostles had the tablets anyway, more likely than not. That was hard to take. In the chaos ahead, they'd be waving those tablets around—*her* tablets—as still more evidence of their own wisdom and holiness.

"I'm sorry that your tablets are gone, Siferra," Beenay said. "But maybe there's still a chance the Apostles didn't steal them. That they'll turn up somewhere."

"I'm not counting on that," said Siferra. And she smiled ruefully and turned away to stare at the darkening sky.

The best she could do by way of comfort was take Athor's line: that the world was ending in a little while anyway, and nothing mattered very much. But that was cold comfort indeed. She fought inwardly against any such counsel of despair. The important thing was to keep on thinking of the day after tomorrow—of survival, of rebuilding, of the struggle and its fulfillment. It was no good to fall into despondency like Athor, to accept the downfall of humanity, to shrug and give up all hope.

A high tenor voice cut suddenly across her gloomy meditations.

"Hello, everybody! Hello, hello, hello!"

"Sheerin!" Beenay cried. "What are you doing here?"

The plump cheeks of the newcomer expanded in a pleased smile. "What's this morgue-like atmosphere in here? No one's losing their nerve, I hope."

Athor started in consternation and said peevishly, "Yes, what *are* you doing here, Sheerin? I thought you were going to stay behind in the Sanctuary."

Sheerin laughed and dropped his tubby figure into a chair. "Sanctuary be damned! The place bored me. I wanted to be here, where things are getting hot. Don't you suppose I have my share of curiosity? I rode in the Tunnel of Mystery, after all. I can survive another dose of Darkness. And I want to see these Stars that the Apostles have been spouting about." He rubbed his hands and added in a soberer tone, "It's freezing outside. The wind's enough to hang icicles on your nose.

156

Dovim doesn't seem to give any heat at all, at the distance it is this evening."

The white-haired director ground his teeth in sudden exasperation. "Why do you go out of your way to do a crazy thing like this, Sheerin? What kind of good can you be around here?"

"What kind of good am I around there?" Sheerin spread his palms in comical resignation. "A psychologist isn't worth a damn in the Sanctuary. Not now. Not a thing I could do for them. They're all snug and safe, laced in underground, nothing to worry about."

"And if a mob should break in during the Darkness?"

Sheerin laughed. "I very much doubt that anyone who didn't know where the entrance was would be able to find the Sanctuary in broad daylight, let alone once the suns have gone out. But if they do, well, they'd need men of action to defend them. Me? I'm a hundred pounds too heavy for that. So why should I huddle in down there with them? I'd rather be here."

Siferra felt her own spirits rise as she heard Sheerin's words. She too had chosen to spend the evening of Darkness at the Observatory, rather than in the Sanctuary. Perhaps it was mere wild bravado, perhaps it was idiotic overconfidence, but she was sure that she could last out the hours of the eclipse—and even the coming of the Stars, if there was anything to that part of the myth—and retain her sanity. And so she had decided not to pass up the experience.

Now it appeared that Sheerin, no model of bravery, had taken the same approach. Which might mean that he had decided the impact of Darkness would not be so overwhelming after all, despite the grim predictions he had been making for months. She had heard his tales of the Tunnel of Mystery and the havoc it had wreaked, even on Sheerin himself. Yet here he was. He must have come to believe that people, some at least, would turn out ultimately to be more resilient than he had expected earlier.

Or else he was simply being reckless. Perhaps he preferred to lose his mind in one quick burst this evening, Siferra thought, rather than stay sane and have to cope with the innumerable and perhaps insuperable problems of the hard times ahead—

No. No. She was falling into morbid pessimism again.

She brushed the thought away.

"Sheerin!" It was Theremon, coming across the room to greet the psychologist. "You remember me? Theremon 762?"

"Of course I do, Theremon," Sheerin said. He offered his hand. "Gods, fellow, you've been rough on us lately, haven't you! But bygones may as well be bygones this evening."

"I wish *he* was a bygone," Siferra muttered under her breath. She scowled in distaste and stepped back a few paces.

Theremon shook Sheerin's hand. "What's this Sanctuary you're supposed to have been in? I've heard a little about it here this evening, but I don't have any real idea of what it is."

"Well," said Sheerin, "we have managed to convince a few people, at least, of the validity of our prophecy of—er—doom, to be spectacular about it, and those few have taken proper measures. They consist mainly of the immediate members of the families of the Observatory staff, certain of the faculty of Saro University, and a few outsiders. My companion Liliath 221 is there at this very moment, as a matter of fact, and I suppose I should be too, but for my infernal curiosity. There are about three hundred people all told."

"I see. They're supposed to hide where the Darkness and the —er—Stars can't get at them, and then hold out when the rest of the world goes poof."

"Exactly. The Apostles have some sort of hideout of their own also, you know. We aren't sure how many people are in it —just a few, if we're lucky, but more likely they've got thousands stashed away who will come forth and inherit the world after the Darkness."

"So the university group," Theremon said, "is intended as a counterforce to that?"

Sheerin nodded. "If possible. It won't be easy. With almost all of mankind insane, with the great cities going up in flames, with perhaps a big horde of Apostles imposing their kind of order on what's left of the world—no, it'll be tough for them to survive. But at least they have food, water, shelter, weapons—"

"They've got more," said Athor. "They've got all our records, except for what we will collect today. Those records will mean everything to the next cycle, and *that's* what must survive. The rest can go hang."

Theremon whistled a long, low whistle.

"You people are completely certain, then, that everything you've predicted is going to come about just as you say!"

"What other position could we possibly take?" Siferra asked harshly. "Once we saw that disaster would inevitably come—"

"Yes," the newspaperman said. "You had to make preparations for it. Because you were in possession of the Truth. Just as the Apostles of Flame are in possession of the Truth. I wish I could be half so certain about anything as all you Truth-possessors are about this evening."

She glowered at him. "I wish you could be out there this evening, wandering through the burning streets! But no—no, you'll be safe in here! It's more than you deserve!"

"Easy," Sheerin said. He took Theremon by the arm. Quietly he said, "No sense provoking people now, friend. Let's go somewhere where we won't bother people, and we can talk."

"Good idea," Theremon said.

But he made no motion toward leaving the room. A game of stochastic chess had begun around the table, and Theremon stood watching for a moment or two in obvious incomprehension as moves were made rapidly and in silence. He seemed amazed by the ability of the players to concentrate on a game, when they all must believe that the end of the world was just hours away.

"Come," Sheerin said again.

"Yes. Yes," said Theremon.

He and Sheerin went out into the hall, followed, an instant later, by Beenay.

What an infuriating man, Siferra thought.

She stared at the bright orb of Dovim, burning fiercely in the sky. Had the sky grown even darker in the past few minutes? No, no, she told herself, that was impossible. Dovim was still there. It was just imagination. The sky looked strange, now that Dovim was the only sun aloft. She had never seen it like that before, such a deep purple hue. But it was far from dark out there: somber, yes, but there was light enough, and everything was still easily visible outside despite the relative dimness of the one small sun.

159

She thought about her lost tablets again. Then she banished them from her mind.

The chess players had the right idea, she told herself. Sit down and relax. If you can.

[23]

Sheerin led the way to the next room. There were softer chairs in there. And thick red curtains on the windows, and a maroon carpet on the floor. With the strange brick-toned light of Dovim pouring in, the general effect was one of dried blood everywhere.

He had been surprised to see Theremon at the Observatory this evening, after the horrendous columns he had written, after all he had done to pour cold water on Athor's campaign for national preparedness. In recent weeks Athor had gone almost berserk with rage every time Theremon's name was mentioned; yet somehow he had relented and permitted him to be here for the eclipse.

That was odd and a little troublesome. It might mean that the stern fabric of the old astronomer's personality had begun to break down—that not only his anger but also his whole inner structure of character was giving way in the face of the oncoming catastrophe.

For that matter Sheerin was more than slightly surprised to find *himself* at the Observatory too. It had been a last-minute decision, a pure impulse of the kind he rarely experienced. Liliath had been horrified. He was pretty horrified himself. He had not forgotten the terrors that his few minutes in the Tunnel of Mystery had evoked in him.

But he had realized, in the end, that he *had* to be here, just as he had had to take that ride in the Tunnel. To everyone else, he might be nothing more than an easygoing overweight academic hack; but to himself he was still a scientist beneath all the blubber. The study of Darkness had concerned him through all his professional career. How, then, could he ever live with himself afterward, knowing that during the most celebrated episode of Darkness in more than two thousand years he had chosen to

160

hide himself away in the cozy safety of an underground chamber?

No, he had to be here. Witnessing the eclipse. Feeling the Darkness take possession of the world.

Theremon said with unexpected frankness, as they entered the adjoining room, "I'm starting to wonder whether I was right to have been such a skeptic, Sheerin."

"You ought to wonder about it."

"Well, I am. Seeing just Dovim up there like that. That weird red color spreading over everything. You know, I'd give ten credits for a decent dose of white light right now. A good stiff Tano Special. For that matter, I'd like to see Tano and Sitha in the sky too. Or, even better, Onos."

"Onos will be there in the morning," put in Beenay, who had just entered the room.

"Yes, but will *we?*" asked Sheerin. And grinned immediately to take the sting from his words. To Beenay he said, "Our journalistic friend is eager for a little nip of alcohol."

"Athor will have a fit. He's given orders for everybody to be sober here this evening."

Sheerin said, "So there's nothing but water to be had?"

"Well—"

"Come on, Beenay. Athor won't come in here."

"I suppose."

Tiptoeing to the nearest window, Beenay squatted, and from the low window box beneath it withdrew a bottle of red liquid that gurgled suggestively when he shook it.

"I *thought* Athor didn't know about this," he remarked, as he trotted back to the table. "Here! We've only got one glass, so as the guest you can have it, Theremon. Sheerin and I can drink from the bottle." And he filled the tiny cup with judicious care.

Laughing, Theremon said, "You never touched alcohol at all when we first met, Beenay."

"That was then. This is now. Tense times, Theremon. I'm learning. A good drink can be very relaxing at times like these."

"So I've heard," Theremon said lightly. He took a sip. It was some sort of red wine, rough and raw, probably cheap jug wine from one of the southern provinces. Just the sort of thing that a

161

lifelong abstainer like Beenay would tend to buy, not knowing any better. But it was better than nothing.

Beenay helped himself to a hearty gulp and passed the bottle to Sheerin. The psychologist up-ended it and held it to his lips for a long slow drink. Then, putting it down with a satisfied grunt and a smack of his lips, he said to Beenay, "Athor seems strange this evening. I mean, even allowing for the special circumstances. What's wrong?"

"Worrying about Faro and Yimot, I suppose."

"Who?"

"A couple of young graduate students. They were due several hours ago and haven't shown up yet. Athor's terrifically shorthanded, of course, because all but the really essential people have gone to the Sanctuary."

Theremon said, "You don't think they deserted, do you?"

"Who? Faro and Yimot? Of course not. They're not the type. They'd give everything to be here this evening taking measurements when the eclipse happens. But what if there's some kind of riot going on in Saro City and they've been caught in it?" Beenay shrugged. "Well, they'll show up sooner or later, I imagine. But if they're not here as we approach the critical phase, things could get a little sticky when the work piles up. That must be what Athor's worrying about."

Sheerin said, "I'm not so sure. Two missing men would be on his mind, yes. But there's something else. He looks so *old*, suddenly. Weary. Defeated, even. The last time I saw him he was full of fight, full of talk about the reconstruction of society after the eclipse—the real Athor, the iron man. Now all I see is a sad, tired, pathetic old wreck who's simply waiting for the end to come. The fact that he didn't even bother to throw Theremon out—"

"He tried," Theremon said. "Beenay talked him out of it. And Siferra."

"There you are. Beenay, did you ever know anyone who was able to talk Athor out of anything? —Here, pass me the wine."

"It may be my fault," Theremon said. "Everything that I wrote, attacking his plan to set up Sanctuary-type shelters all across the country. If he genuinely believes that there's going to be a worldwide Darkness in a few hours and that all mankind will go violently insane—"

"Which he does," said Beenay. "As do all of us."

"Then the failure of the government to take Athor's predictions seriously must be an overwhelming, crushing defeat for him. And I'm responsible as much as anyone. If it turns out that you people were right, I'll never forgive myself."

Sheerin said, "Don't flatter yourself, Theremon. Even if you had written five columns a day calling for a colossal preparedness movement, the government *still* wouldn't have done anything. It might have taken Athor's warnings even less seriously than it did if that's possible, with a popular crusading journalist like you on Athor's side."

"Thanks," Theremon said. "I really appreciate that. —Is there any wine left?" He looked toward Beenay. "And of course I'm in trouble with Siferra too. She thinks I'm too contemptible for words."

"There was a time when she seemed really interested in you," Beenay said. "I was wondering about it for a while, as a matter of fact. Whether you and she were—ah—"

"No," Theremon said, grinning. "Not quite. And we never will, now. But we were very good friends for a while. A fascinating, fascinating woman. —What about this cyclic theory of prehistory of hers? Is there anything to it?"

"Not if you listen to some of the other people in her department," Sheerin said. "They're really scornful of it. Of course, they've all got a vested interest in the established archaeological framework, which says that Beklimot was the first urban center and that if you go back more than a couple of thousand years you can't find any civilization at all, just primitive shaggy jungle-dwelling folk."

"But how can they argue away these recurrent catastrophes at the Hill of Thombo?" Theremon asked.

"Scientists who think they know the real story can argue away anything that threatens their beliefs," Sheerin said. "You scratch an entrenched academic and you'll find he's pretty similar in some ways to an Apostle of Flame, underneath. It's just a different kind of robe they wear." He took the bottle, which Theremon had been idly holding, and helped himself again. "The deuce with them. Even a layman like me can see that Siferra's discoveries at Thombo turn our picture of prehistory

163

inside out. The question isn't whether there were recurrent fires over a period of all those thousands of years. It's *why.*"

Theremon said, "I've seen plenty of explanations lately, all of them more or less fantastic. Someone from Kitro University was arguing that there are periodic rains of fire every few thousand years. And we got a letter at the newspaper from someone who claims to be a free-lance astronomer and says he's 'proved' that Kalgash passes through one of the suns every so often. I think there were even wilder things proposed."

"There's only one idea that makes any sense," Beenay said quietly. "Remember the concept of the Sword of Thargola. You have to dispense with the hypotheses that require extra bells and whistles in order to make sense. There's no reason why a rain of fire should fall on us every now and then, and it's obvious nonsense to talk about passing through suns. But the eclipse theory is accounted for perfectly by mathematical consideration of the orbit of Kalgash as it's affected by Universal Gravitation."

"The eclipse theory may stand up, yes. No doubt it does. We'll find out pretty soon, eh?" Theremon said. "But apply Thargola's Sword yourself to what you've just said. There's nothing in the eclipse theory that tells us that there'll *necessarily* be tremendous fires immediately afterward."

"No," Sheerin said. "There's nothing about that in the theory. But common sense indicates it. The eclipse will bring Darkness. Darkness will bring madness. And madness will bring the Flames. Which wrecks another couple of millenniums of painful struggle. It all comes to nothing tomorrow. Tomorrow there won't be a city standing unharmed in all Kalgash."

"You sound just like the Apostles," Theremon said angrily. "I heard pretty much the same stuff from Folimun 66 months ago. And told you two about it, I recall, at the Six Suns Club."

He gazed out the window, past the wooded slopes of Observatory Mount to where the spires of Saro City gleamed bloodily on the horizon. The newsman felt the tension of uncertainty grow within him as he cast a quick glance at Dovim. It glowered redly at zenith, dwarfed and evil.

Doggedly Theremon went on, "I can't buy your chain of reasoning. Why should I go nuts just because there isn't a sun in the sky? And even if I do—yes, I haven't forgotten those poor bastards in the Tunnel of Mystery—even if I do, and everyone else does, how does that harm the cities? Are we going to blow them down?"

"I said the same thing at first," Beenay put in. "Before I stopped to think things through. If you were in Darkness, what would you want more than anything else—what would it be that every instinct would call for?"

"Why, light, I suppose."

"Yes!" Sheerin cried, shouting now. "Light, yes! Light!"

"So?"

"And how would you get light?"

Theremon pointed to the switch on the wall. "I'd turn it on."

"Right," said Sheerin mockingly. "And the gods in their infinite kindness would provide enough current to give you what you wanted. Because the power company certainly wouldn't be able to. Not with all the generators grinding to a halt, and the people who operate them stumbling around babbling in the dark, and the same with the transmission-line controllers. You follow me?"

Theremon nodded numbly.

Sheerin said, "Where will light come from, when the generators stop? The godlights, I suppose. They've all got batteries. But you may not have a godlight handy. You'll be out there on the street in the Darkness, and your godlight will be sitting at home, right next to your bed. And you want light. So you burn something, eh, Mr. Theremon? Ever see a forest fire? Ever go camping and cook a stew over a wood fire? Heat isn't the only thing burning wood gives off, you know. It gives off light, and people are very well aware of that. And when it's dark they want light, and they're going to *get it.*"

"So they'll burn logs," Theremon said without much conviction.

"They'll burn whatever they can get. They've got to have light. They've got to burn something, and wood won't be handy, not on city streets. So they'll burn whatever is nearest. A pile of newspapers? Why not? The Saro City *Chronicle* will give a little brightness for a while. What about the newsstands that the papers on sale are stacked up in? Burn them too! Burn clothing. Burn books. Burn roof-shingles. Burn anything. The

165

people will have their light—and every center of habitation goes up in flames! There are your fires, Mr. Newspaperman. There is the end of the world you used to live in."

"*If* the eclipse comes," said Theremon, an undertone of stubbornness in his voice.

"If, yes," said Sheerin. "I'm no astronomer. And no Apostle, either. But my money's on the eclipse."

He looked straight at Theremon. Eyes held each other as though the whole matter were a personal affair of respective will powers, and then Theremon broke away, wordlessly. His breathing was harsh and ragged. He put his hands to his forehead and pressed hard.

Then came a sudden hubbub from the adjoining room.

Beenay said, "I think I heard Yimot's voice. He and Faro must have showed up, finally. Let's go in and see what kept them."

"Might as well!" muttered Theremon. He drew a long breath and seemed to shake himself. The tension was broken—for the moment.

[24]

The main room was in an uproar. Everyone clustered around Faro and Yimot, who were trying to parry a burst of eager questions while they removed their outer garments.

Athor bustles through the crowd and faced the newcomers angrily. "Do you realize that it's practically E-hour? Where have you two been?"

Faro 24 seated himself and rubbed his hands. His round, fleshy cheeks were red with the outdoor chill. He was smirking strangely. And he seemed curiously calm, almost as if he had been drugged.

"I've never seen him like that before," Beenay whispered to Sheerin. "He's always been very obsequious, very much the humble junior astronomer deferring to the great people around him. Even to me. But now—"

"Shh. Listen," Sheerin said.

Faro said, "Yimot and I have just finished carrying through a

166

little crazy experiment of our own. We've been trying to see if we couldn't construct an arrangement by which we could simulate the appearance of Darkness and Stars so as to get an advance notion as to how it looked."

There was a confused murmur from the listeners.

"Stars?" Theremon said. "You know what Stars are? How did you find out?"

Smirking again, Faro said, "By reading the Book of Revelations. It seems pretty clear that Stars are something very bright, like suns but smaller, that appear in the sky when Kalgash enters the Cave of Darkness."

"Absurd!" someone said.

"Impossible!"

"The Book of Revelations! That's where they did their research! Can you imagine—"

"Quiet," Athor said. There was a sudden look of interest in his eyes, a touch of his old vigor. "Go on, Faro. What was this 'arrangement' of yours? How did you go about it?"

"Well," said Faro, "the idea came to Yimot and me a couple of months ago, and we've been working it out in our spare time. Yimot knew of a low one-story house down in the city with a domed roof—some kind of warehouse, I think. Anyway, we bought it—"

"With what?" interrupted Athor peremptorily. "Where did you get the money?"

"Our bank accounts," grunted the lanky, pipestem-limbed Yimot 70. "It cost us two thousand credits." Then, defensively, "Well, what of it? Tomorrow two thousand credits will be two thousand pieces of paper and nothing else."

"Sure," Faro said. "So we bought the place and rigged it up with black velvet from top to bottom so as to get as perfect a Darkness as possible. Then we punched tiny holes in the ceiling and through the roof and covered them with little metal caps, all of which could be shoved aside simultaneously at the close of a switch. At least, we didn't do that part ourselves; we got a carpenter and an electrician and some others—money didn't count. The point was that we could get the light to shine through those holes in the roof, so that we could get a Starlike effect."

167

"What we imagined a Starlike effect would be," Yimot amended.

Not a breath was drawn during the pause that followed. Athor said stiffly:

"You had no right to make a private—"

Faro seemed abashed. "I know, sir—but, frankly, Yimot and I thought the experiment was a little dangerous. If the effect really worked, we half expected to go mad—from what Dr. Sheerin says about all this, we thought that would be rather likely. We felt that we alone should take the risk. Of course, if we found that we could retain our sanity, it occurred to us that we might be able to develop immunity to the real thing, and then expose the rest of you to what we had experienced. But things didn't work out at all—"

"Why? What happened?"

It was Yimot who answered. "We shut ourselves in and allowed our eyes to get accustomed to the dark. It's an extremely creepy feeling because the total Darkness makes you feel as if the walls and ceiling are crashing in on you. But we got over that and pulled the switch. The caps fell away and the roof glittered all over with little dots of light."

"And?"

"And—nothing. That was the wacky part of it. So far as we understood the Book of Revelations, we were experiencing the effect of seeing Stars against a background of Darkness. But nothing happened. It was just a roof with holes in it, and bright points of light coming through, and that's just what it looked like. We tried it over and over again—that's what kept us so late —but there just wasn't any effect at all."

There was a shocked silence. All eyes turned to Sheerin, who stood motionless, mouth open.

Theremon was the first to speak. "You know what this does to the whole theory you've built up, Sheerin, don't you?" He was grinning with relief.

But Sheerin raised his hand. "Not so fast, Theremon. Just let me think this through. These so-called 'Stars' that the boys constructed—the total time of their exposure to Darkness—" He fell silent. Everyone watched him. And then he snapped his fingers, and when he lifted his head there was neither surprise nor uncertainty in his eyes. "Of course—"

168

He never finished. Thilanda, who had been up in the Observatory dome exposing photographic plates of the sky at ten-second intervals as the time of eclipse drew near, came rushing in, waving her arms in wild circles that would have been worthy of Yimot at his most excited.

"Dr. Athor! Dr. Athor!"

Athor turned. "What is it?"

"We just found—he came walking right into the dome—you won't believe this, Dr. Athor—"

"Slow down, child. What happened? Who came walking in?"

There were the sounds of a scuffle in the hall, and a sharp clang. Beenay, starting to his feet, rushed out the door and came to a sudden halt, crying, "What the deuce!"

Davnit and Hikkinan, who should have been up in the dome with Thilanda, were out there. The two astronomers were struggling with a third figure, a lithe, athletic-looking man in his late thirties, with strange curling red hair, a thin sharp-featured face, icy blue eyes. They dragged him into the room and stood holding him with his arms gripped tightly behind his back.

The stranger wore the dark robe of the Apostles of Flame.

"Folimun 66!" Athor cried.

And in the same breath, from Theremon: "Folimun! What in the name of Darkness are you doing here?"

Quietly, in a cold, commanding tone, the Apostle said, "It's not in the name of Darkness that I've come to you this evening but in the name of light."

Athor stared at Thilanda. "Where did you find this man?"

"I told you, Dr. Athor. We were busy with the plates, and then we heard him. He had come right in and was standing behind us. 'Where is Athor,' he said. 'I must see Athor.' "

"Call the security guards," Athor said, his face darkening with rage. "The Observatory is supposed to be sealed this evening. I want to know how this man succeeded in getting past the guards."

"Obviously you've got an Apostle or two on the payroll," Theremon said pleasantly. "Naturally they'd have been only too obliging when the Apostle Folimun showed up and asked them to unlock the gate."

Athor shot him a blistering glance. But the look on his face indicated that the old astronomer realized the probable accuracy of Theremon's guess.

Everyone in the room had formed a ring around Folimun now. They were all staring at him in astonishment—Siferra, Theremon, Beenay, Athor, and the rest.

Calmly Folimun said, "I am Folimun 66, special adjutant to His Serenity Mondior 71. I have come this evening not as a criminal, as you seem to think, but as an envoy from His Serenity. Do you think you could persuade these two zealots of yours to release me, Athor?"

Athor gestured irritatedly. "Let him go."

"Thank you," Folimun said. He rubbed his arms and adjusted the set of his robe. Then he bowed in gratitude—or was it only mock gratitude?—to Athor. The air around the Apostle seemed to tingle with some special electricity.

"Now then," Athor said. "What are you doing here? What do you want?"

"Nothing, I suspect, that you would give me of your own free will."

"You're probably right about that."

Folimun said, "When you and I met some months ago, Athor, it was, I would say, a very tense meeting, a meeting of two men who might well have looked upon themselves as princes of hostile realms. To you, I was a dangerous fanatic. To me, you were the leader of a band of godless sinners. And yet we were able to come to a certain area of agreement, which was, you recall, that on the evening of Theptar nineteenth, Darkness would fall upon Kalgash and would remain for many hours."

Athor scowled. "Come to the point, if there is one, Folimun. Darkness *is* about to fall, and we don't have a lot more time."

Folimun replied, "To me, the coming Darkness was being sent upon us by the will of the gods. To you, it represented nothing more than the soulless movement of astronomical bodies. Very well: we agreed to disagree. I provided you with certain data that had been in the possession of the Apostles since the previous Year of Godliness, certain tables of the movements of the suns in the sky, and other even more abstruse data. In return, you promised to prove the essential truth of the creed of our faith and to make that proof known to the people of Kalgash."

Looking at his watch, Athor said, "And I did exactly that. What does your master want of me now? I've fulfilled my end of the bargain."

Folimun smiled faintly, but said nothing.

There was an uneasy stir in the room.

"I asked him for astronomical data, yes," Athor said, looking around. "Data that only the Apostles had. And it was given to me. For that, thank you. In return I did agree, in a manner of speaking, to make public my mathematical confirmation of the Apostles' basic tenet that Darkness would descend on Theptar nineteenth."

"There was no real need for us to give you anything," was the proud retort. "Our basic tenet, as you call it, was not in need of proof. It stands proven by the Book of Revelations."

"For the handful that constitute your cult, yes," Athor snapped. "Don't pretend to mistake my meaning. I offered to present scientific background for your beliefs. And I did!"

The cultist's eyes narrowed bitterly. "Yes, you did—with a fox's subtlety, for your pretended explanation backed our beliefs and at the same time removed all necessity for them. You made of the Darkness and of the Stars a natural phenomenon and removed all their real significance. That was blasphemy."

"If so, the fault isn't mine. The facts exist. What can I do but state them?"

"Your 'facts' are a fraud and a delusion."

Athor's face grew mottled with rage. "How do *you* know?"

And the answer came with the certainty of absolute faith: "I *know*."

The director purpled even more. Beenay started to go to his side, but Athor waved him away.

"And what does Mondior 71 want us to do? He still thinks, I suppose, that in trying to warn the world to take measures against the menace of madness we are somehow interfering with his attempt to seize power after the eclipse. Well, we aren't succeeding. I hope that makes him happy."

"The attempt itself has done harm enough. And what you are trying to achieve here this evening will make things worse."

171

"What do you know of what we're trying to achieve here this evening?" Athor demanded.

Smoothly Folimun said, "We know that you've never abandoned your hope of influencing the populace. Having failed to do it before the Darkness and the Flames, you intend to come forth afterward, equipped with photographs of the transition from daylight to Darkness. You mean to offer a rational explanation to the survivors of what happened—and to put aside in a safe place your supposed evidence of your beliefs, so that at the end of the *next* Year of Godliness your successors in the realm of science will be able to step forward and guide humanity in such a way that the Darkness can be resisted."

"Someone's been saying things," Beenay whispered.

Folimun went on, "All this works against the interests of Mondior 71, obviously. And it is Mondior 71 who is the appointed prophet of the gods, the one who is intended to lead mankind through the period ahead."

"It's high time you came to the point," Athor said in a frigid tone.

Folimun nodded. "The point is simply this. Your ill-advised and blasphemous attempt to gain information by means of your devilish instruments must be stopped. I only regret that I could not have destroyed your infernal devices with my own hands."

"Is that what you had in mind? It wouldn't have done you much good. All our data, except for the direct evidence we intend collecting right now, is already safely cached and well beyond the possibility of harm."

"Bring it forth. Destroy it."

"*What?*"

"Destroy all your work. Destroy your instruments. In return for which, I will see to it that you and all your people are protected against the chaos that is certain to break loose when Nightfall comes."

Now there was laughter in the room.

"Crazy," someone said. "Absolutely nuts."

"Not at all," Folimun said. "Devout, yes. Dedicated to a cause beyond your comprehension, yes. But not crazy. I'm quite sane, I assure you. I think this man here"—he indicated Theremon—"would testify to that, and he's not known for his gullibility. But I place my cause above all other things. This night is crucial in the history of the world, and when tomorrow dawns, Godliness must triumph. I offer you an ultimatum. You people are to end your blasphemous attempt to provide rational explanations for the coming of Darkness this evening and accept His Serenity Mondior 71 as the true voice of the gods' will. When morning comes, you will go forth to do Mondior's work among mankind, and no more will be heard of eclipses, or orbits, or the Law of Universal Gravitation, or the rest of your foolishness."

"And if we refuse?" said Athor, looking almost amused by Folimun's presumptuousness.

"Then," said Folimun coolly, "a band of angry people led by the Apostles of Flame will ascend this hill and destroy your Observatory and everything within it."

"Enough," Athor said. "Call Security. Have this man thrown out of here."

"You have exactly one hour," Folimun said, unperturbed. "And then the Army of Holiness will attack."

"He's bluffing," Sheerin said suddenly.

Athor, as though he hadn't heard, said again, "Call Security. I want him out of here!"

"Damn it, Athor, what's wrong with you?" Sheerin cried. "If you turn him loose, he'll get out there to fan the flames. Don't you see, chaos is what all these Apostles have been living for? And this man's a master at creating it."

"What are you suggesting?"

"Lock him up," Sheerin said. "Stash him away in a closet and slap a padlock on him, and keep him there for the duration of the time of Darkness. It's the worst possible thing we could do to him. If he's locked away like that, he won't see the Darkness, and he won't see the Stars. It doesn't take much of a knowledge of the fundamental creed of the Apostles to realize that for him to be hidden from the Stars when they appear will mean the loss of his immortal soul. Lock him up, Athor. It's not only what's safest for us, it's what he deserves."

"And afterward," breathed Folimun fiercely, "when you have all lost your minds, there'll be no one to let me out. This is a sentence of death. I know as well as you do what the coming of the Stars will mean—I know it far better than you. With your minds gone, you won't give any thought to freeing me. Suffocation or slow starvation, is it? About what I might have expected from a group of—of *scientists*." He made the word sound obscene. "But it won't work. I've taken the precaution of letting my followers know that they are to attack the Observatory precisely an hour from now, *unless* I appear and order them not to. Locking me away, then, will achieve nothing useful to you. Within an hour it'll bring your own destruction upon you, that's all. And then my people will free me, and together—joyously, ecstatically—we will watch the coming of the Stars." A vein throbbed in Folimun's temple. "Then, tomorrow, when you all are babbling madmen, damned forever by your deeds, we will set about the creation of a wondrous new world."

Sheerin glanced doubtfully at Athor. But Athor looked hesitant too.

Beenay, standing next to Theremon, murmured, "What do you think? Is he bluffing?"

But the newspaperman didn't reply. He had gone pale to the lips. "Look at that!" The finger he pointed toward the window was shaking, and his voice was dry and cracked.

There was a simultaneous gasp as every eye followed the pointing finger and, for one moment, stared frozenly.

Dovim was chipped on one side!

[25]

The tiny bit of encroaching blackness was perhaps the width of a fingernail, but to the staring watchers it magnified itself into the crack of doom.

For Theremon the sight of that small arc of darkness struck with terrible force. He winced and put his hand to his forehead and turned away from the window. He was shaken to the roots of his soul by that little chip in Dovim's side. Theremon the skeptic—Theremon the mocker—Theremon the tough-minded analyst of other people's folly—

Gods! How wrong I was!

As he turned, his eyes met Siferra's. She was at the other side

of the room, looking at him. There was contempt in her eyes—
or was it pity? He forced himself to meet her gaze and shook
his head sadly, as though to tell her with all the humility there
was in him, *I fouled things up and I'm sorry. I'm sorry. I'm sorry.*

It seemed to him that she smiled. Maybe she had understood
what he was trying to say.

Then the room dissolved in shrieking confusion for a moment, as everyone began to rush frenziedly around; and a moment after that, the confusion gave way to an orderly scurry of
activity as the astronomers leaped to their assigned tasks, some
running upstairs to the Observatory dome to watch the eclipse
through the telescopes, some going to the computers, some using hand-held instruments to record the changes in Dovim's
disk. At this crucial moment there was no time for emotion.
They were merely scientists with work to do. Theremon, alone
in the midst of it all, looked about for Beenay and found him,
finally, sitting at a keyboard, madly working out some sort of
problem. Of Athor there was no sign at all.

Sheerin appeared at Theremon's side and said prosaically,
"First contact must have been made five or ten minutes ago. A
little early, but I suppose there were plenty of uncertainties
involved in the calculations despite all the effort that went into
them." He smiled. —"You ought to get away from that window, man."

"Why is that?" said Theremon, who had swung around again
to stare at Dovim.

"Athor is furious," the psychologist whispered. "He missed
first contact on account of this fuss with Folimun. You're in a
vulnerable position, standing where you are. If Athor comes by
this way he's likely to try to throw you out the window."

Theremon nodded shortly and sat down. Sheerin looked at
him, eyes wide with surprise.

"The devil, man! You're shaking."

"Eh?" Theremon licked dry lips and then tried to smile. "I
don't feel very well, and that's a fact."

The psychologist's eyes hardened. "You're not losing your
nerve, are you?"

"No!" cried Theremon in a flash of indignation. "Give me a
chance, will you? You know, Sheerin, I wanted to believe all
this eclipse rigmarole, but I couldn't, I honestly couldn't, it all

175

seemed like the sheerest woolly fantasy to me. I wanted to believe it for Beenay's sake, for Siferra's sake—even for Athor's sake, in a strange way. But I couldn't. Not until just this minute. Give me a chance to get used to the idea, all right? You've had months. It's all hitting me at once."

"I see what you mean," Sheerin said thoughtfully. "Listen. Have you got a family—parents, wife, children?"

Theremon shook his head. "No. Nobody I need to worry about. Well, I have a sister, but she's two thousand miles away. I haven't even spoken with her in a couple of years."

"Well then, what about yourself?"

"What do you mean?"

"You could try to get to our Sanctuary. They'd have room for you there. There's probably still time—I could call them and say that you're on the way, and they'd unlock the gate for you—"

"So you think I'm scared stiff, do you?"

"You said yourself you didn't feel so good."

"Maybe I don't. But I'm here to cover the story. That's what I intend to do."

There was a faint smile on the psychologist's face. "I see. Professional honor, is that it?"

"You might call it that." Wearily Theremon said, "Besides, I helped in a big way to undermine Athor's preparedness program, or have you forgotten? Do you really think I'd have the gall now to go running for shelter into the very Sanctuary I was poking fun at, Sheerin?"

"I hadn't seen it that way."

"I wonder if there's any more of that miserable wine hidden around here somewhere. If ever there was a time when a fellow needed a drink—"

"Shh!" Sheerin said. He nudged Theremon violently. "Do you hear that? Listen!"

Theremon glanced in the direction Sheerin was indicating. Folimun 66 stood by the window, a look of wild elation on his face. The Apostle was droning something to himself in a low singsong tone. It made the newspaperman's skin crawl.

"What's he saying?" he whispered. "Can you make it out?"

"He's quoting the Book of Revelations, fifth chapter," replied Sheerin. Then, urgently, "Keep quiet and listen, will you?"

The Apostle's voice rose suddenly in an increase of fervor:

" *'And it came to pass in those days that the sun, Dovim, held lone vigil in the sky for ever longer periods as the revolutions passed; until such time as for full half a revolution, it alone, shrunken and cold, shone down upon Kalgash.*

" *'And men did assemble in the public squares and in the highways, there to debate and to marvel at the sight, for a strange fear and misery had seized their spirits. Their minds were troubled and their speech confused, for the souls of men awaited the coming of the Stars.*

" *'And in the city of Trigon, at high noon, Vendret 2 came forth and said unto the men of Trigon, "Lo, ye sinners! Though ye scorn the ways of righteousness, yet will the time of reckoning come. Even now the Cave approaches to swallow Kalgash; yea, and all it contains."*

" *'And in that moment as he spoke the lip of the Cave of Darkness passed the edge of Dovim so that to all Kalgash it was hidden from sight. Loud were the cries and lamentations of men as it vanished, and great the fear of soul with which they were afflicted.*

" *'And then it came to pass that the Darkness of the Cave fell full upon Kalgash in all its terrible weight, so that there was no light to be seen anywhere on all the surface of the world. Men were even as blinded, nor could one see his neighbor, though he felt his breath upon his face.*

" *'And in this blackness there appeared the Stars in countless number, and their brightness was as the brightness of all the gods in concourse assembled. And with the coming of the Stars there came also a music, which had a beauty so wondrous that the very leaves of the trees turned to tongues that cried out in wonder.*

" *'And in that moment the souls of men departed from them and fled upward to the Stars, and their abandoned bodies became even as beasts; yea, even as dull brutes of the wild; so that through the darkened streets of the cities of Kalgash they prowled with wild cries, like the cries of beasts.*

" *'From the Stars then there reached down the Heavenly Flames, that was the bearer of the will of the gods; and where the Flames touched, the cities of Kalgash were consumed even to utter destruction, so that of man and of the works of man, nothing whatever remained.*

" *'Even then—' "*

There was a subtle change in Folimun's tone. His eyes had not shifted, but somehow it seemed that he had become aware of the absorbed attention of the other two. Easily, without pausing for breath, he altered the timbre of his voice, so that it rose in pitch and the syllables became more liquid.

Theremon, caught by surprise, frowned. The words seemed to be on the border of familiarity. There had been nothing more than an elusive shift in the accent, a tiny change in the vowel stress—yet Theremon no longer had the slightest idea of what Folimun was saying.

"Maybe Siferra would be able to understand him now," Sheerin said. "He's probably speaking the liturgical tongue now, the old language of the previous Year of Godliness that the Book of Revelations was supposedly translated from."

Theremon gave the psychologist a peculiar look. "You know a lot about this, don't you? What's he saying, then?"

"You think I can tell you? I've done a little studying lately, yes. But not that much. I'm just guessing at what he's talking about. —Weren't we going to lock him in a closet?"

"Let him be," Theremon said. "What difference does it make now? It's his big moment. Let him enjoy it." He shoved his chair back and ran his fingers through his hair. His hands weren't shaking any longer. "Funny thing," he said. "Now that it's all actually begun, I don't feel jittery any more."

"No?"

"Why should I?" Theremon said. A note of hectic gaiety had crept into his voice. "There's nothing I can do to stop what's going to happen, is there? So I'll just try to ride it out. —Do you think the Stars are really going to appear?"

"Not a clue," Sheerin said. "Maybe Beenay would know."

"Or Athor."

"Leave Athor alone," said the psychologist, laughing. "He just passed through the room and gave you a look that should have killed you."

Theremon made a wry face. "I'll have plenty of crow to eat when all this is over, I know. What do you think, Sheerin? Is it safe to watch the show outside?"

"When the Darkness is total—"

"I don't mean the Darkness. I can handle Darkness, I think. I mean the Stars."

"The Stars?" Sheerin repeated impatiently. "I told you, I don't know anything about them."

"They're probably not as terrifying as the Book of Revela-

178

tions would want us to think. If that pinpoint-in-the-ceiling experiment of those two students means anything—" He turned his hands palms upward, as though they might hold the answer. "Tell me, Sheerin, what do you think? Won't some people be immune to the effects of the Darkness and the Stars?"

Sheerin shrugged. He pointed to the floor in front of them. Dovim was past its zenith now, and the square of bloody sunlight that outlined the window upon the floor had moved a few feet toward the center of the room, where it lay like the terrible stain of some ghastly crime. Theremon stared at its dusky color thoughtfully. Then he swung around and squinted once more into the sun itself.

The chip in its side had grown to a black encroachment that covered a third of its visible disk. Theremon shuddered. Once, jokingly, he had talked with Beenay of dragons in the sky. Now it seemed to him that the dragon had come, that it had swallowed five of the suns already, that it was nibbling enthusiastically at the only one that remained.

Sheerin said, "There are probably two million people in Saro City who are all trying to join the Apostles at once. They'll be holding one giant revival meeting down at Mondior's headquarters, I'll bet. —Do I think there's immunity to the Darkness effects? Well, we're about to discover if there is, aren't we?"

"There must be. How else would the Apostles keep the Book of Revelations going from cycle to cycle, and how on Kalgash did it get written in the first place? There *must* have been some sort of immunity. If everyone had gone mad, who would have been left to write the book?"

"Very likely the members of the secret cult hid themselves away in sanctuaries until it was over, just as some of us are doing tonight," Sheerin said.

"Not good enough. The Book of Revelations is set up as an eyewitness account. That seems to indicate they had firsthand experience of the madness—and survived it."

"Well," said the psychologist, "there are three kinds of people who might remain relatively unaffected. First, the very few who don't get to see the Stars at all—the blind, let's say, or those who drink themselves into a stupor at the beginning of the eclipse and stay that way to the end."

"They don't count. They're not really witnesses."

"I suppose not. The second group, though—young children, to whom the world as a whole is too new and strange for anything to seem more unusual than anything else. They wouldn't be frightened by the Darkness or even the Stars, I suspect. Those would just be two more curious events in an endlessly surprising world. You see that, don't you?"

Theremon nodded doubtfully. "I suppose so."

"Lastly, there are those whose minds are too coarse-grained to be entirely toppled. The very insensitive might scarcely be affected—the real clods. They'd just shrug and wait for Onos to rise, I suppose."

"So the Book of Revelations was written by insensitive clods?" Theremon asked, grinning.

"Hardly. It would have been written by some of the keenest minds of the new cycle—and it would have been based on the fugitive memories of the children, combined with the confused, incoherent babblings of the half-mad morons, and, yes, perhaps some of the tales that the clods told."

"You'd better not let Folimun hear that."

"Of course, the text would have been extensively edited and re-edited over the years. And even passed on, perhaps, from cycle to cycle, the way Athor and his people hope to pass along the secret of gravitation. But my essential point is this: that it can't help but be a mass of distortion, even if it is based on fact. For instance, consider that experiment with the holes in the roof that Faro and Yimot were telling us about—the one that didn't work."

"What of it?"

"Well, the reason why it didn't w—" Sheerin stopped and rose in alarm. "Uh-oh."

"Something wrong?" Theremon asked.

"Athor's coming this way. Just look at his face!"

Theremon turned. The old astronomer was moving toward them like some vengeful spirit out of a medieval myth. His skin was paper-white, his eyes were blazing, his features were a twisted mask of consternation. He shot a venomous glance toward Folimun, who still stood by himself in the corner on the far side of the window, and another at Theremon.

To Sheerin he said, "I've been on the communicator for the

past fifteen minutes. I talked to the Sanctuary, and to the Security people, and to downtown Saro City."

"And?"

"The newspaperman here will be very pleased with his work. The city's a shambles, I hear. Rioters everywhere, looters, panicky mobs—"

"What about the Sanctuary?" Sheerin asked anxiously.

"Safe. They're sealed off according to plan, and they're going to stay hidden until daybreak, at the earliest. They'll be all right. But the *city*, Sheerin—you have no idea—" He was having difficulty in speaking.

Theremon said, "Sir, if you would only believe me when I tell you how deeply I regret—"

"There's no time for that now," snapped Sheerin impatiently. He put his hand on Athor's arm. "What about you? Are you all right, Dr. Athor?"

"Does it matter?" Athor leaned toward the window, as if trying to see the riots from there. In a dull voice he said, "The moment the eclipse began, everyone out there realized that all the rest of it was going to happen just as we had said—we, and the Apostles. And hysteria set in. The fires will be starting soon. And I suppose Folimun's mob will be here too. What are we to do, Sheerin? Give me some suggestion!"

Sheerin's head bent, and he stared in long abstraction at his toes. He tapped his chin with one knuckle for a time. Then he looked up and said crisply, "Do? What is there to do? Lock the gates, hope for the best."

"What if we were to tell them that we'd kill Folimun if they tried to break in?"

"And would you?" Sheerin asked.

Athor's eyes sparked in surprise. "Why—I suppose—"

"No," Sheerin said. "You wouldn't."

"But if we threatened to—"

"No. No. They're fanatics, Athor. They already know we're holding him hostage. They probably *expect* us to kill him the moment they storm the Observatory, and that doesn't faze them at all. And you know you wouldn't do it anyway."

"Of course not."

"So, then. How long is it until totality?"

"Not quite an hour."

181

"We'll have to take our chances. It'll take time for the Apostles to get their mob together—it's not going to be a bunch of Apostles, I'll bet on that, it's going to be a huge mass of ordinary townspeople stirred up to panic by a handful of Apostles, who'll promise them immediate entrance into grace, promise them salvation, promise them anything—and it'll take more time to get them out here. Observatory Mount is a good five miles from the city—"

Sheerin glared out the window. Theremon, beside him, looked also, staring down the slopes. Below, the farmed patches gave way to clumps of white houses in the suburbs. The metropolis beyond was a blur in the distance—a mist in the waning blaze of Dovim. Eerie nightmare light bathed the landscape.

Without turning, Sheerin said, "Yes, it'll take time for them to get here. Keep the doors locked, keep on working, pray that totality comes first. Once the Stars are shining I think not even the Apostles will be able to keep that mob's mind on the job of breaking in here."

Dovim was cut in half. The line of division was pushing a slight concavity across the middle into the still bright portion of the red sun. It was like a gigantic eyelid inexorably dropping down over the light of a world.

Theremon stood frozen, staring. The faint clatter of the room behind him faded into oblivion, and he sensed only the thick silence of the fields outside. The very insects seemed frightened mute. And things were dimmer and dimmer. That weird blood-hue stained everything.

"Don't look so long at a time," Sheerin murmured in his ear.

"At the sun, you mean?"

"At the city. At the sky. I'm not worried about you hurting your eyes. It's your mind, Theremon."

"My mind's all right."

"You want it to stay that way. How are you feeling?"

"Why—" Theremon narrowed his eyes. His throat was a little dry. He ran his finger along the inside of his collar. Tight. Tight. A hand beginning to close around his throat, was that how it felt? He twisted his neck back and forth but found no relief. "A little trouble breathing, maybe."

"Difficulty in breathing is one of the first symptoms of a

182

claustrophobic attack," Sheerin said. "When you feel your chest tightening, you'd be wise to turn away from the window."

"I want to see what's happening."

"Fine. Fine. Whatever you like, then."

Theremon opened his eyes wide and drew two or three long breaths. "You don't think I can take it, do you?"

Wearily Sheerin said, "I don't know anything about anything, Theremon. Things are changing from moment to moment, aren't they? —Hello, here's Beenay."

[26]

The astronomer had interposed himself between the light and the pair in the corner. Sheerin squinted up at him uneasily. "Hello, Beenay."

"Mind if I join you?" he asked. "My reckonings are set, and there's nothing for me to do till totality." Beenay paused and eyed the Apostle, who was poring intently through a small leather-bound book that he had drawn from the sleeve of his robe. "Say, weren't we going to put him away?"

"We decided not to," Theremon said. "Do you know where Siferra is, Beenay? I saw her a little while ago, but she doesn't seem to be here now."

"Upstairs, in the dome. She wanted to get a view through the big telescope. Not that there's anything much to see that we can't see with our naked eyes."

"What about Kalgash Two?" Theremon asked.

"What's there to see? Darkness in Darkness. We can see the effect of its presence as it moves in front of Dovim. Kalgash Two itself, though—it's just a chunk of night against the night sky."

"*Night,*" Sheerin mused. "What a strange word that is."

"Not any more," said Theremon. "So you don't actually see the wandering satellite at all, even with the big telescope?"

Beenay looked abashed. "Our telescopes really aren't very good, you know. They do fine for solar observations, but let it get just a little dark, and—" He shook his head. His shoulders were thrown back and he seemed to be working hard to pull air into his lungs. "But Kalgash Two is real, all right. The strange zone of Darkness that's passing between us and Dovim—that's Kalgash Two."

Sheerin said, "Have you been having trouble breathing, Beenay?"

"A little." He sniffled. "A cold, I guess."

"A touch of claustrophobia, more likely."

"You think?"

"I'm pretty sure. Anything else feel strange?"

"Well," Beenay said, "I get the impression that my eyes are going back on me. Things seem to blur, and—well, nothing is as clear as it ought to be. And I'm cold, too."

"Oh, that's no illusion. It's cold, all right," Theremon said, grimacing. "My toes feel as if I've been shipping them cross country in a refrigeration car."

"What we need right now," Sheerin said intensely, "is to distract ourselves from the effects we're feeling. Keep our minds busy, that's the thing. I was telling you a moment ago, Theremon, why Faro's experiments with the holes in the roof came to nothing."

"You were just beginning," Theremon replied, playing along. He huddled down, encircling a knee with both arms and nuzzling his chin against it. What I ought to do, he thought, is excuse myself and go upstairs to find Siferra, now that the time before totality is running out. But he found himself curiously passive, unwilling to move. Or, he wondered, am I just afraid to face her?

Sheerin said, "What I was about to propose was that they were misled by taking the Book of Revelations literally. There probably wasn't any sense in attaching any physical significance to the concept of Stars. It might be, you know, that in the presence of total and sustained Darkness the mind finds it absolutely necessary to create light. This illusion of light might be all that the Stars really are."

"In other words," Theremon said, starting to get caught up in it now, "you mean the Stars are the results of the madness and not one of the causes? Then what good will the photographs that the astronomers are taking this evening be?"

"To prove that the Stars are an illusion, maybe. Or to prove the opposite, for all I know. Then again—"

Beenay had drawn his chair closer, and there was an expression of sudden enthusiasm on his face. "As long as you're on the subject of Stars—" he began. "I've been thinking about them myself, and I've come up with a really interesting notion. Of course, it's just a wild speculation, and I'm not trying to put it forth in any serious way. But it's worth thinking about. Do you want to hear it?"

"Why not?" Sheerin said, leaning back.

Beenay looked a little reluctant. He smiled shyly and said, "Well then, supposing there were other suns in the universe."

Theremon repressed a laugh. "You said this was really wild, but I didn't imagine—"

"No, it isn't as crazy as that. I don't mean other suns right close at hand that we somehow mysteriously aren't able to see. I'm talking about suns that are so far away that their light isn't bright enough for us to make them out. If they were nearby, they'd be as bright as Onos, maybe, or Tano and Sitha. But as it is, the light they give off seems to us like nothing more than a little point of illumination, and it's drowned out by the constant glare from our six suns."

Sheerin said, "But what about the Law of Universal Gravitation? Aren't you overlooking that? If these other suns are there, wouldn't they be disturbing our world's orbit the way Kalgash Two does, and why, then, haven't you observed it?"

"Good point," said Beenay. "But these suns, let's say, are really far off—maybe as much as four light-years away, or even more."

"How many years is a light-year?" Theremon asked.

"Not how many. How *far*. A light-year is a measure of distance—the distance light travels in a year. Which is an immense number of miles, because light is so fast. We've measured it at something like 185,000 miles an hour, and my suspicion is that that isn't a really precise figure, that if we had better instruments we'd find out that the speed of light is even a little faster than that. But even figuring at 185,000 miles an hour, we can calculate that Onos is about ten light-*minutes* from here, and Tano and Sitha about eleven times as far as that, and so on. So a sun that's a few light-*years* away, why, that would be really distant. We'd never be able to detect any perturbations they might be causing in Kalgash's orbit, because they'd be so minor. All right: let's say that there are a lot of suns out there, everywhere around us in the heavens, at a distance of four to eight light-years—say, a dozen or two such suns, maybe."

Theremon whistled. "What an idea for a great Weekend Supplement piece! Two dozen suns in a universe eight light-years across! Gods! That would shrink *our* universe into insignificance! Imagine it—Kalgash and its suns just a little trivial suburb of the real universe, and here we've been thinking that we're the whole thing, just us and our six suns, all alone in the cosmos!"

"It's only a wild notion," said Beenay with a grin, "but you see where I'm heading, I hope. During eclipse, these dozen suns would suddenly become visible, because for a little while there'd be no *real* sunlight to drown them out. Since they're so far off, they'd appear small, like so many little marbles. But there you'd have it: the Stars. The suddenly emerging points of light that the Apostles have been promising us."

"The Apostles talk of 'countless numbers' of Stars," Sheerin said. "That doesn't seem like a dozen or two to me. More like a few million, wouldn't you think?"

"Poetic exaggeration," said Beenay. "There just isn't room enough in the universe for a million suns—not even if they were jammed right up against each other so that they touched."

"Besides," Theremon offered, "once we get up to a dozen or two, can we really grasp distinctions of numbers? Two dozen Stars would seem like a 'countless' number, I bet—especially if there happens to be an eclipse going on and everybody is wacky already from staring at Darkness. You know, there are tribes in the backwoods that have only three numbers in their language—'one,' 'two,' 'many,' We're a little more sophisticated than that, maybe. So for us one to two dozen are comprehensible, and then it just feels like 'countless' to us." He shivered with excitement. "A dozen suns, suddenly! Imagine it!"

Beenay said, "There's more. Another cute little notion. Have you ever thought what a simple problem gravitation would be if only you had a sufficiently simple system? Supposing you had a universe in which there was a planet with only one sun. The planet would travel in a perfect ellipse and the exact nature of the gravitational force would be so evident it could be accepted as an axiom. Astronomers on such a world would start off with gravity probably before they even invent the telescope. Naked-eye observation would be enough to let them figure things out."

Sheerin looked doubtful. "But would such a system be dynamically stable?" he asked.

"Sure! They call it the 'one-and-one' case. It's been worked out mathematically, but it's the philosophical implications that interest me."

"It's nice to think about," admitted Sheerin, "as a pretty abstraction—like a perfect gas or absolute zero."

"Of course," continued Beenay, "there's the catch that life would be impossible on such a planet. It wouldn't get enough heat and light, and if it rotated there would be total Darkness half of each day. That was the planet you once asked me to imagine, remember, Sheerin? Where the native inhabitants would be fully adapted to alternating daylight and night? But I've been thinking about that. There wouldn't *be* any native inhabitants. You couldn't expect life—which is fundamentally dependent upon light—to develop under such extreme conditions of light-deprivation. Half of every axial rotation spent in Darkness! No, nothing could exist under conditions like that. But to continue—just speaking hypothetically, the 'one-and-one' system would—"

"Wait a minute," Sheerin said. "That's pretty glib of you, saying life wouldn't have developed there. How do *you* know? What's so fundamentally impossible about life evolving in a place that has Darkness half the time?"

"I told you, Sheerin, life is fundamentally dependent upon light. And therefore in a world where—"

"Life *here* is fundamentally dependent on light. But what does that have to do with a planet that—"

"It stands to reason, Sheerin!"

"It stands to *circular* reason!" Sheerin retorted. "You define life as such-and-such a kind of phenomenon that occurs on Kalgash, and then you try to claim that on a world that's totally unlike Kalgash life would be—"

Theremon burst suddenly into harsh gusts of laughter.

Sheerin and Beenay looked at him indignantly.

187

"What's so funny?" Beenay demanded.

"You are. The two of you. An astronomer and a psychologist having a furious argument about biology. This must be the celebrated interdisciplinary dialogue that I've heard so much about, the great intellectual ferment for which this university is famous." The newspaperman stood up. He was growing restless anyway, and Beenay's long disquisition on abstract matters was making him even edgier. "Excuse me, will you? I need to stretch my legs."

"Totality's almost here," Beenay pointed out. "You may not want to be off by yourself when that happens."

"Just a little stroll, and then I'll be back," said Theremon.

Before he had taken five steps, Beenay and Sheerin had resumed their argument. Theremon smiled. It was a way of easing the tension, he told himself. Everybody was under tremendous pressure. After all, each tick of the clock was bringing the world closer to full Darkness—closer to—

To the Stars?

To madness?

To the Time of the Heavenly Flames?

Theremon shrugged. He had gone through a hundred gyrations of mood in the past few hours, but now he felt oddly calm, almost fatalistic. He had always believed that he was the master of his own destiny, that he was able to shape the course of his life: that was how he had succeeded in getting himself into places where other newspapermen hadn't remotely had a chance. But now everything was beyond his control, and he knew it. Come Darkness, come Stars, come Flame, it would all happen without a by-your-leave from *him*. No sense consuming himself in jittery anticipation, then. Just relax, sit back, wait, watch it all happen.

And then, he told himself—then make sure that you survive whatever turmoil follows.

"Going up to the dome?" a voice asked.

He blinked in the half-darkness. It was the chubby little graduate-student astronomer—Faro, was that his name?

"Yes, as a matter of fact," Theremon said, though in truth he had had no particular destination in mind.

"So am I. Come on: I'll take you there."

A spiral metal staircase wound upward into the high-vaulted

top story of the huge building. Faro went chugging up the stairs in a thudding short-legged gait, and Theremon loped along behind him. He had been in the Observatory dome once before, years ago, when Beenay wanted to show him something. But he remembered very little about the place.

Faro pulled back a heavy sliding door, and they went in.

"Come for a close look at the Stars?" Siferra asked.

The tall archaeologist was standing just inside the doorway, watching the astronomers at their work. Theremon reddened. Siferra wasn't what he wanted to run into just now. Too late he recalled that this was where Beenay had said she had gone. Despite the ambiguous smile she had seemed to cast his way at the moment of the eclipse's beginning, he still feared the sting of her scorn for him, her anger over what she saw as his betrayal of the Observatory group.

But she showed no sign now of hard feelings. Perhaps, now that the world was plunging headlong into the Cave of Darkness, she felt that anything that had happened before the eclipse was irrelevant, that the coming catastrophe canceled out all errors, all quarrels, all sins.

"Quite a place!" Theremon said.

"Isn't it amazing? Not that I really know much of what's going on here. They've got the big solarscope trained on Dovim—it's really a camera more than it is a spyglass, they told me; you can't just squint through it and see the heavens—and then these smaller telescopes are focused deeper out, watching for some sign that the Stars are appearing—"

"Have they spotted them yet?"

"Not so far as anyone's told me," Siferra said.

Theremon nodded. He looked around. This was the heart of the Observatory, the room where the actual scanning of the skies took place. It was the darkest room he had ever been in— not truly dark, of course; there were bronze sconces arrayed in a double row around the curving wall, but the glow that came from the lamps they held was faint and perfunctory. In the dimness he saw a great metal tube going upward and disappearing through an open panel in the roof of the building. He was able to glimpse the sky through the panel also. It had a terrifying dense purple hue now. The diminishing orb of

189

Dovim was still visible, but the little sun seemed to have retreated to an enormous distance.

"How strange it all looks," he murmured. "The sky has a texture I've never seen before. It's thick—it's like some sort of blanket, almost."

"A blanket that will smother us all."

"Frightened?" he asked.

"Of course. Aren't you?"

"Yes and no," Theremon said. "I mean, I'm not trying to sound particularly heroic, believe me. But I'm not nearly as edgy as I was an hour or two ago. Numb, more than anything."

"I think I know what you mean."

"Athor says there's already been some rioting in the city."

"It's only the beginning," Siferra replied. "Theremon, I can't get those ashes out of my mind. The ashes of the Hill of Thombo. Those big blocks of stone, the foundations of the cyclopean city—and ashes everywhere at their base."

"With older ashes below, down and down and down."

"Yes," she said.

He realized that she had moved a little closer to him. He realized also that the animosity she had felt toward him over the past few months seemed to be completely gone, and—could it be?—she appeared to be responding to some ghost of the attraction that he had once had for her. He knew the symptoms. He was much too experienced a man not to know them.

Fine, Theremon thought. The world is coming to an end, and now, suddenly, Siferra is finally willing to put aside her Ice Queen costume.

A weird, gawky figure, immensely tall, came slithering by them in a clumsy jerky way. He offered them a giggly greeting.

"No sign of the Stars yet," he said. It was Yimot, the other young graduate student. "Maybe we won't get to see them at all. It'll all turn out to be a fizzle, like the experiment Faro and I rigged up in that dark building."

"Plenty of Dovim's still visible," Theremon pointed out. "We're nowhere near total Darkness."

"You sound almost eager for it," said Siferra.

He turned to her. "I'd like to get the waiting over with."

"Hey!" someone yelled. "My computer's down!"

"The lights—!" came another voice.

"What's happening?" Siferra asked.

"Power failure," Theremon said. "Just as Sheerin predicted. The generating station must be in trouble. The first wave of madmen, running amok in the city."

Indeed the dim lights in the sconces appeared to be on the verge of going out. First they grew very much brighter, as if a quick final surge of power had gone rushing through them; then they dimmed; then they brightened again, but not as much as a moment before; and then they dropped to just a fraction of their normal light output. Theremon felt Siferra's hand gripping his forearm tightly.

"They're out," someone said.

"And so are the computers—cut in the backup power, somebody! Hey! Backup power!"

"Fast! The solarscope isn't tracking! The camera shutter won't work!"

Theremon said, "Why didn't they prepare for something like this?"

But apparently they had. There came a thrumming from somewhere in the depths of the building; and then the screens of the computers scattered around the room winked back to life. The lamps in their sconces did not, though. Evidently they were on another circuit, and the emergency generator in the basement would not restore them to functioning.

The Observatory was practically in full Darkness.

Siferra's hand still rested on Theremon's wrist. He debated slipping a comforting arm around her shoulders.

Then Athor's voice could be heard. "All right, give me a hand here! We'll be okay in a minute!"

"What's he got?" Theremon asked.

"Athor's brought out the lights," came the voice of Yimot.

Theremon turned to stare. It wasn't easy to see anything, in such a low light level, but in another moment his eyes grew somewhat accustomed to it. There were half a dozen foot-long inch-thick rods cradled in Athor's arms. He glared over them at the staff members.

"Faro! Yimot! Come here and help me."

The young men trotted to the Observatory director's side and took the rods from him. One by one, Yimot held them up, while Faro, in utter silence, scraped a large clumsy match into spluttering life with the air of one performing the most sacred rite of a religious ritual. As he touched the flame to the upper end of each of the rods, the little blaze hesitated a moment, playing futilely about the tip, until a sudden crackling flare cast Athor's lined face into yellow highlights. A spontaneous cheer ran through the great room.

The rod was tipped by six inches of wavering flame!

"Fire?" Theremon wondered. "In here? Why not use god-lights, or something?"

"We discussed it," said Siferra. "But godlights are too faint. They're all right for a small bedroom, just a little cozy presence to get you through the sleeping-period, but for a place this size—"

"And downstairs? Are they lighting torches there too?"

"I think so."

Theremon shook his head. "No wonder the city's going to burn this evening. If even you people are resorting to something as primitive as fire to hold back the Darkness—"

The light was dim, dimmer even than the most tenuous sunlight. The flames reeled crazily, giving birth to drunken, swaying shadows. The torches smoked devilishly and smelled like a bad day in the kitchen. But they emitted yellow light.

There was something joyous about yellow light, Theremon thought. Especially after nearly four hours of somber, dwindling Dovim.

Siferra warmed her hands at the nearest, regardless of the soot that gathered upon them in a fine, gray powder, and muttered ecstatically to herself. "Beautiful! Beautiful! I never realized before what a wonderful color yellow is."

But Theremon continued to regard the torches suspiciously. He wrinkled his nose at the rancid odor and said, "What are those things made out of?"

"Wood," she replied.

"Oh, no, they're not. They aren't burning. The top inch is charred and the flame just keeps shooting up out of nothing."

"That's the beauty of it. This is a really efficient artificial-light mechanism. We made a few hundred of them, but most went to the Sanctuary, of course. You see"—she turned and dusted off her blackened hands—"you take the pithy core of coarse water reeds, dry them thoroughly, and soak them in

192

animal grease. Then you set fire to it and the grease burns, little by little. These torches will burn for almost half an hour without stopping. Ingenious, isn't it?"

"Wonderful," Theremon said dourly. "Very modern. Very impressive."

But he couldn't remain in this room any longer. The same restlessness that had led him to come up here now afflicted him again. The reek of the torches was bad enough; but also there was the cold blast of air coming in through the open panel in the dome, a harsh wintry flow, the icy finger of night. He shivered. He wished that he and Sheerin and Beenay hadn't finished off that whole bottle of miserable wine so quickly.

"I'm going to go back below," he said to Siferra. "There's nothing to see here if you aren't an astronomer."

"All right. I'll go with you."

In the flickering yellow light he saw a smile appear on her face, unmistakable this time, unambiguous.

[27]

They made their way down the clattering spiral staircase to the lower room. Not much had changed down there. The people on the lower level had lit torches there too. Beenay was busy at three computers at once, processing data from the telescopes upstairs. Other astronomers were doing other things, all of them incomprehensible to Theremon. Sheerin was wandering around by himself, a lost soul. Folimun had carried his chair directly beneath a torch and continued reading, lips moving in the monotonous recital of invocations to the Stars.

Through Theremon's mind ran phrases of description, bits and pieces of the article he had planned to write for tomorrow's Saro City Chronicle. Several times earlier in the evening the writing machine in his brain had clicked on the same way —a perfectly methodical, perfectly conscientious, and, as he was only too well aware, perfectly meaningless procedure. It was wholly preposterous to imagine that there was going to be an issue of the Chronicle tomorrow.

He exchanged glances with Siferra.

"The sky," she murmured.

"I see it, yes."

It had changed tone again. Now it was darker still, a horrible deep purple-red, a monstrous color, as though some enormous wound in the fabric of the heavens were gushing fountains of blood.

The air had grown, somehow, denser. Dusk, like a palpable entity, entered the room, and the dancing circle of yellow light about the torches etched itself into ever sharper distinction against the gathering grayness beyond. The odor of smoke here was just as cloying as it had been upstairs. Theremon found himself bothered even by the little chuckling sounds that the torches made as they burned, and by the soft pad of Sheerin's footsteps as the heavyset psychologist circled round and round the table in the middle of the room.

It was getting harder to see, torches or no.

So now it begins, Theremon thought. The time of total Darkness—and the coming of the Stars.

For an instant he thought it might be wisest to look for some cozy closet to lock himself into until it was all over. Stay out of the way, avoid the sight of the Stars, hunker down and wait for things to become normal again. But a moment's contemplation told him what a bad idea that was. A closet—any sort of enclosed place—would be dark too. Instead of being a safe snug harbor, it might become a chamber of terrors far more frightening than the rooms of the Observatory.

And then too, if something big was going to happen, something that would reshape the history of the world, Theremon didn't want to be tucked away with his head under his arm while it was going on. That would be cowardly and foolish; and it might be something he would regret all the rest of his life. He had never been the sort of man to hide from danger, if he thought there might be a story in it. Besides, he was just self-confident enough to believe that he would be able to withstand whatever was about to occur—and there was just enough skepticism left in him so that at least part of him wondered whether anything significant was going to happen at all.

He stood still, listening to Siferra's occasional indrawn breaths, the quick little respirations of someone trying to retain composure in a world that was all too swiftly retreating into the shadow.

Then came another sound, a new one, a vague, unorganized *impression* of sound that might well have gone unnoticed but for the dead silence that prevailed in the room and for Theremon's unnatural focus of attention as the moment of totality grew near.

The newspaperman stood tensely listening, holding his breath. After a moment he carefully moved toward the window and peered out.

The silence ripped to fragments at his startled shout: "*Sheerin!*"

There was an uproar in the room. They were all looking at him, pointing, questioning. The psychologist was at his side in a moment. Siferra followed. Even Beenay, crouched in front of his computers, swung around to look.

Outside, Dovim was a mere smoldering splinter, taking one last desperate look at Kalgash. The eastern horizon, in the direction of the city, was lost in Darkness, and the road from Saro City to the Observatory was a dull red line. The trees of the wooded tracts that bordered the highway on both sides had lost all individuality and merged into a continuous shadowy mass.

But it was the highway itself that held attention, for along it there surged another, and infinitely menacing, shadowy mass, surging like a strange shambling beast up the slopes of Observatory Mount.

"Look," Theremon cried hoarsely. "Someone tell Athor! The madmen from the city! Folimun's people! They're coming!"

"How long to totality?" Sheerin asked.

"Fifteen minutes," Beenay rasped. "But they'll be here in five."

"Never mind, keep everyone working," Sheerin said. His voice was steady, controlled, unexpectedly commanding, as though he had managed to tap into some deep reservoir of inner strength in this climactic moment. "We'll hold them off. This place is built like a fortress. You, Siferra, go upstairs and let Athor know what's happening. You, Beenay, keep an eye on Folimun. Knock him down and sit on him if you have to, but don't let him out of your sight. Theremon, come with me."

Sheerin was out the door, and Theremon followed at his heels. The stairs stretched below them in tight, circular sweeps around the central shaft, fading into a dank and dreary grayness.

The first momentum of their rush had carried them fifty feet down, so that the dim, flickering yellow from the open door of the room behind them had disappeared, and both up above and down the same dusky shadow crushed in upon them.

Sheerin paused, and his pudgy hand clutched at his chest. His eyes bulged and his voice was a dry cough. His whole body was quivering in fear. Whatever the final source of resolve he had found a moment ago now seemed exhausted.

"I can't . . . breathe . . . go down . . . yourself. Make sure all doors are closed—"

Theremon took a few downward steps. Then he turned. "Wait! Can you hold out a minute?" He was panting himself. The air passed in and out of his lungs like so much molasses, and there was a little germ of screeching panic in his mind at the thought of making his way farther below by himself.

What if the guards had left the main door open, somehow?

It wasn't the mob he was afraid of. It was—

Darkness.

Theremon realized that he was, after all, afraid of the Dark!

"Stay here," he said unnecessarily to Sheerin, who was huddled dismally on the staircase where Theremon had left him. "I'll be back in a second."

He dashed upward two steps at a time, heart pounding—not altogether from the exertion—tumbled into the main room, and snatched a torch from its holder. Siferra stared at him, eyes wide with bewilderment.

"Shall I come with you?" she asked.

"Yes. No. No!"

He ran out again. The torch was foul-smelling, and the smoke smarted his eyes almost blind, but he clutched that torch as if he wanted to kiss it for joy. Its flame streamed backward as he hurtled down the stairs again.

Sheerin hadn't budged. He opened his eyes and moaned as Theremon bent over him. The newspaperman shook him roughly. "All right, get hold of yourself. We've got light."

He held the torch at tiptoe height, and, propping the tottering psychologist by an elbow, made his way downward again, protected now by the sputtering circle of illumination.

On the ground floor everything was black. Theremon felt the horror rising within him again. But the torch sliced a way through the Darkness for him.

"The Security men—" Sheerin said.

Where were they? Had they fled? It looked that way. No, there were a couple of the guards Athor had posted, jammed up against the corner of the hallway, trembling like jelly. Their eyes were blank, their tongues were lolling. Of the others there was no sign.

"Here," Theremon said brusquely, and passed the torch to Sheerin. "You can hear *them* outside."

And they could. Little scraps of hoarse, wordless shouts.

But Sheerin had been right: the Observatory was built like a fortress. Erected in the last century, when the neo-Gavottian style of architecture was at its ugly height, it had been designed for stability and durability, rather than for beauty.

The windows were protected by the grillwork of inch-thick iron bars sunk deep into the concrete sills. The walls were solid masonry that an earthquake couldn't have touched, and the main door was a huge oaken slab reinforced with iron at the strategic points. Theremon checked the bolts. They were still in place.

"At least they can't just walk right in the way Folimun did," he said, panting. "But listen to them! They're right outside!"

"We have to do something."

"Damned right," Theremon said. "Don't just stand there! Help me drag these display cases up against the doors—and keep that torch out of my eyes. The smoke's killing me."

The cases were full of books, scientific instruments, all sorts of things, a whole museum of astronomy. The gods only knew what the display cases weighed, but some supernal force had taken possession of Theremon in this moment of crisis, and he heaved and pulled them into place—aided, more or less, by Sheerin—as though they were pillows. The little telescopes and other gadgets within them went tumbling over as he jockeyed the heavy cases into position. There was the sound of breaking glass.

Beenay will kill me, Theremon thought. He worships all that stuff.

But this was no moment for being delicate. He slammed one case after another up against the door, and in a few minutes had built a barricade that might, he hoped, serve to hold back the mob if it succeeded in breaking through the gate.

Somewhere, dimly, far off, he could hear the battering of bare fists against the door. Screams—yells—

It was all like a ghastly dream.

The mob had set out from Saro City driven by the hunger for salvation, the salvation held forth by the Apostles of Flame, which could be attained now, they had been told, only by the destruction of the Observatory. But as the moment of Darkness drew near a maddening fear had all but stripped their minds of the ability to function. There was no time to think of ground cars, or of weapons, or of leadership, or even of organization. They had rushed to the Observatory on foot, and they were assaulting it with bare hands.

And now that they were there, the last flash of Dovim, the last ruby-red drop of sunlight, flickered feebly over a humanity that had nothing left but stark, universal fear.

Theremon groaned. "Let's get back upstairs!"

There was no sign of anyone now in the room where they had been gathered. They had all gone to the topmost floor, into the Observatory dome itself. As he came rushing in, Theremon was struck by an eerie calmness that seemed to prevail in there. It was like a tableau. Yimot was seated in the little lean-back seat at the control panel of the gigantic solarscope as if this were just an ordinary evening of astronomical research. The rest were clustered about the smaller telescopes, and Beenay was giving instructions in a strained, ragged voice.

"Get it straight, all of you. It's vital to snap Dovim just before totality and change the plate. Here, you—you—one of you to each camera. We need all the redundancy we can get. You all know about—about times of exposure—"

There was a breathless murmur of agreement.

Beenay passed a hand over his eyes. "Are the torches still burning? Never mind, I see them!" He was leaning hard against the back of a chair. "Now remember, don't—don't try to look for fancy shots. When the Stars appear, don't waste time trying to get t-two of them in the scope field at a time. One is enough. And . . . and if you feel yourself going, *get away from the camera.*"

At the door, Sheerin whispered to Theremon, "Take me to Athor. I don't see him."

The newspaperman did not answer immediately. The vague forms of the astronomers wavered and blurred, and the torches overhead had become only yellow splotches. The room was cold as death. Theremon felt Siferra's hand graze his for a moment—only a moment—and then he was unable to see her.

"It's dark," he whimpered.

Sheerin held out his hands. "Athor." He stumbled forward. "Athor!"

Theremon stepped after him and seized his arm. "Wait. I'll take you." Somehow he made his way across the room. He closed his eyes against the Darkness and his mind against the pounding chaos that was rising within it.

No one heard them or paid attention to them. Sheerin stumbled against the wall.

"Athor!"

"Is that you, Sheerin?"

"Yes. Yes. Athor?"

"What is it, Sheerin?" Athor's voice, unmistakably.

"I just wanted to tell you—don't worry about the mob—the doors are strong enough to hold them out—"

"Yes. Of course," Athor muttered. He sounded, Theremon thought, as if he were many miles away.

Light-years away.

Suddenly another figure was among them, moving swiftly, a whirling flail of arms. Theremon thought it might be Yimot or even Beenay, but then he felt the rough fabric of a cultist's robe and knew that it must be Folimun.

"The Stars!" Folimun cried. "Here come the Stars! Get out of my way!"

He's trying to get to Beenay, Theremon realized. To destroy the blasphemous cameras.

"Watch—out—" Theremon called. But Beenay still sat huddled in front of the computers that activated the cameras, snapping away as the full Darkness swept down.

Theremon reached out. He caught hold of Folimun's robe,

199

yanked, twisted. Suddenly there were clutching fingers at his throat. He staggered crazily. There was nothing before him but shadows; the very floor beneath his feet lacked substance. A knee drove hard into his gut, and he grunted in a blinding haze of pain and nearly fell.

But after the first gasping moment of agony his strength returned. He seized Folimun by the shoulders, somehow swung him around, hooked his arm around the Apostle's throat. At the same moment he heard Beenay croak, "I've got it! At your cameras, everyone!"

Theremon seemed conscious of everything at once. The entire world was streaming through his pounding mind—and everything was in chaos, everything was screaming with terror.

There came the strange awareness that the last thread of sunlight had thinned out and snapped.

Simultaneously he heard one last choking gasp from Folimun, and a heavy bellow of amazement from Beenay, and a queer little cry from Sheerin, a hysterical giggle that cut off in a rasp—

And a sudden silence, a strange, deadly silence, from outside.

Folimun had gone limp in his loosening grasp. Theremon peered into the Apostle's eyes and saw the blankness of them, staring upward, mirroring the feeble yellow of the torches. He saw the bubble of froth upon Folimun's lips and heard the low animal whimper in Folimun's throat.

With the slow fascination of fear, he lifted himself on one arm and turned his eyes toward the bloodcurdling blackness of the sky.

Through it shone the Stars!

Not the one or two dozen of Beenay's pitiful theory. There were thousands of them, blazing with incredible power, one next to another next to another next to another, an endless wall of them, forming a dazzling shield of terrifying light that filled the entire heavens. Thousands of mighty suns shone down in a soul-searing splendor that was more frighteningly cold in its awful indifference than the bitter wind that shivered across the cold, horribly bleak world.

They hammered at the roots of his being. They beat like flails against his brain. Their icy monstrous light was like a million great gongs going off at once.

My God, he thought. My God, my God, my God!

But he could not tear his eyes away from the hellish sight of them. He looked up through the opening in the dome, every muscle rigid, frozen, and stared in helpless wonder and horror at that shield of fury that filled the sky. He felt his mind shrinking down to a tiny cold point under that unceasing onslaught. His brain was no bigger than a marble, rattling around in the hollow gourd that was his skull. His lungs would not work. His blood ran backward in his veins.

At last he was able to close his eyes. He knelt for a time, panting, murmuring to himself, fighting to regain control.

Then Theremon staggered to his feet, his throat constricting him to breathlessness, all of the muscles of his body writhing in a tensity of terror and sheer fear beyond bearing. Dimly he was aware of Siferra somewhere near him, but he had to struggle to remember who she was. He had to work at remembering who *he* was. From below came the sound of a terrible steady pounding, a frightful hammering against the door—some strange wild beast with a thousand heads, struggling to get in—

It didn't matter.

Nothing mattered.

He was going mad, and knew it, and somewhere deep inside a bit of sanity was screaming, struggling to fight off the hopeless flood of black terror. It was very horrible to go mad and know that you were going mad—to know that in a little minute you would be here physically and yet all the real essence that was *you* would be dead and drowned in the black madness. For this was the Dark—the Dark and the Cold and the Doom. The bright walls of the universe were shattered and their awful black fragments were falling down to crush and squeeze and obliterate him.

Someone came crawling toward him on hands and knees and jostled up against him. Theremon moved aside. He put his hands to his tortured throat and limped toward the flames of the torches that filled all his mad vision.

"Light!" he screamed.

Athor, somewhere, was crying, whimpering horribly like a terribly frightened child. "Stars—all the Stars—we didn't know at all. We didn't know anything. We thought six stars is a universe is something the Stars didn't notice is Darkness forever and ever and ever and the walls are breaking in and we didn't know we couldn't know and anything—"

Someone clawed at the torch, and it fell and snuffed out. In that instant the awful splendor of the indifferent Stars leaped nearer to them.

From below came the sound of screams and shouts and breaking glass. The mob, crazed and uncontrollable, had broken into the Observatory.

Theremon looked around. By the awful light of the Stars he saw the dumbstruck figures of the scientists lurching about in horror. He made his way into the corridor. A fierce blast of chilly air coming through an open window struck him, and he stood there, letting it hit his face, laughing a little at the arctic intensity of it.

"Theremon?" a voice called behind him. "Theremon?"

He went on laughing.

"Look," he said, after a time. "Those are the Stars. This is the Flame."

On the horizon outside the window, in the direction of Saro City, a crimson glow began growing, strengthening in brightness, that was not the glow of a sun.

The long night had come again.

THREE

DAYBREAK

[28]

The first thing of which Theremon became aware, after a long period of being aware of nothing at all, was that something huge and yellow was hanging over him in the sky.

It was an immense blazing golden ball. There was no way he could look at it for more than a fraction of a second, on account of its brilliance. Searing heat was coming from it in pulsing waves.

He huddled in a crouching position, head downward, and crossed his wrists in front of his eyes to protect himself from that great outpouring of heat and light overhead. What, he wondered, kept it up there? Why didn't it simply fall?

If it falls, he thought, it will fall on me.

Where can I hide? How can I protect myself?

For a long moment he hunkered down where he was, hardly daring to think. Then, cautiously, he opened his eyes just a slit. The gigantic blazing thing was still there in the sky. It hadn't moved an inch. It wasn't going to fall on him.

He began to shiver despite the heat.

The dry, choking smell of smoke came to him. Something was burning, not very far away.

It was the sky, he thought. The sky was burning.

The golden thing is setting fire to the world.

No. No. There was another reason for the smoke. He would remember it in a moment, if only he could clear the haze out of his mind. The golden thing hadn't caused the fires. It hadn't even been here when the fires started. It was those other things, those cold glittering white things that filled the sky from end to end—they had done it, they had sent the Flames—

What were they called? The Stars. Yes, he thought.

The Stars.

And he began to remember, just a little, and he shivered

205

again, a deep convulsive quiver. He remembered how it had been when the Stars came out, and his brain had turned to a marble and his lungs refused to pump air and his soul had screamed in the deepest of horror.

But the Stars were gone now. That bright golden thing was in the sky instead.

The bright golden thing?

Onos. That was its name. Onos, the sun. The main sun. One of—one of the six suns. Yes. Theremon smiled. Things were beginning to come back to him now. Onos belonged in the sky. The Stars did not. The sun, the kindly sun, good warm Onos. And Onos had returned. Therefore all was well with the world, even if some of the world seemed to be on fire.

Six suns? Then where were the other five?

He even remembered their names. Dovim, Trey, Patru, Tano, Sitha. And Onos made six. He saw Onos, all right—it was right above him, it seemed to fill half the sky. What about the rest? He stood up, a little shakily, still half afraid of the hot golden thing overhead, wondering now if perhaps he stood up too far he would touch it and be burned by it. No, no, that didn't make any sense. Onos was good, Onos was kind. He smiled.

Looked around. Any more suns up there?

There was one. Very far off, very small. Not frightening, this one—the way the Stars had been, the way this fiery hot globe overhead was. Just a cheerful white dot in the sky, nothing more. Small enough to put in his pocket, almost, if he could only reach it.

Trey, he thought. That one is Trey. So its sister Patru ought to be somewhere nearby—

Yes. Yes, that's it. Down there, in the corner of the sky, just to the left of Trey. Unless that one's Trey, and the other one is Patru.

Well, he told himself, the names don't matter. Which one is which, unimportant. Together they are Trey and Patru. And the big one is Onos. And the other three suns must be somewhere else right now, because I don't see them. And my name is—

Theremon.

Yes. That's right. I'm Theremon.

But there's a number, too. He stood frowning, thinking about it, his family code, that's what it was, a number he had known all his life, but what was it? What—was—it?

762.

Yes.

I am Theremon 762.

And then another, more complex thought followed smoothly along: I am Theremon 762 of the Saro City *Chronicle.*

Somehow that statement made him feel a little better, though it was full of mysteries for him.

Saro City? The *Chronicle?*

He almost knew what those words meant. Almost. He chanted them to himself. *Saro saro saro. City city city. Chronicle chronicle chronicle. Saro City Chronicle.*

Perhaps if I walk a little, he decided. He took a hesitant step, another, another. His legs were a little wobbly. Looking around, he realized that he was on a hillside out in the country somewhere. He saw a road, bushes, trees, a lake off to the left. Some of the bushes and trees seemed to have been ripped and broken, with branches dangling at odd angles or lying on the ground below them, as though giants had come trampling through this countryside recently.

Behind him was a huge round-topped building with smoke rising from a hole in its roof. The outside of the building was blackened as if fires had been set all around it, though its stone walls appeared to have withstood the flames well enough. He saw a few people lying scattered on the steps of the building, sprawled like discarded dolls. There were others lying in the bushes, and still others along the path leading down the hill. Some of them were faintly moving. Most were not.

He looked the other way. On the horizon he saw the towers of a great city. A heavy pall of smoke hung over them, and when he squinted he imagined that he could see tongues of flame coming from the windows of the tallest buildings, although something rational within his mind told him that it was impossible to make out any such detail at so great a distance. That city had to be miles away.

Saro City, he thought suddenly.

Where the *Chronicle* is published.

Where I work. Where I live.

And I'm Theremon. Yes. Theremon 762. Of the Saro City *Chronicle.*

He shook his head slowly from side to side, as some wounded animal might have done, trying to clear it of the haze and torpor that infested it. It was maddening, not being able to think properly, not being able to move around freely in the storehouse of his own memories. The brilliant light of the Stars lay like a wall across his mind, cutting him off from his own memories.

But things were beginning to get through. Colored fragments of the past, sharp-edged, shimmering with manic energy, were dancing around and around in his brain. He struggled to make them hold still long enough for him to comprehend them.

The image of a room came to him, then. *His* room, heaped with papers, magazines, a couple of computer terminals, a box of unanswered mail. Another room: a bed. The small kitchen that he almost never used. This, he thought, is the apartment of Theremon 762, the well-known columnist for the Saro City *Chronicle.* Theremon himself is not at home at this time, ladies and gentlemen. At the present moment Theremon is standing outside the ruins of the Saro University Observatory, trying to understand—

The ruins—

Saro University Observatory—

"Siferra?" he called. "Siferra, where are you?"

No answer. He wondered who Siferra was. Someone he must have known before the ruins were ruined, probably. The name had come bubbling up out of the depths of his troubled mind.

He took another few uncertain steps. There was a man lying under a bush a short distance downhill. Theremon went to him. His eyes were closed. He held a burned-out torch in his hand. His robe was torn.

Sleeping? Or was he dead? Theremon prodded him carefully with his foot. Yes, dead. That was strange, all these dead people lying around. You didn't ordinarily see dead people everywhere like this, did you? And an overturned car over there—it looked dead, too, with its undercarriage turned pathetically toward the sky, and curls of smoke rising sluggishly from its interior.

"Siferra?" he called again.

Something terrible had happened. That seemed very clear to him, though hardly anything else did. Once again he crouched, and pressed his hands against the sides of his head. The random fragments of memory that had been jigging around in there were moving more slowly now, no longer engaged in a frantic dance: they had begun to float about in a stately fashion, like icebergs drifting in the Great Southern Ocean. If he could only get some of those drifting fragments to come together—force them into a pattern that made a little sense—

He reviewed what he had already managed to reconstruct. His name. The name of the city. The names of the six suns. The newspaper. His apartment.

Last evening—

The Stars—

Siferra—Beenay—Sheerin—Athor—names—

Abruptly things began to form connections in his mind.

The memory-fragments of his immediate past had finally started to reassemble themselves. But at first nothing yet made real sense, because each little cluster of memories was something independent unto itself, and he was unable to put them into any kind of coherent order. The harder he tried, the more confused everything became again. Once he understood that, he gave up the idea of trying to force anything.

Just relax, Theremon told himself. Let it happen naturally.

He had, he realized, suffered some great wound of the mind. Although he felt no bruises, no lumps on the back of his head, he knew that he must have been injured in some way. All his memories had been cut into a thousand pieces as though by a vengeful sword, and the pieces had been stirred and scattered like the pieces of some baffling puzzle. But he seemed to be healing, moment by moment. Moment by moment, the strength of his mind, the strength of the entity that was Theremon 762 of the Saro City *Chronicle*, was reasserting itself, putting him back together.

Stay calm. Wait. Let it happen naturally.

He drew in his breath, held it, slowly released it. Breathed in again. Hold, release. Breathe, hold, release. Breathe, hold, release.

In his mind's eye he saw the interior of the Observatory. Remembering, now. It was evening. Only the little red sun was in the sky—Dovim, that was its name. That tall woman: she was Siferra. And the fat man was Sheerin, and the young slender earnest one, he was Beenay, and the fierce old man with the patriarchal mane of white hair was the great famous astronomer, the head of the Observatory—Ithor? Uthor? *Athor*, yes. Athor.

And the eclipse was coming. The Darkness. The Stars.

Oh, yes. Yes. It was all flowing together now. The memories returning. The mob outside the Observatory, led by fanatics in black robes: the Apostles of Flame, that's what they were called. And one of the fanatics had been inside the Observatory. Folimun, his name was. Folimun 66.

He remembered.

The moment of totality. The sudden and complete descent of night. The world entering the Cave of Darkness.

The Stars—

The madness—the screaming—the mob—

Theremon winced at the recollection. The hordes of crazed, frightened people from Saro City breaking down the heavy doors, bursting into the Observatory, trampling each other in their rush to destroy the blasphemous scientific instruments and the blasphemous scientists who denied the reality of the gods—

Now that the memories came flooding back, he almost wished he had not recaptured them. The shock he had felt at the first moment of seeing the brilliant light of the Stars—the pain that had erupted within his skull—the strange horrific bursts of cold energy racing across his field of vision. And then the coming of the mob—that moment of frenzy—the struggle to escape—Siferra beside him, and Beenay nearby, and then the mob surging around them like a river in full spate, separating them, pulling them in opposite directions—

Into his mind came a single last glimpse of old Athor, his eyes bright and glazed with the wildness of utter madness, standing majestically on a chair, furiously ordering the intruders out of his building as though he were not merely the director of the Observatory but its king. And Beenay standing next to him, tugging at Athor's arm, urging the old man to flee. Then the scene dissolved. He was no longer in the great room. Theremon saw himself swept down a corridor, scrambling for a staircase, looking around for Siferra, for anyone he knew—

The Apostle, the fanatic, Folimun 66, suddenly appearing before him, blocking his way in the midst of the chaos. Laughing, holding out a hand to him in a mocking gesture of false friendship. Then Folimun too had disappeared from sight, and Theremon continued frantically onward, down the spiral stairs, tumbling and stumbling, clambering over people from the city who were wedged so tightly together on the ground floor that they were unable to move. Out the door, somehow. Into the chill of night. Standing bareheaded, shivering, in the Darkness that was Darkness no longer, for everything was illuminated now by the terrible, hideous, unthinkable cold blaze of those thousands of merciless Stars that filled the sky.

There was no hiding from them. Even when you closed your eyes you saw their frightful light. Mere Darkness was nothing, compared with the implacable pressure of that heaven-spanning vault of unthinkable brilliance, a light so bright that it boomed in the sky like thunder.

Theremon remembered that he had felt as though the sky, Stars and all, was about to fall on him. He had knelt and covered his head with his hands, futile though he knew that to be. He remembered, too, the terror all about him, people rushing this way and that, the shrieking, the crying. The fires of the blazing city leaping high on the horizon. And above all else those hammering waves of fear descending from the sky, from the remorseless unforgiving Stars that had invaded the world.

That was all. Everything after that was blank, utterly blank, until the moment of his awakening, when he looked up to see Onos in the sky once more, and began to put back together the shards and slivers of his mind.

I am Theremon 762, he told himself again. *I used to live in Saro City and write a column for the newspaper.*

There was no Saro City any longer. There was no newspaper.

The world had come to an end. But he still lived, and his sanity, he hoped, was returning.

211

What now? Where to go?

"Siferra?" he called.

No one answered. Slowly he began to shuffle down the hill once more, past the broken trees, past the burned and over-turned cars, past the scattered bodies. If this is what it looks like out here in the country, he thought, what must it be like in the city itself?

My God, he thought again.

All you gods! What have you done to us?

[29]

Sometimes cowardice has its advantages, Sheerin told himself, as he unbolted the door of the storeroom in the Observatory basement where he had spent the time of Darkness. He still felt shaky, but he had no doubt that he was still sane. As sane as he had ever been, at any rate.

It seemed quiet out there. And although the storeroom had no windows, enough light had managed to make its way through a grating high up along one of its walls so that he was fairly confident that morning had come, that the suns were in the sky again. Perhaps the madness had passed by this time. Perhaps it was safe for him to come out.

He poked his nose out into the hallway. Cautiously he looked around.

The smell of smoke was the first thing he perceived. But it was a stale, musty, nasty, damp, acrid kind of smoke-smell, the smell of a fire that has been extinguished. The Observatory was not only a building made of stone, but it had a highly efficient sprinkler system, which must have gone into operation as soon as the mob began setting fires.

The mob! Sheerin shuddered at the recollection.

The rotund psychologist knew that he would never forget the moment when that mob had come bursting into the Obser-vatory. It would haunt him as long as he lived—those twisted, distorted faces, those berserk eyes, those howling cries of rage. These were people who had lost their fragile grip on sanity even before the totality of the eclipse. The deepening Darkness

212

had been enough to push them over the edge—that, and the skillful rabble-rousing of the Apostles of Flame, triumphant now in their moment of fulfilled prophecy. So the mob had come, by the thousands, to root out the despised scientists in their lair; and there they were, now, rushing in, waving torches, clubs, brooms, anything at all with which they could hit, smash, ruin.

Paradoxically enough, it was the coming of the mob that had jolted Sheerin into being able to get a grip on himself. He had had a bad moment, back there when he and Theremon first went downstairs to barricade the doors. He had felt all right, even strangely buoyant, on the way down; but then the first reality of the Darkness had hit him, like a whiff of poison gas, and he had folded up completely. Sitting huddled up there on the stairs, cold with panic, remembering his trip through the Tunnel of Mystery and realizing that this time the trip would last not only a few minutes but for hour upon intolerable hour.

Well, Theremon had pulled him out of that one, and Sheerin had recovered some of his self-control as they returned to the upper level of the Observatory. But then came totality—and the Stars. Though Sheerin had turned his head away when that ungodly blast of light first came bursting through the opening in the Observatory roof, he had not been able completely to avoid the shattering sight of it. And for an instant he could feel his mind's grip giving way—could feel the delicate thread of sanity beginning to sunder—

But then had come the mob, and Sheerin knew that the issue wasn't simply one of preserving his sanity, any more. It was one of saving his life. If he wanted to survive this night he had no choice but to hold himself together and find a place of safety. Gone was his naive plan to observe the Darkness phenomena like the aloof, dispassionate scientist he pretended to be. Let someone else observe the Darkness phenomena. He was going to hide.

And so, somehow, he had made his way to the basement level, to that cheery little storeroom with its cheery little godlight casting a feeble but very comforting glow. And bolted the door, and waited it out.

He had even slept, a little.

And now it was morning. Or perhaps afternoon, for all he

knew. One thing was certain: the terrible night was over, and everything was calm, at least in the vicinity of the Observatory. Sheerin tiptoed into the hall, paused, listened, started warily up the stairs.

Silence everywhere. Puddles of dirty water, from the sprinklers. The foul reek of old smoke.

He halted on the stairway and thoughtfully removed a fire-hatchet from a bracket on the wall. He doubted very much that he could ever bring himself to use a hatchet on another living thing; but it might be a useful thing to be carrying, if conditions outside were as anarchic as he expected to find them.

Up to the ground floor, now. Sheerin pulled the basement door open—the same door that he had slammed behind him in his frenzied downward flight the evening before—and looked out.

The sight that greeted him was horrifying.

The great hall of the Observatory was full of people, all scrambled together on the floor, sprawled every which way, as though some colossal drunken orgy had been going on all night. But these people weren't drunk. Many of them lay twisted in ghastly impossible angles that only a corpse could have adopted. Others lay flat, stacked like discarded carpets in heaps two or three people high. They too seemed dead, or lost in the last unconsciousness of life. Still others were plainly alive, but sat whimpering and mewling like shattered things.

Everything that once had been on display in the great hall, the scientific instruments, the portraits of the great early astronomers, the elaborate astronomical charts, had been pulled down and burned or simply pulled apart and trampled. Sheerin could see the charred and battered remains jutting up here and there amidst the crush of bodies.

The main door was open. The warm and heartening glow of sunlight was visible beyond.

Carefully Sheerin picked his way through the chaos toward the exit.

"Dr. Sheerin?" a voice said suddenly, unexpectedly.

He whirled, brandishing his hatchet so fiercely that he came close to laughing at his own feigned belligerence.

"Who's there?"

"Me. Yimot."

"Who?"

"Yimot. You remember me, don't you?"

"Yimot, yes." The gangling, gawky young graduate astronomy student from some backwoods province. Sheerin saw the boy now, half hidden in an alcove. His face was blackened with ashes and soot and his clothing was torn, and he looked stunned and shaken, but he seemed otherwise to be all right. As he came forward, in fact, he moved in a far less comical way than usual, none of his jerky mannerisms, no wild swings of his arms or twitches of his head. Terror does strange things to people, Sheerin told himself. —"Have you been hiding here all through the night?"

"I tried to get out of the building when the Stars came, but I got jammed up in here. Have you seen Faro, Dr. Sheerin?"

"Your friend? No. I haven't seen anyone."

"We were together for a while. But then, with all the shoving and pushing, things got so wild—" Yimot managed an odd smile. "I thought they would burn the building down. But then the sprinklers came on." He pointed at the townspeople who lay all around. —"Are they all dead, do you think?"

"Some of them are just insane. They saw the Stars."

"I did too, just for a moment," Yimot said. "Just for a moment."

"What were they like?" Sheerin asked.

"You didn't see them, Doctor? Or is it that you just don't remember?"

"I was in the basement. Nice and snug."

Yimot craned his long neck upward as though the Stars were still blazing in the ceiling of the hallway. "They were—awesome," he whispered. "I know that doesn't tell you anything, but that's the only word I can use. I saw them only for two seconds, maybe three, and I could feel my mind spinning, I could feel the top of my head starting to lift off, so I looked away. Because I'm not very brave, Dr. Sheerin."

"No. Neither am I."

"But I'm glad I had those two or three seconds. The Stars are very frightening, but they're also very beautiful. At least to an astronomer they are. They were nothing at all like those silly little pinpricks of light that Faro and I created in that stupid experiment of ours. We must be right in the middle of an immense cluster of them, you know. We have our six suns in a tight group close by us—some of them closer than others, I mean—and then farther back, five or ten light-years back, or more, there's this whole giant sphere of Stars, which are suns, thousands of suns, a tremendous globe of suns completely enclosing us, but invisible to us normally because of the light of our own suns shining all the time. Just as Beenay said. Beenay's a wonderful astronomer, you know. He'll be greater than Dr. Athor some day. —You didn't see the Stars at all?"

"Just the merest quick glimpse," said Sheerin, a little sadly. "Then I went and hid. —Look, boy, we've got to get ourselves out of this place."

"I'd like to try to find Faro first."

"If he's all right, he's outside. If he isn't, there's nothing you can do for him."

"But if he's underneath one of those heaps—"

"No," Sheerin said. "You can't go poking around those people. They're all still stunned, but if you provoke them there's no telling what they'll do. The safest thing is to get out of here. I'm going to try to make it to the Sanctuary. If you're smart, you'll come with me."

"But Faro—"

"Very well," Sheerin said, with a sigh. "Let's look for Faro. Or Beenay, or Athor, or Theremon, any of the others."

But it was hopeless. For perhaps ten minutes they picked through the heaps of dead and unconscious and semi-conscious people in the hallway; but none of them were university people. Their faces were appalling, horribly distorted by fear and madness. Some stirred when they were disturbed, and began to froth and mutter in a horrifying way. One snatched at Sheerin's hatchet, and Sheerin had to use the butt end to push him away. It was impossible to ascend the stairs to the upper levels of the building; the staircase was blocked by bodies, and there was broken plaster everywhere. Pools of muddy water had collected on the floor. The harsh, piercing smell of smoke was intolerable.

"You're right," Yimot said finally. "We'd better go."

Sheerin led the way, stepping out into the sunlight. After the hours that had just passed, golden Onos was the most welcome sight in the universe, though the psychologist found his eyes unaccustomed to so much bright light after the long hours of Darkness. It hit him with almost tangible force. For a few moments after he emerged he stood blinking, waiting for his eyes to readapt. After a time he was able to see, and gasped at what he saw.

"How awful," Yimot murmured.

More bodies. Madmen wandering in circles, singing to themselves. Burned-out vehicles by the side of the road. The shrubbery and trees hacked up as though by blind monstrous forces. And, off in the distance, a ghastly pall of brown smoke rising above the spires of Saro City.

Chaos, chaos, chaos.

"So this is what the end of the world looks like," Sheerin said quietly. "And here we are, you and I. Survivors." He laughed bitterly. "What a pair we are. I'm carrying a hundred pounds too many around my middle and you've got a hundred pounds too few. But we're still here. I wonder if Theremon made it out of there alive. If anyone did, *he* would have. But I wouldn't have bet very much on you or me. —The Sanctuary's midway between Saro City and the Observatory. We ought to be able to walk it in half an hour or so, if we don't get into any trouble. Here, take this."

He scooped up a thick gray billy-club that was lying beside one of the fallen rioters and tossed it to Yimot, who caught it clumsily and stared at it as though he had no idea what it might be.

"What will I do with it?" he asked finally.

Sheerin said, "Pretend that you'll use it to bash in the skull of anybody that bothers us. Just as I'm pretending that I'd use this hatchet if I needed to defend myself. And if necessary I will. It's a new world out here, Yimot. Come on. And keep your wits about you as we go."

[30]

The Darkness was still upon the world, the Stars still were flooding Kalgash with their diabolical rivers of light, when Siferra 89 came stumbling out of the gutted Observatory building. But the faint pink glow of dawn was showing on the eastern horizon, the first hopeful sign that the suns might be returning to the heavens.

She stood on the Observatory lawn, legs far apart, head thrown back, pulling breath deep down into her lungs.

Her mind was numb. She had no idea how many hours had passed since the sky had turned dark and the Stars had erupted into view like the blast of a million trumpets. All the night long she had wandered the corridors of the Observatory in a daze, unable to find her way out, struggling with the madmen who swarmed about her on all sides. That she had gone mad too was not something she stopped to think about. The only thing on her mind was survival: beating back the hands that clutched at her; parrying the swinging clubs with blows of the club that she herself had snatched up from a fallen man; avoiding the screaming, surging stampedes of maniacs who rumbled arm in arm in groups of six or eight through the hallways, trampling everyone in their way.

It seemed to her that there were a million townsfolk loose in the Observatory. Wherever she turned she saw distended faces, bulging eyes, gaping mouths, lolling tongues, fingers crooked into monstrous claws.

They were smashing everything. She had no idea where Beenay was, or Theremon. She vaguely remembered seeing Athor in the midst of ten or twenty bellowing hoodlums, his thick mane of white hair rising above them—and then seeing him go down, swept under and out of sight.

Beyond that Siferra remembered nothing very clearly. For the whole duration of the eclipse she had run back and forth, up one hallway and down the other like a rat caught in a maze. She had never really been familiar with the layout of the Observatory, but getting out of the building should not have been that difficult for her—if she had been sane. Now, though, with the Stars blazing relentlessly at her out of every window, it was as if an icepick had been driven through her brain. She could not think. She could not think. She could not think. All she could do was run this way and that, shoving leering gibbering fools aside, shouldering her way through clotted gangs of ragged strangers, searching desperately and ineffectually and futilely for one of the main exits. And so it went, for hour after hour, as though she were caught in a dream that would not end.

Now, at last, she was outside. She didn't know how she had gotten there. Suddenly there had been a door in front of her, at the end of a corridor that she was sure she had traversed a thousand times before. She pushed and it yielded and a cool blast of fresh air struck her, and she staggered through.

The city was burning. She saw the flames far away, a bright furious red stain against the dark background of sky.

She heard screams, sobs, wild laughter from all sides.

Below her, a little way down the hillside, some men were mindlessly pulling down a tree—tugging at its branches, straining fiercely, ripping its roots loose from the ground by sheer force. She couldn't guess why. Probably neither could they.

In the Observatory parking lot, other men were tipping cars over. Siferra wondered whether one of those cars might be hers. She couldn't remember. She couldn't remember very much at all. Remembering her name was something of an effort.

"Siferra," she said aloud. "Siferra 89. Siferra 89."

She liked the sound of that. It was a good name. It had been her mother's name—or her grandmother's, perhaps. She wasn't really sure.

"Siferra 89," she said again. "I am Siferra 89."

She tried to remember her address. No. A jumble of meaningless numbers.

"Look at the Stars!" a woman screamed, rushing past her. "Look at the Stars and die!"

"No," Siferra replied calmly. "Why should I want to die?"

But she looked at the Stars all the same. She was almost getting used to the sight of them now. They were like very bright lights—*very* bright—so close together in the sky that they seemed to merge, to form a single mass of brilliance, like a kind of shining cloak that had been draped across the heavens. When she looked for more than a second or two at a time she thought she could make out individual points of light, brighter than those around them, pulsing with a bizarre vigor. But the best that she could manage was to look for five or six seconds; then the force of all that pulsating light would overwhelm her, mak-

219

ing her scalp tingle and her face turn burning hot, and she would have to lower her head and rub her fingers against the fiery, throbbing, angry place of pain between her eyes.

She walked through the parking lot, ignoring the frenzy going on all about her, and emerged on the far side, where a paved road led along a level ridge on the flank of Observatory Mount. From some still-functioning region of her mind came the information that this was the road from the Observatory to the main part of the university campus. Up ahead, Siferra could see some of the taller buildings of the university now.

Flames were dancing on the roofs of some of them. The bell tower was burning, and the theater, and the Hall of Student Records.

You ought to save the tablets, said a voice within her mind that she recognized as her own.

Tablets? What tablets?

The Thombo tablets.

Oh. Yes, of course. She was an archaeologist, wasn't she? Yes. Yes. And what archaeologists did was dig for ancient things. She had been digging in a place far away. Sagimot? Beklikan? Something like that. And had found tablets, prehistoric texts. Ancient things, archaeological things. Very important things. In a place called Thombo.

How am I doing? she asked herself.

And the answer came: *You're doing fine.*

She smiled. She was feeling better moment by moment. It was the pink light of dawn on the horizon that was healing her, she thought. The morning was coming: the sun, Onos, entering the sky. As Onos rose, the Stars became less bright, less terrifying. They were fading fast. Already those in the east were dimmed by Onos's gathering strength. Even at the opposite end of the sky, where Darkness still reigned and the Stars thronged like minnows in a pool, some of the intensity was starting to go from their formidable gleam. She could look at the sky for several moments at a stretch now without feeling her head begin to throb painfully. And she was feeling less confused. She remembered clearly now where she lived, and where she worked, and what she had been doing the evening before.

220

At the Observatory—with her friends, the astronomers, who had predicted the eclipse—

The eclipse—

That was what she had been doing, she realized. Waiting for the eclipse. For the Darkness. For the Stars.

Yes. For the Flames, Siferra thought. And there they were. Everything had happened right on schedule. The world was burning, as it had burned so many times before—set ablaze not by the hand of the gods, nor by the power of the Stars, but by ordinary men and women, Star-crazed, cast into a desperate panic that urged them to restore the normal light of day by any means they could find.

Despite the chaos all around her, though, she remained calm. Her injured mind, numbed, all but stupefied, was unable to respond fully to the cataclysm that Darkness had brought. She walked on and on, down the road, into the main quadrangle of the campus, past scenes of horrifying devastation and destruction, and felt no shock, no regret for what had been lost, no fear of the difficult times that must lie ahead. Not enough of her mind was restored yet for such feelings. She was a pure observer, tranquil, detached. The blazing building over there, she knew, was the new university library that she had helped to plan. But the sight of it stirred no emotion in her. She could just as well have been walking through some two-thousand-year-old site whose doom was a cut-and-dried matter of historical record. It would never have occurred to her to weep for a two-thousand-year-old ruin. It did not occur to her to weep now, as the university went up in flames all around her.

She was in the middle of the campus now, retracing familiar paths. Some of the buildings were on fire, some were not. Like a sleepwalker she turned left past the Administration building, right at the Gymnasium, left again at Mathematics, and zig-zagged past Geology and Anthropology to her own headquarters, the Hall of Archaeology. The front door stood open. She went in.

The building seemed almost untouched. Some of the display cases in the lobby were smashed, but not by looters, since all the artifacts appeared still to be there. The elevator door had been wrenched off its hinges. The bulletin board next to the stairs was on the floor. Otherwise everything apparently was intact. She heard no sounds. The place was empty.

Her office was on the second floor. On the way up the stairs she came upon the body of an old man lying face upward at the first-floor landing. "I think I know you," Siferra said. "What's your name?" He didn't answer. "Are you dead? Tell me: yes or no." His eyes were open, but there was no light in them. Siferra pressed her finger against his cheek. "Mudrin, that's your name. Or was. Well, you were very old anyway." She shrugged and continued upward.

The door to her office was unlocked. There was a man inside.

He looked familiar too; but this one was alive, crouching against the file cabinets in a peculiar huddled way. He was a burly, deep-chested man with powerful forearms and broad, heavy cheekbones. His face was bright with sweat and his eyes had a feverish gleam.

"Siferra? You here?"

"I came to get the tablets," she told him. "The tablets are very important. They have to be protected."

He rose from his crouch and took a couple of uncertain steps toward her. "The tablets? The tablets are gone, Siferra! The Apostles stole them, remember?"

"Gone?"

"Gone, yes. Like your mind. You're out of your mind, aren't you? Your face is blank. There's nobody home behind your eyes. I can see that. You don't even know who I am."

"You are Balik," she said, the name coming unbidden to her lips.

"So you do remember."

"Balik. Yes. And Mudrin is on the stairs. Mudrin is dead, do you know that?"

Balik shrugged. "I suppose. We'll all be dead in a little while. The whole world's gone crazy out there. But why am I bothering to tell you that? You're crazy too." His lips trembled. His hands shook. An odd little giggle burst from him, and he clenched his jaws as though to suppress it. "I've been here all through the Darkness. I was working late, and when the lights started to fail—my God," he said, "the Stars, the Stars. I had just one quick look at them. And then I got under the desk and stayed there through the whole thing." He went to the window. "But Onos is coming up now. The worst must be over. —Is everything on fire out there, Siferra?"

"I came for the tablets," she said again.

"They're gone." He spelled the word out for her. "Do you understand me? Gone. Not here. Stolen."

"Then I will take the charts that we made," she said. "I must protect knowledge."

"Absolutely crazy, aren't you? Where were you, the Observatory? Got a good view of the Stars, did you?" He giggled again and started to cut diagonally across the room, moving closer to her. Siferra's face twisted with disgust. She could smell the odor of his sweat now, sharp and harsh and disagreeable. He smelled as if he hadn't bathed in a week. He looked as if he hadn't slept in a month. "Come here," he said, as she backed away from him. "I won't hurt you."

"I want the charts, Balik."

"Sure. I'll give you the charts. And the photographs and everything. But first I'm going to give you something else. Come here, Siferra."

He reached for her and pulled her toward him. She felt his hands on her breasts and the roughness of his cheek against her face. The smell of him was unbearable. Fury rose in her. How dare he touch her like this? Brusquely she pushed him away.

"Hey, don't do that, Siferra! Come on. Be nice. For all we know, there's just the two of us in the world. You and me, we'll live in the forest and hunt little animals and gather nuts and berries. Hunters and gatherers, yes, and later on we'll invent agriculture." He laughed. His eyes looked yellow in the strange light. His skin seemed yellow too. Again he reached for her, hungrily, one cupped hand seizing one of her breasts, the other sliding down her back toward the base of her spine. He put his face down against the side of her throat and nuzzled her noisily like some kind of animal. His hips were heaving and thrusting against her in a revolting way. At the same time he began to force her backward toward the corner of the room.

Suddenly Siferra remembered the club that she had picked up somewhere during the night in the Observatory building. She was still holding it, loosely dangling in her hand. Swiftly she brought it upward and rammed the top of it against the point of Balik's chin, hard. His head snapped up and back, his teeth clattered together.

He let go of her and lurched a few steps backward. His eyes were wide with surprise and pain. His lip was split where he had bitten into it, and blood was pouring down on one side.

"Hey, you bitch! What did you want to hit me for?"

"You touched me."

"Damn right I touched you! And about time, too." He rubbed his jaw. "Listen, Siferra, put that stick down and stop looking at me that way. I'm your friend. Your ally. The world has turned into a jungle now, and there's just the two of us. We need each other. It isn't safe trying to go it alone now. You can't afford to risk it."

Again he came toward her, hands upraised, seeking her.

She hit him again.

This time she brought the club around and smashed it against the side of his cheek, connecting with bone. There was an audible sharp sound of impact, and Balik jerked to one side under the force of it. With his head turned halfway away from her, he looked at her in utter astonishment and staggered back. But he was still standing. She hit him a third time, above his ear, swinging the club with all her strength in a long arc. As he fell, Siferra clubbed him once more, in the same place, and felt everything give beneath the blow. His eyes closed and he made a strange soft sound, like an inflated balloon releasing its air, and sank down in the corner against the wall, with his head going one way and his shoulders the other.

"Don't ever touch me like that again," Siferra said, prodding him with the tip of the club. Balik didn't reply. He didn't move, either.

Balik ceased to concern her.

Now for the tablets, she thought, feeling wonderfully calm.

No. The tablets were gone, Balik had said. Stolen. And she remembered now: they really were. They had disappeared just before the eclipse. All right, the charts then. All those fine drawings they had made of the Hill of Thombo. The stone walls, the ashes at the foundation lines. Those ancient fires, just like the fire that was ravaging Saro City at this very moment.

Where were they?

Oh. Here. In the chart cabinet, where they belonged.

She reached in, grabbed a sheaf of the parchment-like papers, rolled them, tucked them under her arm. Now she remembered the fallen man, and glanced at him. But Balik still hadn't moved. He didn't look as though he was going to, either.

Out the office door, down the stairs. Mudrin remained where he had been before, sprawled out motionless and stiff on the landing. Siferra ran around him and continued to the ground floor.

Outside, the morning was well along. Onos was climbing steadily and the Stars were pale now against its brightness. The air seemed fresher and cleaner, though the odor of smoke was thick on the breeze. Down by the Mathematics building she saw a band of men smashing windows. They caught sight of her a moment later and shouted to her, raucous, incoherent words. A couple of them began to run toward her.

Her breast ached where Balik had squeezed it. She didn't want any more hands touching her now. Turning, Siferra darted behind the Archaeology building, pushed her way through the bushes on the far side of the pathway in back, ran diagonally across a lawn, and found herself in front of a blocky gray building that she recognized as Botany. There was a small botanical garden behind it, and an experimental arboretum on the hillside beyond that, at the edge of the forest that encircled the campus.

Looking back, Siferra thought she saw the men still pursuing her, though she couldn't be sure. She sprinted past the Botany building and easily leaped the low fence around the botanical garden.

A man riding a mowing machine waved at her. He wore the olive-drab uniform of the university gardeners; and he was methodically mowing the bushes, cutting a wide swath of destruction back and forth across the center of the garden. He was chuckling to himself as he worked.

Siferra went around him. From there it was a short run into the arboretum. Were they still following her? She didn't want to take the time to glance behind her. Just run, run, run, that was the best idea. Her long, powerful legs carried her easily between the rows of neatly planted trees. She moved in steady strides. It felt good, running like this. Running. Running.

Then she came to a rougher zone of the arboretum, all brambles and thorns, everything tightly interwoven. Unhesitatingly Siferra plunged into it, knowing no one would go after her there. The branches clawed at her face, ripped at her clothing. As she pushed her way through one dense patch she lost her grip on the roll of charts, and emerged on the far side without them.

Let them go, she thought. They don't mean anything any more anyway.

But now she had to rest. Panting, gasping with exhaustion, she vaulted across a little stream at the border of the arboretum and dropped down on a patch of cool green moss. No one had followed her. She was alone.

She looked up, through the tops of the trees. The golden light of Onos flooded the sky. The Stars could no longer be seen. The night was over at last, and the nightmare too.

No, she thought. The nightmare is just beginning.

Waves of shock and nausea rolled through her. The strange numbness that had afflicted her mind all through the night was beginning to lift. After hours of mental dissociation, she was starting to comprehend the patterns of things again, to put one event and another and another together and understand their meaning. She thought of the campus in ruins, and the flames rising above the distant city. The wandering madmen everywhere, the chaos, the devastation.

Balik. The ugly grin on his face as he tried to paw her. And the look of amazement on it when she had hit him.

I've killed a man today, Siferra thought in astonishment and dismay. *Me. How could I ever have done a thing like that?*

She began to tremble. The horrifying memory seared her mind: the sound the club had made when she hit him, the way Balik had staggered backward, the other blows, the blood, the twisted angle of his head. The man with whom she had worked for a year and a half, patiently digging out the ruins at Beklimot, falling like a slaughtered beast under her deadly bludgeoning. And her utter calmness as she stood over him afterward—her satisfaction at having prevented him from annoying her any more. That was perhaps the ghastliest part of it all.

Then Siferra told herself that what she had killed hadn't been Balik, but only a madman inside Balik's body, wild-eyed and drooling as he clawed and fondled her. Nor had she really

226

been Siferra when she wielded that club, but a ghost-Siferra, a dream-Siferra, sleepwalking through the horrors of the dawn.

Now, though, sanity was returning. Now the full impact of the night's events was coming home to her. Not just Balik's death—she would not let herself feel guilt for that—but the death of an entire civilization.

She heard voices in the distance, back in the direction of the campus. Thick, bestial voices, the voices of those whose minds had been destroyed by the Stars and would never again be whole. She searched for her club. Had she lost that too, in her frenzied flight through the arboretum? No. No, here it was. Siferra grasped it and rose to her feet.

The forest seemed to beckon to her. She turned and fled into its cool dark groves.

And went on running as long as her strength held out.

What else was there to do but go on running? Running. Running.

[31]

It was late afternoon, the third day since the eclipse. Beenay came limping down the quiet country road that led to the Sanctuary, moving slowly and carefully, looking about him in all directions. There were three suns shining in the sky, and the Stars had long since returned to their age-old obscurity. But the world had irrevocably changed in those three days. And so had Beenay.

This was the young astronomer's first full day of restored reasoning power. What he had been doing for the two previous days he had no clear idea. The whole period was simply a blur, punctuated by the rising and setting of Onos, with other suns wandering across the sky now and then. If someone had told him that this was the fourth day since the catastrophe, or the fifth or sixth, Beenay would not have been able to disagree.

His back was sore, his left leg was a mass of bruises, and there were blood-encrusted scratches along the side of his face. He hurt everywhere, though the pain of the early hours had

227

given way by now to dull aches of half a dozen different kinds radiating from various parts of his body.

What had been happening? Where had he been?

He remembered the battle in the Observatory. He wished he could forget it. That howling, screaming horde of crazed townspeople breaking down the door—a handful of robed Apostles were with them, but mainly they were just ordinary people, probably good, simple, boring people who had spent their whole lives doing the good, simple, boring things that kept civilization operating. Now, suddenly, civilization had stopped operating and all those pleasant ordinary people had been transformed in the twinkling of an eye into raging beasts.

The moment when they came pouring in—how terrible that had been. Smashing the cameras that had just recorded the priceless data of the eclipse, ripping the tube of the great solar-scope out of the Observatory roof, raising computer terminals high over their heads and dashing them to the floor—

And Athor rising like a demigod above them, ordering them to leave—! One might just as well have ordered the tides of the ocean to turn back.

Beenay remembered imploring Athor to come away with him, to flee while there still might be a chance. "Let go of me, young man!" Athor had roared, hardly seeming even to recognize him. "Get your hands off me, sir!" And then Beenay had realized what he should have seen before: that Athor had gone insane, and that the small part of Athor's mind that was still capable of functioning rationally was eager for death. What was left of Athor had lost all will to survive—to go forth into the dreadful new world of the post-eclipse barbarism. That was the most tragic single thing of all, Beenay thought: the destruction of Athor's will to live, the great astronomer's hopeless surrender in the face of this holocaust of civilization.

And then—the escape from the Observatory. That was the last thing that Beenay remembered with any degree of confidence: looking back at the main Observatory room as Athor disappeared beneath a swarm of rioters, then turning, darting through a side door, scrambling down the fire escape, out the back way into the parking lot—

Where the Stars were waiting for him in all their terrible majesty.

With what he realized later had been sublime innocence, or else self-confidence verging on arrogance, Beenay had totally underestimated their power. In the Observatory at the moment of their emergence he had been too preoccupied with his work to be vulnerable to their force: he had merely noted them as a remarkable occurrence, to be examined in detail when he had a free moment, and then had gone on with what he was doing. But out here, under the merciless vault of the open sky, the Stars had struck him in their fullest might.

He was stunned by the sight of them. The implacable cold light of those thousands of suns descended upon him and knocked him groveling to his knees. He crawled along the ground, choking with fear, sucking in sharp gasps of breath. His hands were shaking feverishly, his heart was palpitating, streams of sweat were running down his burning face. When some shred of the scientist he once had been motivated him to turn his face toward that colossal brilliance overhead, so that he could examine and analyze and record, he was compelled to hide his eyes after only a second or two.

He could remember that much: the struggle to look at the Stars, his failure, his defeat.

After that, everything was murky. A day or two, he guessed, of wandering in the forest. Voices in the distance, cackling laughter, harsh discordant singing. Fires crackling on the horizon; the bitter smell of smoke everywhere. Kneeling to plunge his face in a brook, cool swift water sweeping along his cheek. A pack of small animals surrounding him—not wild ones, Beenay decided afterward, but household pets that had escaped —and baying at him as though they meant to rip him apart.

Pulling berries off a vine. Climbing a tree to strip it of tender golden fruit, and falling off, landing with a disastrous thud. The long hours of pain before he could pick himself up and move onward.

A sudden furious fight in the deepest, darkest part of the woods—fists flailing, elbows jabbing into ribs, wild kicks, then stone-throwing, bestial screeching, a man's face pushed close up against his own, eyes red as flame, fierce wrestling, the two of them rolling over and over—reaching for a massive rock, bringing it down in a single decisive motion—

Hours. Days. A feverish daze.

Then, on the morning of the third day, remembering finally who he was, what had happened. Thinking of Raissta, his contract-mate. Remembering that he had promised to go to her at the Sanctuary when his work at the Observatory was done.

The Sanctuary—now where was that?

Beenay's mind had healed enough for him to recall that the place of refuge that the university people had established for themselves was midway between the campus and Saro City, in an open, rural area of rolling plains and grassy meadows. The Physics Department's old particle accelerator was there, a vast underground chamber, abandoned a few years back when they had built the new research center at Saro Heights. It hadn't been difficult to equip the echoing concrete rooms for short-term occupation by several hundred people, and, since the accelerator site had always been sealed off from easy access for security reasons, it was no problem to make the site safe against any sort of invasion by townsfolk who might be driven insane during the eclipse.

But in order to find the Sanctuary, Beenay first had to find out where *he* was. And he had been wandering randomly in a dismal stupor for at least two days, perhaps more. He could be anywhere.

In the early morning hours he found his way out of the forest, almost by accident, stepping forth unexpectedly into what had once been a neatly laid out residential district. It was deserted now, and in frightening disarray, with cars piled up every which way in the streets where their owners had left them when they no longer were capable of driving, and the occasional body lying in the street under a black cluster of flies. There was no sign that anyone was alive here.

He spent a long morning trudging along a suburban highway lined by blackened, abandoned homes, without recognizing a single familiar landmark. At midday, as Trey and Patru rose into the sky, he entered a house through its open door and helped himself to whatever food he could find that had not spoiled. No water came out of the kitchen tap; but he found a cache of bottled water in the basement and drank as much of that as he could hold. He bathed himself in the rest.

Afterward he proceeded up a winding road to a hilltop cul-de-sac of spacious, imposing dwellings, every one of them burned to a shell. Nothing at all was left of the uppermost house except a hillside patio decorated with pink and blue tiles, no doubt very handsome once, but marred now by thick black lumps of clotted debris scattered along its gleaming surface. With difficulty he made his way out onto it and looked out into the valley beyond.

The air was very still. No planes were aloft, there was no sound of ground traffic, a weird silence resounded from every direction.

Suddenly Beenay knew where he was, and everything fell into place.

The university was visible off to his left, a handsome cluster of brick buildings, many of them now streaked with black smoke-stains and some seeming to be altogether destroyed. Beyond, on its high promontory, was the Observatory. Beenay glanced at it quickly and looked away, glad that at this distance he was unable to make out its condition very clearly.

Far away to his right was Saro City, gleaming in the bright sunlight. To his eyes it seemed almost untouched. But he knew that if he had a pair of field glasses he would surely see shattered windows, fallen buildings, still-glowing embers, rising wisps of smoke, all the scars of the conflagration that had broken out at Nightfall.

Straight below him, between the city and the campus, was the forest in which he had been wandering during the time of his delirium. The Sanctuary would be just on the far side of that; he might well have passed within a few hundred yards of its entrance a day or so ago, all unknowing.

The thought of crossing that forest again did not appeal to him. Surely it was still full of madmen, cutthroats, irate escaped pets, all manner of troublesome things. But from his vantage point on the hilltop he could see the road that cut across the forest, and the pattern of streets that led to the road. Stick to paved routes, he told himself, and you'll be all right.

And so he was. Onos was still in the sky when he completed the traversal of the forest highway and turned onto the small rural road that he knew led to the Sanctuary. Afternoon shadows had barely begun to lengthen when he came to the outer gate. Once past that, Beenay knew, he had to go down a long unpaved road that would take him to the second gate, and thence around a couple of outbuildings to the sunken entrance to the Sanctuary itself.

The outer gate, a high metal-mesh screen, was standing open when he reached it. That was an unexpected and ominous sight. Had the mob come roaring in here too?

But there was no sign of mob destruction. Everything was as it should be, except that the gate was open. He went on in, puzzled, and made his way down the unpaved road.

The inner gate, at least, was closed.

"I am Beenay 25," he said to it, and gave his university identification-code number. Moments passed, and lengthened into minutes, and nothing happened. The green scanner eye overhead seemed to be working—he saw its lens sliding from side to side—but perhaps the computers that operated it had lost their power, or had been smashed altogether. He waited. He waited some more. "I am Beenay 25," he said again, finally, and gave his number a second time. "I am authorized to enter here." Then he remembered that mere name and number were not enough: there was a password to say, also.

But what was it? Panic churned his soul. He couldn't remember. He couldn't remember. How absurd, finally to have found his way here and then be stranded at the outer gate by his own stupidity!

The password—the password—

Something to do with the catastrophe, that was it. "Eclipse?" No, not that. He wracked his aching brain. "Kalgash Two?" Didn't seem right. "Dovim?" "Onos?" "Stars?"

That was closer.

Then it came to him.

"*Nightfall*," he said triumphantly.

Still nothing happened, at least not for a long while.

But then, what seemed like a thousand years later, the gate opened to admit him.

He zigzagged past the outbuildings and confronted the oval metal door of the Sanctuary itself, set at a forty-five-degree angle into the ground. Another green eye studied him here. Did he have to identify himself all over? Evidently he did. "I am Beenay 25," he said, preparing for another long wait.

But the gate began immediately to roll back. He stared down into the Sanctuary's concrete-floored vestibule.

Raissta 717 was waiting for him there, scarcely ten yards away.

"Beenay!" she cried, and came rushing toward him. "Oh, Beenay, Beenay—"

Since they had first become contract-mates, two years earlier, they had never been apart longer than eighteen hours. Now they had been separated for days. He pulled her slim form up against him and held her tight, and it was a long while before he would release her.

Then he realized they were still standing in the open gateway of the Sanctuary.

"Shouldn't we go in and lock the gate behind us?" he asked. "What if I've been followed? I don't think I was, but—"

"It doesn't matter. There's no one else here."

"What?"

"They all went yesterday," she said. "As soon as Onos came up. They wanted me to come too, but I said I was going to wait for you, and I did."

He gaped at her, uncomprehendingly.

He saw now how weary and haggard she looked, how drawn and thin. Her once-lustrous hair was hanging in unkempt strings and her face was pale, unadorned. Her eyes were reddened and puffy. She seemed to have aged five or ten years.

"Raissta, how long has it been since the eclipse?"

"This is the third day."

"Three days. That was more or less what I figured." His voice echoed strangely. He glanced past her, into the deserted Sanctuary. The bare underground chamber stretched on and on, lit by a track of overhead bulbs. He saw no one as far as his eye could reach. He hadn't expected this, not at all. The plan had been for everyone to stay hidden down here until it was safe to emerge. In wonder he said, "Where have they gone?"

"Amgando," Raissta said.

"Amgando National Park? But that's hundreds of miles from here! Were they crazy, coming out of hiding on only the second day and going marching off to some place halfway across the country? Do you have any idea what's going on out there, Raissta?"

Amgando Park was a nature preserve, far to the south, a place where wild animals roamed, where the native plants of

233

the province were jealously protected. Beenay had been there once, when a boy, with his father. It was almost pure wilderness, with a few hiking trails cut into it.

She said, "They thought it would be safer to go there."

"*Safer?*"

"Word came that everyone who was still sane, everybody who wanted to take part in the rebuilding of society, should rendezvous at Amgando. Apparently people are converging on it from all over, thousands of them. From other universities, mostly. And some government people."

"Fine. A whole horde of professors and politicians trampling around in the park. With everything else ruined, why not ruin the last bit of unspoiled territory we have, too?"

"That isn't important, Beenay. The important thing is that Amgando Park is in the hands of sane people, it's an enclave of civilization in the general madness. And they knew about us, they were asking us to come join them. We took a vote, and it was two to one to go."

"Two to one," said Beenay darkly. "Even though you people didn't see the Stars, you managed to go nuts anyway! Imagine leaving the Sanctuary to take a three-hundred-mile stroll—or is it five hundred?—through the utter chaos that's going on. Why not wait a month, or six months, or whatever? You had enough food and water to hold out here for a year."

"We said the same thing," Raissta replied. "But what they told us, the Amgando people, was that the time to come was now. If we waited another few weeks, the roving bands of crazed men out there would coalesce into organized armies under local warlords, and we'd have to deal with them when we came out. And if we waited any longer than a few weeks, the Apostles of Flame would probably have established a repressive new government, with its own police force and army, and we'd be intercepted the moment we stepped outside the Sanctuary. It's now or never, the Amgando people said. Better to have to contend with scattered half-insane free-lance bandits than with organized armies. So we decided to go."

"Everyone but you."

"I wanted to wait for you."

He took her hand. "How did you know I'd come?"

234

"You said you would. As soon as you were finished photographing the eclipse. You always keep your promises, Beenay."

"Yes," Beenay said, in a remote tone of voice. He had not yet recovered from the shock of finding the Sanctuary empty. It had been his hope to rest here, to heal his bruised body, to complete the job of restoring his Stars-shattered mind. What were they supposed to do now, set up housekeeping here by themselves, just the two of them in this echoing concrete vault? Or try to get to Amgando all alone? The decision to vacate the Sanctuary made a sort of crazy sense, Beenay supposed—assuming it made any sense at all for everyone to collect at Amgando, it was probably better to make the journey now, while the countryside was in such a high degree of disorder, than to wait until new political entities, whether Apostles or private regional buccaneers, clamped down on all travel between districts. But he had wanted to find his friends here—to sink down into a community of familiar people until he had recovered from the shock of the past few days. Dully he said, "Do you have any real idea of what's going on out there, Raissta?"

"We got reports by communicator, until the communicator channels broke down. Apparently the city was almost completely destroyed by fire, and the university was badly damaged also—that's all true, isn't it?"

Beenay nodded. "So far as I know, it is. I escaped from the Observatory just as a mob came smashing in. Athor was killed, I'm pretty sure. All the equipment was wrecked—all our observations of the eclipse were ruined—"

"Oh, Beenay, I'm so sorry."

"I managed to get out the back way. The moment I was outside, the Stars hit me like a ton of bricks. Two tons. You can't imagine what it was like, Raissta. I'm *glad* you can't imagine it. I was out of my mind for a couple of days, roaming around in the woods. There's no law left. It's everybody for himself. I may have killed someone in a fight. People's household animals are running wild—the Stars must have made them crazy too—and they're terrifying."

"Beenay, Beenay—"

"All the houses are burned. This morning I came through that fancy neighborhood on the hill just south of the forest—Onos Point, is that what it's called?—and it was unbelievable, the destruction. Not a living soul to be seen. Wrecked cars, bodies in the streets, the houses in ruins—my God, Raissta, what a night of madness! And the madness is still going on!"

"You sound all right," she said. "Shaken, but not—"

"Crazy? But I was. From the moment I first came out under the Stars until I woke up today. Then things finally began to knit back together in my head. But I think it's much worse for most other people. The ones who hadn't the slightest degree of emotional preparation, the ones who simply looked up and—bam!—the suns were gone, the Stars were shining. As your Uncle Sheerin said, there'll be a whole range of responses, from short-term disorientation to total and permanent insanity."

Quietly Raissta said, "Sheerin was with you at the Observatory during the eclipse, wasn't he?"

"Yes."

"And afterward?"

"I don't know. I was busy overseeing the photographing of the eclipse. I don't have any idea what became of him. He didn't seem to be in sight when the mob broke in."

With a faint smile Raissta said, "Perhaps he slipped away in the confusion. Uncle is like that—very quick on his feet, sometimes, when there's trouble. I'd hate to have had anything bad happen to him."

"Raissta, something bad has happened to the whole world. Athor may have had the right idea: better just to let it sweep over you and carry you away. That way you don't have to contend with worldwide insanity and chaos."

"You mustn't say that, Beenay."

"No. No, I mustn't." He came up behind her and lightly stroked her shoulders. Bent forward, softly nuzzled behind her ear. —"Raissta, what are we going to do?"

"I think I can guess," she said.

Despite everything, he laughed. "I mean *afterward*."

"Let's worry about that afterward," she told him.

[32]

Theremon had never been much of an outdoorsman. He thought of himself as a city boy through and through. Grass, trees, fresh air, the open sky—he didn't actually *mind* them, but they held no particular appeal for him. For years his life had shuttled along a fixed urban-based triangular orbit, rigidly following a familiar path bounded at one corner by his little apartment, at another by the *Chronicle* office, by the Six Suns Club at the third.

Now, suddenly, he was a forest-dweller.

The strange thing was that he almost liked it.

What the citizens of Saro City called "the forest" was actually a fair-sized woodsy tract that began just southeast of the city itself and stretched for a dozen miles or so along the south bank of the Seppitan River. There once had been a great deal more of it, a vast wilderness sweeping on a great diagonal across the midsection of the province almost to the sea, but most of it had gone to agriculture, much of the remainder had been cut up into suburban residential districts, and the university had taken a goodly nip some fifty years back for what was then its new campus. Unwilling to have itself engulfed by urban development, the university had then agitated to have what was left set aside as a park preserve. And since the rule in Saro City for many years had been that whatever the university wanted the university usually got, the last strip of the old wilderness was left alone.

That was where Theremon found himself living now.

The first two days had been very bad. His mind was still half fogged by the effects of seeing the Stars, and he was unable to form any clear plan. The main thing was just to stay alive.

The city was on fire—smoke was everywhere, the air was scorching hot, from certain vantage points you could even see the leaping flames dancing along the rooftops—so obviously it wasn't a good idea to try to go back there. In the aftermath of the eclipse, once the chaos within his mind had begun to clear a

237

little, he had simply continued downhill from the campus until he found himself entering the forest.

Many others plainly had done the same thing. Some of them looked like university people, others were probably remnants of the mob that had come out to storm the Observatory on the night of the eclipse, and the rest, Theremon guessed, were suburbanites driven from their homes when the fires began to break out.

Everyone he saw appeared to be at least as unsettled mentally as he was. Most seemed very much worse off—some of them completely unhinged, totally unable to cope.

They had not formed any sort of coherent bands. Mainly they were solitaries, moving on mysterious private tracks through the woods, or else groups of two or three; the biggest aggregation Theremon saw was eight people, who from their appearance and dress seemed all to be members of one family.

It was horrifying to encounter the truly crazy ones: the vacant eyes, the drooling lips, the slack jaws, the smeared clothing. They plodded through the forest glades like the walking dead, talking to themselves, singing, occasionally dropping to their hands and knees to dig up clumps of sod and munch on them. They were everywhere. The place was like one vast insane asylum, Theremon thought. Probably the whole world was.

Those of this sort, the ones who had been most affected by the coming of the Stars, were generally harmless, at least to others. They were too badly deranged to have any interest in being violent, and their bodily coordination was so seriously disrupted that effective violence was impossible for them, anyway.

But there were others who were not quite so mad—who at a glance might seem almost normal—who posed very serious dangers indeed.

These, Theremon quickly realized, fell into two categories. The first consisted of people who bore no one any ill will but who were hysterically obsessed with the possibility that the Darkness and the Stars might return. These were the fire-lighters.

Very likely they were people who had led orderly, settled lives before the catastrophe—family folk, hard workers, pleasant cheerful neighbors. So long as Onos was in the sky they were perfectly calm; but the moment the primary sun began to sink in the west and evening approached, fear of Darkness overcame them, and they looked around desperately for something to burn. Anything. Anything at all. Two or three of the other suns might still be overhead when Onos set, but the light of the minor suns did not seem sufficient to soothe the raging dread of Darkness that these people felt.

These were the ones who had burned their own city down around themselves. Who, in their desperation, had ignited books, papers, furniture, the roofs of houses. Now, driven into the forest by the holocaust in the city, they were trying to burn that down too. But that was a harder job. The forest was densely wooded, lush, its thick cover of trees well supplied by the myriad streams that flowed into the broad river running along its border. Pulling down green boughs and trying to set them afire did not provide very satisfactory blazes. As for the carpet of dead wood and fallen leaves that lay on the forest floor, it had been pretty well soaked by the recent rains. Such of it that was capable of being burned was quickly found and used for bonfires, without touching off any sort of general conflagration; and by the second day the supply of such debris was very sparse.

So the fire-lighter people, hampered as they were by forest conditions and by their own shock-muddled minds, were having little success so far. But they had managed to start a couple of good-sized fires in the forest all the same, which fortunately had burned themselves out in a few hours because they had consumed all the fuel in their vicinity. A few days of hot, dry weather, though, and these people might well be able to set the whole place ablaze, as they had already done in Saro City.

The second group of not-quite-stable people roaming the forest seemed to Theremon to be a more immediate menace. These were the ones who had let all social restraints fall away from them. They were the banditti, the hooligans, the cutthroats, the psychopaths, the homicidal maniacs: the ones who moved like unsheathed blades along the quiet forest pathways, striking whenever they pleased, taking whatever they wanted, killing anyone unlucky enough to arouse their irritation.

Since *everyone* had a certain glazed look in his eyes, some merely from fatigue, others from despondency, and others from madness, you could never be sure, whenever you met someone in the forest, how dangerous he was. There was no way of telling at a quick glance whether the person approaching you was merely one of the distraught or bewildered crazies, and therefore basically harmless, or one of the kind who were full of lethal fury and attacked anyone they encountered, with neither rhyme nor reason behind their deeds.

So you quickly learned to be on your guard against anyone who came prancing and swaggering through the woods. Any stranger at all could be a menace. You might be talking quite amiably with someone, comparing notes on your experiences since the evening of Nightfall, when abruptly he would take offense at some casual remark of yours, or decide that he admired some article of your clothing, or perhaps merely take a blind unreasoning dislike of your face—and, with an animal-like howl, he would come rushing at you in mindless ferocity.

Some of this sort, no doubt, had been criminals to begin with. The sight of society collapsing all around them had freed them of all restraint. But others, Theremon suspected, had been placid enough folk until their minds were shattered by the Stars. Then, suddenly, they found all the inhibitions of civilized life fall away from them. They forgot the rules that made civilized life possible. They were like small children again, asocial, concerned only with their own needs—but they had the strength of adults and the will power of the deeply disturbed.

The thing to do, if you hoped to survive, was to avoid those whom you knew to be lethally crazy, or suspected of it. The thing to pray for was that they would all kill each other off within the first few days, leaving the world safe for the less predatory.

Theremon had three encounters with madmen of this terrifying breed in the first two days. The first one, a tall, rangy man with a weird diabolical grin who was cavorting by the side of a brook that Theremon wanted to cross, demanded that the newspaperman pay him a toll to go past. "Your shoes, let's say. Or how about that wristwatch?"

"How about getting out of my way?" Theremon suggested, and the man went berserk.

Snatching up a cudgel that Theremon hadn't noticed until that moment, he roared some sort of war-cry and charged. There was no time to take evasive action: the best Theremon could do was duck as the other man swung the cudgel with horrific force at his head.

He heard the club go whirring by, missing him by inches. It hit the tree beside him instead, cracking into it with tremendous force—a force so great that the impact of it traveled up the attacker's arm, and he gasped in pain as the cudgel fell from his nerveless fingers.

Theremon was on top of him in an instant, seizing the man's injured arm, bringing it sharply upward with merciless force, making him grunt in agony and double up and fall moaning to his knees. Theremon prodded and pushed him down until his face was in the stream, and held him there. And held him there. And held him there.

How simple it would be, Theremon thought in wonder, just to go on holding his head under water until he drowned.

A part of his mind was actually arguing in favor of it. *He would have killed you without even thinking about it. Get rid of him. Otherwise what will you do once you let go of him? Fight him all over again? What if he follows you through the forest to get even with you? Drown him now, Theremon. Drown him.*

It was a powerful temptation. But only one segment of Theremon's mind was willing to adapt so readily to the world's new jungle morality. The rest of him recoiled at the idea; and finally he released the man's arm and stepped back. He picked up the fallen cudgel and waited.

All the fight was gone from the other man now, though. Choking and gasping, he rose from the stream with water flowing from his mouth and nostrils, and sat trembling by the bank, shivering, coughing, struggling for breath. He stared sullenly and fearfully at Theremon, but he made no attempt to get up, let alone to renew the fighting.

Theremon stepped around him, crossed the stream in a bound, and trotted off quickly, deeper into the forest.

The implications of what he had almost done did not fully strike him for another ten minutes. Then he halted suddenly, in a burst of sweat and nausea, and was swept by a fierce attack

241

of vomiting that racked him so savagely that it was a long while before he could rise.

Later that afternoon he realized that his roamings had brought him right to the border of the forest. When he looked out between the trees he saw a highway—utterly deserted—and, on the far side of the road, the ruins of a tall brick building standing in a broad plaza.

He recognized the building. It was the Pantheon, the Cathedral of All the Gods.

There wasn't much left of it. He walked across the road and stared in disbelief. It looked as if a fire had started in the heart of the building—what had they been doing, using the pews for kindling?—and had swept right up the narrow tower over the altar, igniting the wooden beams. The whole tower had toppled, bringing down the walls. Bricks were strewn everywhere about the plaza. He saw bodies jutting out of the wreckage.

Theremon had never been a particularly religious man. He didn't know anyone who was. Like everyone else, he said things like "My God!" or "Gods!" or "Great gods!" for emphasis, but the idea that there might actually be a god, or gods, or whatever the current prevailing belief-system asserted, had always been irrelevant to the way he lived his life. Religion seemed like something medieval to him, quaint and archaic. Now and then he would find himself in a church to attend the wedding of a friend—who was as much of a disbeliever as he was, of course—or else he went to cover some official rite as a news item—but he hadn't been inside any kind of holy building for religious purposes since his own confirmation, when he was ten years old.

All the same, the sight of the ruined cathedral stirred him profoundly. He had been present at its dedication, a dozen years back, when he was a young reporter. He knew how many millions of credits the building had cost; he had marveled at the splendid works of art it contained; he had been moved by the marvelous music of Ghissimal's *Hymn to the Gods* as it resounded through the great hall. Even he, who had no belief in the sacred, could not help feeling that if there was any place on Kalgash where the gods truly were present, it must be here.

And the gods had let the building be destroyed like this! The gods had sent the Stars, knowing that the madness to follow would wreck even their own Pantheon!

What did that mean? What did that say about the unknowability and unfathomability of the gods—assuming they even existed?

No one would ever rebuild this cathedral, Theremon knew. Nothing would ever be as it was.

"Help me," a voice called.

That feeble sound cut into Theremon's meditations. He looked around.

"Over here. Here."

To his left. Yes. Theremon saw the glint of golden vestments in the sunlight. A man half buried in the rubble, far along down the side of the building—one of the priests, apparently, judging by his rich garb. He was pinned below the waist by a heavy beam and was gesturing with what must be the last of his strength.

Theremon started to go toward him. But before he could take more than a dozen steps a second figure appeared at the far end of the fallen building and came running forward: a lean, agile little man who went scrambling over the bricks with animal swiftness, heading for the trapped priest.

Good, Theremon thought. Together we ought to be able to pull that beam off him.

But when he was still some twenty feet away he halted, horror-stricken. The agile little man had already reached the priest. Bending over him, he had slit the priest's throat with one quick stroke of a small knife, as casually as one might open an envelope; and now he was busily engaged in slicing the cords that fastened the priest's rich vestments.

He looked up, glaring, at Theremon. His eyes were fiery and appalling.

"Mine," he growled, like a jungle beast. "Mine!" And he flourished the knife.

Theremon shivered. For a long moment he stood frozen in his tracks, fascinated in a ghastly way by the efficient manner with which the looter was stripping the dead priest's body. Then, sadly, he turned and hurried away, back across the road, into the forest. There was no point in doing anything else.

That evening, when Tano and Sitha and Dovim held the sky

with their melancholy light, Theremon allowed himself a few hours of fragmentary sleep in a deep thicket; but he awoke again and again, imagining that some madman with a knife was creeping up on him to steal his shoes. Sleep left him long before Onos-rise. It seemed almost surprising to find himself still alive when morning finally came.

Half a day later he had his third encounter with one of the new breed of killers. This time he was crossing a grassy meadow close by one of the arms of the river when he caught sight of two men sitting in a shady patch just across the way, playing some sort of game with dice. They looked calm and peaceful enough. But as Theremon came nearer, he realized that an argument had broken out; and then, unthinkably swiftly, one of the men snatched up a bread-knife sitting on a blanket beside him and plunged it with lethal force into the other man's chest.

The one who had wielded the knife smiled across at Theremon. "He cheated me. You know how it is. It makes you damned angry. I can't stand it when a guy tries to cheat me." It seemed all very clear-cut to him. He grinned and rattled the dice. "Hey, you want to play?"

Theremon stared into the eyes of madness.

"Sorry," he said, as casually as he could. "I'm looking for my girlfriend."

He kept on walking.

"Hey, you can find her later! Come on and play!"

"I think I see her," Theremon called, moving faster, and got out of there without looking back.

After that he was less cavalier about wandering through the forest. He found a sheltered nook in what seemed like a relatively unoccupied glade and built a tidy little nest for himself under a jutting overhang. There was a berry-bush nearby that was heavily laden with edible red fruits, and when he shook the tree just opposite his shelter it showered him with round yellow nuts that contained a tasty dark kernel. He studied the small stream just beyond, wondering if it contained anything edible that he might catch; but there seemed to be nothing in it except tiny minnows, and he realized that even if he could catch them he would have to eat them raw, for he had nothing to use as fuel for a fire and no way of lighting one, besides.

Living on berries and nuts wasn't Theremon's idea of high style, but he could tolerate it for a few days. Already his waistline was shrinking commendably: the only admirable side effect of the whole calamity. Best to stay hidden away back here until things calmed down.

He was pretty sure that things *would* calm down. General sanity was bound to return, sooner or later. Or so he hoped, at least. He knew that he himself had come a long way back from the early moments of chaos that the sight of the Stars had induced in his brain.

Every day that went by, he felt more stable, more capable of coping. It seemed to him that he was almost his old self again, still a little shaky, perhaps, a little jumpy, but that was only to be expected. At least he felt fundamentally sane. He realized that very likely he had had less of a jolt during Nightfall than most people: that he was more resilient, more tough-minded, better able to withstand the fearful impact of that shattering experience. But maybe everybody else would start recovering, too, even those who had been much more deeply affected than he had been, and it would be safe to emerge and see what, if anything, was being done about trying to put the world back together.

The thing to do now, he told himself, was to lay low, to keep from getting yourself murdered by one of those psychopaths running around out there. Let them all do each other in, as fast as they could; and then he would come warily creeping out to find out what was going on. It wasn't a particularly courageous plan. But it seemed like a wise one.

He wondered what had happened to the others who had been in the Observatory with him at the moment of Darkness. To Beenay, to Sheerin, to Athor. To Siferra.

Especially to Siferra.

From time to time Theremon thought of venturing out to look for her. It was an appealing idea. During his long hours of solitude he spun glowing fantasies for himself of what it would be like to hook up with her somewhere in this forest. The two of them, journeying together through this transformed and frightening world, forming an alliance of mutual protection—

He had been attracted to her from the first, of course. For all the good that had done him, he might just as well not have bothered, he knew: handsome as she was, she seemed to be the sort of woman who was absolutely self-contained, in no need whatever of any man's company, or any woman's, for that matter. He had maneuvered her into going out with him now and then, but she had efficiently and serenely kept him at a safe distance all the time.

Theremon was experienced enough in worldly things to understand that no amount of smooth talk was persuasive enough to break through barriers that were so determinedly maintained. He had long ago decided that no worthwhile woman could ever be seduced; you could present the possibility to them, but you had to leave it ultimately to them to do the seducing for you, and if they weren't so minded, there was very little you could do to change their outlook. And with Siferra, things had been sliding in the wrong direction for him all year long. She had turned on him ferociously—and with some justification, he thought ruefully—once he began his misguided campaign of mockery against Athor and the Observatory group.

Somehow right at the end he had felt that she was weakening, that she was becoming interested in him despite herself. Why else had she invited him to the Observatory, against Athor's heated orders, on the evening of the eclipse? For a short time that evening there actually had seemed to be real contact blossoming between them.

But then had come the Darkness, the Stars, the mob, the chaos. After that everything had plunged into confusion. But if he could find her somehow, now—

We'd work well together, he thought. We'd be a tremendous team—hard-nosed, competent, survival-oriented. Whatever kind of civilization is going to evolve, we'd find a good place for ourselves in it.

And if there had been a little psychological barrier between them before, he was certain it would seem unimportant to her now. It was a brand-new world, and new attitudes were necessary if you were going to survive.

But how could he find Siferra? No communications circuits were open, so far as he knew. She was just one of millions of people at large in the area. The forest alone probably had a population of many thousands now; and he had no real reason for assuming that she was in the forest. She could be fifty miles from here by this time. She could be dead. Looking for her was a hopeless task: it was worse than trying to find the proverbial needle in a haystack. This haystack was several counties wide, and the needle might well be getting farther away every hour. Only by the wildest sort of coincidence could he ever locate Siferra, or, for that matter, anyone else he knew.

The more Theremon thought about his chances of finding her, though, the less impossible the task seemed. And after a while it began to seem quite possible indeed.

Perhaps his steadily rising optimism was a by-product of his new secluded life. He had nothing to do but spend hours each day sitting by the brook, watching the minnows go by—and thinking. And as he endlessly reevaluated things, finding Siferra went from seeming impossible to merely unlikely, and from unlikely to difficult, and from difficult to challenging, and from challenging to feasible, and from feasible to readily achievable.

All he had to do, he told himself, was get back out into the forest and recruit a little help from those who were reasonably functional. Tell them who he was trying to find, and what she looked like. Spread the word around. Employ some of his journalistic skills. And make use of his status as a local celebrity. "I'm Theremon 762," he would say. "You know, from the *Chronicle*. Help me and I'll make it worth your while. You want your name in the paper? You want me to make you famous? I can do it. Never mind that the paper isn't being published just now. Sooner or later it'll be back, and I'll be right there with it, and you'll see yourself smack in the middle of the front page. You can count on that. Just help me find this woman that I'm looking for, and—"

"Theremon?"

A familiar voice, high-pitched, cheerful. He stopped short, squinted into the brightness of the midday sunlight cutting through the trees, peered this way and that to locate the speaker.

He had been walking for two hours, looking for people who would be glad to get out there and spread the word on behalf of the famous Theremon 762 of the Saro City *Chronicle*. But so far he had found only six people altogether. Two of them had taken to their heels the moment they saw him. A third sat where he was, singing softly to his bare toes. Another, crouching in the fork of a tree, methodically rubbed two kitchen knives together with maniacal zeal. The remaining two had simply stared at him when he told them what he wanted; one did not seem to understand at all, and the other burst into gales of wild laughter. Not much hope of help from any of them.

And now it appeared that someone had found *him*.

"Theremon? Over here. Over here, Theremon. Here I am. Don't you see me, man? Over here!"

[33]

Theremon glanced to his left, into a clump of bushes with huge prickly parasol-shaped leaves. At first he saw nothing unusual. Then the leaves swayed and parted, and a plump, roundish man stepped out into view.

"Sheerin?" he said, amazed.

"Well, at least you're not so far gone that you've forgotten my name."

The psychologist had lost some weight, and he was incongruously dressed in overalls and a torn pullover. A hatchet with a chipped blade was dangling casually from his left hand. That was perhaps the most incongruous thing of all, Sheerin carrying a hatchet. It wouldn't have been very much stranger to see him walking around with a second head or an extra pair of arms.

Sheerin said, "How are you, Theremon? Great gods, you're all rags and tatters, and it hasn't even been a week! But I suppose I'm not much better." He looked down at himself. "Have you ever seen me this skinny? A diet of leaves and berries really slims you down, doesn't it?"

"You've got a way to go before I'd call you skinny," Theremon said. "But you do look trim. How did you find me?"

"By not looking for you. It's the only way, when everything's become completely random. I've been to the Sanctuary, but no one was there. Now I'm on my way south to Amgando Park. I was just ambling along the path that cuts across the middle of the forest, and there you were." The psychologist came bounding forward, holding out his hand. "By all the gods, Theremon, it's a joy to see a friendly face again! —You are friendly, aren't you? You're not homicidal?"

"I don't think I am."

"There are more crazies per square yard in here than I've ever seen in my life, and I've seen plenty of crazies, let me tell you." Sheerin shook his head and sighed. "Gods! I never dreamed it would be this bad. Even with all my professional experience. I thought it would be bad, yes, very bad, but not *this* bad."

"You predicted universal madness," Theremon reminded him. "I was there. I heard you say it. You predicted the complete breakdown of civilization."

"It's one thing to predict it. It's something else again to be right in the middle of it. It's a very humbling thing, Theremon, for an academic like me to find his abstract theories turning into concrete reality. I was so glib, so blithely unconcerned. 'Tomorrow there won't be a city standing unharmed in all Kalgash,' I said, and it was all just so many words to me, really, just a philosophical exercise, completely abstract. 'The end of the world you used to live in.' Yes. Yes." Sheerin shivered. "And it all happened, just like I said. But I suppose I didn't really believe my own dire predictions, until everything came crashing down around me."

"The Stars," Theremon said. "You never really took the Stars into account. They were the thing that did the real damage. Maybe we could have withstood the Darkness, most of us, just felt a little shaken up, a little bit upset. But the Stars—the Stars—"

"How bad was it for you?"

"Pretty bad, at first. I'm better now. And you?"

"I hid away in the Observatory basement during the worst of it. I was hardly affected at all. When I came out the next day, the whole Observatory was wrecked. You can't imagine the carnage all over the place."

Theremon said, "Damn Folimun! The Apostles—"

"They poured fuel on the fire, yes. But the fire would have happened anyway."

"What about the Observatory people? Athor, Beenay, and the rest? Siferra—"

"I didn't see any of them. But I didn't find their bodies, either, while I was looking around the place. Maybe they escaped. The only person I came across was Yimot—do you remember him? One of the graduate students, the very tall awkward one? He had hidden himself too." Sheerin's face darkened. "We traveled together for a couple of days afterward—until he was killed."

"Killed?"

"By a little girl, ten, twelve years old. With a knife. A very sweet child. Came right up to him, laughed, stabbed him without warning. And ran away, still laughing."

"Gods!"

"The gods aren't listening any more, Theremon. If they ever were."

"I suppose not. —Where have you been living, Sheerin?"

His look was vague. "Here. There. I went back to my apartment first, but the whole building complex had been burned out. Just a shell, nothing salvageable at all. I slept there that evening, right in the middle of the ruins. Yimot was with me. The next day we set out for the Sanctuary, but there wasn't any way of getting there from where we were. The road was blocked—there were fires everywhere. And where it wasn't still burning, there were mountains of rubble that you couldn't get past. It looked like a war zone. So we doubled back south into the forest, figuring we'd circle around by way of Arboretum Road and try to reach the Sanctuary that way. That was when Yimot was—killed. The forest must be where all the most disturbed ones went."

"It's where everyone went," Theremon said. "The forest is harder to set fire to than the city is. —Did I hear you tell me that when you finally did get to the Sanctuary you found it deserted?"

"That's right. I reached it yesterday afternoon, and it was wide open. The outer gate and the inner gate too, and the Sanctuary door itself unlocked. Everyone gone. A note from Beenay was tacked up in front."

"Beenay! Then he made it to the Sanctuary safely!"

"Apparently he did," said Sheerin. "A day or two before I

did, I suppose. What his note said was that everybody had decided to evacuate the Sanctuary and head for Amgando Park, where some people from the southern districts are trying to set up a temporary government. By the time he got to the Sanctuary there was no one there but my niece Raissta, who must have been waiting for him. Now they've gone to Amgando also. And I'm heading there myself. My friend Liliath was in the Sanctuary, you know. I assume she's on her way to Amgando with the others."

"It sounds nutty," Theremon said. "They were as safe in the Sanctuary as they could have been anywhere. Why the deuce would they want to come out into all of this insane chaos and try to march hundreds of miles down to Amgando?"

"I don't know. But they must have had a good reason. In any case, we have no choice, do we, you and I? Everybody who's still sane is gathering there. We can stay here and wait for somebody to slice us up the way that nightmarish little girl did to Yimot—or we can take our chances trying to get to Amgando. Here we're doomed, sooner or later, inevitably. If we can make it to Amgando we'll be all right."

"Have you heard anything about Siferra?" Theremon asked.

"Nothing. Why?"

"I'd like to find her."

"She may have gone to Amgando too. If she met up with Beenay somewhere along the way, he would have told her where everybody is going, and—"

"Do you have any reason to think that might have happened?"

"It's only a guess."

Theremon said, "My guess is that she's still somewhere around here. I want to try to track her down."

"But the odds against that—"

"You found *me*, didn't you?"

"Purely by accident. The chances that you'd be able to locate her the same way—"

"Are pretty good," Theremon said. "Or so I prefer to believe. I'm going to attempt it, anyway. I can always hope to get to Amgando later on. *With* Siferra."

Sheerin gave him an odd look, but said nothing.

Theremon said, "You think I'm crazy? Well, maybe I am."

"I didn't say that. But I think you're risking your neck for nothing. This place is turning into a prehistoric jungle. It's become absolute savagery here, and not getting any better as the days go along, from what I've seen. Come south with me, Theremon. We can be out of here in two or three hours, and the road to Amgando is just—"

"I mean to look for Siferra first," said Theremon obstinately.

"Forget her."

"I don't intend to do that. I'm going to stay here and search for her."

Sheerin shrugged. "Stay, then. I'm clearing out. I saw Yimot cut down by a little girl, remember, right before my eyes, no more than two hundred yards from here. This place is too dangerous for me."

"And you think going on a hike of three or four hundred miles all by yourself isn't dangerous?"

The psychologist hefted his hatchet. "I've got this, if I need it."

Theremon fought back laughter. Sheerin was so absurdly mild-mannered that the thought of him defending himself with a hatchet was impossible to take seriously.

He said, after a moment, "Lots of luck."

"You really intend to stay?"

"Until I find Siferra."

Sheerin stared sadly at him.

"Keep the luck you just offered me, then. I think you'll need it more than I will."

He turned and trudged away without another word.

[34]

For three days—or perhaps it was four; the time went by like a blur—Siferra moved southward through the forest. She had no plan except to stay alive.

There was no point even in trying to get back to her apartment. The city still seemed to be burning. A low curtain of smoke hung in the air wherever she looked, and occasionally she saw a sinuous tongue of red flame licking into the sky on

252

the horizon. It appeared to her as if new fires were being started every day. Which meant that the craziness had not yet begun to abate.

She could feel her own mind returning gradually to normal, clearing day by day, blessedly emerging into clarity as though she were awakening from some terrible fever. She was uncomfortably aware that she wasn't fully herself yet—managing any sequence of thoughts was a laborious thing for her, and she lost herself quickly in muddle. But she was on her way back, of that she was sure.

Apparently many of the others around her in the forest weren't recovering at all. Though Siferra was trying to keep to herself as much as she could, she encountered people from time to time, and most of them looked pretty badly deranged: sobbing, moaning, laughing wildly, glaring weirdly, rolling over and over on the ground. Just as Sheerin had suggested, some had suffered such mental trauma during the time of the crisis that they might never be sane again. Huge segments of the population must have lapsed into barbarism or worse, Siferra realized. They must be setting fires for the sheer fun of it now. Or killing for the same reason.

So she moved carefully. With no particular destination in mind, she drifted more or less southward across the forest, camping wherever she found fresh water. The club that she had picked up on the evening of the eclipse was never very far from her hand. She ate whatever she could find that looked edible—seeds, nuts, fruits, even leaves and bark. It wasn't much of a diet. She knew that she was strong enough physically to endure a week or so on such improvised rations, but after that she'd begin to suffer. Already she could feel what little extra weight she had been carrying dropping away, and her physical resilience beginning little by little to diminish. And the supply of berries and fruits was diminishing too, very rapidly, as the forest's thousands of hungry new inhabitants picked it over.

Then, on what she believed was the fourth day, Siferra remembered about the Sanctuary.

Her cheeks flamed as she realized that there had been no need for her to have been living this cave-woman life all week.

Of course! How could she have been so stupid? Just a few miles from here at this very moment, hundreds of university people were tucked away safe and sound in the old particle-accelerator lab, drinking bottled water and dining pleasantly on the canned foods that they had spent the last few months stashing away. How ridiculous to be skulking around in this forest full of madmen, scratching in the dirt for her meager meals and looking hungrily at the little forest creatures that cavorted beyond her reach on the branches of the trees!

She would go to the Sanctuary. Somehow there would be a way to get them to take her in. It was a measure of the extent to which the Stars had disrupted her mind, she told herself, that it had taken her as long as this to remember that the Sanctuary was there.

Too bad, she thought, that the idea hadn't occurred to her earlier. She realized now that she had spent the last few days traveling in precisely the wrong direction.

Directly ahead of her now lay the steep chain of hills that marked the southern boundary of the forest. Looking up, she could see the blackened remains of the posh Onos Heights real estate development along the summit of the hill that rose like a dark wall before her. The Sanctuary, if she remembered correctly, was the opposite way entirely, midway between the campus and Saro City on the highway running along the north side of the forest.

It took her another day and a half to make her way back through the forest to the north side. In the course of the journey she had to use her club twice to fight off attackers. She had three non-violent but edgy staring-matches with young men sizing her up to decide whether she could be jumped. And once she blundered into a sheltered copse where five gaunt wild-eyed men with knives were stalking one another in a circle, like dancers moving in some strange archaic ritual. She got away from there as fast as she could.

Finally she saw the wide highway that was University Road ahead of her, just beyond the forest boundary. Somewhere along the north side of that road was the unobtrusive little country lane that led to the Sanctuary.

Yes: there it was. Hidden, insignificant, bordered on both sides by untidy clumps of weeds and thick grass that had gone to seed.

It was late afternoon. Onos was almost gone from the sky,

and the hard baleful light of Tano and Sitha cast sharp shadows across the land that gave the day a wintry look, though the air was mild. The little red eye that was Dovim moved through the northern heavens, still very distant, still very high.

Siferra wondered what had become of the unseeable Kalgash Two. Evidently it had done its terrible work and moved on. By this time it might be a million miles out in space, curving away from the world on its long orbit, riding on and on through the airless dark, not to return for another two thousand and forty-nine years. Which would be at least two million years too soon, thought Siferra bitterly.

A sign appeared before her:

PRIVATE PROPERTY
NO TRESPASSING
BY ORDER OF BOARD OF PROCTORS,
SARO UNIVERSITY

And then a second sign, in vivid scarlet:

!!! DANGER !!!
HIGH ENERGY RESEARCH FACILITY
NO ENTRY

Good. She must be going the right way, then.

Siferra had never been to the Sanctuary, even in the days when it had still been a physics laboratory, but she knew what to expect: a series of gates, and then some sort of scanner post that would monitor anyone who had managed to get this far. Within minutes she had come to the first gate. It was a double-hinged screen of tightly woven metal mesh, rising to perhaps twice her height, with a formidable-looking barbed-wire fence stretching off at either end and disappearing into the brambled underbrush that grew uncontrolledly here.

The gate was ajar.

She studied it, puzzled. Some illusion? Some trick of her muddled mind? No. No, the gate was open, all right. And it was the correct gate. She saw the University Security symbol on it. But why was it open? There was no indication that it had been forced.

Troubled now, she went through.

The road inward was nothing more than a dirt track, deeply

rutted and cratered. She followed along its edge, and in a little while she saw an inner barrier, no mere barbed-wire fence here but a solid concrete wall, blank, impregnable-looking.

It was broken only by a gateway of dark metal, with a scanner mounted above it.

And this gate was open too.

Stranger and stranger! What about all the vaunted protection that was supposed to have sealed the Sanctuary away from the general madness that had overtaken the world?

She stepped inside. Everything was very quiet here. Ahead of her lay some scruffy-looking wooden sheds and barns. Perhaps the Sanctuary entrance itself—the mouth of an underground tunnel, Siferra knew—lay behind them. She walked around the outbuildings.

Yes, there was the Sanctuary entrance, an oval door in the ground, with a dark passageway behind it.

And there were people, too, a dozen or so of them, standing in front of it, watching her with chilly, unpleasant curiosity. They all had strips of bright green cloth tied about their throats, as a kind of neckerchief. She didn't recognize any of them. So far as she could tell, they weren't university people.

A small bonfire was burning just to the left of the door. Beside it was a pile of chopped logs, elaborately stacked, every piece of wood very neatly arranged according to size with astonishing precision and care. It looked more like some sort of meticulous architect's model than like a woodpile.

A sickening sense of fear and disorientation swept over her. What was this place? Was it really the Sanctuary? Who were these people?

"Stay right where you are," said the man at the front of the group. He spoke quietly, but there was whip-snapping authority in his tone. "Put your hands in the air."

He held a small sleek needle-gun in his hand. It was pointing straight at her midsection.

Siferra obeyed without a word.

He appeared to be about fifty years old, a strong, commanding figure, almost certainly the leader here. His clothing looked costly and his manner was poised and confident. The green neckerchief he wore had the sheen of fine silk.

"Who are you?" he asked calmly, keeping the weapon trained on her.

"Siferra 89, Professor of Archaeology, Saro University."

"That's nice. Are you planning to do any archaeology around here, Professor?"

The others laughed as though he had said something very, very funny.

Siferra said, "I'm trying to find the university Sanctuary. Can you tell me where it is?"

"I think this might have been it," the man replied. "The university people all cleared out of here a few days back. This is Fire Patrol headquarters now. —Tell me, are you carrying any combustibles, Professor?"

"Combustibles?"

"Matches, lighter, a pocket generator, anything that could be used to start a fire."

She shook her head. "Not any of those things."

"Fire-starting's prohibited under Article One of the Emergency Code. If you're in violation of Article One the punishment is severe."

Siferra stared at him blankly. What was he talking about?

A thin, sallow-faced man standing beside the leader said, "I don't trust her, Altinol. It was those professors that started all this. Two to one she's got something hidden away in her clothes, out of sight somewhere."

"I have no fire-making equipment anywhere on me," Siferra said, irritated.

Altinol nodded. "Perhaps. Perhaps not. We won't take the chance, Professor. Strip."

She stared at him, startled. "What did you say?"

"Strip. Remove your clothes. Demonstrate that you have no concealed illegal devices anywhere on your person."

Siferra hefted her club, rubbing her hand uneasily along its shaft. Blinking in astonishment, she said, "Hold on, here. You can't be serious."

"Article Two of the Emergency Code, Fire Patrol may take any precaution deemed necessary to prevent unauthorized fire-starting. Article Three, this may include immediate and summary execution of those who resist Fire Patrol authority. Strip, Professor, and do it quickly."

He gestured with the needle-gun. It was a very serious-looking gesture.

But still she stared at him, still she made no move to remove her garments. "Who are you? What's this Fire Patrol stuff all about?"

"Citizen vigilantes, Professor. We're attempting to restore law and order in Saro after the Breakdown. The city's been pretty much destroyed, you know. Or maybe you don't. The fires are continuing to spread, and there's no functioning fire department to do anything about it any more. And maybe you haven't noticed, but the whole province is full of crazy people who think we haven't quite had enough fires yet as it is, so they're starting even more. That can't go on. We intend to stop the starters by any means available. You are under suspicion of possessing combustibles. The accusation has been placed and you have sixty seconds to clear yourself of the charge. If I were you, I'd start getting my clothes off, Professor."

Siferra could see him silently counting off the seconds.

Strip, in front of a dozen strangers? A red haze of fury surged through her at the thought of the indignity. Most of these people were men. They weren't even bothering to hide their impatience. This wasn't any sort of security precaution, despite Altinol's solemn citing of an Emergency Code. They just wanted to see what her body looked like, and they had the power to make her submit. It was intolerable.

But then, after a moment, she found her indignation beginning to slip away.

What did it matter? Siferra asked herself wearily. The world had ended. Modesty was a luxury that only civilized people indulged in, and civilization was an obsolete concept.

In any case this was a blunt order, at gunpoint. She had wandered into a remote, isolated place far down a country road. No one was going to come to her rescue here. The clock was ticking. And Altinol didn't seem to be bluffing.

It wasn't worth dying just for the sake of concealing her body from them.

She tossed her club to the ground.

Then, in cold anger but without permitting herself to make any outward show of rage, she began methodically to peel away her garments and drop them down beside it.

"My underwear too?" she asked sardonically.

"Everything."

"Does it look as if I've got a lighter hidden in here?"

"You've got twenty seconds left, Professor."

Siferra glowered at him and finished undressing without another word.

It was surprisingly easy, now that she had done it, to stand naked in front of these strangers. She didn't care. That was the essential thing that came with the end of the world, she realized. *She didn't care.* She pulled herself up to her full imposing height and stood there, almost defiantly revealed, waiting to see what they'd do next. Altinol's eyes traveled over her body in an easy, self-assured way. Somehow she found herself not even caring about that. A kind of burned-out indifference had come over her.

"Very nice, Professor," he said finally.

"Thank you." Her tone was icy. "May I cover myself now?"

He waved grandly. "Of course. Sorry for the inconvenience. But we had to be absolutely sure." He slipped the needle-gun into a band at his waist and stood with his arms folded, casually watching her as she dressed. Then he said, "You must think you've fallen in among savages, isn't that so, Professor?"

"Does what I think really interest you?"

"You'll notice that we didn't leer or drool or wet our clothes while you were—ah—demonstrating that you had no concealed fire-making apparatus. Nor did anyone attempt to molest you in any way."

"That was extremely kind."

Altinol said, "I point these things out, even though I realize it's not likely to make much difference to you while you're still this angry at us, because I want you to know that what you've stumbled across here may in fact be the last remaining bastion of civilization in this godforsaken world. I don't know where our beloved governmental leaders have disappeared to, and I certainly don't consider our cherished brethren of the Apostles of Flame to be in any way civilized, and your university friends who used to be hidden out here have picked up and gone away. Just about everybody else seems to be clear out of his mind. Except, that is, for you and us, Professor."

"How flattering of you to include me."

"I never flatter anybody. You give an appearance of having withstood the Darkness and the Stars and the Breakdown better than most. What I want to know is whether you're interested in staying here and becoming part of our group. We need people like you, Professor."

"What does that mean? Scrub floors for you? Cook soup?"

Altinol seemed impervious to her sarcasms. "I mean helping in the struggle to keep civilization alive, Professor. Not to sound too high-pitched about it, but we see ourselves as having a holy mission. Day after day we are making our way through that madhouse out there, disarming the crazies, taking the fire-making apparatus away from them, reserving to ourselves exclusively the right to light fires. We can't put out the fires that are already burning, at least not yet, but we can do our best to keep new ones from being lit. That's our mission, Professor. We are taking control of the concept of fire. It's the first step toward making the world fit to live in again. You seem sane enough to join us and therefore I invite you in. What do you say, Professor? Do you want to be part of the Fire Patrol? Or would you rather try your luck back there in the forest?"

[35]

The morning was misty and cool. Thick swirls of fog blew through the ruined streets, fog so heavy that Sheerin was unable to tell which suns were in the sky. Onos, certainly—somewhere. But its golden light was diffused and almost completely concealed by the fog. And that patch of slightly brighter sky off to the southwest very likely indicated the presence of one of the pairs of twin suns, but whether they were Sitha and Tano or Patru and Trey he had no way of discerning.

He was very tired. It was already abundantly clear to him that his notion of making his way alone and on foot across the hundreds of miles between Saro City and Amgando National Park was an absurd fantasy.

Damn Theremon! Together, at least, they might have stood a chance. But the newspaperman had been unshakable in his confidence that he would somehow find Siferra in the forest. Talk about fantasy! Talk about absurdity!

Sheerin stared ahead, peering through the fog. He needed a place to rest for a while. He needed to find something fit to eat, and perhaps a change of clothing, or at least a way of bathing himself. He had never been this filthy in his life. Or as hungry. Or as weary. Or as despondent.

Through the whole long episode of the coming of the Darkness, from the first moment that he had heard from Beenay and Athor that such a thing was likely, Sheerin had bounced around from one end of the psychological spectrum to the other, from pessimism to optimism and back again, from hope to despair to hope. His intelligence and experience told him one thing, his naturally resilient personality told him another.

Perhaps Beenay and Athor were wrong and the astronomical cataclysm wouldn't happen at all.

No, the cataclysm will definitely happen.

Darkness, despite his own disturbing experiences with it at the Tunnel of Mystery two years before, would turn out not to be such a troublesome thing after all, if indeed it did come.

Wrong. Darkness will cause universal madness.

The madness would be only temporary, a brief period of disorientation.

The madness will be permanent, in most people.

The world would be disrupted for a few hours and then go back to normal.

The world will be destroyed in the chaos following the eclipse.

Back and forth, back and forth, up and down, up and down. Twin Sheerins, locked in endless debate.

But now he had hit the bottom of the cycle and he seemed to be staying there, unmoving and miserable. His resilience and optimism had evaporated in the glare of what he had seen during his wanderings these past few days. It would be decades, possibly even a century or more, before things returned to normal. The mental trauma had scored too deep a scar, the destruction that had already occurred to the fabric of society was too widespread. The world he had loved had been vanquished by Darkness and smashed beyond repair. That was his professional opinion and he could see no reason to doubt it.

This was the third day, now, since Sheerin had parted from

Theremon in the forest and gone marching off, in his usual jaunty fashion, toward Amgando. That jauntiness was hard to recapture now. He had managed to get out of the forest in one piece—there had been a couple of bad moments, times when he had had to wave his hatchet around and look menacing and lethal, a total bluff on his part, but it had worked—and for the last day or so he had been moving in a plodding way through the once-pleasant southern suburbs.

Everything was burned out around here. Entire neighborhoods had been destroyed and abandoned. Many of the buildings were still smoldering.

The main highway running to the southern provinces, Sheerin had believed, began just a few miles below the park—a couple of minutes' drive, if you were driving. But he wasn't driving. He had had to make the horrendous climb up out of the forest to the imposing hill that was Onos Heights practically on hands and knees, clawing his way through the underbrush. It took him half a day just to ascend those few hundred yards.

Once he was on top, Sheerin saw that the hill was more like a plateau—but it stretched on endlessly before him, and though he walked and walked and walked he did not come to the highway.

Was he going the right way?

Yes. Yes, from time to time he saw a road sign at a street corner that told him he was indeed heading toward the Great Southern Highway. How far was it, though? The signs didn't say. Every ten or twelve blocks there was another sign, that was all. He kept going. He had no choice.

But reaching the highway was only the first step in getting to Amgando. He would still be in Saro City, essentially, at that point. Then what? Keep on walking? What else? He could hardly hitch a ride with someone. No vehicles seemed to be running anywhere. The public fuel stations must have gone dry days ago, those that had not been burned. How long was it likely to take him, at this pace, to get down to Amgando on foot? Weeks? Months? No—it would take him forever. He'd be dead of starvation long before he came anywhere near the place.

Even so, he had to go on. Without a sense of purpose, he was finished right now, and he knew it.

Something like a week had passed since the eclipse, maybe more. He was beginning to lose track of time. He neither ate regularly nor slept regularly any more, and Sheerin had always been a man of the most punctual habits. Suns came and went in the sky, now, the light brightened or dimmed, the air grew warmer or grew cooler, and time passed: but without the progression of breakfast, lunch, dinner, sleep, Sheerin had no idea of *how* it was passing. He knew only that he was rapidly running out of strength.

He hadn't eaten properly since the coming of the Nightfall. From that dark moment onward, it had been scraps and shards for him, nothing more—a bit of fruit from some tree when he could find it, any unripe seeds that didn't look as though they'd be poisonous, blades of grass, anything. It wasn't making him sick, somehow, but it wasn't sustaining him very well, either. The nutritional content must have been close to zero. His clothes, worn and tattered, hung from him like a shroud. He didn't dare look underneath them. He imagined that his skin must lie now in loose folds over his jutting bones. His throat was dry all the time, his tongue seemed swollen, there was a frightful pounding behind his eyes. And that dull, numb, hollow sensation in his gut, all the time.

Well, he told himself in his more cheerful moments, there must have been some reason why he had devoted himself so assiduously for so many years to building up such an opulent layer of fat, and now he was learning what that reason was.

But his cheerful moments were fewer and farther between every day. Hunger was preying on his spirits. And he realized that he couldn't hold out much longer like this. His body was big; it was accustomed to regular feedings, and robust ones; he could live only so long on his accumulated backlog of Sheerin, and then he would be too weak to pull himself onward. Before long it would seem simpler just to curl up behind some bush and rest . . . and rest . . . and rest. . . .

He had to find food. Soon.

The neighborhood he was moving through now, though deserted like all the rest, seemed a little less devastated than the areas behind him. There had been fires here too, but not everywhere, and the flames appeared to have jumped randomly past this house and that without harming them. Patiently Sheerin went from one to the next, trying the door of each house that didn't seem to have been seriously damaged.

Locked. Every one of them.

How fastidious of these people! he thought. How tidy! The world has fallen in around their ears, and they are abandoning their homes in blind terror, running off to the forest, the campus, the city, the gods only knew where—and they take the trouble to lock their houses before they go! As if they mean simply to have a brief holiday during the time of chaos, and then go home to their books and their bric-a-brac, their closets full of nice clothing, their gardens, their patios. Or hadn't they realized that everything was over, that the chaos was going to go on and on and on?

Perhaps, Sheerin thought dismally, they aren't gone at all. They're in there hiding behind those locked doors of theirs, huddling in the basement the way I did, waiting for things to get normal again. Or else staring at me from the upstairs windows, hoping I'll go away.

He tried another door. Another. Another. All locked. No response.

"Hey! Anybody home? Let me in!"

Silence.

He stared bleakly at the thick wooden door in front of him. He envisioned the treasures behind it, the food not yet spoiled and waiting to be eaten, the bathtub, the soft bed. And here he was outside, with no way of getting in. He felt a little like the small boy in the fable who has been given the magic key to the garden of the gods, where fountains of honey flow and gumdrops grow on every bush, but who is too small to reach up and put it in the keyhole. He felt like crying.

He realized, then, that he was carrying a hatchet. And he began to laugh. Hunger must have been making him simpleminded! The little boy in the fable perseveres, offering his mittens and his boots and his velvet cap to various animals who are passing by so that they will help him: each one gets on another one's back, and he climbs on the top of the heap and puts the key in the keyhole. And here was not-so-little Sheerin, staring at a locked door, and he was holding a hatchet!

Break the door down? Just break it down?

It went against everything that he thought was right and proper.

Sheerin looked at the hatchet as though it had turned to a serpent in his hand. Breaking in—why, that was burglary! How could he, Sheerin 501, Professor of Psychology at Saro University, simply smash down the door of some law-abiding citizen's house and casually help himself to whatever he found there?

Easily, he told himself, laughing even harder at his own foolishness. This is how you do it.

He swung the hatchet.

But it wasn't all that easy. His starvation-weakened muscles rebelled at the effort. He could lift the hatchet, all right, and he could swing it, but the blow seemed pathetically weak, and a line of fire shot through his arms and back as the blade made contact with the stout wooden door. Had he split the door? No. Cracked it a little? Maybe. Maybe a little chip. He swung again. Again. Harder. There you go, Sheerin. You're getting the hang of it now. Swing! Swing!

He scarcely felt the pain, after the first few swings. He closed his eyes, pulled breath deep into his lungs, and swung. And swung again. The door was cracking now. There was a perceptible crevice. Another swing—another—maybe five or six more good blows and it would break in half—

Food. Bath. Bed.

Swing. And *swing.* And—

And the door opened in his face. He was so astonished that he nearly fell through. He staggered and lurched, braced himself with the haft of the ax against the door-frame, and looked up.

Half a dozen fierce wild-eyed faces looked back at him.

"You knocked, sir?" a man said, and everyone howled in manic glee.

Then they reached out for him, caught him by his arms, pulled him inside.

"You won't be needing this," someone said, and effortlessly twisted the hatchet from Sheerin's grasp. "You can only hurt yourself with a thing like that, don't you know?"

More laughter—a crazed howling. They pushed him into the center of the room and formed a ring around him.

There were seven, eight, maybe nine of them. Men and women both, and one half-grown boy. Sheerin could see at a glance that they weren't the rightful residents of this house, which must have been neat and well maintained before they moved into it. Now there were stains on the wall, half the furniture was overturned, there was a sodden puddle of something—wine?—on the carpet.

He knew what these people were. These were squatters, rough and ragged-looking, unshaven, unwashed. They had come drifting in, had taken possession of the place after its owners fled. One of the men was wearing only a shirt. One of the women, hardly more than a girl, was clad just in a pair of shorts. They all had an acrid, repellent odor. Their eyes had that intense, rigid, off-center look that he had seen a thousand times in recent days. You didn't need any clinical experience to know that those were the eyes of the insane.

Cutting through the stink of the squatters' bodies, though, was another odor, a much more pleasing one, one that almost drove Sheerin out of his mind too: the aroma of cooking food. They were preparing a meal in the next room. Soup? Stew? Something was boiling in there. He swayed, dizzied by his own hunger and the sudden hope of soothing it at last.

Mildly he said, "I didn't know the house was occupied. But I hope you'll let me stay with you this evening, and then I'll be moving along."

"You from the Patrol?" a big, heavily bearded man asked suspiciously. He seemed to be the leader.

Sheerin said uncertainly, "The Patrol? No, I don't know anything about them. My name is Sheerin 501, and I'm a member of the faculty of—"

"Patrol! Patrol! Patrol!" they were chanting suddenly, moving in a circle around him.

"—Saro University," he finished.

It was as though he had uttered a magic spell. They halted in their tracks as his quiet voice cut through their shrill screaming, and they fell silent, staring at him in a terrifying way.

"You say you're from the university?" the leader asked in a strange tone.

"That's right. Department of Psychology. I'm a teacher and I do a little hospital work on the side. —Look, I don't intend to make any trouble for you at all. I just need a place to rest for a few hours, and a little food, if you can spare it. Just a little. I haven't eaten since—"

"*University!*" a woman cried. The way she said it, it sounded like something filthy, something blasphemous. Sheerin had heard that tone before, from Folimun 66 the night of the eclipse, referring to scientists. It was a frightening thing to hear.

"*University! University! University!*"

They began to circle around him again, chanting again, pointing at him, making bizarre signs with their hooked fingers. He could no longer understand their words. It was a raucous nightmare chant, nonsense syllables.

Were these people some subchapter of the Apostles of Flame, convening here to practice an arcane rite? No, he doubted that. They had a different look, too ragged, too shabby, too demented. The Apostles, such few of them as he had seen, had always appeared crisp, self-contained, almost frighteningly controlled. Besides, the Apostles hadn't been in evidence since the eclipse. Sheerin supposed that they had all withdrawn to some sanctuary of their own to enjoy the vindication of their beliefs in private.

These people, he thought, were simply unaffiliated wandering crazies.

And it seemed to Sheerin that he saw murder in their eyes.

"Listen," he said, "if I've disturbed some ceremony of yours in any way, I apologize, and I'm perfectly willing to leave right now. I only tried to come in here because I thought the house was empty and I was so hungry. I didn't mean to—"

"*University! University!*"

He had never seen a look of such intense hatred as these people were giving him. But there was fear there too. They kept back from him, tense, trembling, as if in dread of some terrible power that he might unexpectedly unleash.

Sheerin held his hands out to them imploringly. If only they'd stop prancing and chanting for a moment! The smell of the food cooking in the next room was making him wild. He caught one of the women by the arm, hoping to halt her long

267

enough to appeal to her for a crust, a bowl of broth, anything. But she jumped away, hissing as though Sheerin had burned her with his touch, and rubbed frantically at the place on her arm where his fingers had briefly rested.

"Please," he said. "I don't intend any harm. I'm as harmless as anyone there is, believe me."

"Harmless!" the leader cried, spitting the word out. "You? You, university? You're worse than the Patrol. The Patrol just makes a little trouble for people. But you, you destroyed the world."

"I *what?*"

"Be careful, Tasibar," a woman said. "Get him out of here before he makes a magic on us."

"A magic?" Sheerin said. "Me?"

They were pointing at him again, stabbing the air vehemently, terrifyingly. Some had begun to chant under their breaths, a low, fierce chant that had the rhythms of a motor steadily gaining speed and soon to spin out of control.

The girl who wore only a pair of shorts said, "It was the university that called down the Darkness on us."

"And the Stars," said the man who wore just a shirt. "They brought the Stars."

"And this one might bring them back," said the woman who had spoken before. "Get him out of here! Get him out of here!"

Sheerin stared incredulously. He told himself that he should have been able to predict this. It was an all too likely development: pathological suspicion of all scientists, all educated people, an unreasoning phobia that must be raging now like a virus among the survivors of the night of terror.

"Do you think I can bring back the Stars with a snap of my fingers? Is that what's frightening you?"

"You are university," the man called Tasibar said. "You knew the secrets. University brought the Darkness, yes. University brought the Stars. University brought *doom.*"

It was too much.

Bad enough to be dragged in here and forced to inhale the maddening flavor of that food without being allowed to have any of it. But to be blamed for the catastrophe—to be looked upon as some sort of malevolent witch by these people—

Something snapped in Sheerin.

Derisively he cried, "Is that what you believe? You idiots! You deranged superstitious fools! Blaming the university? *We* brought the Darkness? By all the gods, what stupidity! We were the very ones who tried to warn you!"

He gestured angrily, clenching his fists, clashing them furiously together.

"He's going to bring them again, Tasibar! He'll make it go dark on us! Stop him! Stop him!"

Suddenly they were clustering all about him, closing in, reaching for him.

Sheerin, standing in their midst, held out his hands helplessly, apologetically, toward them and did not try to move. He regretted having insulted them just now, not because it had endangered his life—they probably hadn't even paid attention to the names he was calling them—but because he knew that the way they were was not their fault. If anything it was *his* fault, for not having tried harder to help them protect themselves against what he knew was coming. Those articles of Theremon's—if only he had spoken with the newspaperman, if only he had urged him in time to change his mocking tack—

Yes, he regretted that now.

He regretted all sorts of things, things both done and undone. But it was much too late.

Someone punched him. He gasped in surprise and pain.

"Liliath—" he managed to cry.

Then they swarmed all over him.

[36]

There were four suns in the sky: Onos, Dovim, Patru, Trey. Four-sun days were supposed to be lucky ones, Theremon remembered. And certainly this one was.

Meat! Actual meat at last!

What a glorious sight!

It was food that he had obtained strictly by accident. But that was all right. The novel charms of outdoor life had been wearing thinner and thinner for him, the hungrier he got. By now

269

he'd gladly take his meat any way it came, thank you very much.

The forest was full of all sorts of wild animals, most of them small, very few of them dangerous, and all of them impossible to catch—at least with your bare hands. And Theremon knew nothing about making traps, nor did he have anything out of which he might have fashioned one.

Those children's tales about people lost in the woods who immediately set about adapting to life in the open, and turn instantly into capable hunters and builders of dwelling-places, were just that—fables. Theremon regarded himself as a reasonably competent man, as city-dwellers went; but he knew that he had no more chance of hunting down any of the forest animals than he did of making the municipal power generators start to work again. And as for building a dwelling-place, the best he had been able to do was throw together a simple lean-to of branches and twigs, which at least had kept most of the rain away from him on the one stormy day.

But now the weather was warm and lovely again, and he had actual meat for dinner. The only problem now was cooking it. He was damned if he was going to eat it raw.

Ironic that in a city that had just undergone near-total destruction by fire he should be pondering how he was going to go about cooking some meat. But most of the worst fires had burned themselves out by now, and the rain had taken care of the rest. And though for a while in the first few days after the catastrophe it had seemed as though new fires were still being lit, that didn't seem to be happening any more.

I'll figure something out, Theremon thought. Rub two sticks together and get a spark? Strike metal against stone and set a scrap of cloth ablaze?

Some boys on the far side of a lake near the place where he was camped had obligingly killed the animal for him. Of course, they hadn't known they were doing him any favor—most likely they had been planning to eat it themselves, unless they were so unhinged that they were simply chasing the creature for the sake of sport. Somehow he doubted that. They had been pretty purposeful about it, with a singlemindedness that only hunger can inspire.

The beast was a graben—one of those ugly long-nosed bluish-furred things with slithery hairless tails that sometimes could be seen poking around suburban garbage cans after Onos had set. Well, beauty wasn't a requirement just now. The boys had somehow flushed it out of its daytime hiding place and had driven the poor stupid thing into a little dead-end box of a canyon.

As Theremon watched from the other side of the lake, disgusted and envious at the same time, they chased it tirelessly up and down, pelting it with rocks. For a dumb scavenger it was remarkably agile, scooting swiftly this way and that in its desperation to elude its attackers. But finally a lucky shot caromed off its head and killed it instantly.

He had assumed that they would devour it on the spot. But at that moment a shaggy, shambling figure came into view above them, standing for a moment at the rim of the little canyon, then beginning to climb down toward the lake.

"Run! It's Garpik the Slasher!" one of the boys yelled.

"Garpik! Garpik!"

In an instant the boys scattered, leaving the dead graben behind.

Theremon, still watching, had slipped back into the shadows on his side of the lake. He also knew this Garpik, though not by name: one of the most dreaded of the forest-dwellers, a squat, almost ape-like man who wore nothing but a belt through which an assortment of knives was thrust. He was a killer without motive, a cheerful psychopath, a pure predator.

Garpik stood by the mouth of the canyon for a while, humming to himself, fondling one of his knives. He didn't seem to notice the dead animal, or didn't care. Perhaps he was waiting for the boys to come back. But plainly they weren't planning to do that, and after a time Garpik, with a shrug, went slouching off into the forest, most likely in search of something amusing to do with his weapons.

Theremon waited an endless moment, making certain Garpik didn't intend to double back and pounce on him.

Then—when he could no longer bear the sight of the dead graben lying there on the ground, where some other human or animal predator might suddenly come along to seize it before he did—he rushed forward, circled the lake, snatched the animal up, carried it back to his hiding place.

271

It weighed as much as a small child. It might be good for two or three meals—or more, if he could restrain his hunger and if the meat didn't spoil too quickly.

His head was spinning with hunger. He had had nothing but fruits and nuts to eat for more days than he could remember. His skin had drawn tight over his muscles and bones; what little spare fat he had been carrying he had long since absorbed, and now he was consuming his own strength in the struggle to stay alive. But this evening, at last, he would enjoy a little feast.

Roast graben! What a treat! he thought bitterly. —And then he thought: Be grateful for small mercies, Theremon.

Let's see—to build a fire, now—

Fuel, first. Behind his shelter was a flat wall of rock with a deep lateral crack in it, in which a line of weeds was growing. Plenty of them were long dead and withered, and had dried out since the last rainstorm. Quickly Theremon moved along the rock wall, plucking yellowed stems and leaves, assembling a little heap of straw-like material that would catch fire easily.

Now some dry twigs. They were harder to find, but he rummaged around the forest floor, looking for dead shrubs or at least shrubs with dead branches. The afternoon was well along by the time he had put together enough of that sort of tinder to matter: Dovim was gone from the sky, and Trey and Patru, which had been low on the horizon when the boys were hunting the graben, now had moved into the center of things, like a pair of glittering eyes watching the sorry events on Kalgash from far overhead.

Carefully Theremon arranged his kindling-wood above the dried plants, building a framework as he imagined a real outdoorsman would, the bigger branches along the outside, then the thinner ones crisscrossed over the middle. Not without some difficulty, he skewered the graben on a spit he had made of a sharp, reasonably straight stick, and positioned it a short distance above the woodpile.

So far, so good. Just one little thing missing, now.

Fire!

He had kept his mind away from that problem while assembling his fuel, hoping that it would solve itself somehow without his having to dwell on it. But now it had to be faced. He needed a spark. The old boys'-book trick of rubbing two sticks together was, Theremon was certain, nothing but a myth. He had read that certain primitive tribes had once started their fires by twirling a stick against a board with a little hole in it, but he suspected that the process wasn't all that simple, that it probably took an hour of patient twirling to get anything going. And in any case very likely you had to be initiated into the art by the old man of the tribe when you were a boy, or some such thing, or it wouldn't work.

Two rocks, though—was it possible to strike a spark by banging one against the other?

He doubted that too. But he might as well try it, he thought. He had no other ideas. There was a wide flat stone lying nearby, and after a little searching he found a smaller triangular one that could fit conveniently in the palm of his hand. He knelt beside his little fireplace and began methodically to hit the flat one with the pointed one.

Nothing in particular happened.

A hopeless feeling began to grow in him. Here I am, he thought, a grown man who can read and write, who can drive a car, who can even operate a computer, more or less. I can turn out a newspaper column in two hours that everybody in Saro City will want to read, and I can do it day in, day out, for twenty years. But I can't start a fire in the wilderness.

On the other hand, he thought, I will *not* eat this graben raw unless I absolutely have to. Will not. Will not. Not. Not. *Not!*

In fury he struck the stones together, again, again, again.

Spark, damn you! Light! Burn! Cook this ridiculous pathetic animal for me!

Again. Again. Again.

"What are you doing there, mister?" an unfriendly voice asked suddenly from a point just behind his right shoulder.

Theremon looked up, startled, dismayed. The first rule of survival in this forest was that you must never let yourself get so involved in anything that you failed to notice strangers sneaking up on you.

There were five of them. Men, about his own age. They looked as ragged as anyone else living in the forest. They didn't seem especially crazy, as people went these days: no glassy eyes, no drooling mouths, only an expression that was grim and weary and determined. They didn't appear to be carrying any weapons other than clubs, but their attitude was distinctly hostile.

Five against one. All right, he thought, take the damned graben and choke on it. He wasn't foolish enough to try to put up a fight.

"I said, 'What are you doing there, mister?' " the first man repeated, more coldly than before.

Theremon glared. "What does it look like? I'm trying to start a fire."

"That's what we thought."

The stranger stepped forward. Carefully, deliberately, he aimed a kick into Theremon's little woodpile. The painstakingly assembled kindling-wood went scattering, and the skewered graben toppled to the ground.

"Hey, wait a second—!"

"No fires here, mister. That's the law." Brusquely, firmly, bluntly. "Possession of fire-making equipment is prohibited. This wood is to use for a fire. That's obvious. And you admit guilt besides."

"Guilt?" Theremon said, incredulously.

"You said you were making a fire. These stones, they seem to be fire-making equipment, right? The law's clear on that. Prohibited."

At a signal from the leaders, two of the others came forward. One grabbed Theremon about the neck and chest from behind, and the other took the two stones he had been using from his hands and hurled them into the lake. They splashed and disappeared. Theremon, watching them go, felt the way he imagined Beenay must have felt at seeing his telescopes smashed by the mob.

"Let—go—of—me—" Theremon muttered, struggling.

"Let go of him," said the leader. He dug his foot into Theremon's fire-site again, grinding the bits of straw and stems into the dirt. —"Fires aren't allowed any more," he said to Theremon. "We've had all the fires we're ever going to have. We can't permit no more fires on account of the risk, the suffering, the damage, don't you know that? You try to build another fire, we're going to come back and smash your head in, you hear me?"

"It was fire that ruined the world," one of the others said.

"Fire that drove us from our homes."

"Fire is the enemy. Fire is forbidden. Fire is evil."

Theremon stared. Fire *evil?* Fire *forbidden?*

So they were crazy after all!

"The penalty for trying to start a fire, first offense," the first man said, "is a fine. We fine you this animal here. To teach you not to endanger innocent people. Take it, Listigon. It's a good lesson to him. The next time this fellow catches something, he'll remember that he oughtn't try to conjure up the enemy just because he feels like having some cooked meat."

"No!" Theremon cried in a half-strangled voice, as Listigon bent to pick up the graben. "That's mine, you morons! Mine! *Mine!*"

And he charged wildly at them, all caution swept away by exasperation and frustration.

Someone hit him, hard, in the midsection. He gasped and gagged and doubled over, clutching his belly with his arms, and someone else hit him from behind, a blow in the small of the back that nearly sent him tumbling forward on his face. But this time he jabbed backward sharply with his elbow, felt a satisfying contact, heard a grunt of pain.

He had been in fights before, but not for a long, long time. And never one against five. But there was no running away from this one now. What he had to do, he told himself, was stay on his feet and keep on backpedaling until he was up against the rock wall, where at least they couldn't come at him from the rear. And then just try to hold them off, kicking and punching and if necessary biting and roaring, until they decided to let him be.

A voice somewhere deep within him said, *They're completely nuts. They're perfectly likely to keep this up until they beat you to death.*

Nothing he could do about that now, though. Except try to hold them off.

He kept his head down and punched as hard as he could, while steadily pushing onward toward the wall. They crowded around him, battering him from all sides. But he stayed on his feet. Their numerical advantage wasn't as overwhelming as he had expected. In these close quarters, the five of them were unable all to get at him at once, and Theremon was able to play the confusion to his own benefit, striking out in any direction and moving as quickly as he could while they lumbered around trying to avoid hitting each other.

Even so, he knew he couldn't take much more. His lip was cut and one eye was starting to swell, and he was getting short of breath. One more good punch could send him down. He held one arm in front of his face and struck with the other, while continuing to back toward the shelter of the rock wall. He kicked someone. There was a howl and a curse. Someone else kicked back. Theremon took it on his thigh and swung around, hissing in pain.

He swayed. He struggled desperately for air. It was hard to see, hard to tell what was going on. They were all around him now, fists flailing at him from all sides. He wasn't going to reach the wall. He wasn't going to stay on his feet much longer. He was going to fall, and they were going to trample him, and he was going to die—

Going—to—die—

Then he became aware of confusion within the confusion: the shouts of different voices, new people mingling in the me-lee, a host of figures everywhere. Fine, he thought. Another bunch of crazies joining the fun. But maybe I can slip away somehow while all this is going on—

"In the name of the Fire Patrol, stop!" a woman's voice called, clear, loud, commanding. "That's an order! Stop, all of you! Get away from him! Now!"

Theremon blinked and rubbed his forehead. He looked around, bleary-eyed.

There were four newcomers in the clearing. They seemed fresh and crisp, and were wearing clean clothes. Flowing green neckerchiefs were tied about their throats. They were carrying needle-guns.

The woman—she appeared to be in charge—made a quick imperative gesture with the weapon she held, and the five men who had attacked Theremon moved away from him and went obediently to stand in front of her. She glowered sternly at them.

Theremon stared in disbelief.

"What's all this about?" she asked the leader of the five in a steely tone.

"He was starting a fire—trying to—he was going to roast an animal, but we came along—"

"All right. I see no fire here. The laws have been maintained. Clear off."

The man nodded. He reached down to take the graben.

"Hey! That belongs to me," Theremon said hoarsely.

"No," the other said. "You have to lose it. We fined you for breaking the fire laws."

"I'll decide the punishment," the woman said. "Leave the animal and clear off! Clear off!"

"But—"

"Clear off, or I'll have *you* up on charges before Altinol. Get! Get!"

The five men went slinking away. Theremon continued to stare.

The woman wearing the green neckerchief came toward him.

"I guess I was just in time, wasn't I, Theremon?"

"Siferra," he said in amazement. "Siferra!"

[37]

He was hurting in a hundred places. He wasn't at all sure how intact his bones were. One of his eyes was practically swollen shut. But he suspected he was going to survive. He sat leaning against the rock wall, waiting for the haze of pain to diminish a little.

Siferra said, "We've got a little Jonglor brandy back at our headquarters. I can authorize you to have some, I guess. For medicinal purposes, of course."

"Brandy? Headquarters? What headquarters? What is this all about, Siferra? Are you really here at all?"

"You think I'm a hallucination?" She laughed and dug her fingertips lightly into his forearm. "Is that a hallucination, would you say?"

He winced. "Careful. I'm pretty tender there. And everywhere else, right now. —You just dropped right down out of the sky, is that it?"

277

"I was on Patrol duty, passing through the forest, and we heard the sounds of a scuffle. So we came to investigate. I had no idea you were mixed up in it until I saw you. We're trying to restore order around here somehow."

"*We?*"

"The Fire Patrol. It's as close as there is to a new local government. The headquarters is at the university Sanctuary, and a man named Altinol who used to be some sort of company executive is in charge. I'm one of his officers. It's a vigilante group, really, which has managed to put across the notion that the use of fire must be controlled, and that only members of the Fire Patrol have the privilege of—"

Theremon raised his hand. "Hold on, Siferra. Slow down, will you? The university people in the Sanctuary have formed a vigilante group, you say? They're going around putting out fires? How can that be? Sheerin told me that they had all cleared out, that they had gone south to some sort of rendezvous at Amgando National Park."

"Sheerin? Is he here?"

"He was. He's on his way to Amgando now. I—decided to stick around here a little while longer." It seemed impossible to tell her that he had stuck around on the unlikely chance that he would manage to find *her*.

Siferra nodded. "What Sheerin told you was true. All the university people left the Sanctuary the day after the eclipse. I suppose they're off in Amgando by now—I haven't heard anything about them. They left the Sanctuary wide open, and Altinol and his bunch wandered in and took possession of it. The Fire Patrol has fifteen, twenty members, all of them in pretty good shape, mentally. They've been able to establish their authority over about half the area of the forest, and some of the surrounding territory of the city where people are still living."

"And you?" Theremon asked. "How did you get involved with them?"

"I went into the forest first, once the Stars were gone. But it looked pretty dangerous here, so when I remembered about the Sanctuary, I headed there. Altinol and his people were already there. They invited me to join the Patrol." Siferra smiled in what might have been a rueful way. "They didn't really offer

278

me much of a choice," she said. "They aren't particularly gentle sorts."

"These aren't gentle times."

"No. So I decided, better off with them than drifting around on my own. They gave me this green neckerchief—everybody around here respects it. And this needle-gun. People respect *that* too."

"So you're a vigilante," Theremon said, musing. "Somehow I never figured you for that kind of thing."

"I never did either."

"But you believe that this Altinol and his Fire Patrol are righteous folk who are helping to restore law and order, is that it?"

She smiled again, and again it was not an expression of mirth.

"Righteous folk? *They* think they are, yes."

"You don't?"

A shrug. "They're out for themselves first, and no kidding about that. There's a power vacuum here and they mean to fill it. But I suppose they're not the worst possible people to try to impose a governmental structure right now. They're easier to take than some of the outfits I can think of, at least."

"You mean the Apostles? Are they trying to form a government too?"

"Very likely they are. But I haven't heard anything about them since it all happened. Altinol thinks that they're still hidden away underground somewhere, or that Mondior has led them off to some place far out in the country where they'll set up their own kingdom. But we've got a couple of new fanatic groups that are real lulus, Theremon. You just had a run-in with one of them, and it's only by wild luck that they didn't finish you off. They believe that the only salvation for humanity now is to give up the use of fire completely, since fire has been the ruin of the world. So they're going around destroying fire-making equipment wherever they can find it, and killing anyone who seems to enjoy starting fires."

"I was simply trying to cook some dinner for myself," said Theremon somberly.

Siferra said, "It's all the same to them whether you're cooking a meal or amusing yourself with a little bit of arson. Fire is fire, and they abhor it. Lucky thing for you that we came along in time. They accept the authority of the Fire Patrol. We're the elite, you understand, the only ones whose use of fire will be tolerated."

"It helps to have needle-guns," Theremon said. "That gets you a lot of toleration too." He rubbed a sore place on his arm and looked off bleakly into the distance. —"There are other fanatics besides these, you say?"

"There are the ones who think the university astronomers had discovered the secret of making the Stars appear. They blame Athor, Beenay & Co. for everything that's happened. It's the old hatred of the intellectual that crops up whenever medieval emotions start surfacing."

"Gods! Are there many like that?"

"Enough. Darkness only knows what they'll do if they actually catch any university people who haven't already reached Amgando safely. String them up to the nearest lamppost, I suppose."

Morosely Theremon said, "And I'd be responsible."

"You?"

"Everything that's happened is *my* fault, Siferra. Not Athor's, not Folimun's, not the gods', but mine. Mine. Me, Theremon 762. That time you called me irresponsible, you were being too easy with me. I wasn't just irresponsible, I was criminally negligent."

"Theremon, stop it. What's the good of—"

He swept right on. "I should have been writing columns day in and day out, warning of what was coming, crying out for a crash program to build shelters, to set aside provisions and emergency generating equipment, to provide counseling for the disturbed, to do a million different things—and instead what did I do? Sneered. Poked fun at the astronomers in their lofty tower! Made it politically impossible for anybody in the government to take Athor seriously."

"Theremon—"

"You should have let those crazies beat me to death, Siferra."

Her eyes met his. She looked angry. "Don't talk like a fool. All the government planning in the world wouldn't have changed anything. I wish you hadn't written those articles too, Theremon. You know how I felt about them. But what does any of that matter now? You were sincere in what you felt. You were wrong, but you were sincere. And in any case there's no sense speculating about what might have been. What we have to deal with now is what *is.*" More gently she said, "Enough of this. Are you able to walk? We need to get you back to the Sanctuary. A chance to wash up, some fresh clothes, a little food in you—"

"Food?"

"The university people left plenty of provisions behind."

Theremon chuckled and pointed to the graben. "You mean I don't have to eat *that?*"

"Not unless you really want to. I suggest you give it to someone who needs it more than you do, while we're on our way out of the forest."

"Good idea."

He pulled himself to his feet, slowly and painfully. Gods, the way everything was hurting! An experimental step or two: not bad, not bad. Nothing seemed to be broken after all. Just a little bit misused. The thought of a warm bath and actual substantial food was healing his bruised and aching body already.

He took a last look around at his little flung-together lean-to, his stream, his scruffy little bushes and weeds. His home, these strange few days. He wouldn't miss it much, but he doubted that he'd forget his life here very soon, either.

Then he picked up the graben and slung it over his shoulder. "Lead the way," he said to Siferra.

They had not gone more than a hundred yards when Theremon caught sight of a group of boys skulking behind the trees. They were the same ones, he realized, who had flushed the graben from its burrow and hunted it to its death. Evidently they had come back to search for it. Now, sullenly, they were staring from a distance, obviously annoyed that Theremon was walking off with their prize. But they were too intimidated by the green neckerchiefs of office that identified the Fire Patrol group—or, more likely, simply by their needle-guns—to stake a claim to it.

"Hey!" Theremon called. "This is yours, isn't it? I've been taking care of it for you!"

He flung the carcass of the graben toward them. It fell to the ground well short of the place where they were, and they hung

back, looking mystified and uneasy. They were obviously eager
to have the animal but afraid to come forward.

"There's life in the post-Nightfall era for you," he said sadly
to Siferra. "They're starving, but they don't dare make a move.
They think it's a trap. They figure that if they step out from
those trees to get the animal we'll shoot them down, just for
fun."

Siferra said, "Who can blame them? Everyone's afraid of everyone, now. Leave it there. They'll go after it when we're out
of sight."

He followed her onward, limping as he went.

Siferra and the other Patrol people moved confidently
through the forest, as though invulnerable to the dangers that
were lurking everywhere. And indeed there were no incidents
as the group headed—as rapidly as Theremon's injuries permitted—toward the road that ran through the woods. It was interesting to see, he thought, how quickly society was beginning to
reconstitute itself. In just a few days an irregular outfit like this
Fire Patrol had begun to take on a kind of governmental authority. Unless it was just the needle-guns and the general air
of self-assurance that kept the crazies away, of course.

They came to the edge of the forest, finally. The air was
growing cooler and the light was uncomfortably dim, now that
Patru and Trey were the only suns in the sky. In the past
Theremon had never been bothered by the relatively low light
levels that were typical of the hours when the only illumination came from one of the double-sun pairs. Ever since the
eclipse, though, such a two-sun evening had seemed disturbing
and threatening to him, a possible harbinger—although he
knew it could not be so—of the imminent return of Darkness.
The psychic wounds of Nightfall would be a long time healing,
even for the world's sturdiest minds.

"The Sanctuary is just a little way down this road," Siferra
said. "How're you doing?"

"I'm all right," said Theremon sourly. "They didn't cripple
me, you know."

But it was a considerable struggle to force his sore, throbbing
legs to carry him along. He was intensely gladdened and re-
lieved when at last he found himself at the cave-like entrance to
the underground domain that was the Sanctuary.

The place was like a maze. Caverns and corridors led off in all directions. Vaguely in the distance he saw the intricate loops and coils of scientific-looking gear, mysterious and unfathomable, running along the walls and ceiling. This place, he remembered now, had been the site of the university's atom smasher until the big new experimental lab at Saro Heights opened. Apparently the physicists had left a good deal of obsolete equipment behind.

A tall man appeared, radiating authority.

Siferra said, "This is Altinol 111. Altinol, I want you to meet Theremon 762."

"Of the *Chronicle?*" Altinol said. He didn't sound awed or in any way impressed: he seemed merely to be registering the fact out loud.

"Formerly," said Theremon.

They eyed each other without warmth. Altinol, Theremon thought, looked to be a very tough cookie indeed: a man in early middle age, obviously trim and in prime condition. He was well dressed in sturdy clothing and carried himself with the air of someone who was accustomed to being obeyed. Theremon, studying him, riffled quickly through the well-stocked files of his memory and after a moment was pleased to strike a chord of recognition.

He said, "Morthaine Industries? That Altinol?"

A momentary flicker of—amusement? Or was it annoyance? —appeared in Altinol's eyes. "That one, yes."

"They always said you wanted to be Prime Executive. Well, it looks like you are, now. Of what's left of Saro City, at least, if not the whole Federal Republic."

"One thing at a time," Altinol said. His voice was measured. "First we try to stumble back out of anarchy. Then we think about putting the country together again and worry about who's going to be Prime Executive. We have the problem of the Apostles, for example, who have seized control of the entire north side of the city and the territory beyond, and placed it under religious authority. They won't be easy to displace." Altinol smiled coolly. "First things first, my friend."

"And for Theremon," Siferra said, "the first thing is a bath, and then a meal. He's been living in the forest since Nightfall. —Come with me," she said to him.

Partitions had been set up all along the old particle-accelerator track, carving it up into a long series of little rooms. Siferra showed him to one in which copper pipes mounted overhead carried water to a porcelain tank. "It won't be really warm," she warned him. "We only run the boilers a couple of hours a day, because the fuel supply is so low. But it's bound to be better than bathing in a chilly forest stream. —You knew something about Altinol?"

"Chairman of Morthaine Industries, the big shipping combine. He was in the news a year or two back, something about wangling a contract by possibly irregular means to develop a huge real-estate tract on government land in Nibro Province."

"What does a shipping combine have to do with real-estate development?" Siferra asked.

"That's exactly the point. Nothing at all. He was accused of using improper government influence—something about offering lifetime passes on his cruise line to senators, I think—" Theremon shrugged. "Makes no difference now, really. There's no more Morthaine Industries, no more real-estate developing to be done, no Federal senators to bribe. He probably didn't like my recognizing him."

"He probably didn't care. Running the Fire Patrol is all that matters to him now."

"For the time being," said Theremon. "Today the Saro City Fire Patrol, tomorrow the world. You heard him talking about displacing the Apostles who've grabbed the far side of the city. Well, someone's got to do it. And he's the kind who enjoys running things."

Siferra went out. Theremon lowered himself into the porcelain tank.

Not exactly sybaritic. But pretty wonderful, after all he had been through lately. He leaned back and closed his eyes and relaxed. And luxuriated.

Siferra took him to the Sanctuary dining hall, a simple tin-roofed chamber, when he was finished with his bath, and left him there by himself, telling him she had to make her day's report to Altinol. A meal was waiting for him there—one of the packaged dinners that had been stockpiled here in the months that the Sanctuary was being set up. Lukewarm vegeta-

bles, tepid meat of some unknown kind, a pale green non-alco-
holic drink of nondescript flavor.

It all tasted wondrously delicious to Theremon.

He forced himself to eat slowly, carefully, knowing that his
body was unaccustomed to real food after his time in the forest;
every mouthful had to be thoroughly chewed or he'd get sick,
he knew, though his instinct was to bolt it as fast as he could
and ask for a second helping.

After he had eaten Theremon sat back, staring dully at the
ugly tin wall. He wasn't hungry any more. And his frame of
mind was beginning to change for the worse. Despite the bath,
despite the meal, despite the comfort of knowing he was safe in
this well-defended Sanctuary, he found himself slipping into a
mood of the deepest desolation.

He felt very weary. And dispirited, and full of gloom.

It had been a pretty good world, he thought. Not perfect, far
from it, but good enough. Most people had been reasonably
happy, most were prosperous, there was progress being made
on all fronts—toward deeper scientific understanding, toward
greater economic expansion, toward stronger global cooperation. The concept of war had come to seem quaintly medieval
and the age-old religious bigotries were mostly obsolete, or so it
had seemed to him.

And now it was all gone, in one short span of hours, in a
single burst of horrifying Darkness.

A new world would be born from the ashes of the old, of
course. It was always that way: Siferra's excavations at
Thombo testified to that.

But what sort of world would it be? Theremon wondered.
The answer to that was already at hand. It would be a world in
which people killed other people for a scrap of meat, or because
they had violated a superstition about fire, or simply because
killing seemed like a diverting thing to do. A world in which
the Altinols came forward to take advantage of the chaos and
gain power for themselves. A world in which the Folimuns and
Mondiors, no doubt, were scheming to emerge as the dictators
of thought—probably working hand in hand with the Altinols,
Theremon thought morbidly. A world in which—

No. He shook his head. What was the point of all this dark,
brooding lamentation?

Siferra had the right notion, he told himself. There was no sense in speculating about what might have been. *What we have to deal with is what* is. At least he was alive, and his mind was pretty much whole again, and he had come through his ordeal in the forest more or less intact, aside from a few bruises and cuts that would heal in a couple of days. Despair was a useless emotion now: it was a luxury that he couldn't allow himself, any more than Siferra would allow herself the luxury of still being angry at him over the newspaper pieces he had written.

What was done was done. Now it was time to pick up and move onward, regroup, rebuild, make a fresh start. To look back was folly. To look forward in dismay or despondency was mere cowardice.

"Finished?" Siferra said, returning to the dining hall. "I know, not magnificent food. But it beats eating graben."

"I couldn't say. I never actually got to eat any graben."

"You probably didn't miss much. Come: I'll show you to your room."

It was a low-ceilinged cubicle of no great elegance: a bed with a godlight on the floor beside it, a washstand, a single dangling light fixture. Scattered in one corner were some books and newspapers that must have been left behind by those who had occupied this room on the evening of the eclipse. Theremon saw a copy of the *Chronicle* opened to the page of his column, and winced: it was one of his last pieces, a particularly intemperate onslaught on Athor and his group. He reddened and pushed it out of sight with his foot.

Siferra said, "What are you going to do now, Theremon?"

"Do?"

"I mean, once you've had a chance to rest up a little."

"I haven't given it much thought. Why?"

"Altinol wants to know if you're planning to join the Fire Patrol," she said.

"Is that an invitation?"

"He's willing to take you aboard. You're the kind of person that he needs, someone strong, someone capable of dealing with people."

"Yes," Theremon said. "I'd be good here, wouldn't I?"

"But he's uneasy about one thing. There's room for only one

boss in the Patrol, and that's Altinol. If you joined up, he'd want you to understand right from the beginning that what Altinol says goes, without any argument. He's not sure how good you are at taking orders."

"I'm not so sure how good I am at that either," Theremon said. "But I can see Altinol's point of view."

"Will you join, then? I know there are problems with the whole Patrol setup. But at least it's a force for order, and we need something like that now. And Altinol may be high-handed, but he's not evil. I'm convinced of that. He simply thinks the times call for strong measures and decisive leadership. Which he's capable of supplying."

"I don't doubt that he is."

"Think it over this evening," Siferra said. "If you want to join, talk to him tomorrow. Be frank with him. He'll be frank with you, you can be certain of that. So long as you can assure him that you're not going to be any direct threat to his authority, I'm certain that you and he—"

"No," Theremon said suddenly.

"No what?"

He was silent for a time. At length he said, "I don't need to spend the evening thinking about it. I already know what my answer will be."

Siferra looked at him, waiting.

Theremon said, "I don't want to butt heads with Altinol. I know the kind of man he is, and I'm very sure that I can't get along with people like that for any length of time. And I also know that in the short run it may be necessary to have operations like the Fire Patrol, but in the long run they're a bad thing, and once they're established and institutionalized it's very hard to get rid of them. The Altinols of this world don't give up power voluntarily. Little dictators never do. And I don't want the knowledge that I helped put him on top hanging around my neck for the rest of my life. Reinventing the feudal system doesn't strike me as a useful solution for the problems we have now. So it's no go, Siferra. I'm not going to wear Altinol's green neckerchief. There isn't any future for me here."

Quietly Siferra said, "What are you going to do, then?"

"Sheerin told me that there's a real provisional government

being formed at Amgando Park. University people, maybe some people from the old government, representatives from all over the country coming together down there. As soon as I'm strong enough to travel, I'm going to head for Amgando."

She regarded him steadily. She made no reply.

Theremon took a deep breath. And said, after a moment, "Come with me to Amgando Park, Siferra." He reached a hand toward her. Softly he said, "Stay with me this evening, in this miserable little tiny room of mine. And in the morning let's clear out of here and go down south together. You don't belong here any more than I do. And we stand five times as much chance of getting to Amgando together than we would if either of us tried to make the journey alone."

Siferra remained silent. He did not withdraw his hand.

"Well? What do you say?"

Theremon watched the play of conflicting emotions moving across her features. But he did not dare try to interpret them.

Clearly Siferra was struggling with herself. But then, abruptly, the struggle came to an end.

"Yes," she said at last. "Yes. Let's do it, Theremon."

And moved toward him. And took his hand. And switched off the dangling overhead light, though the soft glow of the godlight beside the bed remained.

[38]

"Do you know the name of this neighborhood?" Siferra asked. She stared, numbed, dismayed, at the charred and ghastly landscape of ruined houses and abandoned vehicles that they had entered. It was a little before midday, the third day of their flight from the Sanctuary. The unsparing light of Onos mercilessly illuminated every blackened wall, every shattered window.

Theremon shook his head. "It was called something silly, you can be sure of that. Golden Acres, or Saro Estates, or something like that. But what it was called isn't important now. This isn't a neighborhood any more. What we have here used to be real estate, Siferra, but these days what it is is archaeology. One of the Lost Suburbs of Saro."

They had reached a point well south of the forest, almost to the outskirts of the suburban belt that constituted the southern fringes of Saro City. Beyond lay agricultural zones, small towns, and—somewhere far in the distance, unthinkably far—their goal of Amgando National Park.

The crossing of the forest had taken them two days. They had slept the first evening at Theremon's old lean-to, and the second one in a thicket halfway up the rugged slope leading to Onos Heights. In all this while they had had no indication that the Fire Patrol was on their trail. Altinol had apparently made no attempt to pursue them, even though they had taken weapons with them and two bulging backpacks of provisions. And surely, Siferra thought, they were beyond his reach by now.

She said, "The Great Southern Highway ought to be somewhere around here, shouldn't it?"

"Another two or three miles. If we're lucky there won't be any fires burning to block us from going forward."

"We'll be lucky. Count on it."

He laughed. "Always the optimist, eh?"

"It doesn't cost any more than pessimism," she said. "One way or another, we'll get through."

"Right. One way or another."

They were moving steadily along. Theremon seemed to be making a quick recovery from the beating he had received in the forest, and from his days of virtual starvation. There was an amazing resilience about him. Strong as she was, Siferra had to work hard to keep up with his pace.

She was working hard, too, to keep her own spirits up. From the moment of setting out, she had consistently struck a hopeful note, always confident, always certain that they'd make it safely through to Amgando and that they would find people like themselves already hard at work there at the job of planning the reconstruction of the world.

But inwardly Siferra wasn't so sure. And the farther she and Theremon went into these once pleasant suburban regions, the more difficult it was to fight back horror, shock, despair, a sense of total defeat.

It was a nightmare world.

289

There was no escaping the enormity of it. Everywhere you turned you saw destruction.

Look! she thought. Look! The desolation—the scars—the fallen buildings, the walls already overrun by the first weeds, occupied already by the early platoons of lizards. Everywhere the marks of that terrible night when the gods had once more sent their curse against the world. The awful acrid smell of black smoke rising from the remains of fires that the recent rains had extinguished—the other smoke, white and piercing, curling upward out of basements still ablaze—the stains on everything—the bodies in the streets, twisted in their final agonies—the look of madness in the eyes of those few lingering living people who now and then peered out from the remains of their homes—

All glory vanished. All greatness gone. Everything in ruins, everything—as if the ocean had risen, she thought, and swept all our achievements into oblivion.

Siferra was no stranger to ruins. She had spent her whole professional life digging in them. But the ruins she had excavated were ancient ones, time-mellowed and mysterious and romantic. What she saw here now was all to immediate, all too painful to behold, and there was nothing at all romantic about it. She had been able readily enough to come to terms with the downfall of the lost civilizations of the past: it carried little emotional charge for her. But now it was her own epoch that had been swept into the discard-bin of history, and that was hard to bear.

Why had it happened? she asked herself. Why? Why? Why?

Were we so evil? Had we strayed so far from the path of the gods that we needed to be punished this way?

No.

No!

There are no gods; there was no punishment.

Of that much, Siferra was still certain. She had no doubt that this was simply the working of blind fate, brought about by the impersonal movements of inanimate and uncaring worlds and suns, drawing together every two thousand years in dispassionate coincidence.

That was all. An accident.

An accident that Kalgash had been forced to endure over and over again during its history.

From time to time the Stars would appear in all their frightful majesty; and in a desperate terror-kindled agony, man would unknowingly turn his hand against his own works. Driven mad by the Darkness; driven mad by the ferocious light of the Stars. It was an unending cycle. The ashes of Thombo had told the whole tale. And now it was Thombo all over again. Just as Theremon had said: *This place is archaeology now.* Exactly.

The world they had known was gone. But we are still here, she thought.

What shall we do? What shall we do?

The only comfort she could find amidst the bleakness was the memory of that first evening with Theremon, in the Sanctuary: so sudden, so unexpected, so wonderful. She kept going back to it in her mind, over and over. His oddly shy smile as he asked her to stay with him—no sly seductive trick, that! And the look in his eyes. And the feel of his hands against her skin— his embrace, his breath mingling with hers—

How long it had been since she had been with a man! She had almost forgotten what it was like—*almost.* And always, those other times, there had been the uneasy sense of making a mistake, of taking a false path, of committing herself to a journey she should not be taking. It had not been that way with Theremon: simply a dropping of barriers and pretenses and fears, a joyful yielding, an admission, finally, that in this torn and tortured world she must no longer go it alone, that it was necessary to form an alliance, and that Theremon, straightforward and blunt and even a little coarse, strong and determined and dependable, was the ally she needed and wanted.

And so she had given herself at last, unhesitatingly and without regret. What an irony, she thought, that it had taken the end of the world to bring her to the point of falling in love! But at least she had that. Everything else might be lost; but at least she had that.

"Look there," she said, pointing. "A highway sign."

It was a shield of green metal, hanging at a crazy angle from a lamppost, its surface blackened by smoke-stains. In three or four places it was punctured by what probably were bulletholes. But the bright yellow lettering was still reasonably legi-

291

ble: GREAT SOUTHERN HIGHWAY, and an arrow instructing them to go straight ahead.

"It can't be more than another mile or two from here," Theremon said. "We ought to reach it by—"

There was a sudden high whining sound, and then a twanging crash, reverberating with stunning impact. Siferra covered her ears. A moment later she felt Theremon hooking his arm through hers, pulling her to the ground.

"Get *down!*" he whispered harshly. "Somebody's firing!"

"Who? Where?"

His needle-gun was in his hand. She drew hers also. Glancing up, she saw that the projectile had struck the highway sign: there was a new hole in it between the first two words, obliterating several of the letters.

Theremon, crouching, was moving in a quick shuffle toward the edge of the nearest building. Siferra followed him, feeling hideously exposed. This was worse than standing naked in front of Altinol and the Fire Patrol: a thousand times worse. The next shot might come at any moment, from any direction, and she had no way to protect herself. Even when she pulled herself around the corner of the building and huddled up against Theremon in the alleyway, breathing hard, her heart pounding, she felt no assurance that she was safe.

He nodded toward a row of burned-out houses on the other side of the street. Two or three of them were intact, down near the opposite corner; and now she saw grimy shadowy faces peering out of an upstairs window of the farthest one.

"People in there. Squatters, I bet. Crazies."

"I see them."

"Not afraid of our Patrol neckerchiefs. Maybe the Patrol doesn't mean anything to them, this far out of town. Or maybe they were shooting at us *because* we're wearing them."

"You think so?"

"Anything's possible." Theremon edged forward a little way. "What I wonder is, were they trying to hit us and is their aim really lousy, or were they just trying to scare us? If they tried to shoot at us and the best they could do was hit the highway sign, then we could try making a run for it. But if it was just a warning—"

"That's what I suspect it was. A shot that went astray isn't likely to have gone astray right into the highway sign. That's too neat."

"Probably so," Theremon said. He scowled. "I think I'm going to let them know we're armed. Just to discourage them from trying to send a few scouts sneaking around one of these houses and coming up on us from the rear."

He looked down at his needler, adjusting the aperture to wide beam and maximum distance. Then he raised it and squeezed off a single shot. A bolt of red light sizzled through the air and struck the ground just in front of the building where the faces had appeared. An angry charred spot appeared on the lawn, and wisps of smoke came curling up.

Siferra asked, "Do you think they saw that?"

"Unless they're so far gone that they aren't capable of paying attention. But my guess is that they saw, all right. And didn't like it much."

The faces were back at the window.

"Stay down," Theremon warned. "They've got some kind of heavy hunting rifle. I can see its snout."

There was another whining sound, another tremendous crash.

The highway sign, shattered, fell to the ground.

"They may be crazies," Siferra said, "but their aim is pretty damned good."

"*Too* good. They were just playing with us when they fired that first shot. Laughing at us. They're telling us that if we show our noses they'll blow us away. They've got us pinned down, and they're enjoying it."

"Can we get out of here down the far end of this alley?"

"It's all rubble back there. And more squatters waiting for us on the other side, for all we know."

"Then what are we going to do?"

"Set that house on fire," Theremon said. "Burn them out. And kill them, if they're too crazy to surrender."

Her eyes widened. "*Kill* them?"

"If they give us no other option, yes, yes, I will. Do you want to get to Amgando, or would you rather spend the rest of your life hiding out here in this alleyway?"

"But you can't just kill people, even though you—even though they—"

Her voice trailed off. She didn't know what she was trying to say.

"Even though they're trying to kill you, Siferra? Even though they think it's fun to send a couple of shots whistling past your ears?"

She made no reply. She had thought she was beginning to understand the way things worked in the monstrous new world that had come into being on the evening of the eclipse; but she realized that she understood nothing, nothing at all.

Theremon had crept out toward the street a short way once again. He was aiming his needler.

The incandescent bolt of light struck the white facade of the house down the street. Instantly the wood began to turn black. Little flamelets sprang up. He drew a line of fire across the front of the building, paused a moment, fired again, tracing a second line across the first.

"Give me your gun," he said. "Mine's overheating."

She passed him the weapon. He adjusted it and fired a third time. An entire section of the house's front wall was ablaze now. Theremon was cutting through it, aiming his beam toward the interior of the building.

Not very long ago, Siferra thought, that white wooden house had belonged to someone. People had lived there, a family, proud of their house, their neighborhood—tending their lawn, watering their plants, playing with their pets, giving dinner parties for their friends, sitting on the patio sipping drinks and watching the suns move through the evening sky. Now none of that meant anything. Now Theremon was lying on his belly in an alleyway strewn with ashes and rubble across the way, efficiently and systematically setting that house on fire. Because that was the only way that he and she could get safely out of this street and continue on their way to Amgando Park.

A nightmare world, yes.

A column of smoke was rising within the house now. The whole left-hand side of its front wall was on fire.

And people were leaping from the second-story windows.

Three, four, five of them, choking, gasping. Two women, three men. They dropped down on the lawn and lay there a moment, as though dazed. Their clothes were ragged and dirty, their hair was unkempt. Crazies. They had been something

294

else, before Nightfall, but now they were simply part of that vast horde of wild-eyed, uncouth-looking drifters whose minds had been unhinged, perhaps forever, by the sudden astounding blast of stunning light that the Stars had hurled against their unprepared senses.

"Stand up!" Theremon called to them. "Hands in the air! Now! Come on, get 'em up!" He stepped out into full view, holding both of the needle-guns. Siferra came out beside him. The house was shrouded in heavy smoke now, and within that dark cloak great frightful gusts of flame were sweeping upward on all sides of the building, blazing like scarlet banners.

Were there people still trapped inside? Who could tell? Did it matter?

"Line up, there!" Theremon ordered. "That's it! Face to the left!" They straggled to attention. One man was a little slow, and Theremon sent a needler beam blazing past his cheek to encourage his cooperation. "Start running, now. Down the street! Faster! Faster!"

One side of the house caved in with a terrible roaring sound, exposing rooms, closets, furniture, like a doll's house that had been cut away. Everything was on fire. The squatters were almost at the corner now. Theremon continued to shout at them, urging them on, aiming an occasional needle-bolt at their heels.

Then he turned to Siferra. "All right. Let's get out of here!"

They holstered their needlers and went running off in the opposite direction, toward the Great Southern Highway.

"What if they had come out firing?" Siferra asked afterward, when they could see the highway entrance itself just a short distance away and were moving through the open fields that led to it. "Would you really have killed them, Theremon?"

He looked at her in a steady, severe way. "If that was the only way we could have gotten ourselves out of that alleyway? I thought I gave you my answer to that before. Of course I would. What choice would I have had? What else could I have done?"

"Nothing, I suppose," Siferra said, her voice barely audible.

The image of the burning house still seared her mind. And the sight of those ragged, shabby people, running down the street.

But they had fired first, she told herself. They had started the trouble. There was no telling how far they would have carried it, if Theremon hadn't hit on the idea of burning the house down.

The house—somebody's house—

Nobody's house, she corrected.

"There it is," Theremon said. "The Great Southern Highway. It's a nice smooth five-hour drive to Amgando. We could be there by dinnertime."

"If we only had something to drive," said Siferra.

"If," he said.

[39]

Even after all he had seen in the course of having come this far, Theremon wasn't prepared for the way the Great Southern Highway looked. A traffic engineer's worst nightmare would not have been as bad.

Everywhere in their crossing of the southern suburbs, Theremon and Siferra had passed abandoned vehicles in the streets. No doubt many drivers, overcome by panic at the moment of the emergence of the Stars, had stopped their cars and fled from them on foot, hoping to find someplace to hide from the terrifying overpowering brilliance that blazed suddenly from the skies.

But the abandoned cars that littered the streets of these quiet residential sectors of the city through which he and Siferra had come so far had been scattered in a sparse random manner, here and there at relatively wide intervals. In these neighborhoods vehicular traffic must have been fairly light at the time of the eclipse, coming as it had after the end of the regular working day.

The Great Southern Highway, though—crowded with late intercity commuters—must have become an utter madhouse in the instant when calamity struck the world.

"Look at it," Theremon whispered, awestruck. "Will you *look* at it, Siferra!"

She shook her head in wonder. "Incredible. Incredible."

There were cars everywhere—clotted masses of them, piled up everywhere in a chaotic scramble, stacked two or three high in places. The wide roadway was almost completely blocked by them, an all but impassable wall of wrecked vehicles. They were facing in every direction. Some were upside down. Many were burned-out skeletons. Bright puddles of spilled fuel gleamed like little crystalline lakes. Streaks of pulverized glass gave the roadbed a sinister sheen.

Dead cars. And dead drivers.

It was the most grisly sight they had seen thus far. A vast army of the dead stretched before them. There were bodies slumped at the controls of their cars, bodies wedged between vehicles that had collided, bodies pinned beneath the wheels of cars. And a host of bodies simply strewn like pitiful discarded dolls along the sides of the road, their limbs frozen in the grotesque attitudes of death.

Siferra said, "Probably some drivers stopped right away, when the Stars came out. But others speeded up, trying to get off the highway and head for home, and went piling into the cars that had stopped. And still other people were so dazed they forgot how to drive altogether—look, they went right off the edge of the road over there, and this one here must have turned around and tried to drive back through the oncoming traffic—"

Theremon shuddered. "A horrendous colossal pileup. Cars crashing in from all sides at once. Spinning around, turning over, flung right across the road to the opposite lanes. People getting out, running for cover, getting hit by other cars just arriving. Everything gone crazy in fifty different ways."

He laughed bitterly.

Siferra said in surprise, "What can you possibly find to laugh about, Theremon?"

"Only my own foolishness. Do you know, Siferra, a wild idea crossed my mind half an hour ago, as we were getting close to the highway, that we could just sit down in somebody's abandoned car and find it fueled up and ready to go, and drive ourselves off to Amgando? Just like that, convenient as could be. I didn't stop to think that the road would be totally blocked —that even if we were lucky enough to find a car we could use, we wouldn't be able to drive so much as fifty feet in it—"

"It'll be hard enough just to walk along the road, in the shape it's in."

"Yes. But we'll have to."

Grimly, they set out on their long journey south.

By the warm Onos-light of early afternoon they picked their way through the carnage of the highway, scrambling over the twisted and battered wreckage of the cars, trying hard to ignore the charred and mutilated bodies, the dried pools of blood, the reek of death, the total horror of it all.

Theremon felt himself growing desensitized to it almost at once. Perhaps that was an even greater horror. But after a short while he simply stopped noticing the gore, the staring eyes of the corpses, the vastness of the disaster that had taken place here. The task of clambering over mountainous heaps of shattered cars and squeezing himself past dangerous jutting masses of jagged metal was so exacting that it required all his concentration, and he quickly ceased to pay attention to the victims of the debacle. He already knew there was no point in searching for survivors. Anyone who had been trapped here this many days would surely have died of exposure by now.

Siferra too seemed to have quickly adapted to the nightmare scene that was the Great Southern Highway. Scarcely saying a word, she picked her way through the obstacles alongside him, now pausing to point to an opening in the tangle of debris, now dropping to her hands and knees to crawl under some overhang of crumpled metal.

They were virtually the only living people using the road. Now and then they caught sight of someone moving southward on foot far ahead of them, or even coming up out of the south heading toward the Saro City end of the road, but there were never any encounters. The other wayfarers would hastily duck down out of sight and lose themselves in the wreckage, or, if they were up ahead, would begin frantically to scramble forward at a pace that spoke of terrible fear, disappearing quickly in the distance.

What are they afraid of? Theremon wondered. That we'll attack them. Is everyone's hand lifted against everyone else, now?

Once, an hour or so from their starting point, they saw a bedraggled-looking man going from car to car, reaching in to fumble in the pockets of the dead, despoiling the bodies of their possessions. There was a great sack of loot on his back, so heavy that he was staggering under the weight of it.

Theremon cursed angrily and pulled out his needle-gun.

"*Look* at the filthy ghoul! *Look* at him!"

"No, Theremon!"

Siferra deflected his arm just as Theremon fired a bolt at the looter. The shot struck a nearby car, and for a moment set up a glittering sunburst of reflected energy.

"Why did you do that?" Theremon asked. "I was only trying to scare him."

"I thought—that you—"

Bleakly Theremon shook his head. "No," he said. "Not yet, anyway. There—look at him run!"

The looter had swung around at the sound of the shot, staring in berserk manic astonishment at Theremon and Siferra. His eyes were blank; a trail of spittle dribbled from his lips. He gaped at them for a long moment. Then, dropping his sack of booty, he went scrabbling away in a wild, desperate flight over the tops of the cars and soon was lost from view.

They went onward.

It was slow, dreadful going. The road-signs that rose high above them on shining stanchions mocked their pitiful progress by telling them what a very small distance from the beginning of the highway they had succeeded in traversing so far. By Onos-set they had gone only a mile and a half.

"At this rate," Theremon said somberly, "it'll take us close to a year to reach Amgando."

"We'll move faster as we get the knack of it," said Siferra, without much conviction.

If only they could have followed along some street parallel to the highway, instead of having to walk on the roadbed itself, it would all have been much simpler for them. But that was impossible. Much of the Great Southern Highway was an elevated road, rising on lofty pillars above wooded tracts, areas of marsh, and the occasional industrial zone. There were places where the highway became a bridge across long open patches of mining scars, or over lakes and streams. For most of the distance they would have no choice but to stick to what had

299

once been the central traffic lanes of the highway itself, difficult as it was to get around the unending array of wreckage.

They kept to the edge of the roadbed as much as they could, since the density of wrecked cars was lower there. Looking over into the districts below, they saw signs of continuing chaos everywhere.

Burned houses. Fires still raging after all this time, stretching to the horizon. Occasional little bands of forlorn refugees, looking stunned and dazed, straggling bewilderedly through the debris-choked streets bound on some hopeless, desperate migration. Sometimes a larger group, a thousand people or more, camped together in some open place, everyone huddled in a desolate, paralyzed-looking way, scarcely moving, their wills and energies shattered.

Siferra pointed to a burned-out church at the crest of a hill just across from the highway. A small group of ragged-looking people were scrambling over its tumbled walls, prying at the remaining blocks of gray stone with crowbars, pulling them loose and hurling them into the courtyard.

"It looks as though they're demolishing it," she said. "Why would they do that?"

Theremon said, "Because they hate the gods. They blame them for everything that happened. —Do you know the Pantheon, the big Cathedral of All the Gods just at the edge of the forest, with the famous Thamilandi murals? I saw it a couple of days after Nightfall. It had been burned down—just rubble, everything destroyed, and one half-conscious priest sticking out of a pile of bricks. Now I realize that it was no accident that it burned. That fire was *deliberately* set. And the priest—I saw a crazy kill him right before my eyes, and I thought it was to steal his vestments. Maybe not. Maybe it was out of mere hatred."

"But the priests didn't cause—"

"Have you forgotten the Apostles so soon? Mondior, telling us for months that what was going to happen was the vengeance of the gods? The priests are the voice of the gods, isn't that so, Siferra? And if they led us into evil, so that we needed to be punished this way, why, the priests themselves must be responsible for the coming of the Stars. Or so people would think."

"The Apostles!" Siferra said darkly. "I wish I could forget them. What do you think they're doing now?"

"Came through the eclipse safe and sound in their tower, I suppose."

"Yes. They must have made it through the night in good shape, prepared for it as they were. What was it Altinol said? That they were already operating a government on the north side of Saro City?"

Theremon stared gloomily at the devastated church across the way. Tonelessly he said, "I just can imagine what sort of government that will be. Virtue by decree. Mondior issuing new commandments of morality every Onos Day. All forms of pleasure prohibited by law. Weekly public executions of the sinful." He spat into the wind. "By Darkness! To think I had Folimun right within my reach that evening and let him go, when I could so easily have throttled him—"

"Theremon!"

"I know. What good would it have done? One Apostle, more or less? Let him live. Let them set up their government, and tell everyone who's unlucky enough to live north of Saro City what to do and what to think. Why should we care? We're heading south, aren't we? What the Apostles do won't affect us. They'll be just one of fifty rival squabbling governments, when things have a chance to settle down. One of five thousand, maybe. Every district will have its own dictator, its own emperor." Theremon's voice darkened suddenly. "Oh, Siferra, Siferra—"

She took his hand. Quietly she said, "You're accusing yourself again, aren't you?"

"How did you know that?"

"When you get yourself so worked up. —Theremon, I tell you you're not guilty of anything! This would have happened no matter what you wrote in the paper, can't you see? One man alone couldn't have made any difference. This is something the world was destined to go through, something that couldn't have been prevented, something—"

"*Destined?*" he said sharply. "What a weird word for you to use! The vengeance of the gods, is that what you mean?"

"I didn't say anything about gods. I mean only that Kalgash Two was destined to come, not by the gods but simply by the laws of astronomy, and the eclipse was destined to happen, and Nightfall, and the Stars—"

"Yes," Theremon said indifferently. "I suppose."

They walked onward, through a stretch of road where very few cars had come to rest. Onos was down now, and the evening suns were out, Sitha and Tano and Dovim. A chilly wind blew from the west. Theremon felt the dull ache of hunger rising in him. They had not taken time to eat all day. Now they halted, camping between two crumpled cars, and unpacked some of the packages of dried food they had brought with them from the Sanctuary.

But, hungry as he was, he found that he had little appetite, and he had to force the meal down mouthful by mouthful. The rigid faces of corpses were staring at him from the nearby cars. While he was on the move he had been able to ignore them; but now, sitting here on what had once been Saro Province's finest highway, he could not screen the sight of them from his mind. There were moments when he felt that he had murdered them all himself.

They built a bed from seat-cushions that had been thrown from colliding cars, and slept close together, a fitful scattered sleep, which could not have been much worse had they tried to sleep on the hard concrete roadbed itself.

During the evening came shouts, hoarse laughter, the distant sound of singing. Theremon awoke once and peered over the edge of the elevated highway, and saw distant campfires in a field down there, perhaps twenty minutes' march off to the east. Did anyone ever sleep under a roof any more? Or had the impact of the Stars been so universal, he wondered, that the whole population of the world had turned itself out of house and home, to camp in the open as he and Siferra were doing, beneath the familiar light of the eternal suns?

Toward dawn he finally dozed. But hardly had he fallen asleep when Onos came up, pink and then golden in the east, pulling him out of fragmentary, terrifying dreams.

Siferra was already awake. Her face was pale, her eyes were reddened and puffy.

He managed a smile. "You look beautiful," he told her.

"Oh, this is nothing," she said. "You ought to see me when I've gone without washing for *two* weeks."

"But I meant—"

"I know what you meant," she said. "I think."

That day they covered four miles, and it was difficult going for them, every step of the way.

"We need water," Siferra said, as the afternoon wind began to rise. "We'll have to take the next exit ramp we see, and try to find a spring."

"Yes," he said. "I guess we'll have to."

Theremon felt uneasy about descending. Since the beginning of the journey they had had the highway virtually to themselves; and by now he had come to feel almost at home, in a strange sort of way, amid the tangle of crushed and ruined vehicles. Down there, in the open fields where the bands of refugees were moving—*Odd,* he thought, *how I call them refugees, as though I'm simply off on some sort of holiday myself*—there was no telling what sort of trouble they would get into.

But Siferra was right. They had to go down and find water. The supply that they had brought with them was all but exhausted. And perhaps they needed some time away from the hellish unending strip of demolished cars and stiff, staring corpses before they resumed their march toward Amgando.

He pointed to a road-sign a short way in front of them. "Half a mile to the next exit."

"We should be able to get there in an hour."

"Less," he said. "The road looks pretty clear up ahead. We'll get ourselves down from the highway and do what we need to do, as fast as we can, and then we'd better get back up here to sleep. It's safer to bed down out of sight between a couple of these cars than to take our chances in the open fields."

Siferra saw the logic of that. In this relatively uncluttered stretch of the road they moved quickly toward the upcoming exit ramp, traveling faster than they had in covering any previous section of the highway. In hardly any time at all they came to the next road-sign, the one that gave quarter-mile warning of the exit.

But then their rapid progress was sharply checked. They found the roadbed blocked at that point by so immense a pileup of crashed cars that Theremon feared for a moment that they would not be able to get through at all.

There must have been some truly monstrous series of crashes

303

here, something dreadful even by the standards of what he and Siferra had already passed through. Two huge transport trucks seemed to be in the middle of it, interlocked face to face like two warring beasts of the jungle; and it appeared that dozens of passenger cars had come barreling into them, flipping up on end, falling back on those who followed them, building a gigantic barrier that reached from one side of the road to the other and outward over the railings at the road's margins. Crumpled doors and fenders, sharp as blades, stuck out everywhere, and acres of broken glass set up a sinister tinkling as the wind played over it.

"Here," Theremon called. "I think I see a way—up through this opening, and then over the left-hand truck—no, no, that won't work, we'll have to go under—"

Siferra came up alongside him. He showed her the problem —a cluster of up-ended cars waiting for them on the far side, like a field of upturned knives—and she nodded. They went underneath instead, a slow, dirty, painful crawl through shards of glass and clotted pools of fuel. Midway through they paused to rest before continuing through to the far side of the pileup.

Theremon was the first to emerge.

"Gods!" he muttered, staring in bewilderment at the scene that lay before him. "What now?"

The road was open for perhaps fifty feet on the far side of the great mass of wreckage. Beyond the clear space a second roadblock lay across the highway from one side to the other. This one, though, had been deliberately constructed—a heap of car doors and wheels neatly piled on the roadbed to a height of eight or nine feet.

In front of the barricade Theremon saw some two dozen people, who had set up a campsite right on the highway. He had been so intent on getting through the tangle of wreckage that he had paid no attention to anything else, and so he had not heard the sounds from the other side.

Siferra came crawling out beside him. He heard her gasp of surprise and shock.

"Keep your hand on your needler," Theremon said quietly to her. "But don't pull it out and don't even think of trying to use it. There are too many of them."

A few of the strangers were sauntering up the road toward

them now, six or seven brawny-looking men. Theremon, motionless, watched them come. He knew that there was no turning back from this encounter—no hope of escape through that maze of knife-sharp wreckage through which they had just wriggled. He and Siferra were trapped in this clearing between the two roadblocks. All they could do was wait to see what happened next, and hope that these people were reasonably sane.

A tall, slouch-shouldered, cold-eyed man came unhurriedly up to Theremon until they were standing virtually nose to nose, and said, "All right, fellow. This is a Search station." He put a peculiar emphasis on the word *Search*.

"Search station?" Theremon repeated coolly. "And what is it that you're searching for?"

"Don't get wise with me or you'll find yourself going over the edge head first. You know damned well what we're searching for. Don't make trouble for yourself."

He gestured to the others. They moved in close, patting Theremon's clothes and Siferra's. Angrily Theremon pushed the questing hands away.

"Let us pass," he said tightly.

"Nobody goes through here without Search."

"By whose authority?"

"By my authority. You going to let us, or we going to have to make you?"

"Theremon—" Siferra whispered uneasily.

He shook her off. Rage was rising in him.

Reason told him that it was folly to try to resist, that they were badly outnumbered, that the tall man wasn't fooling around when he said there'd be trouble for them if they refused to submit to the search.

These people didn't exactly seem to be bandits. There was something official-sounding about the tall man's words, as though this were some kind of boundary, a customs station, perhaps. What were they searching for? Food? Weapons? Would these men try to take the needle-guns from them? Better to give them everything they were carrying, Theremon told himself, than to be killed in a vain and foolishly heroic attempt at maintaining their freedom of passage.

But still—to be manhandled like this—to be forced to submit, on a free public highway—

And they couldn't afford to give up the needle-guns, or their food supply. It was still hundreds of miles to Amgando.

"I warn you," the tall man began.

"And I warn you, keep your hands away from me. I'm a citizen of the Federal Republic of Saro and this is still a road freely open to all citizens, no matter what else has happened. You have no authority over me."

"He sounds like a professor," one of the other men said, laughing. "Making speeches about his rights, and all."

The tall man shrugged. "We've already got our professor here. We don't need any more. And this is about enough talk. Grab them and put them through Search. Top to bottom."

"Let—go—of—me—"

A hand clutched at Theremon's arm. He brought his fist up quickly and jammed it forward into someone's ribs. This all seemed very familiar to him: another scuffle, another beating in store for him. But he was determined to fight. An instant later someone hit him in the face and another man caught him by the elbow, and he heard Siferra cry out in fury and fear. He tried to pull free, hit someone again, was hit again himself, ducked, swung, took a sharp stinging blow in the face—

"Hey, wait a second!" a new voice called. "Hold on! Butella, get away from that man! Fridnor! Talpin! Let go of him!"

A *familiar* voice.

But whose?

The Searchers stepped back. Theremon, swaying a little, struggled to keep his balance as he looked at the newcomer.

A slender, wiry, intelligent-looking man, grinning at him, keen bright eyes peering out of a dirt-stained face—

Someone he knew, yes.

"Beenay!"

"Theremon! Siferra!"

[40]

In a moment everything was changed. Beenay led Theremon
and Siferra to a surprisingly cozy-looking little nest just on the
far side of the roadblock: cushions, curtains, a row of canisters
that appeared to contain foodstuffs. A slim young woman was
lying there, her left leg swathed in bandages. She looked weak
and feverish, but she flashed a brief faint smile as the others
entered.

Beenay said, "You remember Raissta 717, don't you, Theremon? Raissta, this is Siferra 89, of the Department of Archaeology. I told you about her—her discovery of previous episodes
of city-burning in the remote past. —Raissta is my contract-
mate," he said to Siferra.

Theremon had met Raissta a few times over the past couple
of years, in the course of his friendship with Beenay. But that
had been in another era, in a world that was dead and vanished
now. He could barely recognize her. He remembered her as a
slender, pleasant-looking, nicely dressed woman who seemed
always well groomed, always agreeably turned out. But now—
now! This gaunt, frail, haggard girl—this hollow-eyed stringy-
haired ghost of the Raissta he had known—!

Had it really been only a few weeks since Nightfall? It
seemed like years ago, suddenly. It seemed like eons—several
geological epochs ago—

Beenay said, "I have a little brandy here, Theremon."

Theremon's eyes widened. "Are you serious? Do you know
how long it's been since I've had a drink? —How ironic,
Beenay. You, the teetotaler who I had to coax into taking his
first sip of a Tano Special—you've got the last bottle of brandy
in the world hidden away here with you!"

"Siferra?" Beenay asked.

"Please. Just a little."

"Just a little is all we have." He poured three thimble-sized
drinks for them.

Theremon said, as the brandy began to warm him, "Beenay,
what's going on out there? This Search business?"

"You don't know about Search?"

"Not a thing."

"Where have you two been since Nightfall?"

"In the forest, mostly. Then Siferra found me after some hoodlums beat me up, and took me to the university Sanctuary while I recovered from what they did to me. And for the past couple of days we've been trekking down the highway here, hoping to get to Amgando."

"So you know about Amgando, do you?"

"By way of you, at one remove," Theremon said. "I ran into Sheerin in the forest. He was at the Sanctuary right after you must have left it, and he saw your note about Amgando. He told me, I told Siferra. And we set out together to go there."

"With Sheerin?" Beenay asked. "Where is he, then?"

"He isn't with us. He and I split up days ago—he went off to Amgando by himself, and I stayed in Saro to look for Siferra. I don't know what happened to him. —Do you think I could have another little nip of this brandy, Beenay? If you could spare it. And you were starting to tell me about Search."

Beenay poured a second small drink for Theremon. He looked toward Siferra, who shook her head.

Then he said uneasily, "If Sheerin was traveling alone, he's probably in trouble, probably very serious trouble. He certainly hasn't come this way since I've been here, and the Great Southern Highway is the only route out of Saro that anybody could take if he hoped to get to Amgando. We'll have to send out a scouting party to look for him. —As for Search, it's one of the new things that people do. This is an official Search station. There's one at the beginning of every province that the Great Southern Highway runs through."

"We're only a few miles from Saro City," Theremon said. "This is still Saro Province, Beenay."

"Not any more. All the old provincial governments have disappeared. What's left of Saro City's been divided up—I hear that the Apostles of Flame have one big chunk of it, over on the far side of town, and the area around the forest and the university is under the control of somebody named Altinol, who's operating a quasi-military group that calls itself the Fire Patrol. Perhaps you've run into them."

Siferra said, "I was an officer in the Fire Patrol for a few days. This green neckerchief I'm wearing is their official badge of office."

Beenay said, "Then you know what's happened. Fragmentation of the old system—a million petty governmental units springing up like mushrooms everywhere. What you're in now is Restoration Province. It runs from here down the highway about seven miles. When you get to the next Search station, you're in Six Suns Province. Beyond that is Godland, and then Daylight, and after that—well, I forget. They change every few days, anyway, as people wander on to other places."

"And Search?" Theremon prompted.

"The new paranoia. Everyone's afraid of fire-starters. You know what they are? Crazies who thought that what happened at Nightfall was a load of fun. They go around burning things down. I understand that a third of Saro City burned down the night of the eclipse, just from people's panicky wild attempts to drive away the Stars, but that another third of it has been destroyed *since* then, even though the Stars are long gone again. A sick business, that is. So the people who are more or less intact of mind—you're among some now, in case you were wondering—are searching everyone for fire-lighting equipment. It's forbidden to possess matches, or mechanical lighters, or needle-guns, or anything else capable of—"

"The same thing's going on on the outskirts of the city," Siferra said. "That's what the Fire Patrol is all about. Altinol and his people have set themselves up as the only people in Saro who are allowed to use fire."

"And I was attacked in the forest while I was trying to cook a meal for myself," said Theremon. "I suppose they were Searchers too. I'd have been beaten to death if Siferra and her Patrol hadn't come along to rescue me in the nick of time, pretty much the same way you did just now."

"Well," Beenay said, "I don't know who you ran into in the forest. But Search is the formal ritual down here to deal with the same problem. It goes on everywhere, everybody searching everybody else, never any let-up. Suspicion is universal: nobody's exempt. It's like a fever—a fever of fear. Only little elites, like Altinol's Fire Patrol, can carry combustibles. At every border you have to surrender your fire-making apparatus to the authorities, such as they may happen to be at the moment.

You might as well leave those needle-guns here with me, Theremon. You'll never get to Amgando with them."

"We'll never get there without them," Theremon said.

Beenay shrugged. "Maybe, maybe not. But you won't be able to avoid surrendering them as you continue south. The next time you hit Search, you know, I won't be there to call off the Search force."

Theremon considered that.

"How is it that you were able to make them listen to you, anyway?" he asked. "Or are you the head Searcher here?"

With a laugh Beenay said, "The head Searcher? Hardly. But they respect me. I'm their official professor, you see. There are places where university people are loathed, do you know that? Killed on sight by mobs of crazies, because the crazies think we caused the eclipse and are getting ready to cause another one. But not here. Here I'm considered useful for my intelligence— I can compose diplomatic messages to adjoining provinces, I've got ideas about how to take broken things and make them work again, I can even explain why the Darkness isn't going to come back and why nobody will have to look at the Stars again for two thousand years. They find that very comforting to hear. So I've settled in among them. They feed us and take care of Raissta, and I think for them. It's a nice symbiotic relationship."

"Sheerin told me you were going to Amgando," said Theremon.

"I was," Beenay said. "Amgando's the place where people like you and me ought to be. But Raissta and I ran into some trouble on the way down. Did you hear me tell you that crazies are hunting down university people and trying to kill them? We nearly got caught by a bunch of them ourselves, as we were heading south through the suburbs toward the highway. All those neighborhoods on the south side of the forest are occupied by wild squatters now."

"We ran into some," Theremon said.

"Then you know. We were surrounded by a bunch of them. They could tell just by the way we talked that we had to be educated people, and then someone recognized me—recognized me, Theremon, from a picture in the newspaper, from one of *your* columns, one of the times when you were interviewing me about the eclipse! And he said I was from the Observatory, I was the man who had made the Stars appear." Beenay stared off into nowhere for a moment. "We were about two minutes away from being strung up from a lamppost, is my guess. But then came a providential distraction. Another gang showed up—territorial rivals, I suppose—throwing bottles, yelling, waving kitchen knives around. Raissta and I were able to get away. They're like children, the crazies—they can't keep their minds on any one thing very long. But as we were crawling through a narrow path between two burned-out buildings Raissta cut her leg on some broken glass. And by the time we got this far south on the highway it was so badly infected that she couldn't walk."

"I see." No wonder she looks so terrible, Theremon thought.

"Luckily for us, Restoration Province's border guards were in need of a professor. They took us in. We've been here a week, or maybe ten days, now. I figure Raissta may be able to travel again in another week if all goes well, or more likely two. And then I'll have the boss of this province write out a passport for us that might get us safely through the next few provinces down the road, at least, and we'll set out on our way for Amgando. You're welcome to stay here with us until then, and then we can all go south together, if you like. Certainly it'll be safer that way. —You want me, Butella?"

The tall man who had tried to search Theremon in the clearing had poked his head over the curtains of Beenay's little den. "Messenger just came in, Professor. Brought some news from the city, by way of Imperial Province. We can't make much sense out of it."

"Let me see," Beenay said, reaching up and taking a folded slip of paper from the man. To Theremon he said, "Messengers go back and forth between the various new provinces all the time. Imperial's north and east of the highway, stretching up toward the city itself. —Most of these Searchers here aren't too good at reading. Their exposure to the Stars seems to have damaged their verbal centers, or something."

Beenay fell silent as he began to scan the message. He scowled, frowned, pursed his lips, muttered something about post-Nightfall handwriting and spelling. Then after a moment his expression grew dark.

"Good God!" he cried. "Of all the rotten, miserable, terrible—"

His hand was shaking. He looked up at Theremon, wild-eyed.

"Beenay! What is it?"

Somberly Beenay said, "The Apostles of Flame are coming this way. They've assembled an army, and they're going to march down to Amgando, clearing away all the new little provincial governments that have sprung up along the highway. And when they get to Amgando they're going to smash whatever reconstituted governing body it is that has taken form down there and proclaim themselves the only legally empowered ruling force in all of the Republic."

Theremon felt Siferra's fingers digging into his arm. He turned to look at her and saw the horror on her face. He himself must not look very different, he knew.

"Coming—this—way—" he said slowly. "An army of Apostles."

"Theremon, Siferra—you've got to get out of here," said Beenay. "Immediately. If you're still here when the Apostles arrive, everything's lost."

"Go to Amgando, you mean?" Theremon asked.

"Absolutely. Without wasting another minute. The whole university community that was in the Sanctuary is down there, and people from other universities, educated people from all over the Republic. You and Siferra have to warn them to scatter, fast. If they're still in Amgando when the Apostles get there, Mondior will be able to gobble up the whole nucleus of any future legitimate government this country's likely to have, all in one swoop. He might even order mass executions of university people. —Look, I'll write out passports for you that'll get you through the next few Search stations down the line, anyway. But when you've gotten beyond our authority, you'll simply have to submit to Search and let them take whatever they want from you, and then keep on heading south. You can't afford to let yourself be distracted by secondary issues like resisting Search. The Amgando group has to be warned, Theremon!"

"And what about you? Are you just going to stay here?"

Beenay looked puzzled. "What else can I do?"

312

"But—when the Apostles come—"

"When the Apostles come, they'll do what they want with me. Are you suggesting that I leave Raissta behind and run off to Amgando with you?"

"Well—no—"

"Then I have no choice. Right? Right? Here I stay, with Raissta."

Theremon's head began to ache. He pressed his hands against his eyes.

Siferra said, "There's no other way, Theremon."

"I know. I know. But all the same, to think of Mondior and his crew taking a man as valuable as Beenay prisoner—executing him, even—"

Beenay smiled and rested his hand for a moment on Theremon's forearm. "Who knows? Maybe Mondior would like to keep a couple of professors around as pets. Anyway, what happens to me is unimportant now. My place is with Raissta. Your place is on the road—scampering down to Amgando as fast as you know how. Come on: I'll get you a meal, and I'll give you some official-looking documents. And then on your way with you." He paused. "Here. You'll need this, too." He poured the rest of the brandy, no more than an ounce or so, into Theremon's empty glass. —"Down the hatch," he said.

[41]

At the boundary between Restoration Province and Six Suns they had no trouble at all getting through Search. A border official who looked as though he might have been an accountant or a lawyer in the world that no longer existed simply glanced at the passport Beenay had written out, nodded when he saw the florid "Beenay 25" inscription at the bottom, and waved them on through.

Two days later, when they were crossing from Six Suns Province into Godland, it wasn't that simple. Here the border patrol looked like a gang of cutthroats, who would just as soon toss Theremon and Siferra over the side of the elevated highway as look at their papers at all. There was a long uneasy moment as Theremon stood there, dangling the passport like some sort of magic wand. Then the magic worked, more or less.

"This thing a safe-through?" the head cutthroat asked.

"A passport, yes. Exemption from Search."

"Who from?"

"Beenay 25, Chief Search Administrator, Restoration Province. That's two provinces up the road."

"I know where Restoration Province is. Read it to me."

" 'To Whom It May Concern: This is to attest that the bearers of this document, Theremon 762 and Siferra 89, are properly accredited emissaries of the Fire Patrol of Saro City, and that they are entitled to—' "

"The Fire Patrol? What's that?"

"Altinol's bunch," one of the other cutthroats murmured.

"Ah." The head man nodded toward the needle-guns that Theremon and Siferra wore in full view at their hips. "So Altinol wants you to go marching off through other people's countries carrying weapons that could set a whole district on fire?"

Siferra said, "We're on an urgent mission to the people at Amgando National Park. It's vital that we get there safely." She touched her green neckerchief. "You know what this means? What we do is to keep fires from starting, not to start them. And if we don't get to Amgando on time, the Apostles of Flame will come marching down this highway and destroy everything you people are trying to create."

It didn't make a lot of sense, Theremon thought. Their getting to Amgando, far to the south, wasn't going to save the little republics at the northern end of the highway from the Apostles. But Siferra had put just the right note of conviction and passion into her speech to make it all sound very significant, in a jumbled sort of way.

The response was silence, for a moment, while the border patrolman tried to figure out what she was talking about. Then an irritated frown and a perplexed glare. And then, suddenly, almost impetuously: "All right. Go on through. Get the hell out of here, and don't let me see you anywhere inside Six Suns Province again, or we'll make you regret it. —Apostles! Amgando!"

"Thank you very much," said Theremon, with a graciousness bordering so closely on sarcasm that Siferra took him by

314

the arm and steered him quickly through the checkpoint before he could get them into real trouble.

They were able to move quickly in this stretch of the highway, covering a dozen or more miles a day, sometimes even more. The citizens of the provinces that called themselves Six Suns and Godland and Daylight were hard at work, clearing the debris that had littered the Great Southern Highway since Nightfall. Barricades of rubble were set up at regular intervals —nobody was going to be driving the Great Southern Highway again for a long, long time, Theremon thought—but between checkpoints it was possible now to walk at a steady clip, without having to crawl and creep around mounds of hideous wreckage.

And the dead were being taken from the highway and buried, too. Bit by bit, things were beginning to seem almost civilized again. But not normal. Not even remotely normal.

There were few fires now to be seen still burning in the hinterlands flanking the highway, but burned-out towns were visible all along the route. Refugee camps had been set up every mile or two, and as they walked briskly along the elevated road Theremon and Siferra could look down and see the sad, bewildered people of the camps moving slowly and purposelessly about in them as if they had all aged fifty years in that one single terrible night.

The new provinces, Theremon realized, were simply strings of such camps linked together by the straight line of the Great Southern Highway. In each district local strongmen had emerged who had been able to put together a little realm, a petty kingdom that covered six or eight or ten miles of the highway and spread out for perhaps a mile on either side of the roadbed. What lay beyond the eastern and western borders of the new provinces was anybody's guess. No radio or television communications seemed to be in existence.

"Wasn't there any kind of emergency planning at all?" Theremon asked, speaking more to the air than to Siferra.

But it was Siferra who answered him. "What Athor was predicting was altogether too fantastic for the government to take seriously. And it would have been playing into Mondior's hands to admit that anything like the collapse of civilization could happen in just one short period of Darkness, especially a period of Darkness that could be predicted so specifically."

"But the eclipse—"

"Yes, maybe some people in high office were capable of looking at the diagrams and really did believe that there was going to be an eclipse. And a period of Darkness as a result. But how could they anticipate the Stars? The Stars were simply the fantasy of the Apostles of Flame, remember? Even if the government knew that something like the Stars was going to happen, no one could predict the impact the Stars would have."

"Sheerin could," Theremon said.

"Not even Sheerin. He didn't have an inkling. It was Darkness that was Sheerin's specialty—not sudden unthinkable light filling the whole sky."

"Still," Theremon said. "To look around at all this devastation, all this chaos—you want to think that it was unnecessary, that it could have been avoided, somehow."

"It *wasn't* avoided, though."

"It better be, the next time."

Siferra laughed. "Next time is two thousand and forty-nine years away. Let's hope we can leave our descendants some kind of warning that seems more plausible to them than the Book of Revelations seemed to most of us."

Turning, she stared back over her shoulder, peering apprehensively at the long span of highway they had covered in the past few days of hard marching.

Theremon said, "Afraid you'll see the Apostles thundering down the road behind us?"

"Aren't you? We're still hundreds of miles from Amgando, even at the pace we've been going lately. What if they catch up with us, Theremon?"

"They won't. A whole army can't possibly move as quickly as two healthy and determined people. Their transport isn't any better than ours—one pair of feet per soldier, period. And there are all sorts of logistic considerations that are bound to slow them down."

"I suppose."

"Besides, that message said that the Apostles are planning to stop at each new province along the way to establish their authority. It's going to take them plenty of time to obliterate all those stubborn little petty kingdoms. If we don't run into any unexpected complications ourselves, we'll be at Amgando weeks ahead of them."

"What do you think will happen to Beenay and Raissta?" Siferra asked, after a time.

"Beenay's a pretty clever boy. I suspect he'll work out some way of making himself useful to Mondior."

"And if he can't?"

"Siferra, do we really need to burn up our energies worrying ourselves over horrible possibilities that we can't do a damned thing about?"

"Sorry," she said sharply. "I didn't realize you'd be so touchy."

"Siferra—"

"Forget it," she said. "Maybe I'm the touchy one."

"It'll all work out," said Theremon. "Beenay and Raissta aren't going to be harmed. We'll get down to Amgando in plenty of time to give the warning. The Apostles of Flame won't conquer the world."

"And all the dead people will rise up and walk again, too. Oh, Theremon, Theremon—" Her voice broke.

"I know."

"What will we *do?*"

"We'll walk fast, is what we'll do. And we won't look back. Looking back doesn't do any good at all."

"No. None at all," said Siferra. And smiled, and took his hand. And they walked quickly onward in silence.

It was amazing, Theremon thought, how swiftly they were going, now that they had hit their stride. The first few days, when they were coming down out of Saro City and picking their way through the wreckage-strewn upper end of the highway, progress had been slow and their bodies had protested bitterly against the strains that they were imposing on them. But now they were moving like two machines, perfectly attuned to their task. Siferra's legs were nearly as long as his own, and they walked along side by side, muscles working efficiently, hearts pumping steadily, lungs expanding and contracting in flawless rhythm. *Stride stride stride. Stride stride stride. Stride stride stride—*

Hundreds of miles yet to go, sure. But it wouldn't take long, not at this pace. Another month, perhaps. Perhaps even less.

The road was almost completely clear, down here in the rural regions beyond the farthest edge of the city. There hadn't been nearly as much traffic here in the first place as there had been to the north, and it looked as though many of the drivers had been able to get off the highway safely even while the Stars were shining, since they were in less danger of being struck by the cars of other drivers who had lost control.

There were fewer checkpoints, too. The new provinces in these sparsely populated areas covered much greater areas than those up north, and their people seemed less concerned with such things as Search. Theremon and Siferra underwent serious interrogation only twice in the next five days. At the other border points they were simply waved on through without even having to show the papers Beenay had provided for them.

Even the weather was on their side. It was fair and mild almost every day: a few little rain-showers now and then but nothing that caused serious inconvenience. They would walk for four hours, pause for a light meal, walk another four, eat again, walk, stop for six hours or so of sleep—taking turns, one sitting up and watching for a few hours, then the other—and then get up and march onward. Like machines. The suns came and went in the sky in their age-old rhythm, now Patru and Trey and Dovim up above, now Onos and Sitha and Tano, now Onos and Dovim, now Trey and Patru, now four suns at once —the unending succession, the great pageant of the skies. Theremon had no idea how many days had passed since they had left the Sanctuary. The whole idea of dates, calendars, days, weeks, months—it all seemed quaint and archaic and cumbersome to him, something out of a former world.

Siferra, after her spell of brooding and apprehensiveness, became cheerful again.

This was going to be a breeze. They would make it down to Amgando with no trouble at all.

They were passing through a district known as Spring Glen now—or perhaps it was called Garden Grove; they had heard several different names from the people they encountered along the road. It was farm country, open and rolling, and there was little sign here of the hellish devastation that had

318

blighted the urbanized regions: an occasional fire-damaged barn, or a herd of farm animals that seemed to be roaming unattended, and that was about the worst of it. The air was sweet and fresh, the light of the suns was bright and strong. But for the eerie absence of vehicular traffic on the highway, it was possible here to think that nothing extraordinary had happened at all.

"Are we halfway to Amgando yet?" Siferra asked.

"Not quite. I haven't seen a road-sign for a while, but my guess is that—"

He stopped abruptly.

"What is it, Theremon?"

"Look. Look there, to the right. Along that secondary road coming in from the west."

They peered over the edge of the highway. Down below, a few hundred yards away, a long row of trucks was drawn up at the side of the secondary road, where it fed into an approach to the main one. There was a large, bustling camp there: tents, a big campfire burning, some men chopping logs.

Two or three hundred people, perhaps. All of them in black hooded robes.

Theremon and Siferra exchanged astounded glances.

"Apostles!" she whispered.

"Yes. Get down. Hands and knees. Hide yourself against the railing here."

"But how did they manage to get this far south so fast? The highway's upper end is completely blocked!"

Theremon shook his head. "They didn't take the highway at all. Look there—they've got trucks that work. Here's another one, coming right now. Gods, that looks strange, doesn't it, an actual moving vehicle! And hearing the sound of an engine again after all this time." He felt himself beginning to shiver. "They were able to keep a fleet of trucks undamaged, and a supply of fuel. And obviously they've come down from Saro around through the west, on little country roads. Now they're joining up with the main highway, which I suppose is open from here to Amgando. They could be there by this evening."

"This evening! Theremon, what are we going to do?"

"I'm not sure. There's only one wild chance, I guess. —What if we went down there and tried to seize one of those trucks?

319

And drove it to Amgando ourselves. Even if we got there only two hours ahead of the Apostles, there'd be time for most of the Amgando people to escape. Right?"

Siferra said, "Perhaps. It sounds crazy, though. How could we steal a truck? The moment they see us, they'll know we aren't Apostles, and they'll grab us."

"I know. I know. Let me think." After a moment he said, "If we could catch a couple of them at a distance from the others, and take their robes away from them—shoot them with our needlers, if we have to—and then, when we're robed, just walk up to one of the trucks as though we have every right to be doing that, and jump on board and drive off toward the high-way—"

"They'd follow after us in two minutes."

"Maybe. Or maybe if we were calm and cool about it they'd think it was something perfectly ordinary, part of their plan— and by the time they realized it wasn't, we'd be fifty miles down the road." He looked at her eagerly. "What do you say, Siferra? What other hope do we have? Continue toward Amgando on foot, when for us it'll be a journey of weeks and weeks, and they can drive past us in a couple of hours?"

She was staring at him as though he had lost his mind.

"Overpower a couple of Apostles—hijack one of their trucks —go zooming off toward Amgando—oh, Theremon, it'll never work. You know that."

"All right," he said abruptly. "You stay here. I'll try to do it alone. It's the only hope there is, Siferra."

He rose to a half-crouch, and began to scuttle along the side of the highway toward the exit ramp a few hundred yards ahead.

"No—wait, Theremon—"

He looked back at her and grinned. "Coming?"

"Yes. Oh, this is crazy!"

"Yes," he said. "I know. But what else can we do?"

She was right, of course. The scheme *was* crazy. Yet he saw no alternative. Evidently the report Beenay had received had been garbled: the Apostles had never intended to move down the Great Southern Highway province by province, but instead had set out directly for Amgando in a huge armed convoy, taking minor roads which, though not very direct, were at least still open to vehicular transport.

Amgando was doomed. The world would fall by default to Mondior's people.

Unless—unless—

He had never imagined himself as a hero. Heroes were people he wrote about in his column—people who functioned at the top of their form under extreme circumstances, performing strange and miraculous deeds that the ordinary individual would never dream of even attempting, let alone of carrying off. And now here he was in this strangely transformed world, blithely talking of overpowering hooded cultists with his needle-gun, commandeering a military truck, speeding off to Amgando Park to sound the warning of the oncoming attack—

Crazy. Utterly crazy.

But perhaps it might just work, simply because it *was* so crazy. Nobody would be expecting two people to appear out of thin air down here in this peaceful bucolic setting and simply run off with a truck.

They edged their way down the highway ramp, Theremon a short distance in the lead. A thickly overgrown field lay between them and the camp of the Apostles. "Maybe," he whispered, "if we get down and wriggle through the tall grass here, and a couple of the Apostles come wandering out this way for some reason, we can rise up and jump them before they know what's happening."

He got down. He wriggled.

Siferra went right after him, keeping pace.

Ten yards. Twenty. Just keep going, head down and wriggle, over to that little knoll, and then wait—wait—

A voice said suddenly, just behind him, "What do we have here? A couple of peculiar serpents, is it?"

Theremon turned, looked, gasped.

Gods! Apostles, seven or eight of them! Where had they come from? A private picnic in the field? Which he and Siferra had crawled right past, all unknowing?

"Run for it!" he barked to her. "You go this way—I'll go that—"

He began to sprint to his left, toward the towers that supported the highway. Maybe he could outrun them—disappear into the wooded country on the other side of the road—

No. No. He was strong and fast, but they were stronger, faster. He saw them coming up alongside him.

"Siferra!" he yelled. "Keep going! Keep—going!"

Perhaps she had actually made it to safety. He couldn't see her now. The Apostles were all around him. He reached for his needle-gun, but one of them caught his arm immediately, and another got him by the throat. The gun was yanked from his hand. Legs poked between his, entangling him, tripping him. He fell heavily, rolled over, looked up. Five hooded faces, unsmiling, rigid, looked back. One of the Apostles had his own needle-gun aimed at his chest.

"Get up," the Apostle said. "Slowly. With your hands in the air."

Awkwardly Theremon stumbled to his feet.

"Who are you? What are you doing here?" the Apostle demanded.

"I live around here. My wife and I were just taking a shortcut through these fields, back to our house—"

"The nearest farm is five miles away. A very long shortcut." The Apostle gestured with a nod of his head toward the camp. "Come with us. Folimun will want to talk to you."

Folimun!

So he had survived the night of the eclipse after all. And was in charge of the expedition against Amgando!

Theremon glanced around. No sign of Siferra at all. He hoped she was back on the highway by now, heading for Amgando as fast as she could go. A slim hope, but the only one left.

The Apostles marched him toward the camp. It was a weird sensation to be among so many hooded figures. Scarcely any of them paid attention to him, though, as his captors nudged him along, into the largest of the tents.

Folimun was seated at a bench near the back of the tent, looking through a sheaf of papers. He turned his chilly blue eyes on Theremon and his thin, sharp face softened for an instant as a smile of surprise crossed it.

"Theremon? You here? What are you doing—covering us for the *Chronicle?*"

"I'm traveling south, Folimun. Taking a little holiday, since

322

things are a little unsettled back in the city. Would you mind asking these thugs of yours to let go of me?"

"Release him," Folimun said. —"Where are you heading, exactly, eh?"

"That's of no importance to you."

"Let me be the judge of that. Going to Amgando, are you, Theremon?"

Theremon offered the cultist a cold level stare. "I don't see any reason why I should tell you anything."

"After all that I told you, when you interviewed me?"

"Very funny."

"I want to know where you're heading, Theremon."

Stall, Theremon thought. Stall him as long as you can.

"I decline to answer that question, or any other you might happen to have for me. I'll discuss my intentions only with Mondior himself," he said in a steady, determined tone.

Folimun made no reply for a moment. Then he smiled again, a quick on-off. And then, suddenly, unexpectedly, he broke into actual laughter. Theremon wondered if he had ever seen Folimun laugh before. "Mondior?" Folimun said, his eyes glinting with amusement. "There is no Mondior, my friend. There never was."

[42]

It was hard for Siferra to believe that she had actually managed to escape. But that was indeed what appeared to have happened.

Most of the Apostles who had surprised them in the field had gone after Theremon. Looking back once, she had seen them surrounding him like hunters' hounds surrounding their prey. They had knocked him down; he would certainly be captured.

Only two of the Apostles had split off to pursue her. Siferra had jabbed one in the face, hard, with the flat of her hand at the end of her stiff outstretched arm, and at the speed she was traveling the impact had sent him reeling to the ground. The remaining one was fat and ungainly and slow; in moments Siferra left him far behind.

She doubled back the way she and Theremon had come, toward the elevated highway. But it seemed unwise to go up onto it. The highway was too easily blocked, and there was no safe way down from it except at the exit ramps. She would only be putting herself at risk of running into a trap if she went up there. And even if no roadblocks lay ahead, it would be a simple thing for the Apostles to come after her in their trucks and pick her up, a mile or two down the way.

No, the thing to do was to run into the woods on the far side of the road. The Apostles' trucks wouldn't be able to follow her there. She could lose herself easily enough in those low shrubby trees, and hide there until she had figured out her next move.

And what could that be? she wondered.

She had to admit that Theremon's idea, wild as it was, still was their only hope: steal a truck somehow, drive down to Amgando and sound the alarm before the Apostles could get their army on the move again.

But Siferra knew there wasn't the remotest chance that she could simply tiptoe up to an empty truck, jump in, and drive it away. The Apostles weren't that stupid. She'd have to order one of them at gunpoint to switch the truck on for her and surrender its controls to her. And that involved carrying out the whole bizarre maneuver of trying to overpower a stray Apostle, getting his robe, slipping into the camp, locating someone who could open up one of the trucks for her—

Her heart sank. It was all too implausible. She might just as well consider trying to rescue Theremon while she was at it— go marching in with her needle-gun blazing, take hostages, demand his immediate release—oh, it was absolute foolishness, a silly melodramatic dream, a gaudy maneuver out of some cheap children's adventure book—

But what will I do? What will I do?

She huddled down in a copse of tightly woven little trees with long feathery leaves and waited for time to pass. The Apostles gave no sign of breaking camp: she could still see the smoke of their bonfire against the twilight sky, and their trucks were still parked where they had been along the road.

Evening was coming on. Onos was gone from the sky. Dovim hovered on the horizon. The only suns overhead were her two least favorite ones, bleak and cheerless Tano and Sitha, casting their cold light from their distant location at the edge of the universe. Or what people had *thought* was the edge of the universe, rather, in those far-off innocent days before the Stars appeared and revealed to them just how immense the universe really was.

The hours ticked interminably by. No solution to the situation made sense to her. Amgando seemed lost, unless someone else had managed to get a warning to them—certainly there was no way she was going to get down there ahead of the Apostles. Rescuing Theremon was an absurd idea. Her chances of stealing a truck and getting to Amgando by herself was only slightly less preposterous.

What then? Simply sit back and watch while the Apostles took command of everything?

There seemed to be no alternative.

At one point during the evening she thought that the only path open to her was to walk into the Apostles' camp, surrender, and ask to be imprisoned with Theremon. At least they would be together then. It astonished her how much she missed him. They had not been out of each other's company in weeks, she who had never lived with a man in her life. And all during the long journey from Saro City, though they had bickered now and then, even quarreled a little, she had never tired of being with him. Not once. It had seemed the most natural thing in the world for them to be together. And now she was alone again.

Go on, she told herself. Give yourself up. Everything's lost anyway, isn't it?

It grew darker. Clouds veiled Sitha and Tano's frosty light, and the sky turned so dusky that she half expected the Stars to reappear.

Go ahead, she thought bitterly. Come out and shine. Drive everyone crazy all over again. What harm can it do? The world can only be smashed once, and that's been done already.

But the Stars, of course, did not appear. Veiled as they were, Tano and Sitha nevertheless afforded enough light to mask the glow of those distant points of mysterious brilliance. And as the hours went by, Siferra found herself swinging completely around from her mood of total defeatism to a new sense of almost reckless hope.

When all is lost, she told herself, there's nothing left to lose. Under cover of this evening gloom she would slip into the Apostles' camp and—somehow, somehow—take one of their trucks. And rescue Theremon, too, if she could manage it. And then off to Amgando! By the time Onos was in the sky tomorrow morning, she'd be down there, among her university friends, in plenty of time to let them know that they had to scatter before the enemy army arrived.

All right, she thought. Let's go.

Slowly—slowly—more cautiously than before, just in case they have sentries hidden in the grass—

Out of the woods. A moment of uncertainty, there: she felt tremendously vulnerable, now that she had left the safety of that tangle of shrubbery behind. But the dimness still protected her. Across the cleared place, now, that led from the woods to the elevated highway. Under the great metal legs of the roadbed and into the unkempt field where she and Theremon had been surprised that afternoon.

Get down and wriggle, now, the way they had before. Once again across the field—looking this way and that, scanning for sentries who might be on duty at the perimeter of the Apostles' camp—

Her needle-gun was in her hand, set for minimum aperture, the sharpest, most highly focused, deadliest beam the gun could produce. If anyone came upon her now, so much the worse for him. There was too much at stake to worry about the niceties of civilized morality. While still half out of her mind she had killed Balik in the Archaeology lab, not meaning to, but he was dead all the same; and, a little to her surprise, she found herself quite ready to kill again, this time intentionally, if circumstances required it of her. The important thing was to get a vehicle and get out of here and carry the news of the Apostles' army's approach to Amgando. Everything else, including considerations of morality, was secondary. Everything. This was war.

Onward. Head down, eyes raised, body hunched. She was only a few dozen yards from the camp now.

It was very silent over there. Probably most of them were

asleep. In the murky grayness Siferra thought she could see a couple of figures on the far side of the main bonfire, though the smoke rising from the fire made it difficult to be sure. The thing to do, she thought, was to slip into the deep shadows behind one of the trucks and toss a rock against a tree some distance away. The sentries would probably investigate; and if they fanned out separately, she could slip up behind one of them, jab the needler into his back, warn him to keep quiet, make him strip off his robe—

No, she thought. Don't warn him of anything. Just shoot him, quickly, and *take* his robe, before he can call out an alarm. These are Apostles, after all. Fanatics.

Her own newfound cold-bloodedness amazed her.

Onward. Onward. She was almost at the nearest truck now. Into the darkness on the side opposite the campfire. Where's a rock? Here. Here, this is a good one. Shift the needler to the left hand for a moment. Now, toss the rock at that big tree over there—

She raised her arm to make the throw. And in that moment she felt a hand seize her left wrist from behind and a powerful arm clamp across her throat.

Caught!

Shock and outrage and a jolt of maddening frustration went coursing through her. Furiously Siferra lashed out with her foot, kicking backward with all her strength, and connecting. She heard a grunt of pain. Not enough to break the man's strong grip, though. Twisting halfway around, she kicked again, and attempted at the same time to pass the needle-gun from her left hand to her right.

But her assailant pulled her left arm upward in a short, sharp, agonizing gesture that numbed her and sent the needler spilling out of her hand. The other arm, the one that was pressing against her throat, tightened to choking intensity. She coughed and gasped.

Darkness! Of all the stupidity, to let someone sneak up on her while she was sneaking up on them!

Tears of rage burned her cheeks. In fury she kicked backward again, and then again.

"Easy," a deep voice whispered. "You could hurt me that way, Siferra."

"Theremon?" she said, astounded.

"Who do you think it is? Mondior?"

The pressure at her throat eased. The hand that clutched her wrist released its grasp. She took a couple of tottering steps forward, fighting for breath. Then, numb with confusion, she swung around to stare at him.

"How did you get free?" she asked.

He grinned. "A holy miracle, it was. An absolute holy miracle. —I watched you the whole time, coming from the woods. You were very good, really. But you were concentrating so hard on getting here unnoticed that you didn't notice me circling around behind you."

"Thank all the gods it was you, Theremon. Even if you did give me the shock of my life when you grabbed me. —But why are we standing here? Quick, let's grab one of those trucks and clear out of here before they see us."

"No," he said. "That isn't the plan any more."

She gave him a blank look. "I don't understand."

"You will." To her amazement he clapped his hands and called loudly, "Over here, fellows! Here she is!"

"*Theremon!* Are you out of your—"

The beam of a flashlight struck her in the face with an impact nearly as devastating as the one the Stars had had. She stood blinded, shaking her head in bewilderment and consternation. There were figures moving all around her, but it was another moment before her eyes adapted sufficiently to the sudden brightness for her to make them out.

Apostles. Half a dozen of them.

She glared accusingly at Theremon. He seemed calm, and very pleased with himself. Her dazed mind could barely begin to accept the awareness that he had betrayed her.

When she tried to speak, nothing but blurted monosyllables would emerge. "But—why?—what?—"

Theremon smiled. "Come on, Siferra. There's someone I want you to meet."

[43]

Folimun said, "There's not really any need to glower at me like that, Dr. Siferra. You may have trouble believing it, but you are among friends here."

"*Friends?* You must think I'm a very gullible woman."

"Not at all. Quite the contrary."

"You invade my laboratory and steal priceless research materials. You order your horde of berserk superstitious followers to invade the Observatory and wreck the equipment with which the university astronomers are trying to perform unique, essential research. Now you hypnotize Theremon into doing your bidding, and send him out to capture me and turn me over to you as a prisoner. And then you tell me that I'm among friends?"

Theremon said quietly, "I haven't been hypnotized, Siferra. And you aren't a prisoner."

"Of course not. And this is all just a very bad dream, too: Nightfall, the fires, the collapse of civilization, the whole thing. An hour from now I'll wake up in my apartment in Saro City and everything will be just the way it was when I went to sleep."

Theremon, facing her across the middle of Folimun's tent, thought that she had never looked more beautiful than she did right then. Her eyes were luminous with anger. Her skin seemed to glisten. There was an aura of intensely focused energy about her that he found irresistible.

But this was hardly the moment to tell her anything like that.

Folimun said, "For stealing your tablets, Dr. Siferra, I can only offer my apologies. It was a shameless act of theft, which I assure you I never would have authorized except that you made it necessary."

"*I* made it—"

"You did. You insisted on keeping them in your possession—on placing those irreplaceable relics of the previous cycle in jeopardy at a time when chaos was about to break loose and, for

329

all you knew, the university buildings were going to be destroyed down to the last brick. We saw it as essential that they be placed in safekeeping, that is to say, in our own hands, and since you would not authorize that we found it necessary to take them from you."

"I found those tablets. You'd never have known they existed if I hadn't dug them up."

"Which is beside the point," Folimun said smoothly. "Once the tablets were discovered, they became vital to our needs—to humanity's needs. We felt that the future of Kalgash was more important than your personal proprietary interest in your artifacts. As you will see, we have translated the tablets fully now, making use of the ancient textual material already available to us, and they have added greatly to our understanding of the extraordinary challenges that civilized life on Kalgash must periodically confront. Dr. Mudrin's translations were, unfortunately, extremely superficial. But the tablets provide an accurate and convincing version, uncorrupted by centuries of textual alteration and error, of the chronicles that have come down to us under the name of the Book of Revelations. The Book of Revelations, I must confess, is full of mysticism and metaphor, adopted for propagandistic purposes. The Thombo tablets are straightforward historical accounts of two separate advents of the Stars thousands of years ago, and of the attempts made by the priesthoods of the time to warn the populace of what was about to happen. We can demonstrate now that throughout history and prehistory on Kalgash, small groups of dedicated people have struggled again and again to prepare the world for the disruption that repeatedly falls upon it. The methods they used, obviously, were insufficient to the problem. Now at last, aided as we are by a knowledge of past mistakes, we will be able to spare Kalgash from another devastating upheaval when the present Year of Godliness comes to its end two thousand years from now."

Siferra turned to Theremon. "How smug he sounds! Justifying his own burglary of my tablets by telling me that they'll enable him to set up an even more efficient theocratic dictatorship than they had hoped! Theremon, Theremon, why did you sell me out like this? Why did you sell *us* out? We could have been halfway to Amgando by this time, if only—"

Folimun said, "You'll be in Amgando tomorrow afternoon, Dr. Siferra, I assure you. All of us will be in Amgando by tomorrow afternoon."

"What will you do?" she asked hotly. "March me in chains at the rear of your conquering army? Tie me up and make me walk in the dust behind Mondior's chariot?"

The Apostle sighed. "Theremon, explain things to her, if you please."

"No," she said. Her eyes were blazing. "You poor brainwashed ninny, I don't want to hear the gibberish this maniac has poured into your mind! I don't want to hear anything from any of you! Let me alone. Lock me up, if you like. Or turn me loose, if you can bring yourself to do it. I can't possibly harm you, can I? One woman against a whole army? I can't even cross a field without having someone come up and surprise me from behind!"

Theremon, dismayed, reached toward her.

"No! Keep away from me! You disgust me! —But it isn't your fault, is it? They've done something to your mind. —You'll do it to me too, won't you, Folimun? You'll make me into an obliging little puppet. Well, let me ask just this one favor. Don't force me to wear an Apostle's robe. I can't stand the idea of walking around inside one of those ridiculous things. Take my soul away, if you have to, but let me dress as I please, all right? All right, Folimun?"

The Apostle laughed faintly. "Perhaps it would be best if I left the two of you alone. I see that nothing's going to be accomplished so long as I'm part of the conversation."

Siferra cried, "No, damn you, I don't want to be left alone with—"

But Folimun had already risen and walked quickly from the tent.

Theremon turned toward Siferra, who backed away from him as though he were carrying some plague.

Softly he said, "I wasn't hypnotized, Siferra. They haven't done anything to my mind."

"Of course you'd say that."

"It's true. I'll prove it to you."

She stared at him bleakly, coldly, making no response.

Very quietly he said, after a moment, "Siferra, I love you."

"How long did it take the Apostles to program *that* line into you?" she asked.

He winced. "Don't. Don't. I mean it, Siferra. I won't try to tell you that I've never said those words to anyone before. But this is the first time I've meant them."

"Oldest line in the book," said Siferra derisively.

"I suppose I deserve that. Theremon the ladies' man. Theremon the seducer-about-town. Well, all right. Forget I said it. —No. No. I'm serious, Siferra. Traveling with you these past weeks—being with you morning and afternoon and evening— there hasn't been a moment when I haven't looked at you and thought to myself, This is the woman I was waiting for all these years. This is the woman I never dared to imagine I would find."

"Very touching, Theremon. And the best way you could find to show your love was to grab me from behind, practically breaking my arm in the process, and turn me over to Mondior. Right?"

"Mondior doesn't exist, Siferra. There's no such person."

For an instant he saw a flicker of surprise and curiosity cut through her hostility.

"What?"

"He's a convenient mythical construct, put together by electronic synthesis to make speeches on television. No one's ever had an audience with him, have they? He's never been seen in public. Folimun invented him to be a public spokesman. Since Mondior never appears in person, he can be on television in five different countries at once, all over the world—nobody could ever be sure where he really was, and so he could be displayed simultaneously. Folimun's the real boss of the Apostles of Flame. He simply masquerades as a public-relations officer. In fact he calls all the shots, and has for the past ten years. Before that there was someone named Bazret, who's dead now. Bazret was the one who invented Mondior, but Folimun's brought him to his present eminence."

"Folimun told you all this?"

"He told me some. I guessed the rest, and he confirmed it. He'll show me the Mondior apparatus when we're back in Saro City. The Apostles plan to restore television transmissions in another few weeks."

"All right," Siferra said harshly. "The discovery that Mondi-or's a fake so overwhelmed you with its slimy cleverness that you decided on the spot that you absolutely had to join up with Folimun's outfit. And your first assignment was to turn me in. So you skulked around looking for me, and took me by surprise, and thereby made certain that the people down in Amgando would fall into Folimun's clutches. Nicely done, Theremon."

"Folimun's heading for Amgando, yes," Theremon said. "But he doesn't intend to harm those who have gathered there. He wants to offer them posts in the new government."

"Gods almighty, Theremon, do you believe—"

"Yes. Yes, Siferra!" Theremon held his hands out, fingers spread wide in an agitated gesture. "I may be a mere coarse journalist, but at least grant me that I'm no fool. Twenty years in the newspaper business has made me an excellent judge of character, at the very least. Folimun impressed me in a strange way from the first time I met him. He seemed very much the opposite of crazy, very complex, very sly, very sharp. And I've been talking with him for the past eight hours. Nobody's been sleeping here this evening. He's laid his whole plan bare. He's shown me his entire scheme. Would you grant, for the sake of argument, that it's possible for me to get an accurate psychological reading on someone during the course of an eight-hour conversation?"

"Well—" she said grudgingly.

"Either he's completely sincere, Siferra, or he's the best actor in the world."

"He could be both. That still doesn't make him someone we'd want to trust."

"Maybe not. But I do. Now."

"Go on."

"Folimun is a totally ruthless, almost monstrously rational man who believes that the only thing that's of any real importance is the survival of civilization. Because he's had access, through his age-old religious cult, to historical records of previous cycles, he's known for many years what we've all just learned in the hardest possible way: that Kalgash is doomed to be shown a view of the Stars once every two thousand years and that the sight of them is so overwhelming that it'll shatter

333

ordinary minds and give even the strongest ones a bad time for days or weeks. —He's willing to let you see all their ancient documents, by the way, when we're back in Saro City."

"Saro City has been destroyed."

"Not the part of it controlled by the Apostles. They made damned well sure nobody would be setting any fires within a mile of their tower on all sides."

"Very efficient of them," Siferra said.

"They're efficient people. All right: Folimun knows that in a time of total madness the best hope of pulling things together is a religious totalitarianism. You and I may think the gods are just old fables, Siferra, but there are millions and millions of people out there, believe it or not, who have a different view of things. They've always been uneasy about doing things that they consider sinful, for fear the gods will punish them. And now they have an absolute *dread* of the gods. They think the Stars might come back tomorrow, or the day after tomorrow, and finish off the job. —Well, here are the Apostles, who claim a direct pipeline to the gods and have all sorts of scriptural passages to prove it. They're in a better position to set up a world government than Altinol, or the little provincial overlords, or the fugitive remnants of the former governments, or anyone else. They're the best hope we have."

"You're serious," Siferra said in wonder. "Folimun hasn't hypnotized you, Theremon. You've managed to do it to yourself!"

"Look," he said. "Folimun's been working all his life toward this moment, knowing that his is the generation of Apostles on whom the responsibility for ensuring survival will fall. He's got all sorts of plans. He's well on his way to establishing control over enormous territories north and west of Saro City, and next he's going to take charge of the new provinces along the line of the Great Southern Highway."

"And establish a theocratic dictatorship that will begin its rule by executing all the atheistic, cynical, materialistic university people like Beenay and Sheerin and me."

"Sheerin's already dead. Folimun told me his people found his body in a ruined house. He was apparently killed some weeks back by a band of anti-intellectual crazies."

Siferra looked away, unable for a moment to meet Ther-

334

emon's eyes. Then she stared at him more angrily than before and said, "There you are. First Folimun sends his goons crashing into the Observatory—Athor was killed too, wasn't he?—and then he eliminates poor harmless Sheerin. And then all the rest of us will be—"

"He was trying to *protect* the Observatory people, Siferra."

"He didn't go about it very well, did he?"

"Things got out of hand. What he wanted to do was rescue all the scientists before the rioting started—but because he was operating under the guise of a wild-eyed fanatic, he had no way of persuading them to hear what he was offering, which was to give them safe-conduct to the Apostles' Sanctuary."

"After the Observatory was wrecked."

"That wasn't his first choice either. The world was crazy that night. Things didn't always follow his scheme."

"You're very good at making excuses for him, Theremon."

"Maybe so. Hear me out, anyway. He wants to work with the surviving university people, and the other sane and intelligent ones who have gathered at Amgando, to rebuild humanity's pool of knowledge. He—or the supposed Mondior, rather—will be in charge of the government. The Apostles will keep the unstable and superstition-ridden populace pacified by religious domination, at least for a generation or two. Meanwhile the university people will help the Apostles assemble and codify the knowledge they've managed to save, and together they'll guide the world back to a rational state—as has happened so many times before. But this time, perhaps, they'll be able to begin the preparations for the next eclipse a hundred years or so in advance, and head off the worst of the upheaval, the mass insanity, the torchings, the universal devastation."

"And you believe all this?" Siferra asked. There was the bite of acid in her voice. "That it makes sense to stand back and applaud while the Apostles of Flame spread their poisonous irrational totalitarian creed throughout the world? Or what's even worse—that we should join forces with them?"

"I hate the idea," Theremon said suddenly.

Siferra's eyes widened. "Then why—?"

"Let's go outside," he said. "It's almost dawn. Give me your hand?"

"Well—"

"It wasn't just a line, when I told you I love you."

She shrugged. "One thing has nothing to do with another. The personal and the political, Theremon—you're using one to muddle the other."

"Come," he said.

[44]

They stepped from the tent. The early light of Onos was a pink glow on the eastern horizon. High overhead, Tano and Sitha had emerged from the clouds, and the twin suns, now at their zenith, had a radiance that was strange and wonderful to behold.

There was one more. Far off in the north the small hard red sphere that was the little sun Dovim was shining like a tiny ruby set in the forehead of the sky.

"Four suns," Theremon said. "A sign of luck."

All about them in the Apostles' camp there was the bustle of activity. The trucks were being loaded, the tents were coming down. Theremon caught sight of Folimun far across the other side, directing a team of workers. The Apostle leader waved to Theremon, who nodded in return.

"You hate the idea that the Apostles will rule the world," Siferra said, "and yet you're still willing to give your allegiance to Folimun? Why? What sense does that make?"

Quietly Theremon said, "Because there's no other hope."

"Is that what you think?"

He nodded. "It began to sink in, after Folimun had been talking with me for a couple of hours. Every rational instinct in me tells me not to trust Folimun and his crew of fanatics. Whatever else he may be, there's no doubt that Folimun's a power-hungry manipulator, very ruthless, very dangerous. But what other chance is there? Altinol? All the petty little bosses along the highway? It could take a million years to weld all the new provinces into a global economy. Folimun's got the authority to make the whole world kneel to him—or to Mondior, rather. —Listen, Siferra, most of mankind is lost in madness. There are millions of crazies loose out there now. Only strong-minded ones like you and me and Beenay have been able to recover, or very stupid ones; but for the others, the mass of humanity, it'll be months or years or never before they can think straight again. A charismatic prophet like Mondior, much as I loathe the idea, may be the only answer."

"No other option, then?"

"Not for us, Siferra."

"Why not?"

"Look, Siferra: I believe that what matters is healing. Everything else is secondary to that. The world has suffered a terrible wound, and—"

"Has inflicted a terrible wound on itself."

"That's not how I see it. The fires were a response to a vast change of circumstances. They never would have happened if the eclipse hadn't yanked our curtain away and shown us the Stars. —But the wounds go on and on. One leads to another, now. Altinol is a wound. These new little independent provinces are wounds. The crazies killing each other in the forest—or hunting down fugitive university professors—are wounds."

"And Folimun? He's the biggest wound of all!"

"Yes and no. Of course he's peddling fanaticism and mysticism. But there's discipline there. People *believe* in what he's selling, even the crazies, even the ones with sick minds. He's a wound so big he can swallow all the others. He can heal the world, Siferra. And then—from within—we can try to heal what *he* has done. But only from within. If we join him, we stand a chance. If we set ourselves up in opposition, we'll be swept aside like fleas."

"What are you saying, then?"

"We have our choice between rallying behind him and becoming part of the ruling elite that will bring the world back from insanity, or becoming wanderers and outlaws. Which do you want, Siferra?"

"I want a third choice."

"There isn't any. The Amgando bunch doesn't have the force of will to form a workable government. People like Altinol don't have the scruples. Folimun already controls half of what used to be the Federal Republic of Saro. He's certain to prevail over the rest. It'll be centuries before the reign of reason returns, Siferra, regardless of what you and I do."

"So you say it's better to join him, and try to control the direction in which the new society goes, than to oppose him simply because we don't like the kind of fanaticism he represents?"

"Exactly. Exactly."

"But to cooperate in handing the world over to religious fanaticism—"

"The world has made its way up from religious fanaticism before, hasn't it? The important thing now is to find some way out of the chaos. Folimun and his crew offer the only visible hope of that. Think of their faith as a machine that'll drive civilization, at a time when all the other machinery is broken. That's the only thing that counts now. First fix the world; then hope our descendants will get tired of the mystical fellows in the robes and hoods. Do you see what I'm saying, Siferra? Do you?"

She nodded in a strange, vague way, as though she were responding in her sleep. Theremon watched as she walked slowly away from him, toward the clearing where they had been surprised by the sentries of the Apostles the evening before. It seemed like years ago.

She stood a long while by herself there, in the light of the four suns.

How beautiful she looks, Theremon thought.

How I love her!

How strange this all has turned out to be.

He waited. All about him the breakup of the Apostles' camp was reaching a pitch of activity, robed and hooded figures running back and forth past him.

Folimun came over. "Well?"

"We're thinking it over," Theremon said.

"We? I had the impression you were with us, no matter what."

Theremon eyed him steadily. "I'm with you if Siferra is. Otherwise no."

"Whatever you say. We'd hate to lose a man with your skills at communication, though. Not to mention Dr. Siferra's expertise with the artifacts of the past."

Theremon smiled. "Let's see how skillful I've been at communicating just now, eh?"

Folimun nodded and walked away, back to the trucks that were being loaded. Theremon looked toward Siferra. She was facing the east, toward Onos, while the light of Sitha and Tano descended on her in a dazzling stream from above, and out of the north came the slender red spear of Dovim's beam.

Four suns. The best of omens.

Siferra was coming back, now, trotting across the field. Her eyes were shining, and she seemed to be laughing. She came running up to him.

"Well?" Theremon asked. "What do you say?"

She took his hand in hers. "All right, Theremon. So be it. Almighty Folimun is our leader, and I will follow him withersoever he telleth me to go. With one condition."

"Go on. What is it?"

"The same one I mentioned when we were in his tent. I won't wear the robe. I absolutely will not. If he insists on the robe, the deal is off!"

Theremon nodded happily. It was going to be all right. After Nightfall came daybreak, and rebirth. Out of the devastation a new Kalgash would rise, and he and Siferra would have a voice, a powerful voice, in creating it. "I think that can be arranged," he replied. "Let's go talk to Folimun and see what he says."